"Prepare to be amazed by *The Illusionist's Apprentice*. Wren Lockhart, the talented magician at the heart of Kristy Cambron's spellbinding tale of Jazz Age Boston, is the fierce, brilliant, guarded headliner you've been waiting for. This novel will have your pulse pounding and your mind racing to keep up with reversals, betrayals, and surprises from the first page to the last. Like her characters, Cambron works magic so compelling and persuasive, she deserves a standing ovation."

—GREER MACALLISTER, BESTSELLING
AUTHOR OF *THE MAGICIAN'S
LIE* AND *GIRL IN DISGUISE*

"With rich descriptions, attention to detail, mesmerizing characters, and an understated current of faith, this work evokes writers such as Kim Vogel Sawyer, Francine Rivers, and Sara Gruen."

—*LIBRARY JOURNAL*, STARRED REVIEW,
FOR *THE RINGMASTER'S WIFE*

"Mixing fictional characters with true historical figures is a daunting task, but author Kristy Cambron achieves such excellence in that vein that the reader is compelled to devour the author's note at the end, just to find out which characters lived among us . . . and which were constructed on the page. Historical fiction lovers will adore this novel! A vivid and romantic rendering of circus life in the Jazz Age, *The Ringmaster's Wife* features two rich love stories and a glimpse into our nation's live entertainment history. Highly recommended!"

—*USA TODAY* HAPPY EVER AFTER

"Cambron takes a real person, Mable Ringling, and breathes fictional life into her while staying true to what is known about this compelling woman. The novel is an intriguing look into circus life in the 1920s . . . but the author's gift for writing beautifully crafted sentences will draw readers into the story and the fascinating world of the circus."

—*RT Book Reviews*, 4 stars,
for *The Ringmaster's Wife*

"Cambron vividly depicts circus life during the 1920s, when the vast menagerie moved in 100-car trains and the Ringlings were establishing themselves in Sarasota, Fla., society. With a strong supporting cast of friends and family—including a nemesis or two—the women experience heartbreak, loss, hope, and triumph, all set against the colorful backdrop of the 'Greatest Show on Earth.'"

—*Publishers Weekly*,
for *The Ringmaster's Wife*

"A novel that is at once captivating, deeply poignant, and swirling with exquisite historical details of a bygone world, *The Ringmaster's Wife* will escort readers into the center ring, with its bright lights, exotic animals, and a dazzling performance that can only be described as the Greatest Show on Earth!"

—*Family Fiction*

"In true Kristy Cambron fashion, *The Ringmaster's Wife* is packed with emotional depth and characters who charm their way into your heart within the first pages. But perhaps most alluring about this story is the colorful world it's set in—from England to the Chicago World's Fair to the ever-moving backdrop of the circus world, I felt fully immersed. Engaging and poignant, this is a must-read!"

—*Melissa Tagg*, author of *From the Start* and *Like Never Before*

"A soaring love story! Vibrant with the glamour and awe that flourished under the Big Top in the 1920s, *The Ringmaster's Wife* invites the reader to meet the very people whose unique lives brought The Greatest Show on Earth down those rattling tracks. Through each of Rosamund's and Mable's stories, author Kristy Cambron offers the rare delight of witnessing a heartrending portrayal of love in the midst of circus life . . . and how one so deeply amplified the other."

—JOANNE BISCHOF, AWARD-WINNING
AUTHOR OF *THE LADY AND THE LIONHEART*

"The second installment of Cambron's Hidden Masterpiece series is as stunning as the first. Though heartbreaking in many places, this novel never fails to show hope despite dire circumstances. God's love shines even in the dark."

—*RT BOOK REVIEWS*, 4½ STARS,
TOP PICK! FOR *A SPARROW IN TEREZIN*

"In her second book, the author again interweaves a story from the present with a tale from the past. Both Sera and Kája must find courage to battle for a future against impossible circumstances."

—*CBA RETAILERS + RESOURCES*,
FOR *A SPARROW IN TEREZIN*

"Fans of the author's first book will gravitate to this tale of the power of faith and love to cope with impossible situations, although the grim realities depicted cannot be ignored. A must for book groups and genocide studies teachers and students."

—*LIBRARY JOURNAL*, STARRED REVIEW,
FOR *A SPARROW IN TEREZIN*

"Alternating points of view skillfully blend contemporary and historical fiction in this debut novel that is almost impossible to put down.

Well-researched yet heartbreaking scenes shed light on the horrors of concentration camps, as well as the contrasting beauty behind the prisoner's artwork. Two stories are carefully intertwined and demonstrate that there is always hope in God despite the monstrosities inflicted by man."

—*RT Book Reviews*, 4¹/₂ stars,
TOP PICK! for *The Butterfly
and the Violin*

"In her historical series debut, Cambron expertly weaves together multiple plotlines, time lines, and perspectives to produce a poignant tale of the power of love and faith in difficult circumstances. Those interested in stories of survival and the Holocaust, such as Elie Wiesel's 'Night,' will want to read."

—*Library Journal*, for *The
Butterfly and the Violin*

"This amazing book was emotionally engaging and very hard to put down. Its message of trusting God no matter the circumstances is one that will stay with your customers."

—*CBA Retailers + Resources*, for
The Butterfly and the Violin

"In chapters alternating between past and present, debut novelist Cambron vividly recounts interwoven sagas of heartache and recovery through courage, love, art, and faith."

—*Publishers Weekly*, for *The
Butterfly and the Violin*

THE
ILLUSIONIST'S
APPRENTICE

BOOKS BY KRISTY CAMBRON

The Ringmaster's Wife

THE HIDDEN MASTERPIECE NOVELS
The Butterfly and the Violin
A Sparrow in Terezin

the
Illusionist's
Apprentice

KRISTY CAMBRON

THOMAS NELSON
Since 1798

The Illusionist's Apprentice

Copyright © 2017 by Kristy Cambron

Published in Nashville, Tennessee, by Thomas Nelson. Thomas Nelson is a registered trademark of HarperCollins Christian Publishing, Inc.

Published in association with the Books & Such Literary Management, 52 Mission Circle, Suite 122, PMB 170, Santa Rosa, California 95409-5370, www.booksandsuch.com.

Interior design by: Mallory Collins

Thomas Nelson titles may be purchased in bulk for educational, business, fund-raising, or sales promotional use. For information, please e-mail SpecialMarkets@ThomasNelson.com.

Scripture quotation is from the *Holy Bible*, New Living Translation. © 1996, 2004, 2007, 2013 by Tyndale House Foundation. Used by permission of Tyndale House Publishers, Inc., Carol Stream, Illinois 60188. All rights reserved.

Library of Congress Cataloging-in-Publication Data

Names: Cambron, Kristy, author.
Title: The illusionist's apprentice / by Kristy Cambron.
Description: Nashville, Tennessee : Thomas Nelson, [2017]
Identifiers: LCCN 2016044577 | ISBN 9780718041502 (paperback)
Subjects: | GSAFD: Christian fiction.
Classification: LCC PS3603.A4468 I45 2017 | DDC 813/.6--dc23 LC record available at https://lccn.loc.gov/2016044577

Printed in the United States of America

17 18 19 20 21 LSC 5 4 3 2 1

For the real Jenny Wren:
because sisters have the magic of memories
and secrets all their own.

The world is full of obvious things
which nobody by any chance ever observes.

—Sherlock Holmes,
The Hound of the Baskervilles (1902)

CHAPTER 1

O death, where is your victory?
O death, where is your sting?

—1 Corinthians 15:55

December 31, 1926

Mount Auburn Cemetery

Cambridge, Mass.

Agent Elliot Matthews stared down a firing squad.

The potential executioners held firm in their stance with camera lenses and pencils cocked, all ready to fire. And fire they would, splashing sensational bulletins across the next day's newspaper headlines.

A slew of brash young journalists assembled in the famed Mount Auburn Cemetery, focused on the job at hand. They stood in formation at the front of the crowd, photographers tinkering with cameras and reporters tapping pencils against notepads, all with the itchiness of glorious anticipation.

Elliot hated feeling hemmed in, with the press and scores

of onlookers closing ranks. He wanted a full view in the event something erupted without warning, so he and his partner melted along the side of the gathering, opting for a perch along the old stone fence bordering Bigelow Chapel. They were still surrounded by the overhang of trees, but at least they would have a clear view of the front row.

The faces in the crowd weren't morose like one would expect to find in a cemetery on such a frigid day. They smiled and chatted, their curiosity piqued as they waited for the show to begin. Police stood by, too, poised to arrest anyone who dared to cause a stir.

And that's all Elliot could think it was. A *stir*.

A media frenzy in what should have been a place for mourners and gravediggers. Instead, a crowd of onlookers—spiritualists and press—had shown up at the public invitation printed in the *Boston Globe* the previous Monday: *Famed Medium Horace Stapleton to Defy Death in Public Ceremony on New Year's Eve.*

What a terrible waste. Elliot had seen a crowd of mourners fill a cemetery before—one too many times—and didn't want to be haunted by the host of memories the current setting dared trigger. Not wishing to think back on things he couldn't change, Elliot turned away and settled his attention on the landscape. If his objective was to forget, staring down lifeless trees seemed safer than watching a bunch of nail-biters in trench coats and fedoras.

The canopy of trees formed a bower on all sides. Mist invaded, curling around the trunks of aged sycamores and maples. An icy drizzle coated the leafless limbs, making the scene look like a fragile glass world.

"See that?" Elliot elbowed his partner.

Agent Connor Finnegan responded with a full-body turn and a squint in Elliot's direction. "Noticing something, boss?"

He coughed into his palm, a puff of breath on air. "Besides the zoo in front of us?"

"The trees." Elliot motioned to the line of sycamores and the only spot broken in the row of trees shadowing the chapel's stone border. "Odd. In a well-known and meticulously manicured cemetery like this, the grounds keepers leave a spot untended in full view of the chapel. It's just there. Barren. Lifeless. Like a tree fell and they neglected to replace it."

"But it's all barren, isn't it?" Connor looked around. "Everything and everyone's dead here. Shame we have to spend our New Year's Eve in a cemetery. We've been summoned to the event of the year—"

"Says who?" Elliot shot back before he could help himself. It wasn't the time to get caught up in the happenings of the society column. Connor should know that.

"Says me. And anyone with a brain rattling in his head. At the event of the year—maybe the decade—with scores of reporters and all of Boston's high society present, we have to spend it looking at a couple of trees on a hill?" He clapped his hands together in front of him, his brow furrowed. "Sometimes I wish this job had a little more action to it."

Connor was a roughneck of an agent with a thick New Englander's accent and shades of pretension he shouldn't yet own for barely a year with the Bureau. But he wore it well. He could be laid back when it suited him, but obviously not when forced to brave the punishing midwinter temperatures for a mockery of a display.

"More action isn't always a good thing. But yeah, Ace. That's why we're here. To notice what other people don't, action or not."

"Trees . . . Figures." Connor heaved a sigh. "Don't tell me we were sent all the way out here to look at landscaping. Notice something more interesting, why don't you? You tell me that missing tree is somehow connected to a dame and maybe then I'll listen. How 'bout you find a nice pair of gams for us to appreciate while we wait for the show to start."

"Classy."

"I submit that class wasn't a requirement when I applied for this job."

"And we never said you shouldn't look for it down the road either." Elliot tossed the thought away and turned his wrist to check his watch. "It's nearly noon."

"Good." Connor rubbed his hands together. "Because my face is starting to freeze. The sooner this clown starts and finishes his show, the better. My insides are screaming for a cup of joe. And I can't tell you how many party invites I had for tonight, and I'm poised to miss out on all of them if something doesn't happen soon."

Needing something mundane to occupy his mind, Elliot pulled the ivory-faced lighter from his pocket—the one his father used to own. It had been his favorite, one Elliot remembered now only in memories of days before the Great War. But even those had begun to fade as time passed. He flipped it back and forth between his fingers, waiting for the show to begin.

The crowd hushed then, drawing their attention.

"It appears he's not going to make you wait any longer." Elliot tipped his chin forward. "Look."

On the hinges of his words, a figure broke through the mass of people, the center of the crowd parting around him.

Flashbulbs flickered, lighting up the man's purple velvet coat and top hat. He was rail thin but elegant, moving with haughty purpose as the sheen on his long coat reflected the light with each drawn-out stride.

"That's Stapleton."

"Doesn't look like much." Connor curled up the side of his lip. "But he makes up for what he lacks in stature with gumption, eh? Houdini's not even two months cold in his grave, and this guy's already organized a public parade to discount his memory."

"Entertainers thrive on their media attention. We knew it wouldn't be long before characters like Stapleton would step out in the public eye again. They'll try to discredit Houdini's memory or make a bigger name for themselves now that he's out of the picture."

"So you don't believe Stapleton is a real medium?"

"Doesn't matter what I think. In this line of work, it only matters what we can prove. Remember that. Stapleton's an illusionist. That's a fact. Beyond that, I wouldn't try to guess."

The showman climbed two steps onto a platform that had been erected—a clumsy but wide setup of wood and paper streamers that had been strewn about and were now frozen by the misty rain that still clung to the morning air. The paper became a skeletal backdrop that danced in its fight with the wind, lending a macabre feel to the makeshift stage.

In front of the setup, the chilling image of an open grave.

In clear view of the press, the excavated earth was piled into a mound behind the pit, its top darkened by the rain. Gravediggers stood off to the side, heads down against the wind, holding fast to shovels and picks.

The crowd rumbled with murmurings. Stapleton raised his arms, quieting them with confident control. "It has been said that no man holds the authority over death." His voice boomed, an Irish accent clinging to his words.

Connor rolled his eyes heavenward. "Five clams says the accent's a fake."

"Shh." Elliot frowned, though not from Connor's comic zeal. Somehow, he knew what was coming next.

Stapleton held the crowd's undivided attention. "Many have claimed to be great illusionists. And that is *all* they are. Trick-makers. They grasp your money in their pockets, tearing your eyes from the truth with evil deceit. But I ask you—who here has lost someone? Any sweethearts whose futures with their soldiers were cut short? Any mothers who've buried their husbands or sons? Would you not wish to hear from your beloved just once more? Could mere illusionists help you in this endeavor? I think not."

Elliot had to swallow the distaste growing more bitter in his mouth.

Both he and Connor had been assigned to the case as silent observers—proof that the federal government would investigate claims of fraud into characters who would mislead the public. But they were on strict orders not to get involved—unless, of course, they had to keep the peace.

If he had his way, Elliot would cuff Stapleton and haul him before a judge on principle alone. To manipulate the hearts of hurting people was beyond dastardly, but this man seemed to be almost enjoying it.

"So what is truth? I seek to enlighten you. With no trickery. No illusions . . ." Stapleton punched a fist in the air, professing, "Just plain and simple *power* from the other side. Power to give you back what you've lost . . . And I shall put this power on display today, right before you."

Elliot's brows tipped up. *Well, Houdini may have dealt a blow to this man's career once, but Stapleton certainly has no confidence problem now.*

"That's right. My dear members of the press," Stapleton

shouted, looking down at the crowd with a thick layer of sympathy. "Many of you have stood watch all night, in the deteriorating weather, inspecting each shovelful of dirt and every swing of the pickax as it was brought down to cut the earth before me. We have representatives here and a medical doctor selected by our distinguished Mayor Nichols's office, as well as both state and federal law enforcement and a few choice guests to whom I have extended personal invitations—all to lend credence to what you are about to witness.

"You've been shown the authentication of the plot by which we now stand, for a Mr. Victor Peale, who has been confined to the grave these twenty years. And yes—you've doubted, even as you watched with your own eyes . . ."

Stapleton pointed a bony finger at the crowd, singling out the presence of disbelievers like a plague among them. "But I submit before you, humble as I may, that death is not the final chapter."

Connor groaned, making Elliot crack an unwanted smile. He glanced away from Stapleton's onstage antics, opting to scan the faces of the people packed in before them. Watching. Willing them to see truth. To turn around and go back home. Didn't they realize it was an outlandish claim from a career illusionist? That it was not possible to bring a man back from the grave after that much time? Yet they stood on. Transfixed. Their mouths gaping and confidence clinging to his words.

A shame. The man is just beating his gums, but they're still eating it up.

Stapleton's spell fell to blanket the gathering like snow. Who would be bought in after the show? Who would eventually fork out money—and worse, their *hope*—to this character in the days and weeks to follow?

Elliot shook his head for the poor souls. The man's claims were clearly too sensational to be true. He couldn't help but pity the lot of them. Then something odd caught his eye, drawing his attention away: a flash of fiery crimson buried behind a sea of black woolen coats and hats.

A figure stood off to the side of the crowd, alone.

Sheltered by the haven of a great oak, she was hidden beneath a crimson hood and cape that spilled down to dust the frozen ground at her feet. The garment hid fragments of dress quite eccentric for a woman: a high-collared man's shirt peeking out at the neck, a gold bow tie, black trousers, and matching over-the-knee riding boots. And while the dress piqued Elliot's notice, it was the woman's reaction to Stapleton's words that would not allow him to look away.

Hers was an aura of contradiction.

She owned flaming-red hair with blunt-cut bangs and waves that just peeked out from the hood. And though she projected the illusion of poise, the tips of her hair had caught on the wind and brushed the side of her face, seemingly without her care. Her lips were pursed and her glare pierced the stage, as if she possessed emotion barely held at bay. She clutched at the front of her cape with one gloved hand and held a gleaming black walking stick in the other. She leaned on it, like a stake she was attempting to drive into the ground.

Elliot tipped his head to one side. *It's a disguise.*

A good one, no doubt.

Anyone looking at her would notice the peculiar clothing first. But the woman's mannerisms were decidedly forced. Something had infuriated her, and Elliot wanted to know what it was.

"Connor," he asked, dropping his voice low. Elliot tipped

his chin toward the cloaked figure. "Have you ever seen her before?"

Connor tossed a glance in the woman's direction, then turned back to Stapleton's onstage flailings. "She's one of that lot."

"What lot?"

"You know. The *vaude* performers. Like Stapleton. Though she's one of the more infamous ones on the circuit."

Elliot watched her, the curiosity of her presence holding his attention fast. "A vaude performer, hmm?"

"Don't tell me you've never been to one of those seedy song-and-dance halls before. Or with your father's money, at least one of the more well-to-do theaters?" Connor failed to veil the mocking in his tone. "If I didn't know of your years at the Bureau, I'd have guessed you were the rookie instead of me. It's vaudeville, Elliot. And Wren Lockhart is her name."

Elliot gritted his teeth each time his family's money was brought into a similar conversation, as if that assured his position in society without any merit to his own choices. But Connor was young and just shy of tactless, so Elliot let it slide. "That's her real name?" Elliot paused. "Or stage name?"

"What does it matter, really? She's one of them. But if it's stems you're looking to gaze at, please don't let it be the type in trousers. I'd think you'd have a swankier view with the dancers. I know I'd much prefer it."

"I'm not gazing at anything," Elliot snapped, keenly feeling the dig at his clumsy understanding of entertainment trends. "It's just . . ."

"What?"

Elliot shook his head, still watching the woman. "Something. I'm not quite sure yet."

"Well, you'd better get sure." Connor took a cigarette out of his inside pocket. He struck a match against his thumb and cupped his hand to tender the end with a deep inhale. "Because here we go."

Stapleton had moved on from the theatrics of his grand entrance to the marvel of the main act. He stood with his shoulders back and chin notched high. A rich, almost grandfatherly warmth spread over his face as he smiled. "And now? It begins."

The sudden roar of an engine ripped through the air.

An auto chugged forward, taking the slack out of a length of chain against a pulley hoisted to the side of the stage. Metal popped and tightened and the crowd jumped.

"He's not . . . ," Connor whispered, the cigarette dangling off his bottom lip, threatening to flutter to the ground.

"Oh, but I believe he is," Elliot said, just as the corner of a coffin appeared at the inside edge of the grave, rising up, up, up. The chains creaked with the tension of metal-to-metal friction.

Connor swore under his breath and spat the cigarette from his lips to grind it out beneath the sole of his shoe. He grumbled about not getting paid enough for something or another.

"And now, ladies and gentlemen"—Stapleton's voice slithered through the trees—"the moment you have all been waiting for. The power no one before has harnessed! I shall defy the laws of nature . . ."

The auto slowed, then kicked into reverse, lowering the coffin into the gravediggers' waiting arms. They steered it to the platform with a soft *thud*, then backed away from it.

The crowd let out a collective gasp.

"It is quite alright, I assure you. But who among you can claim the fortitude to stare death in the face?" Stapleton scanned the mass of onlookers with a raised eyebrow. "Who dares to open this crypt and give a man back his life? Who will aid me in summoning his soul from the depths of the hereafter to life among us once again?"

The crowd pulsed with energy. Women edged back, abhorred by the thought of being chosen to resurrect a decayed corpse. Members of the press leaned in, craning their necks to see, though none proved bold enough to volunteer. So all waited. Looking left to right. Watching. Expecting *something*—they just didn't know what.

Elliot kept his feet firm, only migrating his glance from Stapleton, to the crowd, and back to the cloaked woman perched at the fringe of the action. She hadn't moved a muscle, just stood there, haunting the shadowed outline of the oak.

"What's this?" Stapleton bellowed. "Women, have you no husbands who can stand up to the confines of a mere wooden box? We've already opened the grave for you. You have but to urge your man forward to lift the coffin lid and marvel at the wonders inside! Can no one help me?"

"I'll do it." A female voice sliced through the tension.

All heads turned at once, eyes fixated on the woman weaving from the back of the gathering to the front of the crowd.

She was impeccably dressed, made noticeable by a saucy walk. Her heels barely touched the frozen grass as she sauntered by in her fox-trimmed coat. She tossed a coy grin to a few members of the press and rubbed gloved hands against her shoulders, theatrically playing out a mock shiver in comment to the cold. "I'd hate to make this crowd endure another moment in the glacial elements while they wait for one of our courageous men to step forward. I will take up your challenge, good sir."

Connor chuckled and tipped his fedora back a shade from his brow.

Elliot could read the measure of his thoughts. And they wouldn't be far from every other man's at the moment. If Stapleton's intention was to wow the international press, then the surprising turn of events was quite in his favor, to the point of being downright historic.

"I have a constitution sturdy enough to lift the lid." The woman slipped up onstage with flashbulbs snapping at her gold-trimmed cloche hat and bobbed brunette curls framing her cheery face. She winked in the direction of the gravediggers. "If these men onstage will help me."

"And what is your name, miss?"

"I am *Mrs.* Amberley Dover."

A rumble of murmurs grew out of her declaration, yet she stood on in defiance, the tips of her heels mere inches from the death box onstage.

"Swell dame. I wonder who she is. Asking purely for the case file of course." Connor kept his voice just low enough to be heard over the crowd's chatter.

"You may know your vaudes, Connor, but I know Boston's elite. That young woman is the widow of Mr. Stanley Dover—of the Boston Dovers—and owes much to his railroad-financed inheritance."

"Would you look at that? She's not afraid a bit," Connor said, starstruck as the woman lifted the lid with dainty fingertips. He leaned in, watching as one of the gravediggers applied the muscle, and she applied smiles and winks for the crowd. "Looks as though he's gained a high-society femme fatale as his ally. Think you can introduce me?"

"Regardless of who'd like to be in her social circle, I'd say she's out of everyone's league here. That woman is rumored to be

wealthier than the king of England. And no, I'm not the introducing kind. If you want to meet her, you're on your own."

"Now, Elliot, don't judge her because of her money. We
ought to at least see what she has to say about all this. It's the
gentlemanly thing to do."

"She's also a fashionable flirt, and I'd say that's being rather
kind." Elliot noted the way Wren Lockhart straightened her
stance and raised her chin higher when Mrs. Dover sauntered
across the stage. "But I also have to wonder why she's here, now
that you mention it. She's known to be a supporter of spiritualism, but under normal circumstances I don't think she'd be
caught dead on a stage like this."

"Nice pun."

"She's an elitist, so it's no pun." Elliot darted his gaze back
and forth between the woman in red and the action onstage.
"But it is an observation. As is something else." He edged forward into the crowd.

"Elliot?" Connor barked out a whisper. "Where are you
going?"

The woman by the oak had begun to move. Not so much that
anyone would notice, but Wren Lockhart had been withdrawing
from the crowd with furtive steps the instant Mrs. Dover had
appeared in the spotlight.

Instinct told him he shouldn't let the woman go—not without at least some inquiry as to her presence here. It could have
been innocent, but his gut had taken to fierce nagging, forcing
his feet to move.

"Elliot!"

Connor's voice bled into the background as Elliot wove
through the throngs of people, peering past men with bowlers

and ladies' fur-trimmed hats, keeping his gaze locked on Ms. Lockhart's cape.

The crowd surged, crying out in a marvelous gasp.

And Elliot lost sight of the woman in red.

He took his gaze away from where she stood for mere seconds, just in time to see that the coffin lid had been opened wide.

"And now, the doctor chosen by our mayor's office will examine the corpse to ensure he is, in fact, dead." Stapleton waved his arm wide, inviting the doctor to share the stage. It took but a moment for the aged doctor with stethoscope in hand to climb the stairs and examine the corpse. He confirmed with a nod of the head as flashbulbs burst.

"Does the man have a heartbeat, Doctor? Any breath sounds or signs of life at all?"

The doctor shook his head. "No heartbeat. No breath. This man is most certainly dead."

Stapleton hesitated, then a syrupy smile eased across his lips. "We have confirmation, dear ladies and gentlemen. There is a corpse here on the stage. But I ask you . . . how can this be"—he waved his open hand out over the coffin—"when I've brought him back from the grave?"

The crowd hushed.

Elliot wasn't sure what, if anything, was in the coffin. Up to that moment, it could have all been a farce. Maybe still was. But then he saw a man, his skin ashen and hair mussed about his brow, began to rise from the depths of the wooden box.

Elliot darted a glance back at Connor. His partner tipped his shoulders up in a shrug of total bewilderment. It was an illusion, no doubt, but a cracking good one.

"Yes," Stapleton shouted out with triumph. "Come back to

us, sir! You are welcome here, Mr. Peale. Come back from the depths . . ."

And to the utter shock of the crowd, the corpse-man sat up fully.

His eyelids fluttered against the light of day, then opened.

He looked around as if in a trance. Every twitch of muscle and tremble of what should have been rotting flesh precipitated another gasp. He shook out his arms, as if his long slumber could be shrugged off as easily as the sleeves of his suit coat.

Mr. Peale raised shaky legs over the side of the casket and, to a reverberating chorus of shrieks and popping flashbulbs, stepped onto the stage.

The gravediggers darted back, and one fell off the rear of the platform completely, then scurried to disappear behind the auto-and-pulley contraption.

If this is an act, it appears the gravediggers had no knowing part in it.

Elliot couldn't be sure of Mrs. Amberley Dover, however.

Her face had drained of all color but the lipstick on her open mouth. She stood frozen, her gaze following Mr. Peale's wobbly steps as he moved across the stage. She tore her glance over to Stapleton, her eyes questioning like a lost bird. He shook his head, ever so slightly, then turned to address the crowd.

If she's in on this, she isn't playing it well.

"There is nothing to fear, friends!" Stapleton eased an arm out toward Mr. Peale. "Look at him. He is no monster. No Frankenstein creation. This is one of our own—a Bostonian. A man whose life was stolen in his prime. And now, I give it all back . . ."

Mr. Peale had risen from the dead—at least that's what the

crowd was led to believe. Though the evidence was quite compelling, Elliot wouldn't be so easily taken in.

He looked away from the stage and regained a visual of the bright crimson of Ms. Lockhart's cape, peeking out from behind the sea of dark suits. She held his gaze for a few seconds. Then, as if on cue, her attention slid back to Stapleton, who'd taken the corpse-man by the elbow, ushering him to center stage.

Flashbulbs burst to life as journalists shot out questions in rapid succession.

"What have you seen?"

"What is it like on the other side?"

"Speak!" They raised their arms, grasping out to him.

"Tell us what you know!"

"Yes. Do speak to us, sir." Stapleton nodded beneath the brim of his top hat. "Tell us why you've come back . . . Share the secrets of the beyond!"

The crowd waited, eerily silent as Peale's lips began to move.

Elliot's thoughts were blazing so fast through his mind, he hadn't an instant to collect them. Connor moved in closer to the stage to his right. And as the crowd watched, the corpse became fully man and *spoke*.

"I am Victor Peale," he said in a shaky voice. "I have seen the beyond . . ."

His voice grew stronger. *He* grew stronger and shook his elbow out of Stapleton's grasp to approach the front of the stage. The ladies shrieked as the men shuffled them backward on the frozen grass.

"I have come back from the other side . . ." Mr. Peale paused. Shook his head, ruffling hair to fall over his forehead. He tensed a chiseled jaw. "I have come back to . . ."

Stapleton approached his side. "Yes, Mr. Peale. Dear sir." He waved a hand out to hush the crowd again. "What is it you have come back to tell us?"

There was no warning. Victor Peale's eyes simply rolled back in his head and he pitched forward, diving from the stage into a heap at the foot of the crowd.

Elliot's suspicions were confirmed, but in the worst way. The world would not see a man raised from the dead that day, but the newspapers would certainly have their headlines. He charged forward through the chaos of screams and wilting ladies, as did Connor and several of the clothed policemen.

"Back up. We're federal agents." Connor pushed his way in. He flashed his credentials to the policemen attempting to pull them back behind the press.

And all at once, they were surrounded.

Looking on were astonished faces and the flashing of camera bulbs. As Connor knelt to see to the motionless Mr. Peale, Elliot craned his neck, stretching to his full height above the crowd, searching for the spot by the oak where she'd stood.

Empty.

All had been drawn in to the madness—except for Wren Lockhart. She'd swept up her curious air of oddity at the moment everyone else's attentions had been affixed to the stage, disappearing into the cemetery's icy landscape at the very height of the chaos.

"It doesn't make sense," Elliot said.

"I'll say it doesn't." Connor rocked back on his heels. He slid off his fedora and slapped it against his knee. "You can all move back now. We'll not hear anything further from this man today. He's dead."

CHAPTER 2

JANUARY 12, 1927

85 MOUNT VERNON STREET

BOSTON, MASS.

"There's a man here to see you." Irina bounded through the door to Wren's private office.

The sound of creaking floorboards drew Wren's attention to her business manager, who'd begun moving about in a flurry.

"I'm up to my elbows in all this." Wren held a hand over the mound of mail littering her desk. "Could you please make our excuses?"

"Not today, Wren. Excuses won't be enough." She rushed through the French doors to Wren's adjoining bedchamber and dropped an armful of linens on the coverlet of the four-poster bed. "I've brought things for you to dress."

Irina continued, opening the oversized wardrobe on the far wall. She plucked out a pair of riding boots, then tossed them with a thump in the center of the ornamental rug covering the hardwood floor.

Wren turned away. Irina was in one of her moods. As Wren's manager, she was ambitious, always pushing Wren for public appearances—like photos with the mayor, an extra stage show squeezed in wherever possible. It had to be some such nuisance after the events of New Year's Eve. The spotlight had been thrust on vaudeville, thanks to Horace Stapleton. No doubt Irina saw an advantage in it.

Despite Irina's overachieving nature, devising a workable escape plan was all Wren could think of at the moment. And this one wasn't unlocking chains in a water tank or vanishing from inside the depths of a wardrobe. That she'd done onstage for years and could manage with her eyes closed. But escaping from her present circumstances felt far more impossible.

Wren needed to think, not have her office invaded.

She stared down at the stack of mail on her desk. The pink stationery with gold foil lettering on the top of the pile—she wished she could forget she'd ever seen it. It was an invitation to a lavish soirée in honor of grieving widow Amberley Dover's upcoming birthday. It had arrived by messenger mere hours after Victor Peale had met his demise at the cemetery. And there it remained days later, looking back at her with defiance every time she dared to consider answering it.

"Irina, if it's a member of the press, then he should already know my answer. I've had no comment for nearly two weeks, and I will refuse any today. That goes for tomorrow too. If they keep this up, I may have the telephone disconnected. Those vultures will have to write their stories without my assistance. Period."

Irina shook her head, concern flashing in her green eyes. "It's not the press."

Wren leaned back in her wooden swivel chair and parted the ivory lace drapes with her fingertips. The snow-blanketed landscape showed no tire tracks to mar the smooth drive. The street was still quiet, the sun just peeking through the maze of trees below.

"I didn't hear a car come up."

"The man claims he parked on the street and walked up across the ridge."

"Someone walked through the snowdrifts?" Wren released the drapes to float back into place and shrugged. "That's bold. Who is it then?"

Wren suppressed the thought of Mrs. Dover's invitation. She couldn't remember the last time they'd entertained a social call nor been invited for one.

"It's the law."

Wren waved her off with a flick of the wrist and turned back to her letters. The way Irina had charged in had almost made her think it was something serious. But a policeman stopping by her front stoop was nothing to worry about. They'd never been able to intimidate her before, and Stapleton's fiasco at the cemetery wouldn't change that.

What could they possibly say to sway her into making a statement now?

Her mind flashed back to the cemetery—to the man who'd locked his gaze with hers. The one whose blue eyes seemed able to look straight through her. Whoever he was, he knew how to handle himself. The way he scanned the crowd instead of watching the stage spoke volumes. If Wren had to wager a guess, she'd have put her money on the fact that he was a lawman.

And that meant she'd employ a wide berth in the opposite direction.

"As if the police have nothing better to do than to bother us. Take the gentleman's card please, and tell him we'll be in touch."

Wren returned to writing an address on her envelope. "That should send him on his way."

"Not this time. He says you've already done that. Twice this week alone . . ." Irina paused, staring back with eyebrows slightly raised.

"Well?" Wren's stomach started to sink. It wasn't like Irina to be so coy about anything. "Then what does he want when he should already know our answer?"

"He's an agent from the Federal Bureau, and he claims he'll stay here until you consent to speak with him." Irina moved about the room again, her words hanging in the air as she pulled a brush from the vanity drawer. "Furthermore, he says he'll take you to the downtown office if he must, but he's giving you the choice as to where you'd prefer to answer his questions—as a courtesy."

The manner of anyone to make such a demand could prick Wren's temper on the best of mornings. But not two weeks after the grand fiasco at Mount Auburn Cemetery? She had nothing to do with Stapleton's public failure, except to feel that the man had brought ruin raining upon himself and now could stew in it.

"He said it was a courtesy?"

"Right before I left him in the entry." Irina tipped her head toward the door that led to the hall. "He's waiting there now."

Wren dropped her pen and stood. "Irina? Stop." The unwelcome sensation of fear pricked at her spine. "In the ten years we've worked together, you've never been this insistent. Tell me. What's happened?"

Irina moved around to the side of the bed and set down an unbuttoned linen shirt and tuxedo jacket. "He knows who you are, Wren. I have no idea how, but he knows."

Wren swallowed hard and looked down at the soft ivory sweater and paisley drop-waist skirt she wore. They were airy and feminine—things she desperately wanted to feel—rather than having to put on the street costume and play her part of the eccentric illusionist while inside her own home.

"How can you be sure?"

Irina sighed, a slight crease to her brow. "Because he didn't ask to see you," she said, her voice hushed as if the gentleman could hear through the floorboards. "He said he wants to speak with Jennifer Charles. And he seems to think she's here."

Wren's throat went dry. Why in the world would anyone want to know about that name? It had been buried. Long ago buried in her past. Who could want to unearth it now?

"I see . . . ," she managed, though the words came out on a rough whisper.

One last look at the invitation on top of the stack. It would have to wait yet again. She crossed the room, ready to do battle if that's what lay ahead.

"Make sure all of the doors are locked down the length of the hall." Wren straightened her spine. "And see that things aren't disturbed upstairs. I'll do my best to get rid of him. When I pull the chord in the library, you'll know he's ready to leave—and quickly."

"Of course."

Time to go to work . . .

She swept up the costume from the bed. "Oh, and Irina? Make him wait. A good twenty minutes at the very least, so he knows where we stand."

❉

Ms. Lockhart's entry hall was not dissimilar from the many high-society homes Elliot had seen before. Hers boasted inlaid mahogany floors, an impressive, storybook staircase curving up a wall papered in tones of burnished cream and gold, a chandelier wrapped with gold-tipped leafy vines twinkling from the ceiling overhead, and lush ivory nail-head chairs lining the back wall.

And the house smelled of warm cinnamon mingling with a strong odor of something Elliot could only guess was curry. The mix of spicy aromas swept through the entry of the ornate brick mansion, enveloping him the instant he'd stepped inside.

Not altogether cold.

Thick robin's-egg blue and gold brocade curtains painted the length of wall from floor to ceiling at the opposite end of the entry. They were drawn tight over what? Doors? Hidden rooms? Elliot had to wonder if that was their purpose—to make one question everything the eye couldn't see behind them.

The atmosphere is careful. Almost too controlled . . . Ms. Lockhart sees to every detail.

Elliot had set out to learn as much as he could about the infamous Wren Lockhart in the past days. Though her three-story home looked quite stately from the street, with tall, arched windows that overlooked Boston's famous Common, it was rumored to hold a menagerie of marvels on the inside. And he was here to learn if this, and his own suspicions about Ms. Lockhart, were indeed true.

"Sir?"

He turned. The woman who'd shown him in stood just behind, an aloof air surrounding her.

"It's not sir. Agent Matthews suits me fine. We hold no pretenses at the Bureau."

"Very well, Agent Matthews. If you'll come this way."

The woman leading him down the hall must be the one he'd heard about—Ms. Lockhart's business manager. With an avant-garde tunic in shades of rust and jade and deep-chocolate hair cropped tight like a man's, she was the only woman in Boston who could fit the description of an islander from the South Pacific. The tight, sculpted coif at her brow highlighted dark-rimmed eyes of a striking and almost iridescent green. Her oversized gold earrings swayed with each step she took.

She appeared quite controlled—every bit the type of individual Elliot expected for someone in Ms. Lockhart's employ. She didn't utter a word when she opened the door to a moderately sized library at the end of a hall. Floor-to-ceiling windows were tightly shuttered and a fire sizzled in the hearth, orange and yellow flickers dancing through the darkness.

"Do come in, Agent Matthews." She swept in before him, moving to the desk in the center of the room to flick on a lamp with an intricate filigree shade. Light bathed the space in a hue of warm gold. The room greeted Elliot with oddities that cried out for attention from a hundred different directions.

A taxidermist's talent was perched high above the mantel: a big-game cat's head, labeled *ocelot*, mounted on a carved-wood plaque, with spotted fur and fangs bared a few inches long. Its oversized glass eyes were eerily lifelike, watching him as he waited in the doorway.

On either side of the room were wooden built-ins lined with apothecary jars, which the woman busied herself with inspecting. Towers of ancient books, dusty and worn, were set in thick stacks on an ornately carved desk. Potted plants and rows of canisters bearing chalkboard labels tied with twine round their lids lined deep windowsills. The far wall held an oversized world map, a gold-framed oil painting of a pirate character, and an impressive collection of swords artfully displayed on hooks, their blades burnishing in the firelight.

Elliot wasn't easily intimidated.

He'd walked into crime scenes that could turn even a seasoned veteran's stomach and had weathered them without cracking the veneer of his exterior, no matter what was going on inside him. But the library wasn't exactly what he'd expected. It was at once curious and threatening—the oddest sort of combination—as if a sideshow caravan had broken down and camped the contents of its wagons inside the four walls. It was such a contrast to the pristine entry hall that Elliot had to question what could be the motive to receive guests in spaces that were such polar opposites of one other.

In truth, he'd never seen anything like it.

"Please. Do make yourself comfortable." The woman motioned him to the pair of high-back leather chairs by the fire. "Ms. Lockhart will be down momentarily."

Elliot crossed the room, to which the woman nodded and left the door open a shade behind her. He settled on the edge of the chair with his feet firmly planted on the hardwood floor, hands gathered in a loose fist in front of him.

A deep-chested grandfather clock chimed loudly from its perch on the far wall—nine o'clock. The fire danced, popping and sizzling with the ticking of the clock, lulling into a soft melody about the room.

He looked around.

And waited.

Elliot tapped his shoes against the hardwood, staring through the crack in the door as the minutes ticked by. He unbuttoned his jacket and leaned back into the chair. He checked the clock again, finding that his initial interest in the room's contents had faded into apathy, followed by full-fledged irritation when nearly a half an hour had ticked by.

He finally blew out his breath in a sigh and slapped his hands to his knees, ready to jump up and start tearing open doors if that's what it took to get five minutes out of the woman's busy schedule.

The door creaked across the room and suddenly, there she was—standing in the doorway, her golden eyes and porcelain skin bathed in the firelight. Her flaming hair was wavy and unbound, wild to a blunt point inches below her jawline. She wore gentleman's attire again, but this time a tuxedo jacket in navy, a matching bow tie, and trousers of a light tan.

Lovely wasn't a word she probably wished would be used to describe her. *Mysterious. Confident,* maybe, that she didn't have to dress like a lady. But despite the gentleman's attire, Elliot found himself irritated by more than the time he'd been kept waiting. Wren Lockhart must command just about every room she walked into, down to the way she stood with shoulders back, spine straight and, without shame at her boldness, met people eye to eye.

The way she seemed to be staring straight through him now. He'd never have owned up to it, but that confidence was decidedly memorable.

He stood and angled his head in a slight nod.

"Good morning." She offered the greeting from deeply painted lips. "My apologies to have kept you waiting."

A hint of a British accent? Unexpected . . .

Wren kept her gaze directed on Elliot as she stepped into the library. The manager woman returned and stood behind, awaiting instructions from her mistress.

"Irina? Tea for two, please."

"Of course, Ms. Lockhart." Irina offered the slightest of coy smiles, then tipped her head to Elliot. As if she knew some secret delight he didn't and only played the part of the respectful ser-vant for the merits of his benefit.

"And you may close the door," Wren added just as the woman was stepping out.

Something exchanged between the women—they made a silent connection with their eyes.

Wren waited until Irina had clicked the door closed before she crossed the room. "I hope Darjeeling is acceptable, Mr. . . ."

"Elliot Matthews." He nodded and remained standing until she decided to sit. "Or Agent Matthews. And whatever you have will be fine. To be honest, I'm not much for tea anyway."

She said nothing right away, just eased down into the chair across from the one he'd vacated moments before, keeping her back pin-straight and crossing her legs at the ankle. "Very well, Agent Matthews. To what do I owe the honor of a visit from Boston's finest? I'm afraid I'm unaccustomed to calls this early in the day."

He followed her lead and sat, then pulled a notepad and pen-cil from his inner jacket pocket. "I'm from the Federal Bureau of Investigation, madam. The Boston field office. And I am sorry about the timing of this visit. It couldn't be helped. But if you'll allow me, I'm just here to ask a few questions in the death inves-tigation of Victor Peale. Would that be alright?"

"Who?"

"Victor Aurelius Peale." *This is going to be like pulling teeth . . .* "The man who died at the cemetery on New Year's Eve," he added, though it was perfectly clear Ms. Lockhart knew of whom he spoke. It had been the talk of Boston since it happened. And she'd been there. Plain as day. Occupying a spot under an old oak. Seething beneath layers of crimson satin.

Wren clicked her tongue against the roof of her mouth, as if the recollection of the day's events was falling back into place in her mind. "You're quite certain that's his name? And that he was alive to begin with? I read in the papers that it's still up for debate whether he really is dead."

The lady had cheek.

In spades.

And though Elliot could assess many things about this woman, his ability to anticipate her next moves proved elusive. He managed to fight against a smile trying to ease across his lips.

If she wanted a cat-and-mouse game of wits, she'd get one.

"We are certain of his name . . . as much as we can be at this point. But yes, the medical examiner has confirmed he is dead. Do you always answer questions with a question?"

She paused. "Well, that all depends, Agent Matthews. Should I suspect there's a hidden motive behind this inquisition? Or is it simply a friendly call? Because if it's friendly, we can enjoy our tea and talk about the art on the walls. But if it's something different, I do wish you'd come out with it. I am a very busy woman."

"Very well. I have to question everyone who was at the cemetery when Victor Peale's death occurred. On principle, of course."

"And how do you know I was there?"

The veil fell and Elliot smiled this time. "Because you know *I* saw you there."

Wren drummed her slender fingertips in a silent melody against the armrest of her chair. "So you did. May I also assume Horace Stapleton was the first in line for your questioning?"

"Naturally. But we're considering all angles, so to speak."

"You mean you're considering all motives."

"Motives for what?"

"Precisely." She tipped her head toward the door to the hall. "No partner? I thought you Bureau boys traveled together. Like a pair of well-worn shoes."

Just who was conducting this interview?

"Well, yes. We do work in teams, Ms. Lockhart. My partner is outside having a smoke."

"I see." She clasped her hands in her lap. "You will have to tell him he missed out on a warm fire and pleasant conversation. And our tea, when it arrives. Or perhaps you're a bourbon man? But alas, I loathe it and won't allow a single drop under my roof—that, too, on principle."

"While I applaud you for following the law to the letter, I really won't be here long enough for a drink of anything." Elliot flipped the notepad open to a fresh page. "I'd just like to get down to business, then be on my way, if that's alright?"

"Certainly."

"Good. Have you always worked as a magician?"

Wren brought the tips of her fingers together in a steeple under her chin but said nothing right away.

He wrote *Confident* at the top of the page.

"I have never worked as a magician, Agent Matthews."

Elliot glanced up, meeting her challenge. "Then the newspapers have it wrong? You haven't given shows all over the world? Taken to, uh . . ." He flipped a few pages back in his pad. "*Wanderlust*, I believe the press called it. I wonder if you could comment on that."

She narrowed her eyes, a sure sign his question was ill appreciated. "I don't see the relevance of that question. And I'd contend that newspapers manage to get few things correct," she said matter-of-factly. "You asked if I'd always worked as a magician. The answer is no. I never have. I'm an illusionist, and there is quite a difference. I've never claimed the use of magic. I don't believe in it."

"You're a religious woman then?"

"Faith and religion can be two different things. I prefer not to confuse them. And as to wanderlust? Well, that is the newspapers' opinion. I simply don't bother to correct them. As I said, I haven't the time."

"I'll make note of that—*no newspapers*." He jotted down *Clever* as the next word on his list. "And how long have you lived at this estate?"

"Six years."

"Does anyone else live here at the house with you?"

Her eyes turned playful, sparkling in their golden depths. "Is that a backhanded way of inquiring as to whether I'm married, Agent Matthews?"

"No—" He faltered for a breath, then sat up a little straighter, covering the hitch. "I need an account of everyone under this roof in the event I have to come back."

"Irina, my business manager, whom you met at the door, lives here at the estate. We have Mr. Adler on staff from time to time. He comes twice a week to tend the garden and grounds, but that's usually only in season."

"No other permanent staff?" He added *Independent* to the list, then looked up as she gave a slow shake of her head, a cool smile easing onto her lips.

"Not at the moment."

"And why is that? It's quite a large estate house from the looks of it."

"It is. But you see, if I need something done then I take care of it myself. We typically bring new staff in only for a party or an event, but that is planned well in advance and all candidates are thoroughly screened to my satisfaction."

"Right." Elliot nodded, underlining *Independent* on his list for good measure. "And did your staff attend Horace Stapleton's show with you?"

"No. I don't employ staff, as I've said, so I attended alone. My manager stayed on to watch over my affairs here, which she always does."

"So you won't be surprised when I corroborate these details."

"Of course not." She paused. "And when the questions about Victor Peale begin, let me know. I do so want to be on my toes."

Elliot cleared his throat. If he wanted to battle with the wry wit of Wren Lockhart, he'd have to hit harder.

A lot harder. "Very good. Last question, Ms. Lockhart, and it looks like I can be out of your way for now." Elliot punctuated the statement by locking eyes with hers in an iron glare. "Is it true that your real name is Jennifer Charles?"

Her features iced over, chilling the temperature of the room despite the warmth of the fire. She raised her chin, as if the question were a marked intrusion into a place she'd put up a fight to keep hidden.

Checkmate.

Turns out he'd struck the chord he'd intended.

Wren held his stare far longer than most men would have. "Where did you come across that name?"

He didn't miss a beat and answered, "In a file."

"What file?"

"I'm afraid that's Bureau business, madam."

The firelight danced across her face. She paused, seemingly to choose her words carefully. "Yet you still asked questions that anyone could learn about me if they did a bit of research.

I'd say that file of yours must be full of some rather remarkable holes."

"Oh no, Ms. Lockhart. We have quite enough to fill as many files as we'd like. I was only asking the questions to ascertain whether or not you'd be honest with me."

Wren's eyes flashed with anger. "Excuse me, but am I being implicated in some sort of crime?"

"Not at all. Unless, of course, you have something to hide."

"What could I have to hide? I've welcomed you into my home, haven't I?"

"You have . . . yes."

"Well then." She dropped her hands to the armrests, triumph evident. "I ask you. What more can you have to question me about?"

Elliot scanned the room, settling his glance on a door nestled in a shadowed back corner. It was tucked away, as if forgotten between dusty bookcases and a velvet curtain that had been drawn over a great portion of it.

He allowed his gaze to linger on the possibility of hidden mysteries she might be concealing behind it, before shifting his focus back to her.

"I believe you have nothing to hide—at least not of a criminal nature." He pointed his pencil toward the hidden door. "It's what's behind doors like that I find holds my interest, Ms. Lockhart. Not the distractions you want others to see in this room."

Elliot jotted down one more word, then tucked the pad and pencil back in the inside coat pocket. He exchanged them for a single scrap of paper he held in his fingertips.

"When Victor Peale's body was examined, we found several items on his person. Curiously, we found a book tucked in an inside pocket of his jacket." He held up a piece of paper between his fingertips. "And a piece of paper that had been slipped in the front cover, similar to this one: a scrap with two names written on it."

"Which book?" Her voice was soft and controlled, as if she asked out of making polite conversation, instead of the keen interest that he knew held her captive.

Why not ask me the names? Why not ask why a piece of paper would remain intact seemingly after so long in a grave?

"A copy of Sir Arthur Conan Doyle's *The Hound of the Baskervilles*. First edition, as a matter of fact."

"Sharing information are you, Agent Matthews?"

"Whatever I need to in order to get what I want, Ms. Lockhart."

She rose and crossed the room to the mantel, wasting no time to summon Irina with a tug on the gold chord against the wall. "I'm afraid that's all I have time for today. I have a prior engagement I must attend to, so if you'll excuse me."

Elliot patted the scrap of paper on the armrest and stood.

Slowly.

With marked intention.

"Well then . . . I do thank you for your time."

Wren took a confident step toward him, the heel of her boot clipping against the hardwood floor. She looked him square in the eyes. "You're intruding upon things of which you know nothing, Agent Matthews. Vaudeville is a complex world—so much more than what you might see on a stage. But it is also a notoriously closed world to outsiders. Be aware that what you'll unearth by digging into Stapleton's life may turn out to be more than you bargained for. Dig too deep and you could find yourself buried in the aftermath."

"Sharing information?" He reached back into his jacket pocket and raised an eyebrow. "Should I be taking notes?"

"Write whatever you'd like. It was merely a piece of advice. And as a matter of record, I prefer to stand on truth. The ground there is much more solid. But I will tell you this: I fiercely protect every corner I own. I won't be intimidated, especially by an agent who thinks he can do so in *my* home."

"Of that I have no doubt, Ms. Lockhart. And I assure you"— Elliot buttoned his jacket—"it was meant to be a friendly call. I'll see myself out."

"No need. Irina will meet you outside the door with your coat and hat. To make quite sure you don't get lost on your way to the front gate. I bid you a good day."

"Until we meet again." He nodded to her just as the library door was opened from the hall.

Irina was there, just as Ms. Lockhart had predicted, waiting on the other side with his coat and hat in hand. Elliot accepted them, adding, "Good day," to Wren before he was followed down the hall and tossed out by the seat of his trousers.

The pleasant smell of cinnamon curry from the mansion died as the door was shut behind him. The sound of turning bolts cut through the air. The wind kicked up with its relentless sting, reminding Elliot once again that it was early January.

He pulled the collar of his trench coat up around his chin to fend off its onslaught and trekked through the ankle-deep snow on the path to the curb.

"What took you so long?" Connor blasted him the instant Elliot slipped into the passenger side of their car. "I was nearly fitted for a pine box out here!"

"I was just engaged in a little chess match, that's all. Took longer than I thought. But my hunch was right: this Jennifer Charles and Wren Lockhart are one and the same."

"Well, praise be for that much." Connor fired up the engine, then angled the car out onto the snow-covered street.

"It means the pieces on the game board are in play, and Ms. Lockhart now knows where we stand. She knows more about Peale's death than she's willing to admit—at least right now. And whatever she's uneasy about regarding her real name could be why she's been putting us off. We'll just have to do our best to change her mind about getting involved."

"Well, you could have at least let me go in with you. Never heard of a partner who prefers interviewing potential witnesses alone, especially when it's January and the mansion is sure to have a fireplace or two."

"I wanted to see her reaction to my questions. She wouldn't have been as open with two of us in the room. But never fear, you'll get to see her up close when we drop in at her next show."

"A show? When?"

"Saturday night, as a matter of fact."

Connor gave him an exasperated glare, muttering, "I'm putting in for a transfer."

"No you're not. You want to get to the bottom of this as much as I do." Elliot chuckled. Connor's gruff exterior hid an almost childlike curiosity about the unexplained. This mystery was simply too good for him to walk away from. "As soon as the medical examiner's report comes back, you and I both know this case will become the media frenzy Stapleton wanted—except he could be arrested for killing a man instead of bringing him back to life.

"Everyone saw Peale walk across that stage. He wasn't a

phantom or a vapor created by smoke and mirrors. However it happened, Peale was alive—for a few moments, anyway. And now he's dead. And Stapleton may have to answer for it."

"And you think she can stop that?"

Elliot shook his head. "No. But she can help us uncover the truth, and it's almost the same thing. Truth is the illusion we always chase."

The car chugged past the Beacon Hill landscape. Elliot continued thinking on the encounter as snowy scenes passed by the window. How long did it take for the ever-composed Wren Lockhart to snap up the paper he'd left on the chair's armrest?

On it was written: *Jennifer Charles*, the name Wren wanted to remain buried deep in her past. Beneath it: *Ehrich Weisz*, the real name of the infamous Harry Houdini, the legend they both knew she'd apprenticed under. And though Elliot could imagine what must have been going through her mind, it was the conclusions he'd written on his own paper that told him what he needed to know about Ms. Lockhart.

Confident, clever, independent, and *sad.*

CHAPTER 3

THE CASTLETON THEATRE

SCOLLAY SQUARE

BOSTON, MASS.

Wren was fairly certain she was being followed.

She thought she caught sight of a figure as it cut a ghostly path through the glow of the lamplights along old Trenton Street. The shadow appeared to be trailing her a little more than a block behind. She quickened her pace, marching through the shroud of darkness that hovered between the downtown buildings, bound for the back alley entrance to the Castleton Theatre.

Braggarts were known to frequent the hidden corners and alleys of the theater district, even in the winter. And though patrons trickled out from theaters—potential witnesses who might deter criminal intentions—the hour was still late and the alleys dark enough that she didn't want to tempt trouble to glance her way.

Wren kept the white-knuckled grip on her walking stick,

ready to defend herself if need be. Though she doubted anyone would dare to challenge her.

Not on this night.

Not when she'd had to contend with a visit from the FBI and an urgent summons to the Castleton on the very same day. If anyone provoked a confrontation in her present mood, they'd soon regret it.

A stray cat hissed, overturning a crate in its haste to flee from Wren's approach.

She jumped back, almost falling prey to a wide patch of ice under a nearby waterspout. The heel of her boot slipped, throwing her against the side of the building, shoulder smashing brick.

"Blasted cat!" She cracked the end of her cane against one of the upturned crates, sending it flying out of her path. "Be off with you!"

The cat scurried away, hissing out its final threats.

"You're on edge," she muttered to herself, running her hand down the length of her arm to dust off any dirt that may have marred her cloak. "Calm down. Stand tall."

Wren stopped long enough to glance over her shoulder. Whoever might have been there hadn't followed her into the alley. She drew in a deep breath and let it out, by degrees, before edging past the ice to knock on the stage-side door. She kicked her boots against the brick wall to free them of latent snow and waited.

Nothing.

She knocked harder, this time pounding with her gloved fist against the aged wood. When no one answered, she tried the tarnished brass knob. It squeaked, giving easily. The door groaned on rusty hinges as she opened it wide.

Wren stepped under the low door frame, making sure to clear the edge of her top hat.

The theater's back halls were dank and dimly lit. The one working lightbulb hung from the ceiling far to one end and let off weak light at best.

"Why is no one posted at this door?" she called out.

The scurrying of tiny feet froze her, the hair on the back of her neck spiking to attention. Whether roaches or rats it didn't matter, she bemoaned the prospect of either uninvited guest. She'd never been so grateful she wore boots that protected her legs up to the knees.

Wren rapped her knuckles against the nearest wall, trying to get someone's attention. When no one responded, she stepped over a pile of soiled linens mounded next to the door, covering the lingering odors of sweat and lye with her gloved hand pressed against her nose.

"Hello?" She tried not to trip over formless obstacles lining the walls. She bumped into a metal bucket and mop, sending both clattering to the floor. "Honestly!" She knelt and groped out in the darkness. "Tulley?"

"Wren—"

She stood and turned toward the voice, only to plow front-first into the stage manager.

The collision rocked her onto her backside, knocking off her hat. She absorbed the impact with her outstretched hand, then grimaced when the leather of her glove pulled against something sticky the instant she lifted it from the floor.

The man offered her a hand up, scruffy bearded face looking down, the burn of the lightbulb casting a glow behind him. It outlined a linen shirt and a red-and-black-striped vest at his shoulders.

"Between the ice in the alley and the traps set up in this hall, I'm surprised I'm still in one piece."

"Come on." Tulley sighed and hooked an arm under her elbow. "I'll help you up."

"I can do it." She released herself from his grip. "But thank you." She pushed up from the ground. When she was sure her feet were level on the floor, she inhaled. Squared her shoulders.

He picked up her top hat and dusted it against his sleeve before offering it back to her.

"It's us that thank you for coming tonight, Wren. We had no one else to call."

"Apparently it's quite good that I did. The laundry, Tulley." Wren extended her arm wide to question the deplorable conditions surrounding them, down to the end of the halls by the smell of it. "I don't think it's too much to ask for an explanation."

"I know, I know. Don't say it." He moved past her, grumbling, "Where's that switch?"

He lit a match, then ran his hand along the wooden framing against the back wall.

"The wiring's all shot. Been on the fringe for months, but it's taken a turn now. The lights keep going out back here, and we've taken to using candles in the dressing rooms. The girls are all threatening to quit, and I don't blame them. The other theaters on the block don't have to deal with such conditions."

She sighed. "Did you tell Josiah?"

"Of course I told him. Last month, and the month before that, when the stage lights went out midshow. But our proprietor lets every complaint fall on deaf ears."

"What did he say?"

"Nothing of substance these days. Just yells at the performers and then slinks away again to find his bottle." Tulley covered a yelp as the match burned down and singed his fingertips. "Ah, there it is."

She heard him flicking a switch back and forth. The lights primed, flashed weakly, then hummed and lit up the hall in both directions, tiny rows of bulbs illuminating an outline of the floor.

Wren sighed, taking in the sight of the hall. *Deplorable* would be a kind description for what they'd found themselves in. *Maybe it would have been better to keep the lights off . . .*

"Good. That'll do for now." She turned to take in her first full look at Tulley.

The half-moons under his eyes and creased brow told tales of the last few weeks. His shirt was hastily tucked. Bow tie crooked up on one side. And the mature brown-and-gray hair that had always been parted with such care was mussed now, curling down against his forehead in a haphazard frenzy.

Like the theater halls, the wiring, and the dancers, he was clearly exhausted.

"I'd ask what's so important that you'd call me away from Beacon Hill at this time of night, but by the looks of things, I can guess."

"Believe me, Wren, if we had anyone else to bother with the day-to-day operations, we would have. I waited as long as I could to tell you. Even if you are a silent owner, you have the right to know, despite what Josiah wants."

She read indecision in his eyes. Whatever he was skirting around telling her, it couldn't be good or he'd have just come out with it. "What is it?"

"We've got enough cash on the books to last out the month, but not much longer. I hate to tell you this . . ." He paused and sighed deep. Bravery needed, apparently. "But we're going to have to close. Unless, that is, you've got a miracle up your sleeve."

"I can procure a number of things from my sleeve. I'm not sure a miracle would be one of them." Wren leaned her cane against the wall and laid her hat on a stray chair nearby, then spotted the bucket and mop she'd kicked over. She went on talking as she righted them and began tidying up the nearest corner.

"Is it really that bad?"

"It's been a slow fade for years, Wren. But I don't need to tell you that."

A survey of the hall told her the laundry and pest problems were the least of their worries. Wren looked up, finding water damage to the ceiling. Water dripped somewhere behind her— probably plumbing that was about to go. And with faulty wiring, the theater was a hazard no matter how you spelled it.

For the safety of everyone involved, maybe the best thing to do was to close. It broke her heart to think of it, but what else was there to do?

"Why is no one watching this door?"

"I have no one to post here. After the last gent quit, Josiah refused to hire anyone else."

"We need to get someone here pronto." She looked out to the alley again, then slid over to pull the door closed tight.

"I'm tending backstage while trying to take tickets at the front door, managing the deliveries, organizing the crew onstage. I tell you, if I had anywhere else to go, I'd be there right now. But the people here depend on me to see this through. I won't leave in the midst of a crisis. Once we right these wrongs, however, I'm afraid I'll be packing my suitcase with everyone else."

Tulley wasn't angry, though he had every right to be. The honesty in his words, the obvious care in his voice, and the effort to keep everyone else going—they were all evident.

Wren saw the sparkle and swish of a brunette woman in a dancer's costume slip around the corner carrying an armful of programs.

"Cleo? Is that you?"

The woman turned, her exotic face softening, obviously cheered to hear Wren's voice. "My dear, Wren. You have returned," she said, the Cajun French accent tingeing her words even as she slowed, breathing deep as though winded. She smiled in the depths of smoke-blue eyes, a reprieve evident. Her slight readjustment shifted the stack of programs in her arms.

"Tulley and I will manage the programs."

"You have no idea how relieved I am to hear that." Cleo wasted no time in hoisting them over to Tulley.

Wren nodded. That was good enough for her. "Fine. Tulley, I'm putting you in charge of the front door tonight. I'll personally double your pay for the added inconvenience. Agreed?"

"Well, of course he agrees," Cleo cut in and tilted her head down to adjust the costume cinching at her waist. "We all will. Might as well have someone who has authority around here. The rest of the girls are threatening to walk out."

Wren sighed, now fully bathed in the Castleton's troubles.

Once upon a time, it had been one of the most prestigious theaters in vaudeville. An icon in Scollay Square once, owned by her mother's family. But the passage of two decades was all it took for everything to fall into rot. The truth of the matter was without Wren, the Castleton would die. And she knew, deep down, that if the theater died, one of the last remaining memories of her mother would too.

It was a legacy in Boston's theater district no longer.

"Let's fix what we can control now and worry about tomorrow then, okay? I'm more concerned about the riffraff who will try to walk in with no one posted at the door." Wren swiped her cane from its perch against the wall. "Look, I'll handle Josiah, alright? Just please get someone to watch this door, preferably not a young chap fresh from the schoolhouse. We need someone reliable to man this post. I thought I caught sight of someone lurking around as I crossed into the alley, and that means thieves have their eye on this door as a weak spot. We don't have much any thief would want to steal at this point, but I'd like to at least ensure the safety of everyone backstage."

Wren checked her watch. Already quarter to eight. "Is there a set starting at the top of the hour?"

Cleo nodded. "The Mermaid show."

"Fine. You're the most experienced onstage. You go ahead and direct the newer girls through the rest of the show, at least until we can figure things out. Do you have a pianist?"

Tulley scoffed. "I wish. He quit last week too. Was lured over to Keith's Theatre by some nonsense about running water and electricity. I tried to tell him such things were a fantasy in theater life, but he didn't seem to buy that. Especially not when Keith is scooping up our paying customers like fish in a barrel. I've got one of the gents from the comedy duo doubling up to play."

Wren nodded, her heart weighted like a stone in her chest. She surveyed the squalor around them. Off in the distance, a muted melody drifted from the main hall as the hum of patrons chattered to find their seats.

Doubling up acts on the already exhausted players? She couldn't have that.

"Go on, Cleo." She nudged her on with a brush of the shoulder. "I'll stop by the backstage dressing rooms and reassure the rest of the girls before showtime. And then I'll find someone to play piano for the remaining acts. Agreed?"

"Anything for you, boss lady," she said with a wink and slipped around the corner.

Wren made sure the footsteps died away before she asked, "Where is he? Josiah. Is he still here?"

Tulley drew in a deep breath, shifting the stack of programs into one arm so he could straighten his uniform with a tug to the bottom of his vest. "Passed out on the cot in the back office." Shades of genuine sympathy settled on his face.

"He's been drinking again . . . ," Wren whispered, more to herself than the manager before her.

"Never stopped, to my knowledge. Josiah now keeps the VIP rooms stocked—even with corn whiskey if he has to. He's taken to keeping glass vials of it in the hollowed-out legs of the upholstered chairs, just in case the coppers bust in. But the few customers we have left know they can come here and he'll have it. So we're still selling tickets, at least until we all get hauled downtown by the Prohibition Unit."

"You knew about this?"

His nod was heavy with regret. "Yes. And we've tried, but no one can seem to stay on top of where he gets it or where he chooses to hide it. The chair legs were a new one. I came upon it by accident when I moved the furniture around to put a bucket down for a roof leak. I haven't done anything about it because I wanted to tell you first."

Wren sighed. "Fine. I'll handle that too. I'll check on him and be back out in a few minutes. Have someone make a pot of strong coffee and bring it back in ten minutes, okay?"

Tulley nodded, keeping his thoughts to himself. It was as if he already knew what she'd say and do. He reached over for a lantern hanging from the shepherd's hook on the wall.

"Take this at least, in case the lights go out again. Can't have you falling down on the job. We'd all be lost without you, Wren. I hope you know that."

She nodded, feeling weak and forced into accepting praise she didn't deserve. "I haven't saved anything yet."

If Wren had any true gumption, she'd stand up to Josiah. She'd give the man a piece of her mind and a stiff clip to the chin, if that's what it took to knock some sense into him. Someone should make him realize what he was doing to the people working for him, what he was doing to the theater that had belonged to his late wife's family. But he was past hope. Seeing any shades of redemption, she feared, was a dream long dead.

Tulley may have held out hope that Josiah would pull some measure of character to the surface. But Wren knew better. No one was to know that Josiah Charles was Wren Lockhart's father—and that's the way it would stay—but he'd still never change, not until he was cold in his grave.

Wren took the lantern in hand with a soft "thank you," curling her fingers around the handle. She held it at her side, looking down the hall toward her father's tiny back office.

"Wren?"

She turned at the sound of Tulley's voice, feeling the weight of the Castleton's world bearing down upon her shoulders. "Yes?"

He offered a forced but supportive smile. "Happy New Year."

❄

Josiah thrashed about like a roaring lion the instant the gush of icy water splashed over the cot. Wren had deposited her walking stick and hat on the desk and rolled her sleeves to the elbows. She stood back in the doorway of the tiny back office, bucket in hand, ready in the event he decided to charge and needed a second wave to cool him off.

A black costume boot lay on the ground at his feet. He swiped at the makeshift weapon, ready to throw. "Who'd dare wake a man in such a state!"

"You're not going to throw that and you know it."

Josiah eyed her behind heavy lids.

Wren stood firm as she clicked the door closed behind her, making sure she erased every emotion from her face. He squinted for long seconds, then as recognition seeped in, he lowered the makeshift weapon with a *thud* to the floor.

Grumbling, he ran a hand through the scratchy gray beard at his chin. "What are you doing here?"

Wren stood tall, eyeing him, refusing to back down no matter how her father attempted to play her. She crossed the room, eased the top of the boot from his still clenched fist, then set it on the floor behind them. "Tulley sent for me."

"Then he's fired," he growled, gravel rumbling in his throat with each syllable.

Wren slammed the bucket to the floor and pulled a stool over to the side of the cot. She leaned down until she was eye to eye with her father. "You can't fire him. Not when we're about to close down and he'll be out of a job anyway. Look at this place. It's crumbling around you. Tulley is the only one keeping you going. I'd say if anything, you owe him your right arm for putting up with such misery at your expense."

"He's paid well for his services."

"Tulley's paid a pittance for what he does. And I am through standing idly by while you abuse his loyalty. Either take the money I've offered and make the necessary repairs, or close down for good. Those are your options." Wren shook her head in disgust.

The man before her was a shell of a graying, bitter man who chose to drown his sorrows in anything that came his way,

Prohibition laws or not. It was the oddest thing for Wren to be questioned by a federal agent that morning, only to find herself in the presence of a bootlegger mere hours later.

Beads of water dripped off the tips of his hair and trailed down his nose as he stared back, derision burning in his eyes. She was Wren Lockhart to him now, the illusionist he couldn't help but despise for the measure of success she'd managed to find without him—or perhaps despite him.

He took in her trousers and gentleman's boots. "Your mother would weep if she could see what you've become."

Wren didn't miss a beat. "I'm sure she would, knowing what's happened since she's been gone."

Josiah turned away, squeezing his eyes shut from the sight of her. "You have contracts to appear in your own list of theaters, don't you? The ones your famous magician friend favored? But now he's in his grave, you think you can crawl back here and order us around? Just because you and that sister of yours share ownership of this rat-infested mausoleum."

"Don't bring anyone else into this. It's about you."

"And you don't know anything about the happenings here."

She ignored the barb, dropping her voice low. "I know that the Federal Bureau of Investigation knows who I am. And if the agent who visited me this morning knows who Jennifer Charles is, I can guarantee he'll find my father if he wants to. It won't take them long to dredge up an old case locked in a police desk drawer somewhere and start asking some tough questions about the Charles family. I'm not confident you'd be ready to answer them. If we want to protect Charlotte, we have to work together.

"So if I were you"—she offered him a swatch of linen—"I'd get sober and wash some of that dirt from your face before the authorities get here, because I can promise you they're not likely to leave you alone. And if they turn over your chairs to find one drop of alcohol, they'll lock you up without batting an eyelash. I'm through cleaning up your messes."

"A man is dead, and the Stapleton friend of yours is behind bars for doing it. It's all over the street. Seems like the coppers have enough on their hands without coming after a washed-up entertainer like me, especially when they could come after a toffee-nosed vaude like you."

"Stapleton is no friend of mine." She shook her head. "This Victor Peale is in the grave and I'm sorry for it, but he bargained with the wrong people and now there's nothing more to be done. We have to think of the living, not the dead."

"That's rather callous, even for you. It wasn't one of your onstage tricks that killed him, was it?"

Though she fought never to show it, hatred simmered somewhere deep within Wren at the part she had to play. She was one woman onstage, but someone else entirely in the back halls of the Castleton. There she couldn't hide her past. It was staring her in the face like an unforgiving beast, ready to strike at the weakest parts of her heart.

"You know better than to ask if I'd share a stage with a man like Horace Stapleton."

"Then why did the FBI question you?"

Wren gave quick thought to the image of Agent Matthews's scrap of paper. She seriously doubted anyone else had the vault of their past cracked open as hers had most recently been—and all because of a name she thought had been long buried.

Someone wanted that past dredged up again. Trouble was, she didn't know who.

"I imagine they're doing a sweep by interviewing any entertainers who've crossed paths with Stapleton in the past. But it doesn't matter now." She dismissed the worry that had been building in her midsection all day. "I'll handle the FBI. You just manage your theater and care for the people in it. That's all I ask."

"You don't want much, do you?" Josiah rubbed a palm over his brow, smearing the line of dirt and sweat in the crease across his forehead. He glanced at the clock on the wall. It had gone silent, likely ages ago. "What time is it?"

"It's late. Too late for changing anything now." She nodded to the desktop in the corner. A stack of clothing was piled next to her walking stick and top hat. "Outside of your shirt. I left a clean one over there, along with one of Tulley's vests. Put them on. And I'll have some strong coffee sent back."

Josiah swayed on the side of the cot and nearly fell back down, bracing his arm against the wooden frame. He brushed a hand over the days' growth of whiskers at his chin and coughed, the rumble taking over his chest. "I won't take your money." Though weak and hungover, he was adamant, coughing out the vow. "Not a single penny. I'd rather starve."

"I'm under contract at the Bijou through July, then I set sail for Europe. I'll be gone for a late-summer tour. That's a long time to have to go without food."

"Are you going to manage your uncle's estate?" He tried to bait her with the reminder that his own brother's fortune had been left solely in Wren's care.

She ignored it. "I have business, yes, but it doesn't concern anyone else."

"And what about your sister?" Spittle dropped off his bottom lip.

Oh no you don't. You're not changing the subject to go down that road now . . .

"Please do not pretend to have an interest in her now. We're talking about the Castleton. By the time I return I expect you will have cleaned up this mess or closed and boarded the front doors. It's your choice, but you will make one. And if you resist, I'll go to the authorities and turn you in myself. Don't make the error of believing that's an empty threat."

"I suppose I'll have to contend with the FBI while you're gone."

"I already told you—let me worry about them. It may be resolved already." Wren stood, dismissing the threat of Agent Matthews's interest in her past. "But if it's not, I have more than one trick up my sleeve. And I'll use every one of them to make the past disappear."

Josiah's body trembled slightly. He sat up, still squinting at her.

Muffled sounds of music floated in, cutting through the chasm of silence that had fallen between them. She waited. Listening to the sounds of jubilant applause from the auditorium. Wishing things were different somehow, that silence wasn't the one thing they could share.

Silence and pain.

"Why are you helping me?" he accused, his whisper coarse.

"Because we both love Charlotte and will do anything to protect her." Wren swallowed hard and looked away, casting the momentary rise of emotion in her throat to the wayside.

"If anything's true, I suppose that is."

Of course. He had two daughters, but only one needed anything from him.

"It is. I'm still your daughter." She took the linen towel from him, laid it on the side of the cot, then headed for the door. "And unfortunately for us both, that fact will never change."

CHAPTER 4

January 15, 1927

Bijou Theatre

Washington Street

Boston, Mass.

"Undercommit offstage, then overdeliver every time you're on it."

If Wren closed her eyes long enough, she could hear her mentor's words of advice ringing in her ears. She drew in a deep breath, letting the memory of them sink deep.

"No matter what's occurred—especially if you find yourself in a fix that you can't see your way out of—the crowd must walk away believing you did exactly what you said you would, without any break in the story. Make them believe it."

Wren stood backstage at the Bijou Theatre, the lively tapping of an index finger against her crossed arms the only indication she was energized before a show. She waited now in the fallen darkness of the stage wing, peeking out from behind the drawn curtain.

As she did today, Wren always looked to ensure her assigned

man had been placed in the audience—the one who'd been hired and coached before the show. Everything else was a mystery to him, save for the fact that he'd be seated in the fourth row, third seat in from the center aisle. And when Wren called for a volunteer from the audience, the man knew his pay depended upon standing up and doing exactly what he was told to do once on her stage.

Irina informed Wren moments before that she'd selected a man with a gray bowler hat and round, wire-rimmed spectacles sitting on the edge of a hawk-like nose. Wren couldn't miss him. Or she wasn't *supposed* to miss him. But as of yet, he hadn't found his seat—even though the band was cuing up to signal showtime was drawing near.

The lights flickered against the soaring ceiling vaults of the Bijou, stirring theater guests from their pockets of conversation in private boxes or along the aisles. Wren stood tall, quiet as always, watching as elegantly dressed ladies and tuxedo-clad gentlemen found their seats as the lights dimmed across the balcony and the main floor.

The curtain would part in a matter of moments.

Where is he?

Wren turned, taking a quick inventory of her show props behind the curtain, making sure everything was in order. A spindle-legged parlor chair and a crystal vase were center stage, waiting for her opening act. A tall wardrobe with an affixed gold-gilt mirror she used for one of her vanishing tricks was off to the side, with an oblong table holding various handcuffs and chains with locks positioned behind it. A pulley and wooden frame more than ten feet high was shrouded in darkness behind her—the contraption that would hoist her in the air and drop her into a large glass-walled tank for her final act.

She squeezed her palms, making certain she could feel the

clicks of the tiny metal files taped under her gloves—counting one in each hand. If she dropped one or an edge snagged in the fabric of her costume, it could spell disaster when she had to pick a lock. It had happened only once, and she managed to play it off without notice, but since then she left nothing to chance and doubled up on everything.

A small disturbance erupted from the back of the auditorium, drawing her attention to the part in the curtain.

Wren peered out. A slew of press had arrived—bolstered by a wave of ready flashbulbs and chattering reporters who'd trained their eyes on the stage. They swarmed in a pack that floated out from the cover of the balcony and down the center aisle, not stopping until they'd settled in the front rows.

Every muscle in her body tensed as the press came into view.

What are they all doing here? We've never had this many press at a show.

She had to consider that they weren't lined up merely to see a good show. Gut instinct told her it was the scene at Mount Auburn Cemetery all over again, except this time the venue was a plush theater with gilt ceilings and chandeliers instead of the wide-open sky and a main act who wasn't after a media frenzy to infect the show. After Victor Peale's dramatic death, the newspapers were making as many broad assumptions as they could, and now they flocked to vaudeville for their next story.

It appeared as if her show had sold out for a reason—and not particularly the one she'd hoped for. The proprietor must have saved back seats, then let the lot in like cattle in a corral.

The final shimmer of a symbol sounded offstage and the band hushed, done tuning their instruments. Ready or not, it was showtime.

Wren closed her eyes and drew in a steadying breath.

She opened them again, feeling that on this night, the stakes were much higher. She banished an uncharacteristic wave of fear with a shrug, shaking it off the shoulders of her tuxedo jacket without another thought. She drew in another deep breath, ready to emerge with the melody the band was poised to play.

One more glance at the audience before we go. She parted the edge of the curtain with her index finger. *Just to make sure my man is in place . . .*

He'd removed his hat, but Mr. Spectacles was indeed seated in the fourth row, third chair from the center aisle. Normally relief would wash over her that all things were in place, but Wren's heart sank a measure when an even bigger distraction came into view.

There sat another patron, parked in the row directly behind her planted man.

His was a familiar face, framed by wheat-blond hair and the same set jaw and sharp blue eyes she'd had to contend with in her library just days before. Now those eyes were actively engaged in surveying every inch of the Bijou's elegant auditorium—including the stage.

Her stage.

The one she was poised to step out on in a matter of seconds.

Any moment the curtain would part, and the last man who stood between her and a public thrashing—maybe even the end of her career—was none other than Agent Elliot Matthews.

❊

"Collar still choking you?" Connor ceased crowd-gazing and mouthed the words with unfiltered amusement from across the lobby alcove.

Elliot hadn't even noticed, but he must have tugged at his tuxedo collar one time too many. The incessant nagging of his bow tie forced Elliot to pull at it every few seconds. Add that to the fact his shoes were straight-out-of-the-box tight, and he was losing the battle of comfort from head to foot. Still, he shook his head and tipped his chin to the crowd, directing them back to the task at hand.

Connor rolled his eyes in reluctant submission and slipped back into the throngs of people gathered around them.

Though the scene threatened to twist knots in Elliot's stomach, instincts won out so that both he and Connor had donned their best suits and melted into the crowd at the Bijou's Saturday headlining show.

It reminded Elliot that he hated being trussed up.

That he'd once fled his family's world of operas and high-society shows for good reason. But everything told him that Wren Lockhart could be the key to their rapidly ballooning death investigation, and if he wanted to get to the bottom of it, some sacrifices would have to be made. She entertained a certain measure of fame on the vaudeville circuit, and in order to enlist her help, they'd have to understand her world.

Gents scooted in with diamond-frosted flappers hanging on their arms. Guests chattered as they waltzed by, anticipating the delights of the sold-out Wren Lockhart show. Gleeful as the evening looked to be, they were too interested in their own world to notice what Elliot had seen happening—that a man had been pulled from the crowd by a mysterious woman with cropped brown hair and striking green eyes.

The man's presence was inconsequential to the patrons in the lobby. He'd appeared clueless as Irina had directed him to an alcove beneath the grand staircase.

Elliot had looked for Connor, who'd noticed the exchange, too, and locked gazes across the lobby. They'd both seen the man emerge from the hall and weave into the crowd, moving in unnoticed. Almost, that is. They had but to stop him and offer a fistful of dollars more than Ms. Lockhart to find out why her business manager had been slinking around the shadows of the lobby.

Elliot sat in the row behind the man now, in view of the fact he'd been hired as a plant in the audience. That meant he wanted to stay close-by. It ensured Ms. Lockhart would see him from the stage.

Connor slipped into the seat next to him and immediately began to fidget, tapping his feet and drumming fingers against his knee.

"Would you pipe down?" Elliot nudged Connor with his elbow. "It's not that bad. If I can put up with this collar, then you can sit still for five minutes."

"I'm sorry, Elliot. But I told you I'd rather be chasing rum-runners down a dusty back road outside the city than to be here, hamming it up with 'polite' society. My only passing interest is that one of these hoity-toities might have a single daughter they're looking to pawn off on a lug. Though I'm not sure how I'd like being tied to an apron string, even if it is threaded in gold, you know?"

"Well, you're on the clock, so I'd say you won't have to worry about it tonight. And I had to fork over all my cash for these seats—"

"Which I suppose I owe you for now," Connor cut in.

"It was a sold-out show and it cost me a pretty penny to get us in here tonight. The least you could do is pretend you're enjoying yourself, if only to keep up appearances."

"I told you." Connor gave a mock shiver to his shoulders.

"I'm all nerves around these people. *You* might be used to these high-society dames, but I'm not partial."

Elliot rolled his eyes. "You don't mind a spray of bullets from a tommy gun, yet you worry about a bunch of middle-aged ladies in opera dresses. Seems logical."

"Logical or not—" He huffed, tipping his head to pan the seating behind them. "See that? A full balcony that wraps around and only a handful of exits in this entire auditorium. I'd have to climb over about a hundred people to chase a crook out any one of them. This place is a rattrap."

"Who's going to cause a disturbance in the middle of an upscale theater?" Elliot scanned the stage, looking over all angles. "I'll handle how to get us backstage after the show. You just keep your eyes peeled and take in as much as you can. I need you to be our eyes and ears tonight."

"That's the nicest thing you've said to me all week, boss. That redhead's a pretty thing. Odd, but pretty." Connor tilted his eyebrows in the direction of the stage and the performer who would soon grace it. "Normally I wouldn't want to work around the clock like you seem to enjoy, but in this case . . . don't mind if I do."

The evening may have been too much for Connor to entertain unless there was a female to gaze at, but Elliot took the rest of the scene in—from the ornate wainscoting around the auditorium to the length and lighting of the stage to the band in the orchestra pit below.

Everything is professional.

Detailed.

Controlled . . .

Exactly what he would have expected for a Wren Lockhart show. Save for one thing: Elliot had thrown a wrench in her plans, and if she wasn't keen to it yet, she soon would be. Wren would tell him more with her response to his presence than she could with words.

The lights dimmed and the crowd quieted, giving way for the band to play a rendition of the Original Memphis Five's popular song "Fireworks," the ceiling vaults echoing the jazzy tune out over the audience. The tune seemed to carry the curtain with it, parting the thick cascade of red velvet down the middle, revealing a figure standing under a solitary spotlight.

Wren looked down at the tips of her boots, fiery wavy hair outlining her visage. Trouser- and boot-clad legs were crossed one over the other, one toe tapping in time with the music. Her crimson tuxedo jacket was framed in the overhead light, her arms tucked behind her back. The rest of the brass came to life, cutting through the welcome of applause with their song. She lifted her head and went to work then, ushering the auditorium full of guests into the depths of her world.

Wren moved to one side and revealed a delicate, spindle-legged wooden chair positioned center stage. From behind her back she pulled a crystal vase, the beveled edges in its surface glinting from the spotlight's beam as if it had been fashioned from a thousand tiny diamond chips.

She held up the vase and did a little skip and a dance across the stage, allowing the light to fracture through it as the music began to fade.

"It was Socrates who said, 'The greatest way to live with honor in this world is to be what we pretend to be.'" Wren placed the vase on the seat of the spindle chair as the band music eased off. "How many of us pretend here tonight? Certainly we all wish to live well. To live with honor while we're in this world. So was our philosopher wise in his judgment? Or can we prove him misguided? Perhaps we'll see if his conclusions were well placed."

A young girl appeared on the wings of Wren's opening, a spotlight raining down on her as she seemed to float down the aisle, cutting through the dimmed light of the auditorium.

She wore a day dress in childlike pink, as if the enchantment of spring had broken into their cold January world for a moment. She carried an oversized flower basket hooked under one elbow, the woven sea grass cradling a robust bouquet of peonies and roses in an array of bright pinks and rouge.

Wren made a slight movement with her eyes and nodded, nudging the little girl on in whatever silent question she'd asked. "Children. Flowers. Do they pretend at all? Yes, they grow in beauty and grace. And all too soon, with the ebb and flow of seasons, they mature. Blooming into what they were meant to be. With no pretense. No masks. Just beauty in every honest bloom."

With her black Mary Janes dancing, the little girl waltzed about, deep-brown ringlets bobbing against her shoulders with each skipped step. She selected a single stem after another, curtsying to delighted ladies along the center aisle as she dropped a magnificent bloom in their opera-gloved hands.

"And if cared for properly, if given light and room to grow, these beauties bring joy to all who come in contact with them," Wren added, head high. "They defy Socrates's definition of honor without thinking twice as to what they *should* be—only who and what they *are*."

The girl had gifted all of her blooms by the time she reached the front row. She gave an aristocratic curtsy to the press seated there and then skipped off into the shadows past the stage.

"And so I ask you, dear guests. Are we only who we pretend

to be? To each whom a flower has been given—are people as transparent as the bloom you now hold in your hands?" She gazed around, searching the crowd. "From whence does real beauty come? Is it in outward adornments? Or, rightly placed, does it grow from what is inside the measure of one's heart?"

Wren stood back from the vase, the transparent crystal bathed in the stream of light. "Grow," she stated.

Nothing happened.

All was silent and still, save for the subtle hum of the band in the background and a light cough from somewhere in the depths of the audience.

Wren played to the crowd, raising an eyebrow as if the vase had a personality all its own, and stubborn was what it wished to be at the moment. She stepped back, crossing her arms over her chest and tilting her head to one side. She tapped her toe in mock perplexity while she waited.

A chorus of muted chuckles followed.

"Grow," she said, louder this time, resting her hands on her hips.

The crowd watched, hushed, the few gifted with blooms twirling the flowers in their fingertips.

The lot of them, Elliot included, sat on the edges of their seats with wonder at what the illusionist was poised to do with a lonely spindle-legged chair and an empty vase. Even Connor looked interested, which was a win in itself.

Wren shrugged to the audience, as if the props hadn't the inclination to cooperate on that night. She looked out over the crowd, her eyes searching. And finally, they landed on a spot offstage and she smiled brightly.

She crooked her finger and waited until the sound of *clip-clopp*ing Mary Janes echoed against the hardwood of the stage.

The little girl had returned and soon joined her under the stage lights.

Wren knelt, cupping her hand to whisper in the little girl's ear. The girl giggled and nodded as if whatever idea exchanged had been full of a fairy's delights.

The little girl walked over to the chair, then hesitated for the briefest of seconds to nibble the corner of her bottom lip. She then closed her eyes and leaned up on the tips of her toes, as if ready to wish, blowing air over the vase to extinguish the flame of imaginary candles.

Wren nodded approval, then with feeling, whispered, *"Grow."*

The crowd gasped in awe. The little girl jumped and clapped as the depths of the empty vase burst forth with pops of color.

Stems sprouted up, defying gravity and time with green shoots that reached for the grand heights of the Bijou's ceiling. Leaves unfurled like delicate scrolls waking from slumber. Stems stretched into vines. And buds formed like miniature bells on a string, then burst into a song of color as flowers exploded, painting the mass of green in ivory and pinks. Crimson and coral.

The flowers bloomed to the astonishment of the crowd.

Wren looked on, as if the vines and their hidden beauty had performed well for her, just as she'd expected. She crossed the stage and picked up a pair of shears that had been set on the chair. She ran leather-gloved fingertips over the softness of the petals.

To a handful of select flowers Wren took the shears, clipping the stems. "Do these flowers pretend at all?" She tossed the blooms to grasping hands in the audience. "They're beautiful, are they not? Beautiful without invention or pretense."

She selected a last flower from the vase, a bright pink, and clipped its stem. And to the little girl who stood in wonder at the side of the stage, Wren approached, then handed her the perfect bloom.

"Now it's your turn, little one. And you will grow soon enough." She patted her cheek. "But not tonight. You may bow to our guests."

The little girl smiled, front teeth missing, and bowed low. The crowd erupted in applause as she trotted back offstage. Wren took center stage again, standing under the spotlight with her brilliant blooms, and the crowd hushed once more.

"Before we continue, might I have a volunteer from the audience? Someone who is quite certain they live a life of honor."

Wren peered out into the crowd, the lights along the rows of seats carrying a dim glow all the way to the back of the auditorium. She paused, seconds only, Elliot judging that she waited for her planted man to make his move. And though hands were flying up in droves, she didn't call on them. She watched as the man stood, then opened her mouth to speak.

Elliot shot to his feet before Wren could protest. "Right here. I'm your volunteer," he called out.

Connor sighed. "Matthews," he moaned under his breath, shaking his head. "You can't be serious."

Elliot stripped out of his tuxedo jacket and lobbed it in Connor's lap. "See you on the other side I guess." He headed for the stage without waiting for welcome. Instead, he proceeded down the aisle and trotted up the stairs, stopping only when he stood opposite Wren and her chair of blooms.

He arched an eyebrow, offering a silent challenge in her direction.

"Thank you, sir. We can see how eager you are to participate this eve." She tossed a knowing smile at the crowd.

Flashbulbs encased them in pops of light as laughter flavored the background.

"Like everyone here." Hands in his pockets, Elliot looked out over the span of filled seats for the first time. "My curiosity is piqued."

"Very well. We shall attempt to satisfy it. But first I must ask any volunteer if he has been on this stage before."

Elliot shook his head. "I can honestly say I've never met the Wren Lockhart who stands onstage with me now."

She gave him a look that suggested "I'll ignore your cheek" and continued. "Good." She crossed the stage, then handed him the shears. "Then you may pick one, sir. Choose the bloom that is pretending."

"Pretending what?" He reached out to take the tool in hand.

Wren notched her chin, as if the answer were simple. "The one that is lying, of course. Choose and clip the stem that is guilty of inauthenticity. We believe you to have honor, and as such, you should be able to find the masked culprit among the rest of the innocent."

Elliot cleared his throat, humored that they traded barbs onstage no one else in the audience might decode, save for Connor or Irina. He accepted the challenge, turning back to the vase.

The blooms were indeed brilliant. Fragrant even, which was a surprise.

Elliot inspected them with a skeptical eye. He stood mere inches away, but for the life of him, he couldn't see anything illegitimate. They could have been spring blooms in the entryway to a ladies' parlor for how real they were. Even still, Elliot's mind was bent on realism, and it pricked at the illusion before him.

What his eyes saw in the moment couldn't be trusted.

She couldn't be trusted. Not yet, anyway. Not while she held them all under the grand spell of her onstage illusions.

One dark flower stood out among the bunch—bloodred as the coat she wore and as vibrant as her smile. The hue grew still darker at the center of the bud, as if the flower's heart were a hidden shade of black.

He took it in hand and clipped the stem with a single swipe. Elliot advanced two steps, and in a flash of chivalry he hadn't expected, bowed to Wren, presenting the bloom to her.

"Ms. Lockhart," he whispered so only she could hear. "May I have a word with you after the show?"

She shook her head, ever so slightly.

"Thank you, sir," Wren announced, but refrained from accepting the gift. "But I fear my heart is already spoken for. You'll have to save that bloom for another young lady."

The crowd gasped behind Elliot then, not at Wren's words, but at something else. He hadn't time to process, not even as his eyes told him he was witnessing the impossible.

The blooms in the vase sagged, their brilliance withering away.

Their vibrant hues had begun to fade into a wretched mass of wilting brown. Petals broke away and fluttered to the stage, the peonies' vines curling and leaves turning black as death.

To the astonishment of all, the vase full of flowers disintegrated into lifeless stems and a ring of ash around the vase.

Elliot turned to Wren, shock reverberating through him.

She looked back, not with the haughtiness he expected. She'd clearly bested him and could have held her superiority over him. But instead, her countenance held an openness that didn't speak of victory. In fact, it looked real. As if it had pained her to reveal the truth that delicacy could die away and ash could so easily take the place of something beautiful.

"I believe you've chosen with wisdom, sir," she said with a nod to him. "You've found the one bloom that is truly beautiful at its core. This one looked different from the rest, but you didn't judge it harshly. You saw it not for what it is . . ." Wren turned toward the chair again, then cupped her hands around the pile of the ash. She sifted it from palm to gloved palm, then turned to face the crowd. ". . . but for what it could be." And with that, she tossed the ash into the air.

The ash took flight, sailing over the audience on the wings of a bird that fluttered and soared high, chirping as it disappeared over the balcony.

The crowd erupted, clapping and whistling in delight. Elliot stole a final glance over at Wren, who didn't return the gesture. She looked to her crowd, a softness in the smile that eased over her lips as the wave of applause washed over them.

"Thank you." She held her arm out to him. "A round of applause for our volunteer, please."

Elliot returned the final peony to the vase.

It rested against the crystal rim, the lone splash of color set against the remainder of the wilted bunch. He trotted down the stairs and found his place next to Connor but stayed on his feet, applauding with the rest of the audience.

He'd forgotten just about everything in that moment.

That they had a job to do that amounted to more than awe at stage tricks. They had the truth to unearth, to find justice for a man who'd lost his life. But somewhere between the astonishing sight of flowers blooming out of thin air and the enchantment of a little girl's wide-eyed wonder, Elliot began to feel he might have misjudged Wren Lockhart.

He'd been unyielding, accusatory even, in the way he'd questioned her. He wasn't sure how she did it, but the real illusion wasn't that flowers grew or wilted away before their eyes, or that a bird could rise from the ashes of death. It was how Wren had mystified them all, winning over a packed house of Boston society in the span of a few heartbeats.

She'd shown a genuine softness onstage that he hadn't anticipated. And the crowd reveled in it. Elliot looked around, seeing the faces of men and women, members of the press . . . even Connor, all left spellbound by the woman in red.

"I'll say this for her," Connor chimed in over the crowd. "She certainly isn't like any witness we've had before. Someone will have to keep a keen eye on that one."

"Yes." Elliot nodded, watching as Wren eased into her next act onstage. "Someone will."

CHAPTER 5

"Gentlemen here to see you, Ms. Lockhart."

Wren leaned against the table as she pressed the tips of her hair into a linen hand towel, soaking up the moisture left over from the water tank escape she'd just completed onstage. She glanced up at the sound of Irina's voice, finding her standing guard at the stage door like the protector of a castle drawbridge.

"Let me guess . . ."

"I'll give you two guesses but you'll only need the one," Irina replied, eyebrows raised.

Of course the agents had found their way backstage.

Wren had been expecting them. But she was exhausted in mind and body—as usual, quite spent after a show. She was also soaked to the skin and not at all interested in trading wits with two bothersome agents.

She sighed though, finding no way around it now.

Wren ran a hand through the mass of damp waves at her nape, then straightened her posture and nodded for them to be let in. "Thank you, Irina."

Her business manager melted into the background as the men swept into her backstage world.

The shorter of the two men sidestepped a wooden stool and the wardrobe in his path, avoiding a crash with a half stumble. He righted himself, nonplussed, and crossed the length of the alcove to her side.

Wren looked to Agent Matthews, but he appeared not to have noticed the blunder. He hung back, taking in the full layout of the backstage area. His inspection dusted from corner to corner of her stage props and floor to ceiling. If anything, the man was curious. Too curious. That kind of inquisitive spirit was a most unwelcome quality of any guest's foray into an illusionist's world.

"Agent Matthews? It's a pleasure to see you again." She drew his gaze from the spindle chair that had been pushed up against the wall, the vase still cradling the crimson peony from the opening act they'd shared. "And may I assume you are Mr. Finnegan?"

Connor stepped up, eager to thrust out his hand, looking positively delighted that she knew his name before he'd offered it.

"Agent Connor Finnegan, Ms. Lockhart. Boston Bureau. It's a pleasure, ma'am." He stood with his hand outstretched.

With picks and tape that she hadn't yet had the chance to remove from the inside of her gloves, the last thing Wren could do was accept his hand. She folded her towel instead, then leaned against a nearby table, crossing one arm over the other.

"Yes. We haven't met, but I recognized your name associated with Agent Matthews's in the newspapers. If you'll permit me, sir, I'm soaked to the skin. Might I defer a handshake until the next time we meet?"

"Oh, yes." Connor shifted back, a clumsy smile on his face. "Yes, of course."

"Is this a good time?" Elliot cut in matter-of-factly. He

continued loitering at the edge of the backstage shadows, quite opposite from the ardent advances of his partner.

"That all depends on why you're here, doesn't it?"

Connor shoved his hands in his pants pockets. "However did you manage to escape from a pair of handcuffs behind your back, while under water no less? And conjuring a bird from ash?" He winked. "Care to tell us how you did it?"

"That's an age-old question, Mr. Finnegan. One that would put people like me out of business." Wren pressed her lips into a knowing smile.

"Well, I admit I didn't expect to enjoy the show, if you don't mind me saying."

"It's quite alright. But we managed to change your mind anyway?"

"Changed my mind? And then some."

She turned to Elliot. "And what about you, Agent Matthews? Did you enjoy the show?"

"He did. But he wouldn't dare admit it." Connor chuckled and rolled back on his heels, a boyish grin on his face. "As to the handcuffs you used—I bet we'd be the ones who were sorry if we ever had to arrest you."

"Then let's hope it never comes to that." She dropped the towel to the tabletop.

Wren was owning the definition of aloof at the moment.

It was much smarter to reveal nothing but carefully masked lightheartedness with the more jovial Agent Finnegan. But his partner? Wren couldn't place Agent Matthews's intentions at all, and that unnerved her. Best to hurry them along with their questions, then away from her stage and, hopefully, shoo them out of her life completely.

Wren clasped her hands in front of her. "If you'll forgive me, gentlemen, I'm quite tired and still have a bit to do before we can lock up tonight. So, is there something I can help you with?"

"That all depends." Elliot took a step forward into the full light.

She tilted her head a fraction. "A rather intriguing answer."

"We have a proposition for you, Ms. Lockhart."

"I'm afraid I'm already booked up. I have a few months left on my contract here. After that, I'm away to Europe for a late-summer tour."

"We're not offering you a job."

"What then?"

"A chance to seek justice," Elliot answered. "Or truth. Whichever interests you most."

"The truth about what?" Wren darted her glance between the men.

"Horace Stapleton. Since he will likely be indicted for murder."

"Murder." Wren sighed, half expecting it would come to this. Still, it was grating to hear it stated as fact. "Alright then. Go on. What does this have to do with me?"

Elliot nodded. "It's more than that. The case is building up to a possible charge of premeditation, if the evidence proves it. And that presents some challenges we hadn't anticipated."

"Such as?"

"I don't believe he did it. But we need your help to untangle the mess he's made."

Wren knew it was a losing battle to hide astonishment from her face now. To charge a showman as dim-witted as Horace Stapleton with the crime of calculated murder was laughable. But the absurdity to think she'd dare to get involved left her nearly speechless. Hadn't the press caused this with their theories and moral judgments inked in the newspapers every day? The last thing a showman needed was bad press. This reeked of nothing but. She couldn't get involved.

"We've surprised you," Connor stated. "You haven't seen the papers to know it had come to this?"

She shook her head, damp hair clinging to her jaw. "I've been working all day. And I try to steer clear of the newspapers' speculations as a rule."

"Then you need to have a clear understanding of why we're here." Elliot pulled a chair over in front of her. "Should we sit down?"

She nodded and sat. Elliot waited for Connor to scoot up a stool of his own before joining them.

"Regardless of how you want to stay out of it, that's not likely to be a possibility now. Given that Stapleton's name is attached to vaudeville, all manner of illusionists will find themselves under the spotlight. And that gang of press that was sitting in your front row tonight? They may try to tail you."

"But why? I've done nothing wrong."

"May I be frank, Ms. Lockhart?"

"I prefer it, as a matter of fact."

"Then you won't need to forgive me for stating that a woman who makes flowers grow out of thin air or owns a house of oddities and goes about in gentlemen's clothing is going to be labeled an eccentric. Anyone who is that unconventional is assured to be a source of fascination for both the press and society at large. Judgments come packing along with your profession, I'm afraid, and the public has now been drawn behind the curtain of your world."

"I don't care what people think."

"And we're not here to judge you."

She narrowed her eyes. "Yet what you're saying is . . . I've done this to myself? I deserve to be hounded by the press and law enforcement because I'm different? In the court of public opinion, I'm already guilty by association?"

If Wren thought the men might be backing down, Elliot proved the opposite by leaning forward, elbows braced on his knees. He stared back, blue eyes fixed on her face.

"No. You don't deserve the bad press. I think George Valentine would agree with you that it can be very damaging to one's livelihood." He dropped his voice to a gruff whisper. "As would Ann O'Delia Diss Debar. Joaquín Argamasilla. Mina Crandon, also known as Margery. And one Horace Stapleton, just to name a few."

She allowed a veil of innocence to overpower her face. "To name a few what?"

"You know as well as I do that's a short list of the more notable spiritualists Harry Houdini publicly debunked in the last few years leading up to his death."

Wren straightened her spine. "Frauds he exposed, you mean."

"Or mediums you systematically defrauded—*together*."

"I never made claims against anyone."

He didn't believe her, of course. The tight line to his jaw and the unwavering focus in his eyes confirmed it.

"Maybe not, but you had a hand in building the evidence against some of them. And I can see by your expression that you think those people deserved it. Maybe they did. But whatever they did or didn't do is not my concern."

Wren didn't deny it. Who knew what was documented in that file of his? But she didn't want to live under a cloak of dishonesty either.

Best to evade.

"I fail to see how any of this is relevant to your current case, Agent Matthews. Badgering me won't get you any closer to the truth of a man's death, especially when I had nothing to do with it."

"We're not here to accuse you of anything. But right now our position is problematic. You see, Stapleton's bail has been set high with the severity of the crime, but he claims he hasn't the ability to post bond. So he'll stay put until a trial date is set. We thought that might encourage him to talk. But even with the threat of a drawn-out trial, it hasn't budged him. And the initial evidence we can find points to the fact that Stapleton's claims are real. It looks as though he indeed raised Victor Peale from the dead."

"Though that's clearly impossible."

"We know it is, Ms. Lockhart. But Stapleton suggests Peale died again in the moments after he was brought back, and that is the man's own misfortune. Stapleton only claims responsibility for summoning his spirit from the other side."

"You're here to solicit my help in solving a murder."

"Not solving outright. Helping to uncover the truth, yes. Stapleton's not talking. He won't refute anything. Seems to think the charges are baseless when he gets off scot-free, but he's not willing to destroy his career to prove himself innocent. He's making this a matter of spiritualism, claiming a connection with the other side that law enforcement couldn't understand—or find criminal. The courts will have to unfurl the legalities of that. And I'm sorry, but you were brought into this matter, along with Mr. Houdini, when your names were written on the paper we found on Peale's body."

"I had nothing to do with that."

"We believe you." Elliot raised his hands, palms forward.

"But it's why your name was there in the first place that we have to investigate. It's as if someone knew Peale was going to die and your name would be found on his body afterward. You were drawn into the mix because someone knows of your past connection to Stapleton, and we believe they want to exploit it."

The image of the pink-filigree party invitation invaded her thoughts. "Amberley . . . ," she whispered.

"We're not sure of Mrs. Dover's involvement. But it would speed things along if you could share what you may know about her connection to all of this," Connor added.

Elliot sent Connor a look, clearly bidding silence in their proceedings.

The more seasoned of the two seemed gifted with the ability to look through a person. His clear-blue eyes didn't waver, as if too knowledgeable of things they shouldn't have been.

She swallowed hard, considering.

"We're not asking for ourselves, Ms. Lockhart. A man is dead, and we're charged with finding the guilty party. Moreover, if Stapleton is exonerated after a trial, he'll walk out of his jail cell a free man to take advantage of the unsuspecting public with outlandish claims again. He'll just find new hearts to prey upon. I would think you of all people can sympathize with that. We need to ensure whomever is responsible is prosecuted but at the same time, prove Stapleton's claims as false."

The words she'd spoken onstage but an hour prior came back to haunt her.

Stapleton had swindled money from grieving widows and parents with empty cradles for years, always claiming to have a mystical connection to the grave. But now he'd found himself in real criminal trouble, and all the showmanship in the world couldn't free him from his iron cage.

"I can't possibly help you without giving myself away or revealing the secrets of every other illusionist on vaudeville. Once it gets out that I'm helping you, I'd be cut off from everyone I care about, from everything I've built. It would spell the end of my career."

"We'll protect you," Elliot answered without pause. "We won't reveal anything that would be detrimental. Your file would be sealed. As far as the press knows, we're hounding every notable vaudeville performer. It's logical that you would be a target of our investigation."

"I don't need protection. Furthermore, you can't promise me that, especially not after that stunt you pulled onstage tonight. You've linked me to the FBI, yet you tell me no one will know. Secrets always come up for air. They're never content to stay buried for long. You cannot know what you're asking me," Wren fired back, not comforted in the least when anyone asked for her blind trust or offered promises of protection in return.

She'd find them broken all too soon.

"We'd thought of that. But we can spin this any way we need to," Elliot countered. "The FBI might be questioning you just because you're an illusionist. Wouldn't the public take issue with that? You'd earn their sympathies along with Stapleton. And we would be pursuing you, but you could rebuff the request—at least in the public's view. No one would have to know you're helping us."

Connor stared down at the tips of his shoes. He seemed almost pained by their putting her through her paces, and that was a small amount of solace. And though Elliot's eyes reflected sincerity, they were far more unwavering than Connor's.

Elliot was after truth. She doubted anything mattered more to him.

"What about Bess?"

He furrowed his brow. "Houdini's wife?"

"Yes. How could I dare reveal her husband's secrets when she's still overcome with grief at his passing?"

"You know Houdini's secrets?" Connor piped up, clearly intrigued.

Wren bit her tongue, frustrated at what she'd revealed. "I won't definitively state what I do or don't know, certainly not in a backstage area and without assurances that my words wouldn't be repeated."

Elliot exchanged glances with Connor, adding, "But you know more about Harry Houdini's stage secrets than you're leading everyone to believe, don't you? It's why you're still an ardent supporter of defrauding spiritualists. Are you carrying on his work?"

It was common knowledge that she'd once worked with the famed illusionist's show. The biting fact was, they'd managed to strike at a tender place within Wren, one in which the words had tumbled from her lips and there was no seizing them back.

She'd tossed a strong bargaining chip on the table. Now she'd stiffen her spine and see what they intended to do with it.

"If I agree to answer your questions, we pick up where Harry left off with Stapleton without drawing anyone else in. I won't be the traitor to reveal secrets of the stage, outside of what may have occurred at that cemetery. We keep him from being charged with murder by proving him a fraud, if that's what it takes. But we leave the name of Houdini out of it. Those are my terms."

"I don't believe you would be a traitor to anyone," Elliot said with a quiet poignancy that willed her to trust something in him. After waiting several long seconds for a response, he added, "But I'm also not too proud to say we need your help."

Wren connected her gaze with his, trying to read whether there was honor in them.

Would he remain faithful to his promise to protect her name? Wren Lockhart was entangled in the case now whether she wanted to be or not. But Jennifer Charles—there was far more at stake for her.

"Jennifer Charles," she said. "I won't agree unless you bury that name. If one mention of her makes it into the papers, I'm walking. No second chances."

Elliot nodded. "Done."

Wren sighed. It was about as uncertain a deal as she could make.

"I will help you then, gentlemen. On one final condition," she whispered.

Elliot looked over at Connor. Skepticism melted away from both of their faces. "Alright. What do you want?"

Wren stood and could feel their gazes follow her as she crossed the room to the wardrobe with the mirrored front. She opened it, the door creaking out in protest. Irina had left her crimson cape hanging there. From the secret pocket sewn into the seam, Wren pulled a pink-filigree invitation with gold-foil script.

She crossed back over to where the men sat.

"I believe the fiasco in the cemetery was merely the opening act to a bigger show." Wren held the invitation out to Elliot. He took it in hand, his eyes questioning. "Amberley Dover is hosting a party next month. This will get you in."

Wren lifted her chin a notch. "If anyone was involved in Victor Peale's death, she's going down with them."

CHAPTER 6

April 2, 1907

The Castleton Theatre

Scollay Square

Boston, MASS.

"You like the box?" Jenny's uncle Franklin smiled, his eyes bright.

She unwrapped the gold-foil paper to find a beautiful box, with lacy paper cutouts raised on the top. It was a rich robin's-egg blue—because her uncle must have known she didn't favor pink.

"I found the box in a shop along the Avenue des Champs-Élysées, just for you."

"Along a what?" Jenny ran her hand over the luxurious box, hardly able to take her eyes off it to get to the birthday gift inside. It was heavy, weighting the box in her lap.

"Why, the Champs-Élysées. A most famous street in Paris, of course. You can't tell me you've never heard of it?" He gave her a *tsk, tsk* look, as if every proper young lady should know the layout of France's most famous, modern city.

"No. But would you take me one day?"

"To Paris?" He crossed his arms over his chest, play-thinking.

Her eyes must have lit up, because the mocking melted from his face and was soon replaced with warmth again. "Certainly. If it's alright with your mother and father."

"Maybe you could take Charlotte too. She likes pretty things. If Paris has more things like this, she'd be happy there."

"Well, we'll have to see about that, I think."

"But you'll leave again soon, won't you? To go back to London."

He looked down, as if her question had given him pause.

"Yes. I have some . . . things . . . lingering there that need my attention. I can't leave them now. But you needn't worry about that. Even across an ocean, I'll always be here if you need me. You can rest assured of that."

Jenny looked away, finding the pretty box an easier focus than thinking about him leaving again.

Her momma was sick again.

She was often sick, but this day was different. It was Jenny's birthday. And they were meant to have tea and cakes and take a walk to the big Common Park to feed the birds. Instead, her father had woken Jenny as the sun came up, not even letting her put on her favorite dress for the occasion, and took her along with him to the theater. At least Uncle Franklin had come to see her. And to her surprise, he'd brought her a present all the way from across the sea!

He sat on the front of the stage next to her, dangling his long legs off the side by her little ones. She tried to smile at him. Momma had always told her she should be grateful when she was given a gift. And this might be the most beautiful one she'd ever received just based on the box.

She shook it lightly. What made the weight shift inside?

"Jenny? What is it?"

Tears welled up in her eyes. She couldn't fight them back.

She could turn back to her uncle—the man who looked like what her father would if he ever smiled—and wish, especially on days like this, that he was her father instead.

Her mother had scolded her the one time she'd said it out loud, that it was a wicked thought and she should hush. Franklin was a kind man and an entertainer, too, like her father, but he lived far away, and rarely came home to visit. But when he did reappear, Jenny just kept the longings to herself.

"Momma is sick today," she admitted, holding on to her box as if the one pretty thing she had at the moment would vanish on air if she let loose of it.

"Sick?" He furrowed his brow. "What do you mean, sick? I saw her just yesterday and she was quite well."

Jenny tipped her shoulders in a light shrug. "I don't know. I didn't see her. Father said she was sick, so I had to come with him."

"And where is Charlotte now?"

"Home. In the nursery."

Franklin nodded, as if he were a wise old owl and knew some secrets he hadn't yet told. He scanned the empty auditorium, seeming to look all the way to the back where she could barely see through the darkness.

"Do you know where I might find your father?"

She shook her head. "I don't know. But he likes the rooms in the back. The nice ones. With the dancers. I have to go fetch him. Knock on the doors sometimes. He gave me a walking stick to do it so he can hear and I won't have to come in."

"I see." Franklin hopped down to the floor. He stood before her, looking up into her eyes. He dotted a finger to the soft skin on the apple of her cheek and offered a smile. "Those freckles get more pronounced every day, don't they? Just like your dear mom." He patted her hand atop the box. "They suit you."

She brightened. "They do?"

"Yes. They do." His eyes lingered on her for a long moment.

She wasn't sure, but he looked like he'd wanted to say something and didn't.

"Uncle?"

He cleared his throat. Maybe he was sick, too, because he didn't seem able to speak for a moment. But he summoned a smile anyway.

"How about I give you something else to cheer you on your birthday? Share a secret perhaps, from one grown-up to another? You are six years old today. I think that's quite old enough to share in the entertainers' code."

"An entertainers' code? Yes, please!"

It was interesting. Exciting! She could know something only the showmen did, and that was better than a box from Paris.

"There's a secret door over there." He tipped his chin up to the stage. "Right in the center. A trapdoor for the vanishing acts. And there's a switch in the floor, stage-side right. A stage assistant steps down on it at the right time, and *poof*! The trapdoor opens and the illusionist disappears. Only, the crowd thinks he's vanished into thin air."

Jenny turned, staring back at the empty stage behind them.

A secret door! It was like a hidden-away enchantment, one that only a few were graced with the knowledge of. She smiled, exchanging sadness for a lovely escape.

"What's behind the door?" she whispered, near breathless at the thought.

"You mean, what's beneath it? Why, an entire corridor! Rooms with hidden spaces and tucked-out-of-the-way memories of yesterday. Posters. Old stage props, that sort of thing. There's even a great big sign, with lettering for yours truly—when I used to be on the stage here. But shhh. Only illusionists know about the door. You have to keep it a secret. Promise?"

"I can keep a secret . . . I think." She raised an eyebrow, playacting.

He laughed, a small chuckle that rumbled in his chest. "I believe you. And you just sit here with your gift. Take your time opening it." He leaned in to whisper, a comical bent to his features. "I had the shop girl put mounds of perfumed paper in it just for you. Blue, of course. Your favorite color."

Jenny nodded, feeling the oddest sense of trust wash over her whenever he was around. Suddenly the theater didn't seem so dark in the back. And the days she missed her momma not so sad. When Franklin was there, her world had a bit of light and warmth she couldn't feel otherwise.

Uncle Franklin turned to walk to the right stage curtain, a bit of hustle in his steps. He pivoted, pointing to a door in the shadowed alcove underneath the balcony. "Is this it? The door to the VIP rooms?"

"The new rooms Father likes so much?"

Franklin nodded, though his forehead wrinkled like her father's when he was angry. Maybe her uncle was angry about something too.

"Yes. I need to speak with him. Now."

"That's the door, Uncle Franklin. But pull the curtain back over it. No one's supposed to know it's there. It's another secret. Entertainers' code, you know." She smiled, trying to be brave and show him she remembered things that should be hidden.

He winked, silently sending her back to her fanciful world of birthdays and blue perfumed paper. Then he stepped through the door into the hall beyond and left her alone in the vast auditorium, the lovely box in her hands.

Jenny opened the lid. Slowly, carefully, as though the paper were made of the finest silk, she pulled back the layers of blue to find a book. A thick volume of deep blue, with gold letters on the front.

She couldn't read many of the words, but she did read *Fairy* and *Book* in the title, and a wave of excitement washed over her. The lady on the cover certainly looked fairy-like, with her flowing dress and golden harp and bright flaming hair just like Jenny had.

Careful not to smudge the cover, she lifted it out, then brushed her fingertips over the title. She knew about fairy tales. Her momma had told her about them many times. But this was different. This book had a beauty to it that could be her someday. With flaming red hair and music floating around, with no fear to steal her smile away.

No longer caring whether she'd mar the cover, Jenny hugged the book to her chest. Tight. In a birthday hug that she'd not received from anyone yet. She then put it back, mindful to wrap the folds of the paper just so, and replaced the box lid with the utmost care.

It was a birthday she knew she'd always remember somehow, for her uncle Franklin had given her the image of a hero when she most needed one. He'd shared a secret, even if the door wasn't truly enchanted. And in the life she lived—with shades of darkness in the span of the bright red of theater seats all around—that one glimpse of light made her believe someone was out there who would fight for her.

Somewhere there was a hero waiting to rescue her.

❋

JANUARY 21, 1927

BIJOU THEATRE

WASHINGTON STREET

BOSTON, MASS.

"What's this?"

Irina was trying to move a chair and hadn't seen the book on the seat. It flipped off the edge and landed with a *crack* against the hardwood floor, the sound echoing through the backstage rafters.

"That's mine." Wren had been wringing water out of her hair after the water escape she'd just finished onstage. She wiped her palm on a towel nearby and held out her hand.

"I've never seen it before." Irina bent to retrieve it. She eyed the cover, then tipped her brow up. "Reading fairy stories? Wouldn't our friend Houdini have laughed at that? Who knew that the mysterious Wren Lockhart has a softer side?"

Wren brushed her palm down the spine and over the cover, shaking off imaginary dust. "It was a gift I received on my sixth birthday." She slipped the book inside a hidden drawer at the side of the long worktable they used in the shows. A soft smile eased across her lips. "And you already knew I had a softer side."

"Well, that book must be a favorite if you keep it under lock and key."

"It was given to me the day before my mother died. So yes,

it's dear. But it's been on the shelf for ages. I almost never get it down to look at it."

Irina stood by, still gripping the chair back. "Yet in all the years you and I have worked together, I've never even seen you with it. What made you get it out tonight?"

Wren turned her back to her friend and went back to fiddling with the wardrobe. Anything to avoid digging any deeper into what was stirring inside her at the moment.

She heard the sound of Irina's wooden chair creak as she sat. "It was those agents, wasn't it? First the one who came snooping around the house. Then both of them nosing around our back-stage area—where no one else is supposed to be given access, I might add." Irina folded her arms across her chest and frowned. "I knew I shouldn't have let them come back that night. Now it's troubled you for an entire week."

Wren waved off the idea that Agent Matthews or Agent Finnegan had truly upset her. They hadn't really. But they made her think, and on some days, that could be even worse, if left to her own devices.

"They didn't cause me any trouble."

"No? Well, they sure didn't come to sing you a lullaby." Irina stood and stepped up to her side. "Wren. I've known you a long time. Since we took a chance and boarded that steamship from England. I remember those early days, when we both sought the American shore as a fresh start. The only thing that could possibly have you thinking about childhood fairy tales again is that they questioned you about your family. So tell me, what did they say?"

"It's not that really. They . . ." Wren ran a hand across her neck, her hair almost dried and taken to riotous curls against her jawline.

"Yes?"

"They want me to work with them to bring Horace Stapleton to justice."

"What?" Irina nearly shrieked. She grasped Wren's elbow, staring in disbelief.

"Well, not take him down. They want to find out the truth. They said that Stapleton will likely be charged with murder and—"

"Murder? Not possible, Wren. Whoever that man pretending to be Victor Peale was, he dropped dead of his own misfortune. It was clearly just an elaborate stage illusion gone wrong. You and I both know that. And I thought you wanted to stay out of it." Irina sighed as she moved over to the table and counted their locks and chains. "Helping the FBI is not even on the same continent as staying out of it."

"But what if it wasn't an accident? They seem to think something more is going on. After the few things I've learned about the case already, I'm inclined to agree with them. But it also doesn't make sense that Stapleton would bring a man back from the dead only to kill him a moment later." Wren chewed on her thumbnail as she tried to slow the thoughts sailing through her mind.

"And they want you to do the dirty work for them, to tell them everything about your life on vaudeville? Do you realize what will happen? If you walk into that Bureau office and spill the secrets of illusionists, your career will be over. You'll be hated—no, *we'll* be hated, and I don't think you want that to happen."

"They're not asking for everyone's secrets onstage. They're not even asking for mine."

"Then . . . ?" Irina cocked her head slightly.

"They want to know how Stapleton managed it. That's all.

They want another illusionist to come in and prove he's a fraud—which we both know is the case."

"You have to know what they're really after."

Wren had wondered from the start... "Harry," she whispered.

"Yes. Now that he's gone, only one or two people on earth know how he managed it all." Irina paused. "That information could be very lucrative for the wrong person—and dangerous for you."

Wren was skilled in the art of hiding her emotions. She'd worked hard to become so. But not with Irina. She was a confidant, her business partner and friend who knew the inner workings of her stage illusions. Of course, Wren had kept a few things to herself. Harry had cautioned her long ago not to let anyone become privy to her deepest secrets, at least not until she had explicit trust in them.

Perhaps it was her tumultuous upbringing and the fact that she'd buried Jenny Charles in name long ago, but Wren found it difficult to fully trust anyone.

"Dangerous? Certainly not. They just want someone who thinks like Stapleton would to examine the case and see what sticks out."

Irina shook her head. "And what about Amberley Dover—your former friend? Why do they think she was at the cemetery? Surely there's an explanation for why she came sauntering out of the woodwork."

Wren pinched the bridge of her nose, then squeezed her eyes tight, not ready to see her friend's response to what she was about to say. "I gave them Amberley's invitation. And I accepted. I'm going to her party."

"Wren, you can't."

"Amberley is hiding something—that much is clear. And she

had no qualms about standing up before God and Boston when she slinked up onto Stapleton's stage. There has to be a reason for it. I have to put the past aside and find out what's happening."

Wren looked to her friend, the like-minded manager who always wanted the best for her, and exhaled. "Please support me in this? My gut is telling me something is going on."

Irina sighed. "Ugh. 'Please'? You never say that word."

"I know, but I need you to be with me on this. Someone is digging up Jennifer Charles, and whoever it is, they're trying to come after me too. I can't stand by and just ignore it—especially not when I have Charlotte to think about."

"Are they looking to dredge up old wounds?" Irina rested a hand on Wren's forearm, concern creeping over her features.

The note in Victor Peale's book had been a warning, and a none-too-subtle one at that. "If they uncover anything about Charlotte, I'll hide her at a moment's notice. I just have to keep the agents close until I can find out more about Stapleton. About Amberley. And certainly about who's digging into my past and why. Even if I'm turning the FBI in circles, they'll need to be circles that are within my reach."

"And that starts with attending Amberley Dover's birthday party, doesn't it?"

The last thing Wren wanted was a public showdown with the illustrious and toxic-tongued Amberley Dover. But that was what it looked like Wren was about to get. Add the FBI agents into the mix, and she had a real storm brewing.

"Do you want me to go with you?"

Wren shook her head. "Thanks, but no. This is something I have to do on my own. It will bring me comfort to know you're watching over things while I'm gone."

"Try to lay low at the party if you can help it. Just learn what you can and try to find out what Amberley's up to without tipping her off."

"You don't have to worry about that. I plan to stay out of it, unless of course Amberley has her own agenda. Then I'll just have to make decisions on the fly."

Irina sighed and stretched her arms. "But that's what you're good at, isn't it? Let's get the rest of this packed up." She smiled, though reluctance was veiled somewhere behind the words. "And then we'll have to figure out what you're going to wear to that party."

Wren had thought of it too. She'd have to show up to the event in true Wren Lockhart-style, donning her best tuxedo and knee-high boots. Her satin top hat would go nicely, as would a silky gentleman's shirt in a deep black. And there was one other little surprise she'd thought of—though she'd tell no one about this addition.

The FBI agents may have been hot on her trail, but a girl still needed to have at least one secret that was all her own.

CHAPTER 7

JULY 23, 1924

10 LIME STREET

BOSTON, MASS.

Wren stepped into the waiting car in front of Harry Houdini.

He slid into the backseat bench beside her without a word. Having just left the sweltering-hot fourth-story séance room of famed Boston medium Mina "Margery" Crandon, it didn't surprise Wren that even the great Harry Houdini had been drawn to silence.

He was no doubt lost in the measure of his thoughts as the driver pulled their car into the flood of automobile traffic on Lime Street. They'd dressed for the occasion—he in a smart suit and she in her usual costume of linen shirt and crisp trousers. But the late-July heat threatened to bake them in the back of the auto, even though the windows had been opened.

Wren fanned a gloved hand in front of her face and waited on Harry, as she usually did, knowing that the gears were cranking in his mind and he'd comment when he was ready.

He stared out the car window as buildings and pedestrians passed by.

They neared Charles Street, and Boston's Public Garden came into view, the man-made structures of the streets they'd left behind now replaced with a bowery of beautiful shade trees and low-hanging clouds that painted cottony-white brushstrokes across the summer sky.

"What did you see in there?" Harry finally asked.

Wren tapped her walking stick against the floor, thinking over the events of the last hour.

"It was a clever setup—simple and manageable. She claimed to summon spirits from the other side. They responded on cue, in the voice of her brother and the ringing of a bell. Her guests seemed to leave satisfied, so in that way, I'd say she put on a rather seamless show."

"Seamless." He pursed his lips. "Yet you're not convinced?"

"No. I am not. And I can tell you're not either or you wouldn't have asked me."

Margery Crandon had indeed put on a show to be remembered. It was Wren's first séance, and though many in Boston's social circles thoroughly enjoyed such diversions, she could only hope it would be her last.

"Tell me what we know thus far, Wren. Facts only."

"Margery is a medium. Late thirties. A flapper, if I can say it, because I believe it to be fact. She claims both brains and beauty and has become quite popular in the parlors of Boston's elite. Her apparent connection to the afterlife has come to the attention of *Scientific American* magazine. By all accounts, she's vying for the twenty-five-hundred-dollar prize the magazine committee is offering to any medium able to display irrefutable evidence of psychic phenomena."

"That sounds rather textbook. And as one such committee member with a trained eye, I summoned myself to show up at her doorstep and investigate the authenticity of her claims."

And you brought me along. Though she still wasn't entirely sure why.

"So you are still not convinced," he added, his counsel to her always frank. "Why? Did you see something that causes you to doubt?"

"Everything about it causes me to doubt, but that's just instinct. If you're asking me personally, then I'd say it's because my faith must always be stronger than what my eyes can see. However, if you're asking Wren the illusionist, then I'd say that you once told me a showman must always make the crowd believe the story she tells. That's what she did: staged a story for everyone gathered around that table. It was an ingenious act, but that's all it was—an *act*. And so now, the choice is mine, whether I'll believe it or stand firm on what I know to be truth."

Harry nodded, a knowing smile turning up the corners of his mouth. "Fair enough. Was there any other reason?"

"The fact that Amberley Dover was there," she replied, unable to avoid a slight frown.

Harry turned to her. Raised an eyebrow, showing the subtlety of his surprise. "Besides the obvious social connection, an odd choice. My former employee and a friend of yours, I understand?"

Wren sighed. "We were friends once. Going back to the first days you brought me into your show. But it was a matter of faith that came between us. She favored mysticism on the stage and didn't mind trickery if it gave people what they wanted. I couldn't see anything but darkness in it. My faith wouldn't bend and neither would her will. So we fell out over it. We haven't spoken since."

Harry nodded, releasing a slight grunt under his breath. "And now she's known as a pretty young socialite who dabbles in spiritualism in her free time. But she was brought in as a silent observer, wasn't she? Why would you suspect her?"

"Amberley was anything but silent. She jabbered on like a magpie. If there really were spirits there, I'm surprised they could manage to get a word in at all. The voices of the afterlife have nothing on her."

"So she's a talker. But where's your evidence?"

Wren tipped her shoulders up in a shrug. "It's a hunch. She didn't mind trickery in the past. Why would that change now?"

"Hunches carry no weight, and you certainly can't defend them."

"The choice is not so odd, sir, when you think about it. Amberley's husband has had a long friendship with Dr. Crandon. It goes to say that Margery's husband and a close acquaintance would have an association that would overstep the boundaries of truth. I can see how a medium would solicit the help of a friend, especially one who has such impressive social standing as Amberley Dover enjoys."

"Circumstantial. You need hard evidence, Wren. Think back. What were we allowed to see in that room? What did your ears tell you when the lights were dimmed? Look at the connections for how the unexplained could be, in fact, explainable. There's always evidence, if you look behind the curtain. And there's always a curtain. You just have to be smarter than they are about how you peek behind it. So I'll ask you again, and think carefully before you answer—what did you see in there? Think about it as an illusionist would."

Wren was certain he'd already worked out how the medium managed to fool so many unsuspecting housewives in their parlor séance parties. Either Amberley had been drawn in by her interest in mysticism, or she was in on some scheme. Harry evidently knew, but he wanted Wren to draw the conclusions on her own.

She went back over the last hour in her mind, gazing out as trees flashed by the car windows. Her thoughts shifted into the layout of the room at 10 Lime Street.

Amberley was seated at Margery's right side: pretty, painted, wide-eyed, and staring daggers at Wren from across the table. Malcom Bird, a committee member of *Scientific American*, sat on her left, quiet and observant. Wren and Harry occupied chairs across from them.

The unease Wren had felt around that table returned to flutter about her midsection. Her senses had been on high alert in that attic room . . . her eyes watching . . . her heart beating faster . . . her mind telling her to cling to her faith. That the séance was a charade. That she should hold fast to what her heart knew until she could escape the darkness permeating the room . . . not to give in to the belief that spirits of the dead could come back to the living.

Not when she knew better.

The room spun in her mind, her memory clicking through the mental pictures she'd taken: the fall of shadows in the fourth-story room, making every pinprick of light stand out from the dark. It fell into place then, something that had been overlooked. Their séance hadn't been in a high-society parlor. Instead, Margery had controlled the atmosphere herself, down to the light, the furnishings, and the collection of people in the room.

"Amberley was brought in to be the distraction—*for us.* Could the contention in our past have been exploited so we'd focus on *who* was in the room and not *what*?"

He seemed to already know that and nodded her along, a distant smile pressed on his lips. "Good. What else?"

"The room was minimally set up—just chairs, a table, and a cabinet—and was checked before and after the séance itself. But that simplicity aids in belief, doesn't it? And if she doesn't charge for her services, which she almost never does, it's that much more credible. She doesn't prey on guests around her table. Instead, she's benevolent. She's one of them, essentially. With a house in the heart of the city and furnishings similar to those they might have in their own homes. It makes her abilities seem more extraordinary when set against a common backdrop."

"That works in her favor. So how did she do it?"

"I think someone smuggled in a bell for her."

"You think it was Amberley."

She cleared her throat, challenge evident in the timing.

Harry nodded, choosing not to dissent. "Fine. And if so, the bell was—"

"Under the table," she whispered, finishing his thought as the possibilities came together, like puzzle pieces falling into place. "She used her foot, didn't she?"

"Precisely."

Wren crossed her arms over her chest.

So simple. Ingenious really, when you thought about all the pomp and circumstance that went into the show itself. By comparison, the real answer was unsophisticated. Was it possible that the calling of spirits and conversing with the dead came down to a woman who could artfully slip her foot from her shoe and, under cover of a tablecloth, grasp a bell handle to ring with her toes?

"So you'll discredit them?"

"I will render my opinion in a public forum, yes." He nodded, his brow creased. "I'd only have played my hand if I found her claims to be false. I've seen enough now to believe that they are."

"And what of the ability to converse with those who have passed on? She claims she can bring people back from the dead—if only to talk for a while. How can you possibly disprove something like that, especially when so many ardently believe in her, Amberley Dover included?"

"Wren, you told me you once lost someone very dear to you."

She drew in a sharp breath, absorbing his swift change in subject.

"Yes. I did lose someone once." She avoided revealing emotion with her quiet tone.

Those memories had been locked away, deep down so she rarely visited them. Conversations with Harry were always focused on fact. They weren't in the habit of discussing anything but illusions and the business of a traveling stage show. Yet now his deliberations seemed weighted solely in the opposite direction.

The newfound depth upended her thoughts.

"The person you lost, what would you give to speak with them again? If only for a moment?"

Wren considered it, though the answer was always there, occupying a secret place at the edge of her heart.

"I'd give everything I own without a second thought."

"As would I, Wren."

Harry turned away from the view beyond the vehicle window to look at her. She saw pain there, in his eyes. It clung to his face, genuine and heartbreaking.

"And that's why what we're doing is so important. We've just been through a terrible war, followed closely by the devastation of the Spanish flu. Couple those together and few in this country have been left untouched by death's hand. Countless hurting souls are drifting in the wake of loss. And mediums have built a following of thousands based, not in the merits of their actual abilities, but on the clever time and place they're able to employ them."

Wren thought about the searing pain of loss. How it had changed everything for her. How her early years had been shadowed by it in some measure, and even now, after all the time that had passed, the pain could still manage to pulse raw under the surface.

So many others struggled with the same wandering through grief. She swallowed hard, trying to force the emotion back down to its hiding place within her heart.

"I see how it could happen, how people could believe in mediums, especially if they're grasping for a bygone life. But I still hated being in that room today. It felt like supporting a lie."

"We must help others see it as you do," Harry said. "And as for Amberley, I share a word of caution. She's gone down a very different path. A journey like that could shake the very core of what you yourself believe in. No matter what friendship you might have had once, you cannot allow yourself to be taken in by her version of truth. I'm not saying you can't seek restoration of a lost friendship. Believe me, I speak from a place of understanding. But you're in a position that ensures you must tread carefully around her from now on. Your faith must not be built on a weak foundation."

Yes, he knew firsthand how the differences in faith beliefs could sever even the deepest bonds of friendship. He'd lost out over the defaming of spiritualists, and his friendship with a close author friend had been the casualty.

Wren hastily wiped at a tear with her gloved hand, lest Harry see it.

"Too many days the sun is shining, but I still can't seem to feel it. Does that make any sense at all?" The truth made her eyes continue to tear despite her inner demand that they cooperate and reveal nothing of the emotion that clawed at her insides.

"It does to me. Wren, no matter what any proprietor will tell you, vaudeville is not about money. Nor prestige. It puts a spotlight on the beliefs held in our very core. You may lose relationships over them. And you'll find that the longer you're a part of this world, you may be asked to sacrifice even more of who you are. As an entertainer, your job is to weave a story onstage—performing illusions that thrill the hearts and minds of the audience. Unfortunately, those who resort to false truths or claim the ability to harness magic that doesn't exist will always draw a crowd. But you're better than that. Frauds should be pitied. And then they should be publicly defamed for the damage they do to the hearts of the grieving."

"I could have been someone in the crowd once, someone vulnerable and hurt, who searched for belief like Amberley does. But at what point do people own their own faith? When can we finally let go of someone we've lost? For the life of me, I don't have the answer."

"When we die, Wren." Harry's voice was weighted with the strangest layer of sadness.

Sunshine cast beams of light against shadows as the car turned toward Tremont Street and the booming theater district that had become their temporary performance home.

"As for returning from the dead, I know this with certainty: it's humanly impossible."

❈

FEBRUARY 5, 1927

THE STATLER HOTEL

BOSTON, MASS.

"It's humanly impossible . . ." Wren whispered Harry's words aloud, remembering the day over two years before, when they'd driven along these very streets from Beacon Hill through the Boston Public Garden.

Harry had spoken to her in a way he'd never done before or after, sharing the depth of conviction for why he'd invited her to Margery Crandon's home that day. The conversation replayed in her mind as she drove along now, feeling numb as she angled her coal-black Pierce Arrow over the icy streets.

It had been over three weeks since Agents Matthews and Finnegan had ventured backstage at the Bijou Theatre and asked her to become part of their plan to unearth the truth about Horace Stapleton. And now, with Amberley's party looming before her, all Wren could think of was Harry's warning to tread carefully where her former friend was concerned.

Wren eased her car to a stop in front of the soon-to-open Statler Hotel and glanced up as a uniformed man opened the door, offering his hand to help her out.

She nodded her thanks but kept her hand on her walking stick.

No picks were taped in her gloves this night, but it was a common practice for her to project a detached manner at all times. If she refrained from taking a gentleman's hand as a rule, it would never catch her off guard when she was indeed gloved up.

"We'll take it for you, madam."

She nodded to the valet, leaving the car in his care.

The Statler Hotel was an imposing structure from the sidewalk along Providence Street. Lights glowed out from windows more than ten stories up.

Wren stepped through the gilded glass front doors, tipping her head to the doorman as she passed. The lobby smelled of fresh paint and furniture polish, mixed with savory food, the aroma of which presumably floated out from the Imperial Ballroom to mingle amongst the gathering of chic society guests.

Whispers echoed behind her as she breezed through the lobby. She could feel the sting of eyes boring into her back. No bother. One couldn't venture out in her attire and expect to receive a usual welcome. She'd dressed in her most notable outfit: an ivory, fox-trimmed coat and sleek suit, with a black silk shirt and gold-stud cuff links peeking out at her wrists, glittering against her matching gloves.

Wren's boots clicked against the marble floor, her strides wide and her cadence strong. She scanned the crowd for the familiar faces of Agents Matthews and Finnegan. They were sure to have faded into the background somewhere, keeping an eye out for her entrance. But other than their ghostly presence, Wren knew she was walking into the lions' den alone.

"Your invitation, madam?"

The question jarred Wren from her thoughts.

A man, tuxedo-clad and white-gloved, stood guard at the door to the ballroom fete.

"It appears that I neglected to bring it along." Wren kept her spine pin-straight and her chin high, an air of superiority fully in place. "Will that be a problem?"

"I'm sorry, madam, but without an invitation . . ."

"Do you know who I am?" She hated sounding so pretentious. But since it was the only way to get in the party, she'd swallow the bitter taste of it and square her shoulders.

He shook his head. "My apologies. I'm afraid I don't."

Probably younger than her twenty-six years, he looked provincial and untested—that much was evident by the shifty-footed stance he employed. He looked to the line of people forming behind her, flip-flopping his glance from her to an older, tuxedo-clad staff member off to the side, probably a manager of some sort.

Wren stood tall and tapped her walking stick on the marble floor. "I do not usually require an invitation."

"I'll vouch for her," came a singsong voice from the direction of the stairs behind them.

A hush fell in the lobby alcove, drawing Wren to turn around.

Amberley, the widow-turned-heiress, floated down the grand staircase in an ensemble of black-and-gold beads, sewn over silk in a deep and luxurious blood orange. Glittering diamonds winked out from her lobes and sparkled on the headband woven through the coif at her nape. Evening gloves nipped at her upper arms to the edge of a nude mink shawl. She surveyed the scene, elegant and self-important, toying with a long-stemmed cigarette holder in her hand.

"After all, we are old friends. Don't you know who she is, sir? This is the famed illusionist Wren Lockhart. I'd hate to think she'd not be admitted to a celebration of gaiety such as this." Amberley spoke through a honeyed smile, with lips that curved up in welcome.

It took nothing for her to cut through the short lobby to the party doors. She slinked along, her heels oddly silent against the marble floor, like a feline taking a post-nap stroll. To anyone on the outside looking in, her greeting would have appeared quite refined, even cordial. But Wren knew better. Amberley's smile may have been sugarcoated, but the depths of her eyes proved glacial.

"Yes, of course, Mrs. Dover." The young man bowed in apology, then turned his attention to the line of party guests.

Amberley waltzed through the doors ahead of Wren, though the glittering host slowed her steps in expectation that Wren would follow. "Misplaced your invitation? I was sure I sent it out several weeks ago. You should have put it in a safe place until this evening."

"I must have mislaid it. Silly me." Wren kept her gaze on the ballroom, inspecting the layout of revelry before her.

Round tables with silver candelabras and elaborate floral concoctions dotted the back half of the ballroom. Guests flitted around the dance floor at the front, beneath a wide stage with a brass band and pianist playing jazzy tunes to billow off the arched two-story ceiling.

"Well, I'm delighted that I came down to the lobby when I did. I'd hate to think of the write-up in the paper if the infamous Wren Lockhart was turned away from a party like this. What would those society column readers say then?"

"What do they ever say when lies are printed?"

"Oh, Wren! You do brighten every room with your cheek, don't you?" Amberley tossed her head and laughed, bouncing the row of sculpted curls against her brow. "But if you're concerned about what the press may write tonight, perhaps you should go speak to them straightaway. Get on their good side early." She angled her cigarette holder toward the back of the room. "See? They're just there, positioned by the far wall. You could even have your photo taken, if you'd like."

"Not particularly. No."

"And waste the delights of this gorgeous getup? Oh dear." Amberley ran her gloved hand against the lapel of Wren's tuxedo jacket. "You really must try to live a little, darling."

"I try to at least once a day."

The blatant cat-and-mouse game Amberley had initiated was tiring Wren—and quickly. She scanned the room, looking for help. Though she was reluctant to admit it to herself, the FBI accomplices were nowhere to be seen. She might be without an ally in the entire ballroom. Perhaps they'd been called away for another case, or worse, had left her to fend off the bejeweled wolves on her own.

It still hadn't been made clear why Wren was invited to the party in the first place. But the last thing she would do now would be to give Amberley the satisfaction of asking outright. So if she preferred to employ false gaiety in her manners, Wren would grit her teeth and withstand it.

"You know, Wren, we have come a long way from Lime Street, haven't we? Or other streets before that." Amberley tilted her head slightly, as if she were working something out in her mind. "I wonder, just to liven things up, would you consent to perform something for my guests tonight? Like the old days."

Wren's refusal would have been swift if Amberley hadn't stopped it in full force on the first syllable by tugging on her arm like coaxing a toddler.

"Oh, you know how I enjoy your parlor tricks. Fun little distractions at society parties." She winked. "You must say yes. It would be such a treat for everyone."

"I've never performed a trick in my life."

"Oh yes, you are particular. I should have said *illusions*."

Amberley didn't give Wren a chance to respond.

The birthday girl flitted off like a jovial butterfly, fluttering past the throngs of guests to the front stage. She climbed the stairs and crossed the stage, then whispered in the band leader's ear. He halted the music full stop, then instructed his pianist to give an introduction. The musician's fingers sailed over the ivories and the horns sang, belting out notes from the jaunty tune "Prohibition Blues" as they moved back to clear a space on the stage.

The audience waited, gleeful at the prospect of a show but oblivious to Amberley's intentions. It was a setup, of course. Amberley's chance to publically humiliate Wren in the way she'd been lambasted after Margery Crandon's public fall nearly three years before.

Wren had half expected Amberley to try and turn the tables.

She watched as Amberley took over the microphone. She whispered something to the band leader, then turned to the throngs of partygoers with a honeyed smile, chatting her thanks for their attendance of her birthday celebration.

"May I have this dance?" Elliot had managed to sneak up, just a step behind, and whisper the request.

Wren straightened her shoulders on principle. "I don't dance."

As usual, he didn't try to hide a laugh at her coiled response. "Yes, I forgot. Anything fun must be outlawed, unless, of course, it's performed on a stage. Strike dancing from Wren's list of hobbies. She's addicted to work, just like I am."

Annoyance mounted and Wren exhaled. Elliot Matthews was far too relaxed at the moment. She glanced over. He was scanning the room, as was his usual practice. His eyes watched everything. Calculating, as if he couldn't have cared less for a grand party unless it profited his investigation.

"You look a bit nervous, Ms. Lockhart."

"I do not because I am not."

"Mrs. Dover's playing to the crowd like a pro. So she sent you an invitation to get you up onstage without notice and, in doing so, embarrasses you in the most public way she could."

"It certainly looks that way."

Elliot stepped up beside her. For some reason she was surprised to see he hadn't arrived at the party in a wrinkled shirt and trench coat. Instead, he'd made an effort again, just like her performance night at the Bijou. He looked as clean-cut and dignified as any guest here.

"How many tuxes do you own?"

He sipped on a drink that matched the deep orange-red of Amberley's gown. "I could ask you the same thing, Ms. Lockhart."

"Unappreciated, but duly noted. Though I wish your attention to detail would prove more worthwhile than noticing what people are wearing."

He leaned closer to her. "Or drinking. I'd have this party shut down if it wouldn't ruin our undercover sting." He held up his tumbler. "Someone's spiked this. These high-society crowds will just never learn, will they?" Not missing a beat, he slipped the glass on a waiter's tray as he swept by.

Wren exhaled in exasperation, dropping her voice low. "Look at Amberley. You're really not supposed to be talking to me. Or have you forgotten? That was your idea when we planned this. I was supposed to get in, find out why Amberley invited me, and if possible learn what I can about her little exposé on Stapleton's stage. Then I melt into the background—certainly without making friends with the FBI. But now you're dropping it all flat because you've stepped into a lavish speakeasy and you want a little tipsy-talk?"

"And dancing. Don't forget that, even though you turned me down."

"I turn everyone down, Agent Matthews," she fired back, trying to keep her response at a decibel low enough to still retain the confines of a private conversation.

"Well, I'm talking to you now because our agreement was before Amberley upped the stakes. She's plotting something."

"Of course she is."

He tilted his head toward the stage. "You've got to admit that the woman has some grit about her."

"When all is said and done, I don't think you'll be prepared to handle her brand of it."

Wren turned her gaze, eager to change the subject, to lose him, or both. She surveyed the reveling crowd. "Where is Agent Finnegan, should this night turn sour and we need an extra badge?"

"Wouldn't we like to know? I lost him somewhere between the words 'nice clambake' and 'I think I'll just go question that group of ladies by the cake table.' He's likely taken with one of them and found a quiet corner in which to hear all of her secrets." Elliot sighed, his eyes taken to scanning the length of the ballroom. "I'll think about firing him tomorrow. But right now you might want to keep focused on our hostess."

Wren shifted her eyes back to the stage, the silky form of Amberley absorbing the crowd's reverence from above. She moved about, then pointed to her audience.

"Don't look now." Elliot whistled low. "You're being summoned to court."

Amberley smiled to the crowd. ". . . Yes, Ms. Lockhart is here! Right in the back of this ballroom." She eased her arm out to point at Wren. "And she has consented to entertain us tonight."

She snapped her fingers against the microphone. "Up to the stage, Wren. Won't you, my dear?"

Wren's pulse burned. She didn't take to being summoned like a lapdog.

"I didn't know you were anyone's 'my dear,'" Elliot said, coughing the last two words under his breath as she edged away.

Wren ignored his brass and kept moving forward. Flappers in beaded dresses and gentlemen in their best dinner jackets parted, smiling and clapping as she threaded her way through the dazzling sequined sea.

"And wouldn't you know it? Our famous illusionist has brought a friend. Dare I say, an escort? Well, we know him at the very least to have been her assistant onstage for one of her last shows. Agent Elliot Matthews?" Amberley sang out. "You're here somewhere, aren't you?" She raised a gloved hand to her brow, shielding her eyes from the blast of the stage lights. "Yes . . . in the back. Won't you join us onstage?"

Wren paused, enough to turn around and catch Elliot's steady gaze. They were too far apart to speak, but she could guess what was going through his mind.

Elliot had linked them together by volunteering for her stage show at the Bijou. The papers had snapped photographs and reported the news in the wake of Stapleton's arrest, including the fact that the FBI agent was in some familiarity with Wren Lockhart.

If there had been any hope for Elliot to stay incognito and learn just why Amberley had sent the party invitation in the first place, it was dead now. The birthday queen had her own agenda. And whatever her association with Horace Stapleton or the deceased Victor Peale, they weren't likely to find out a pittance from the stage.

Wren swallowed hard and continued walking forward, knowing that Elliot was following somewhere behind. "Here we go."

CHAPTER 8

Elliot wasn't in the habit of being caught center stage, but since he'd met Wren, the practice was occurring with irritating regularity.

Always composed, she seemed undaunted by the impromptu show she was asked to give. What's more, if she'd been annoyed when he'd approached her in the audience, any irritation had dissolved now. The transformation from the Wren who'd quipped with him in the audience versus the professional now taking command of the stage was nothing short of a wonder.

She'd show no fear, of that he was certain.

"Thank you, Amberley." Wren's smile veiled the ire he knew she had toward Amberley's intentions.

The spotlights shone down on Wren, standing tall with light outlining the frame of her crisp ivory suit and black boots.

"Might your guests enjoy an escape demonstration? Not from this glamorous party though, I assure you. Isn't it splendid, ladies and gentlemen? Mrs. Dover has gone all out for us tonight." She extended an arm out to bow in the birthday girl's presence.

Amberley shifted in her heels but smiled on with a glaze of haughtiness covering her face.

"Not a bluenose in this bunch, to be sure," Wren added. Whistles and hollers billowed up from the crowded dance floor. "So now, I ask all of you—how does one escape from an unwanted entanglement? Or from a handcuff, perhaps? Not an engagement ring, mind you. I am quite sure every lovely lady in this room would not wish to free herself from that kind of handcuff. But what of the other kind—the darker, more mysterious entanglements of sin and deceit that seek to snare us? Would that handcuff be easier to shake?"

Wren shifted her attention to Elliot. "You are a law enforcement officer, Agent Mathews."

He nodded, leaning in to the microphone. "Some say it, yes. On my better days, Ms. Lockhart."

"Of course you are," she answered in animated fashion, drawing the crowd under her spell as she toyed with the wit of his response. "And might I please have a handcuff from you?"

He raised his eyebrows in comical fashion, then patted his jacket as if looking for a jewelry store box he'd misplaced. "Which handcuff? Are you referring to the real thing or an engagement ring? If it's the latter, I'm afraid I must have left it in my other tux."

The crowd awed, as if witnessing a sweet moment between a couple.

The slightest trace of irritation marred Wren's brow, even through the painted-on smile. This was her show evidently. He could play along but not steer it.

"How flattering of you, Agent Matthews. But the one escape act I'm best at is fleeing any sort of matrimonial entanglement."

She eased back a step, putting distance between them, enough so she could extend her hands, wrist on top of wrist, before him. "What I would like is for you to handcuff me. Surely you have a pair under that jacket somewhere."

The crowd responded with jeers and delighted laughter as Elliot pulled the handcuffs from his belt.

"But you'll want to take off your gloves, certainly. Your jacket too," Amberley piped in. "I'll hold them for you."

Wren said nothing, just flitted a glance over at him.

Elliot's breath caught in his chest for a split second. How did Wren plan to get out of this mess, especially when Amberley kept digging a deeper hole for her to climb out of? Whether Wren had a fail-safe in her pocket or in the palm of her hand, he couldn't know. But she would have to employ it now.

Pausing only a second, Wren beamed to the crowd. "Well, that would make things easier, wouldn't it?"

She shed her jacket and pulled off her gloves, finger by finger, then laid them over the graceful arm Amberley had offered. Wren then extended her arms out in an elegant wave, showing that nothing was concealed in her palms.

As confident as ever, Wren turned back to Elliot with her arms stretched out in front of her, waiting. Beads of sweat began to form on his brow. He could feel them building under the swelter of the spotlights.

He released one handcuff from his palm, dropping it down on the chain. Metal glinted in the light as he stepped up to Wren, then eased his fingertips around the warmth of one of her wrists. "Are you sure you want me to do this?" he whispered, the question barely audible.

Wren nodded, ever so slightly, not backing down.

"Thank you, Agent Matthews." She faced the crowd, holding

her bound wrists high above her head. She parted her arms, clinking the metal several times. "You can see—they're quite real."

Amberley, no doubt thinking she'd won, stood off to the side. She looked to be relishing the moment that was about to come, absently stroking the mink shawl at her collar as if it were a beloved pet.

Elliot hated to admit it, but he doubted too.

He'd registered the slightest bit of hesitation in Wren's eyes. And he felt it—the tiniest reaction when he'd taken her hand in his and slid the metal rings around her wrists, then locked them tight. Maybe the handcuffs she used in her stage show had been doctored in some fashion—made easier to break free from. But there was no mistaking it now: Wren was in a proper fix with real FBI-issued handcuffs binding her wrists.

Amberley had set her up to fail, and do so miserably in public fashion. Which, if what Wren had told him was correct, was what she'd done to Amberley when Houdini had dethroned Margery.

"Agent Matthews, I do hate to trouble you." Wren looked properly sorry, playing to the crowd with drooped shoulders. "But I wonder if I might borrow your jacket. You see, this metal is terribly cold against my skin. It might help if you could lay your jacket over my hands. Warm them up a bit?"

Elliot had no idea what she was poised to do, he simply followed her instruction and slipped out of his jacket, then laid the black fabric over her wrists.

"And now, ladies and gentlemen." Wren's voice cut across the silent expectation of the party guests. "I ask you to raise your glasses, in honor of our illustrious hostess, Mrs. Amberley Dover."

The crowd obeyed, watching, waiting for Wren's next move. Would she manage to free herself from the handcuffs? Or would she be caught in Amberley's well-constructed trap in front of every important name in Boston society?

"Excuse me, sir." She addressed the band leader. "May we have a chorus of 'Happy Birthday'? It's only fitting, isn't it, that we celebrate tonight?"

"Right you are, Ms. Lockhart." The band leader brought his musicians to attention, several men grabbing up horns and the pianist waking up his fingers to dance over the ivories once more. Jazzy music rang out and Wren, perched behind the microphone, led them with the clear tone of a lark's song.

All eyes were peeled on her. On the black tuxedo jacket that moved only slightly, not nearly enough for hands to slip out of a pair of handcuffs or expert fingers to somehow file through metal.

She sang out, showing off talent Elliot hadn't known she possessed. It was one thing to capture a packed auditorium with words and illusions. But she was winning them now with yet another talent.

By the end of the song, the partygoers were on the edges of their seats, smiling and applauding Wren, who whipped the jacket off her wrists to reveal freed hands.

Elliot couldn't hide his smile.

In one hand, Wren showed off the handcuffs. In the other, she grasped a small bell. She rang it against the microphone as the crowd's cheering and clapping filled the Imperial Ballroom's vaulted ceiling.

Wren turned to Amberley, presenting the bell with a deep, flamboyant curtsy.

Amberley's cheeks were nearly set aflame with anger when Wren took her coat and gloves back, then bowed with a triumphant smile. "It's time this was returned to you. Happy birthday, Amberley."

�֍

"Wren?"

She'd hoped to slip out of the front lobby doors unseen. But she turned at the sound of the shout to see Elliot trailing down the steps behind her. He chased her down to the street, his labored breathing puffing out on a frozen cloud.

"You're leaving," he said when he caught up to her.

Wren handed the valet her ticket, thanking him with a quick nod. "Of course. I did what I came to do. We found out why Amberley invited me tonight—to humiliate me in kind. What else is there to stay for?"

Elliot stared back at her, unabashed wonder lighting his face in a wide grin. So offbeat for the carefully controlled investigator. "How did you do it?"

"Do what?"

"That. In there onstage." He held out his handcuffs. "These are real, you know."

She gave in to a tiny laugh. "I figured that out when you clamped them around my wrists—pretty tight, I might add. Remind me never to let you back up on one of my stages. You're a hazard to the conventions of a well-planned show."

He shook his head, reaching out to halt her with a light touch to her elbow.

She froze.

This wasn't an action in jest. He was deadly serious.

"No. You bested Amberley tonight. But it's as if you knew this would happen. And after what you told me about the séance and the bell that played a part in exposing her as having defrauded people . . . You planned it all, didn't you? Was this some sort of revenge?"

Wren eased back from his touch, suddenly feeling the onslaught of the cold. She tugged the collar of her coat higher around her chin and shrugged, as if he'd made it all up. "I don't know what you mean," she stated flatly, moving a step back as the valet turned the car over to her. "Good night, Agent Matthews."

Wren walked around the back of the car, heading to the driver's side door. She grabbed the handle in haste, and her glove slipped on a coating of ice. She fumbled the walking stick in her hand and it fell into the slush at her feet.

Get out of here. He's asking too many questions. Getting closer . . .

There had been a split second onstage that she couldn't stand to relive, especially not with him so near.

Never before had Wren doubted her abilities—onstage or off. But she doubted now. The one thing she knew she'd fail miserably at was to hide the fact that he'd affected her. The brush of his hand against her skin had stirred in the pit of her stomach. The brush of familiarity was something she desperately wished to forget.

Wren dipped her gloved fingertips in the snow, retrieving the walking stick, then flung open the door.

"Connor drove me here, but seeing as he's out of pocket . . ." Elliot had slid over to occupy the driver's seat of her Pierce Arrow. "It appears as if I need a lift home."

"This is *my car*." Irritation flooded in. "I'm sorry, but no one drives it except me."

Elliot ignored her, which he seemed too skilled at doing. The valet had left the engine running, but Elliot had settled into the driver's seat without a second thought. "You're not sorry. And I should have known you weren't the chauffer type." He tossed a glance to the passenger door still being held open by the valet. "We need to talk. Are you going to get in or not?"

The nerve! Never before had anyone been so bold as to order her around, and certainly not to make himself at home in the driver's seat of her car. But standing in the cold, arguing in front of the valet and partygoers whispering as they walked by, didn't seem to help matters.

Wren sighed and walked around to the passenger side, then slid in as the valet closed the door behind her. "I told you before, Agent Matthews, I value my privacy above all things. And I don't take to interference in my affairs. Not from anyone."

"It's not interfering to share a drive home, especially when we need to talk without the press hounding us. Think of it as we're just—sharing the same oxygen for a while."

She twisted her hands in her lap, her fight for composure losing the battle at her fingertips. Realizing he might see the evidence of her unease, she ceased fidgeting and calmed her fingers. It felt good to draw in a deep breath, too, especially when she needed an extra shot of moxie to give him the full force of her opinion.

"I'll tell you in as blunt a manner as possible, I am not a chorus girl who will swoon at some gentleman's smile. I meant what I said onstage," she bit out, refusing to look at him. She fixed her glare on the frozen landscape out the window. It was safer. "I have no interest in any entanglements. If I live alone and drive alone, it's what I want. And no matter how many smooth talkers come along, I won't be convinced otherwise. If we have to work together for your case, then so be it. But rest assured, if you try one thing, I will not hesitate to plant the end of my walking stick into your midsection."

Elliot didn't respond.

She heard only the cadence of the engine and the sound of tiny raindrops pelting the windshield and roof with their icy spray. When she was certain she'd made her point, Wren finally turned to look at him, expecting the words to have cut as deep as she'd intended. Instead, she was met with a pair of blue eyes that sparkled through the dim light of the downtown streetlamps. He was amused and didn't mind showing it.

"My, you're arrogant, aren't you?" He laughed, edging the car onto the street. "Have you always been like this?"

"Like what?"

Elliot scoffed. "You know. Thinking you're above Amberley's petty ways when you're so much like her you two could be sisters. Did you stop to think that not every man in that ballroom wanted you?"

She caught his eye roll, which only fanned the flame of her irritation. "I never said that!"

"Listen, I don't want to argue with you. And I don't want to interfere in your life. We're stuck with each other until this case is over, so you might as well drop the queen act and try to be civil." He steered the car in a turn, misjudging the distance of the curb. The back wheel thumped over it, jarring Wren in her seat.

The sound of a loud *pop* shut off her reply, followed by another.

"Oh no." She turned to look over her shoulder, certain after that rub up against the rough curb he'd managed to flatten one of her tires on a sharp edge. "I knew I shouldn't have let you drive."

Elliot shot a glance out the back, then, without warning, slammed his foot on the gas pedal.

"What are you doing?" she yelled, her heart rising to her throat. Wren grasped the door frame with her fingernails as wheels skidded on ice and her back fused to the seat.

They fishtailed, the car's back end swimming wildly against the road.

"Hold tight!" Elliot turned the car to whisk down a side street.

"Hold tight for what?"

They came up over a slight rise, and the flood of two head-lights illuminated the car's interior through the back window. A *pop* cut through the night, followed by another, with the sound of metal *chinking* at the back of the car.

She gasped, despite her attempts to focus on what was happening. Another high-pitched *chink* struck, crackling the glass around a tiny circle in the windshield above Elliot's head.

"Get down!"

With a firm grip, his palm pushed the back of her head below the line of the front seat. He turned the car from right to left, whizzing down Boston's webbed tangle of streets, jostling them about like prisoners in a chucked tin can.

The shadows of gangly tree limbs flew by the windows, along with the sight of random brick buildings lining both sides of the street, and intermittent light from the streetlamps that whizzed by the car.

Elliot was silent, eyes focused on the maze of streets.

Cracks of gunfire sprayed the back of the car like errant fireworks tied to the bumper. He responded by speeding down another back alley, then turned tight to the left, fighting to lose whoever was tailing them. A shot of white-hot pain seared down the length of Wren's left arm. Without thinking, she reacted by trying to rise again, only to feel Elliot's arm wrap her shoulders and haul her down against his side.

"Wren, get down! What's the matter with you? You're not bulletproof, you know."

"We've got to get out of here." Her breathing was choppy and shallow. "Someone's shooting at us."

"Well, they're not throwing confetti, that's for sure. Hang on." He took a sharp turn down a residential street. Bowers of shade trees obscured the streetlamps' light.

Wren wasn't used to the uncertainty coursing through her body. She fought to calm down, think logically, her mind sorting through scenarios that might help them in the moment.

The pops of metal had eased, the headlights behind them fading somewhere in the distance.

"Was that for you . . . or me?" she whispered, half afraid to hear Elliot's answer.

"Why would it be for you?" He looked her dead in the eyes for a split second. "Either way, I couldn't care less right now. We're in this car together. All that matters is making sure we've lost them. I'll think about why someone's trying to put a bullet in one or both of us after that."

Somehow it felt safer knowing there was a cascade of row houses nearby. Perhaps they could find help, even ditch the car and rush into one of the family homes to hide out until the authorities could show up.

"We could stop here. Ring for help?" Wren pointed her index finger to the rows of front doors with people inside, guaranteed to have telephones and doors that locked tight.

"We're not stopping." He turned the car again.

Wren looked up, seeing the terse line of his jaw and his eyes focused on the road out in front of them. Elliot was steady in the moment. As if he'd done this very thing time and time before.

Maybe this sort of madness was just another day at the office to him.

Ignoring the shock and pain felt easier as they drove along—almost saving to her in a way—so Wren drew her arms in around her middle, making herself as small as possible. And to her surprise, she allowed Elliot to take the role of hero for the moment.

He checked the rearview mirror again and again, eyes flitting from the shadows in their wake to the span of open road out in front of them.

"Where are you going?"

"Somewhere safe."

And that was all he offered.

Wren hoped he wasn't bringing them to the Federal Bureau office—the last thing she wanted to entertain was more agents' questions—but she hadn't the ability to think straight enough to render a guess. They sped along for what seemed like hours. Quiet. Each lost in the depth of their own thoughts as ice-rain pelted the windows and the engine chugged through the streets.

Wren closed her eyes for a few moments, drifting between her inclination to demand control of the wheel herself or to submit to blind trust in a man she barely knew.

Still, her shoulder nagged. She eased her hand over it, trying to rub out the throbbing with every bump and divot in the road. Eliot took one final turn, a sharp left that sent her sliding against the door again. Her eyes shot open, flooding her with the interior view of a carriage house with low, raftered ceilings and whitewashed stalls on one side of them.

Elliot eased the car to a stop. "Stay here."

He'd pulled a revolver from his shoulder holster, then jumped from the driver's side of the car, leaving the door to swing open in his wake.

Wren couldn't see much past the side of the car, just the sight of his feet pounding dirt on his way to the open doors. She slid across the seat so she could have a clearer view, stopping just behind the wheel.

The sound of Elliot's muffled footsteps died away soon after, and Wren could only see horse stalls and hay bales. Lanterns were perched on the wall, the ghostly glow of one dusting light against wooden rafters against the vaulted ceiling. Her frantic heartbeats wreaked havoc on the confines of her chest. The call of the wind whistled as it struck the carriage house walls over and over, the weather having kicked into a frenzy in the time they'd been driving.

Wren exhaled, letting go of a breath she hadn't realized she'd held captive for so long. Suddenly the burning pain returned. Now that she had time to think they might be safe, pain seared down the length of her arm.

Wren's heart nearly stopped when a path of red soaked through the outer layer of her coat sleeve, then trailed down to gather in a dark pool at her cuff.

Elliot returned, startling her from the sight of her own blood seeping from her body.

He didn't hold a gun but a lantern. It illuminated his face, his eyes registering calm and concern. "Don't worry. They're gone. We lost them awhile back."

Wren didn't hide her sigh of relief. He'd come back for her.

"I . . . I think I'm hurt," she managed as calmly as she could muster the words.

She tried to show him the injury, but her arm wouldn't work. It turned lax, burning and useless in her lap.

Elliot nodded, placed the lantern down on the running board, and slipped his arms out of his jacket. Gentle fingertips eased under her arm and raised the elbow, and he wrapped the jacket tight around the wound.

"Come on." Elliot reached in for her, careful not to graze her shoulder, then swept his other arm under her legs, and to her surprise, Wren let him, opting to be carried out instead of trying and failing to walk.

"We'll be safe here."

"Where is here?" She battled to keep her head up.

The air seemed colder than it was at her home on Beacon Hill, the wind whipping her hair in a frantic dance about her cheek. The air smelled fresh and clean, so unlike the city, salty and alive even in the frigid cold of February.

With her energy spent and an unfamiliar numbness invading her arm, she felt overcome with exhaustion. Wren gave up the fight to stay strong on her own, allowing her chin to droop down against Elliot's shoulder.

"Stay awake, Wren. Keep your eyes open." His pace quickened, leading them along the cobblestone path of a garden that lay quiet and still, sleeping through the height of their New England winter.

"Is that a garden?" she whispered. Even her voice felt foreign, weighted.

"It was once." He carried her up the path to a large house perched on the slight crest of a hill. "But don't worry about that now. We've got a bigger concern."

Lamplight glowed soft in the windows.

Her eyelids drifted closed with the welcome of it.

They were at someone's home, weren't they? A safe place, by the looks of it. Somewhere out of the storm . . .

"Wren, I'd say you were wrong about having completed your purpose at Amberley's party tonight. It appears as though someone wants one or both of us dead, and I'm not prepared to comply."

CHAPTER 9

July 2, 1910

Piccadilly Circus

London, England

Jenny shuffled her performance spot between street corners near Leicester Square and Coventry Street to the busy entrance of the Piccadilly Tube station. The heaviest pedestrian traffic was sure to filter past there during the day.

She'd carried her leather-strapped wooden box through the streets, looking the part of a young shoe shine in worn trousers, shirt, and suspenders, her long fiery hair braided and tucked tight in a woolen newsboy cap. It's where she'd been that Saturday afternoon, watching patrons trickle out of the matinee performance at the Criterion Theatre. Truth was, though, she had no interest in shining shoes at all.

Those customers had to be turned away frequently.

The wooden box with chipped blue paint and the sign that read *Shine* in wobbly white letters was all a ruse to fool the coppers, should they come poking around.

Hers was a street game—a *thimblerig*—because it had begun

with street gamblers hiding a pea or small stone under sewing thimbles. She used three shells, because they were easier to slide about the top of her upturned box, giving the illusion that one could follow the path of the pea beneath.

It wasn't a true con, as she never took wagers from patrons. Instead, they paid a flat fee, and if they could guess how she managed to consistently best them with the pea moving under one of three shells, they'd win. In truth, she wanted only to see if her illusion was good. If patrons could guess the sleight of hand behind her tricks, she'd know where to adjust so the performance could be seamless the next time.

And one day, Jenny dreamed, she'd entertain like the performers in the Castleton Theatre. Only, she wouldn't play the part of a comedy act or fill a spot in a girls' chorus line. Jenny was an illusionist. No one needed to tell her. It was just there, inherent and engraved on her innermost heart. And one day she'd answer that call.

"Are you shining today?"

Jenny looked up, squinting in the sun.

She found herself in the shadow of a man she'd noticed before. He'd just exited the theater, a well-dressed gentleman of medium height, with a muscular build and dark curly hair peeking wildly from his brow. With his hands in the pockets of his tweed suit, he waited for her answer, offering a slight smile.

"I might be." She shifted the wide leather strap to more evenly distribute the weight on her shoulder. "Depends on who's asking."

The man lifted a shoe in a comical flat-footed pose, showing off the invisible dust of his travels. "A weary man who can sure use one, as you can see."

Jenny checked over her shoulder.

He'd stopped to talk with a gaggle of on-duty police-men near the entrance only moments before. Surely, he knew that street games—even if they were innocent of a gambling nature—were something she could be hauled into the nearest police station for.

If the man wanted a shine, perhaps she could squeeze them in the edge of an alleyway. And if she saw a measure of trust in him, then she could inquire as to his interest in a game. It couldn't hurt to try and work him out. And if he wasn't inter-ested, at the very least she'd earn a coin or two for her trouble and could be on her way after.

"Over here." She nodded and swept her box into the corner by a downspout and an alleyway that would ensure they went unnoticed. "Out of the sun."

He followed and she laid out her box, the angled shoe plat-form pointed to the sky. He leaned an elbow on the brick building and placed his first shoe into the groove. She went to work, open-ing her flimsy drawer to her shoeshine kit, taking polish and brushes from inside.

"How are the wages along this street?"

Jenny shrugged.

Her greatest protection was to fly by the world unnoticed. To be of no importance to anyone. Best then to keep the conver-sation light.

"I've seen you working along this street before, I think. Do you live close-by?"

Her stomach tightened. Jenny knew she didn't look as though she belonged to London's more affluent corners. Surely he could see the hole in the knee of her pants and the yellowed tinge to her once-white button-down. She'd dirtied them on purpose and worked quite hard to make them appear as naturally worn as she could.

Why would he ask such a question?

"Do I look like I live in this part of the city?"

"Not necessarily. I hear there are some interesting characters in Bloomsbury. But I don't know that anyone really *looks* like where they live. Just making polite conversation."

"Sorry, sir, but I'm afraid conversation isn't going to shine your shoes any faster."

"Right you are." He nodded as she lowered her gaze to refocus on her task. "But you don't mind if I talk while you work, do you? I'm an entertainer by trade. It's what we do."

Jenny's heart pricked at his admission.

An entertainer!

She covered her immediate interest and kept working, dusting and polishing the first of his two oxfords, urging the black-and-white wing tip to a right shine.

He pointed down the street toward Leicester Square. "I performed right over there for a time, at the Hippodrome. Spring 1904. You would have been . . ." He furrowed his brow, then let loose with a chuckle. "Well, you would have been quite young, I'm sure."

"Still am, sir." She whipped her dry towel over the tips of his shoe. It gleamed, singing like a Sunday smile. "Next."

He looked down, surprised, it seemed, that she'd done half the job in such a short time. He slipped his second shoe into the polishing spot and turned his attention to his wristwatch.

"Are you going to ask me what I do?"

She shrugged. "Very well, sir. What do you do?"

"I make things disappear. And I escape from tight spots—

from persons or places that try to tie me down. I imagine an entertainer's life is a fairly similar gig to your job here."

Jenny looked up again, this time just with her eyes edging under the brim of her hat. He kept his gaze on his watch.

Was he timing her?

Still polishing, she asked, "What do you escape from?"

"I started with small things: picking locks around the house. Child's play, really. It became something of a habit. And then I got better. Had more fun with it. So I graduated to picking all the locks in the shops of the little town where I lived. When I tired of that, I moved on to picking handcuffs at the local jail. Fell into that one, really. But I learned a valuable lesson when I had to pick a lock and there was no choice but to allow a prisoner to watch me do it."

Jenny hesitated, her hands pausing for a split second, feeling the direction of their conversation edging too close to her reality. It was polite to nod as he talked, but she readied her feet to move should she need to pack up and bolt in an instant.

"In a sense, I had to give up my secret then and there for how I did one of my signature tricks." He dropped his voice low, so only she could hear. "And I vowed after that, I'd never reveal how I performed any of my illusions again. Not to anyone, unless I had complete trust in them. Because that illusion is all I have. Once it's broken, the story dies forever."

Jenny cleared her throat. Why had he taken his words in the direction he had? She checked over her shoulder, then quickly gathered her things, shoving them into the drawer without care.

"Impressive," he finally said, turning his focus from his watch to admiring her handiwork with his shoes. He dug through his pocket, chinking change. "How much?"

"No charge, sir." Jenny jerked the leather box strap over her shoulder.

"No charge, you say?" His brows drew closer, doubt evident. He dropped the change back into his pocket. "Why ever not? You've done a fine job. And faster than any shine I've ever seen, I might add."

The crowd passing along the sidewalk had grown—ladies whisking by in their long dresses, men with bowler hats and bow ties. They had no idea the game of cat-and-mouse playing out beside them.

This man, whoever he was, knew too much. And Jenny's feet itched to run away from him, to weave into the crowd and leave him and his polished shoes far behind before she was handed over to the authorities.

"Thank you, sir. I'll just be on my way."

She tried to slip away, but he stopped her, laying a hand on the leather shoulder strap from behind.

With fists balled and ready for a fight, Jenny turned to face him.

His wasn't a face that accused. Actually, he looked kind. Interested, even, in what her life on the streets might have been like. He ignored the fists she'd frozen in front of her face and held out a business card in his fingertips. "Your payment, miss."

She hesitated, wanting to run but fear making her feet sink as if the pavement was quicksand under the soles of her shoes. She stood still, terrified that he'd discovered she was a girl and not a boy and, worse yet, had known about her con all along.

He tipped his head to her. "For a job well done."

Jenny reached out with trembling fingers and took the card. The man nodded, satisfied.

"Is this a trick?"

He shook his head and laughed, of all things. "No. I'd never resort to trickery."

"I don't understand . . ."

"A word of advice, young lady?" He leaned down, putting them face-to-face. "Never reveal your secrets to anyone. If people can guess how you perform an illusion, then your story wasn't strong enough. The last thing you should do is pay them to learn how you hide that pea. Do you understand me?"

Jenny couldn't think of the right words to say, though her mouth was too dry to speak anyway. She absorbed the shock of all that he seemed to know about her. A nod was easiest to handle, so that's what she did. And trusted that he'd not turn her in to the authorities.

"When you're ready, say sixteen years old, you come and find me. I just might need another pair of hands and a clever mind like yours."

"You're . . . offering me a job?"

"Offering you the grunt work in an entertainer's traveling show? Probably. But you've got talent. And passion. And I can promise you that combination doesn't come along often. Not even in Piccadilly. So, miss, you know me. Might I have your name?"

"Jennifer Charles," she mumbled, grasping the card tight in her hand. "But I go by Jenny."

"Jenny. That's fine for now. I'll remember it." He smiled. "But you'll need a new name down the road. Think about it now, who you want to be on the stage. That girl will need a name all her own. And before she comes back, she'll need to know exactly who she is."

"You think I'm destined for a stage?"

"We're destined for a lot of things. Make sure your dreams are worthwhile." He winked, stepping out into the afternoon sun. But he paused in his stride and turned back around. "Oh, one last thing." He pointed to the shiny buckle shoes on her feet, the pair her nanny had put out for her that day. "Get different shoes, Jenny. Today. There's an old cobbler's shop but one street over. Check the waste bins in the back. Find an old, mismatched pair and wear them at all times. And shore up your accent. You sound like you're from anywhere but London. If your customers believe the details of your story, then they'll buy what you're selling. It's how we live that will convince them what is truth and what is an illusion."

He tipped his head and walked away from her then, moving past the throngs of pedestrians to step into a sleek black chariot of an auto that had been waiting by the curb.

Jenny looked down at the card in her hand again, inspecting it more closely. It was plain ivory with a gold border and curling, almost mysterious, black lettering printed with his name on the front. She flipped to the back.

Blank.

It had no street number. No way to find him again or send word through the post.

"Wait!" she called out as the car drove off, drawing notice from people moving with the ebb and flow of sidewalk traffic. They parted in a small circle around her, cautious against anyone shouting out in the middle of a crowd. "Wait, sir!"

But he was gone, his car having vanished.

Jenny was left to stare down at the card in her fingertips, her heart beating a frenzied dance in her chest. Numb, she looked left to right as the crowd moved by. The only thing she could think to do was to ask at the Hippodrome. He said he'd performed there some time ago.

What year was it?

She wracked her brain. *Why didn't I pay better attention to the details of what he said?*

Then . . . *the Criterion*!

The theater popped in her mind—it was the only course of action she could take.

Jenny readjusted the strap on her shoulder, keeping her box firm at her side, then trotted up the sidewalk to the front doors of the theater. A man in a suit stepped from the archway before she'd made it two paces in, hooking her by the elbow.

"Hey there, son. Mind you, we don't take to scamps around here. You just move it along, eh?"

"I'm looking for . . ." She pulled her elbow from his grasp. "Some help."

"And we cannot help you here. That's certain."

"No, I . . ." It made sense to give up the explanation that she wasn't a shoe-shine boy. He didn't look inclined to listen anyway. "You see, I received a business card from a gentleman just now after I shined his shoes. But the card has no address. He stepped out of this theater not long ago, so I thought you might know where I can find him."

She held the card up in front of the man, gripping it firm with two hands.

"You. A kid? You received this from Harry Houdini?"

She nodded, hoping she looked confident enough to believe it herself. "Yes."

"Harry Houdini, the famous escape artist? You want me to believe he actually spoke to someone the likes of you?"

"Just now on the street." She pointed toward the shaded alleyway where she'd shined his shoes. "Over there."

Laughter rumbled up from his chest until he snorted and coughed.

Jenny settled back, stiffening her spine while she waited for the lump to compose himself.

"Listen, son. You can have your little cons, but you street chaps aren't swift enough to pull one over on me." He wiped a tear from the corner of his eye, then straightened his tie and vest. He waved her off with a flick of the wrist, then turned his gaze somewhere above her head. "If that man had walked into this theater, I would know. His name means something. And yours, if you even have one, *does not*. So be off with you. I have work to do."

There was nothing to do but turn away.

The summer sun bore down hotter somehow as Jenny melted through the crowd outside the Criterion, not caring for any more patrons that day. She had a card in her hand. One that was foiled in gold and with a strong name in block letters. A name that people knew. And respected. One that meant the man behind the stage curtain had once reinvented himself too. He could have left his own past behind, if he'd wanted, and become someone new up on stage.

She shuffled along the sidewalk in her fancy shoes, wondering if it was all real. If Houdini had actually meant what he'd said. In six short years, she could be anyone she wanted. She could think up a new name, just like he'd said.

A new name for a life she'd imagine.

"I'll start again," she whispered, feeling the sting of tears prick at her eyes. "And I'll make my life whatever I want it to be."

❋

A cathedral-blue sky behind the shadows of buildings painted the streets of Piccadilly in Wren's subconscious.

But it faded and soon she was tucked back in the memory of her childhood home. Before she'd gone to live with her uncle in London. Before her world had changed and she'd become the new itinerant version of herself on that street corner. Dwindling off in the distance, like a whisper on the wind, someone was calling her name. Her *real* name. Patting her cheek to awaken her.

Jenny . . .

She hadn't heard her mother's voice in ages. Warmth radiated in the embrace of fingertips to skin. She pressed her palm against the hand, gripping tight, not wanting to leave. Not wanting to wake up in the world of Wren Lockhart.

Wake up, Jenny. You can wake up now . . .

Her eyelids fluttered, still heavy. She fought the pull to fall back into sleep's remembrance and blinked awake.

A fire sizzled through its orange and yellow dance, flickering light around a parlor decorated in soft shades of buttercup and white. The fall of night still occupied corners the firelight couldn't reach, even from an oversized hearth across the room. She could see little through the windows' ivory gauze curtains flanking the sides, save for the presence of a few curious lights that twinkled in the far-off depths of the ink sky.

"You're awake. And you have some color back. That's good." Elliot cut into her thoughts, stepping into view at the foot of the settee.

Wren cleared her throat softly, trying to summon her wits enough to speak. "What time is it?"

He checked his watch. "Nearly three."

Remembering her injury, Wren drew her hand up to her shoulder. The tuxedo jacket was gone, replaced by the torn fabric of her silk shirt and layers of bandages tightly wound around her upper arm. A sling had been fashioned over her neck, gently hugging her arm to her chest.

"The bullet went through muscle, but you're going to be fine. Had to toss your jacket, though. Sorry about that. I know it was tailored. But I won't tell you what it looked like."

"So it was a bullet after all." She ran her fingertips over the rows of bandages around her shoulder.

He nodded. "You'll be sore for a while but should have full use of your arm again soon. Provided you rest, of course."

"Rest? I have months of shows left on the books. The timing on all this couldn't be worse."

She closed her eyes on a sigh, silently adding: *And an auto mechanic to find . . . and gun-wielding strangers to avoid,* thinking of the car outside with fresh holes cut in the back.

"I think you're without an option on that now. But it'll keep, for tonight at least." Elliot knelt, offering a cup with steam that curled up from the confines of delicate yellow-and-white porcelain. "Here. I didn't know how you like it."

Wren eased up to a sitting position, her shoulder crying out in protest. Her head swam. She steadied her good hand at her temple until the wave of sickness passed.

"Take it slow." Elliot leaned in, offering her an arm.

When she swung her stocking feet over the settee to the hardwood floor, he handed her the cup, and after pausing and seeming to judge if she was able to stay upright on her own, he edged back into the wingback chair across from her.

She eased the rim of the cup to her lips, breathing in the spicy scent. "Tea . . ." Wren smiled, uncaring that she was predictable in this one thing.

It was a touch bitter without her favorite firewood honey to soften it, but the liquid was hot and she closed her eyes, letting it warm her from the inside out.

"I thought you might not like coffee. I couldn't find any

Darjeeling, but it's some English something or other I found in the pantry. I figured it would do."

"Thank you." It felt right to open her eyes again. To connect with him as she said it. Finding his features void of anything close to "I told you so" somehow made it easier. "I mean it. Thank you, Agent Matthews."

He seemed to understand that she meant it for far more than the tea.

"You're welcome. And it's Elliot from now on. No more of this agent stuff. We've just been through the wringer. And as I spent the better part of an hour cleaning blood from the front seat of your car, I suppose we could do without formalities."

His focus had been so sharp in the frenzied moments before they'd reached the carriage house, but now Elliot seemed without worry. He'd leaned back, legs crossed out in front of him, his shirt unbuttoned at the collar and rolled at the cuffs. Content to stare into the fire-dance and sip from his mug as if they hadn't a bumper full of bullet holes, nor any other care in the world.

"So, where are we?" Wren suddenly felt uncomfortable with how content he seemed in her presence.

He turned his attention from the fire back to her. "In Winthrop. At my aunt's summer cottage."

The uninterrupted expanse of darkness beckoned her gaze out beyond the windows. It just registered that what she'd thought was the sound of rough wind before had actually been the toiling of the sea.

"I suspected we were outside the city."

"That would be the North Shore." He tilted his head toward the windows. "It was all I could think of at the time, getting us someplace that had no connection to Wren Lockhart. And heading back to the party or trying to take you home to Beacon Hill would have been expected."

Wren's thoughts connected like falling dominoes and she looked up, the possibility of what might have been suddenly overtaking her.

"If you hadn't gotten in that car with me outside the hotel . . . What would have happened if I'd driven away alone?"

"But you didn't drive away alone."

"I would have. Surely I would." Fear rocked her. Wren sat up tall, sliding to the edge of the settee, ready to stand.

Charlotte.

"And what about my home? Irina? I have to find out if everyone's safe."

Elliot's brow creased with a tiny tilt of his chin in her direction. But he remained silent, raising a hand to settle her. "Wren—it's alright. I telephoned, told Irina what happened and that I'd keep you outside the city for tonight. I've already sent a car with two men to watch over your house, so everything's been looked after. We'll have to discuss the security at your estate later, but for the moment, you don't need to worry."

Wren swallowed hard. She was grateful, of course, even if she couldn't tell him the entire reason why.

"Did you sleep?" she asked. Quickly. Without thinking of anything but trying to change the subject from the flurry of unrestrained fears that pricked her heart.

"Why? Do I look tired?" Elliot tipped the corners of his mouth into a faint smile and ran a hand over his brow to tousle his hair. "That's what the coffee was supposed to help with. But the answer is no. Couldn't take the chance that someone had followed us. Not with you knocked out like you were."

"I haven't—" She looked around, only then considering

she may be an unwanted guest in someone's home. "Caused a problem, have I? For anyone here, I mean."

He responded with an aloof tip of the brow. "I seem to remember you bristling when I asked you that same question. But since you're asking"—he held up his left hand, bare ring finger exposed—"there's no one to impose upon. My aunt passed last year and left me this house. I have an apartment in the city so I rarely come back. It's really kept up by the grounds keeper and his wife now. They live nearby and insisted on staying on tonight though, for propriety's sake, even though I tried to explain that no one even knows we're here."

Praise be for the lack of light in the room or he'd have seen that she'd actually blushed through his entire explanation.

"And a doctor, I'd assume?"

"Yes. No matter what some might think of the FBI, we're not all experts at bullet wounds. I called my father's old physician. He's a kind man who won't ask questions. And Mr. and Mrs. Framley have cared for the house for years. They loved my aunt, so they'll be loyal to her nephew. The point is, we're here and you're safe. That's what matters. We'll work through the rest of the details tomorrow."

All too suddenly, returning assassins and their bullets no longer seemed the imminent threat.

If Wren stayed in a fire-bathed parlor—in the growing comfort of this man's presence—there was real danger that informality could gain a foothold between them. Her mind signaled caution as she studied him.

Elliot watched the fire dance. He was stoic—content to sit alongside her, sipping coffee, without the necessity of words. That ease jarred her. The more time she spent with this man, the more her privacy was slowly being chipped away.

First, her home. Her library, which was rarely used and certainly not a place to receive nosy FBI agents. After that, her stage—the one place that had always been hers alone. And now, the safety and protection of those she loved. The graze of the bullet cut much further than her skin; it threatened every convention she'd built around her carefully protected world.

Elliot sighed and leaned forward. "Wren, I know you're thinking something through. I can see it on your face. I'm just wondering if it's the same thing I am."

"And what is that?"

"If the bullets were meant for me or, I'm praying not, if they were for you—or *Jennifer Charles*."

As muscles go, Wren's took on a life of their own, tensing in reaction.

"Now, before you run out of here, I remember that you warned me. I know you don't want to hear that name. But I think you may have to. Someone intentionally drew Jennifer Charles into the story surrounding Victor Peale's death. It seems credible that Amberley could be involved somewhere, especially if she's trying to even some score with you. And now after all this tonight, my gut is telling me that's too much overlap to be mere coincidence. You won't want to broach the subject of your past but, Wren . . . This is serious. You may not have a choice at this point."

"That name is . . ." Wren paused. "I . . ."

"Yes?" He raised his eyebrows.

"I thank you for your help, Agent Matthews, but I must be going," she blurted out, clinking the teacup in its saucer on a telephone table nearby.

"But you've just been shot." He got to his feet and placed his mug on the mantel, watching with wide eyes as she swept past him to retrieve her boots from the corner by the hearth.

"I don't want to cause any trouble for your family."

"There's no family here to be concerned over. I already told you—it's just me."

"Then I've caused enough trouble for you."

"Forgive me for pointing it out, but you can barely stand at the moment. While I don't want to make a mountain out of a nick in the arm, it did require a couple of stitches. And you did lose consciousness for a time. I'd say that makes a couple of compelling reasons for you to stay put."

"Well, I'm awake now."

"But it's the middle of the night. And whoever was after us is still out there. Those weren't rubber bullets they were firing, you know. You can't drive, so how are you planning to get home without killing yourself in the process? Keen on walking back to Boston, are you?" Elliot stared back at her, a sense of confusion marring his brow.

It felt easier to turn away, not to delve into the depths of her unease with all manner of closeness. So she did, diverting her eyes to fumble through the impossible task of trying to tug her boots on with one hand.

"I'll manage. I always do," she stated flatly, the leather awkward in her weak grasp. It took all the gumption she could summon not to wince with the pain that stabbed at the left side of her body when she slid each boot up her leg. She slammed her eyes shut for a second, absorbing the pain.

"So that's it? No explanation. You're just walking out."

"I know it doesn't make sense to the FBI, but I live a certain kind of life. If someone wants a fight, I aim to give it to them. I'm no rabbit. And I don't bend. Not for anyone. I stand my ground."

"We don't know what ground you stand on right now—that's the problem. I can't protect you if you go."

That was it. The quiet side of Elliot's manner had been pushed too far and he was reasoning near the top of his voice.

"And I'm not asking for the federal government's protection. I appreciate your help, Agent Matthews. I do. But I just can't stay. And I can't explain why except to say that people depend on me and I won't let them down."

Elliot stepped up to her, stopping only inches away. He didn't touch her—just lowered his body to look straight into her eyes.

"It's Elliot," he added, his voice at a coarse whisper. "I won't answer to anything else from here on out."

"You won't have to worry about a here on out. I can't continue with the investigation, not if it means giving up my privacy. The government will have to build its case without me."

"You're right about that." Regret laced his tone. "Because the next time those guys come after you, they'll finish the job. Hired guns rarely miss on the first try. Never on the second."

"How do you know they were hired guns?"

"Because they let you live, Wren. It wouldn't have happened if they'd had a personal vendetta. But it doesn't mean they won't try again."

She tried to evade the finality of his words, scanning the parlor for her things.

Her jacket had been discarded. Her coat was folded on the end of the settee. She swept it over her arm and turned away, searching for her walking stick. She spotted it in the corner, gleaming black and silver-tipped, shining in the firelight.

She'd snap it up on her way out.

"You'll be wanting these, too, if you're bent on leaving," Elliot said from behind.

Understanding flooded her and she froze. Glanced down to the uncuffed wrist of her remaining shirt-sleeve.

Empty.

She spun on her heel to find Elliot standing, arm extended, two gold cuff links glittering out from his palm.

"It's how you unlocked the handcuffs, isn't it? The metal hook affixed to these, along with the bell, concealed inside your sleeve." He searched her face. "Though I still haven't worked out how you prevented it from ringing until you made your grand reveal on Amberley's stage."

He reached for her hand and opened her palm, then gentle hands closed her fist around the gold trinkets.

"I took them off first thing, hiding them from the physician. I figured you were entitled to at least one secret, even if you were about to bleed to death before our eyes."

No one had confronted her about working out her illusions. Not since the day Harry Houdini himself had picked out her *thimblerig* on a Piccadilly street corner. Yet here he was, a man who knew so little about her, finding a way to pry open one of the locked doors to her life.

"Don't worry." He eased back from her. "I hadn't planned on telling anyone how you did it. Something about the entertainers' code, right?"

"You're an entertainer now?"

He shook his head, gazing at her with eyes so open and honest that she felt a brush of vulnerability wash clean over her. And guilt, knowing that he'd thought of her. Helped her. Risked his own life, too, when bullets were raining down on their car. And here she was, keeping a death grip on her privacy.

"No. Not an entertainer. Just working with one," he whispered. "And I wish to earn her trust."

"Trust isn't part of my life."

"So you'd rather take risks with both of our lives, when you know I'll only pick up and follow you?" He unrolled his shirt-sleeves and buttoned them at the wrist. "Well, let's go then. Best bundle up. The temperature's dropping out there, and you're down a layer without your jacket."

Wind battered the windows, nudging the panes with pin-pricks of ice. It was one of those rare moments when falling snow didn't come gently. It battled its way to the ground, wreaking havoc like tiny nails tossed against the panes of glass.

"It's your choice whether you stay, Wren. I won't force you, even if it is for your own welfare. But if you feel you absolutely must leave, then I'll go with you."

The firelight danced across his face, illuminating a terse jaw and an immovable will.

It surprised Wren that she rather liked the fact that someone would stand up to her. It added an assurance she hadn't known—maybe not ever. Though the timing and the person standing in front of her made it more fear-inducing than comfortable.

"Why would you go with me?"

"It's what I do, Wren. It's my job, to protect people."

She swallowed, judging the risks he'd laid on the table as the fire popped and danced behind them.

More nails. More pelted glass.

The gale raked against the walls, stirring the cottage with aged groans from the wooden rafters overhead.

"By the sound of it, a storm is coming."

"I think it's already here." He waited with his hands at his sides. "The question is, do you want to face it alone or with help?"

She acquiesced with a nod, crossing again to ease down onto the settee. "I suppose it seems wise to stay for a bit, under the circumstances."

He gave a slight smile, only giving off a hint of satisfaction that he'd won the battle. She reached over and allowed the cuff links to roll from her palm to the tabletop nearby.

They both watched them fall, the golden secrets left exposed between them. The simple inroads of trust now placed out in the open too.

"You said we need to talk about the case?" Wren reached for her teacup and took another sip.

"Yes, but not here. I need my files to go over the details with you. We'll have to do that tomorrow or the next day—if you're feeling up to it."

"Then what?"

He shook his head. "We'll get there when we get there. In the meantime, you sleep."

"And if I were to follow your orders—which I'm not—what do you propose to do?"

"I'll stay awake."

"You're mad if you think I'm going to let you sit here and be the hero who watches over things alone. That's not who I am. So I'm afraid you'll be sorely disappointed that I'm staying awake with you until sunup." She returned his smile with a genuine one of her own. "Then *I'm* driving us home."

CHAPTER 10

FEBRUARY 6, 1927

85 MOUNT VERNON STREET

BOSTON, MASS.

"You cook?"

It wasn't the way he'd intended to greet Wren the following afternoon, but astonishment carried the thought straight from Elliot's mouth before he could stop it.

He'd stepped into the back entrance to her Beacon Hill estate house, not sure what he'd find. The last thing he expected to see was Wren, hair soft and loosely waved in a navy checked scarf and clad in a pinstriped apron over her linen shirt and trousers.

Wren didn't look up as he clicked the back door closed behind him, just continued dicing celery and new potatoes at the center butcher's block.

"Good afternoon. You're early." Wren gave her customarily aloof welcome. She wiped her hand on her apron and glanced up at the clock on the wall. "I didn't expect you until four o'clock. It's barely three."

"Yes, well. I'm always early. And something about making sure innocent civilians aren't threatened with bullets whizzing by makes me want to err on the side of caution."

Elliot had been taken aback at the casual nature of her transformation. It amused him to see the infamous vaudeville star doing something as normal as cooking for herself. With her wealth and success, he'd not have believed it—even though she'd already claimed to have no service staff outside of her manager.

"Irina gave you my instructions?" She cupped the vegetables in her good hand, crossed the kitchen to the stove, and dropped the lot in a copper soup pot with curls of steam rising from its top.

"She sent them and a key over by messenger, yes. Park in the back. Come through the iron gate to the kitchen—which I almost didn't find—with the brick fence and the cover of trees positioned right up against the house. But the mudroom door was unlocked, so here I am."

The last bit exasperated him to no end.

Wren was intelligent. And private to a fault. Maybe too much for her own good. It just wasn't like her to be nonchalant about locking her back door, especially when she'd been chased down and pierced by a bullet just hours before.

"You know, considering what happened last night, it's not exactly safe to leave your doors wide open."

"We needed clams so Irina stepped out to Long Wharf to fetch them. I heard your auto engine, and it would have been a waste to go back and lock the door twice." Wren turned back around to the butcher's block. "But then you locked it behind you just now, didn't you?"

She was certainly proving a quick study about others' habits.

"No Agent Finnegan today?" Wren looked past him into an empty mudroom.

Elliot shook his head. "He has another assignment."

Did she think it would be that easy for him to fall victim to her change of subject? He frowned. "You know, there should be a car out there. I ordered one to stay put. Any idea why they're absent?"

Wren kept her gaze down as she continued chopping, slowly but surely, even though her injured arm didn't provide much help.

"Oh, you mean the two plain clothes officers who were idling their engine at my gate all through the morning?" She tried to shrug, then seemed to think better of it with her injury. "I sent them away."

"And how did you manage that—against my distinct orders, I might add? It's common practice to have security after something like what happened last night. There is such a thing as witness protection, Wren."

"But I'm not your witness."

"Regardless, you are important to this case. Someone trailed you last night. That should be enough to allow some small measure of protecting to occur."

"Well, I wouldn't be too hard on your men for leaving. I did march out there brandishing the blade from inside my walking stick and told them they had five seconds to remove themselves from my property or else find out what kind of mood I was in."

"You pulled a knife on federal officers . . ." He nearly slapped a hand to his forehead. "You can't do that."

"I know how that bothers your very precise sensibilities, Agent Matthews. But might I add that the iron gate and brick fence are more than six feet high and the kitchen door was left open for you. Any other time it's locked tight. But I doubt if anyone who really wanted entrance into this house would find their path blocked by a gate or a glass-paned kitchen door. Seems to me they'd just come in whether I want them to or not."

She tipped her glance to a walking stick leaning in the corner of the kitchen. "It's been within reach all along."

Wren seemed quite serious about her capability to defend herself, wounded shoulder and all. Elliot doubted it but sighed. It would do no good to battle with her when he wasn't likely to win anyway. To get agreement for a security detail to watch over her, Elliot would have to find a way to make Wren think it was her idea—or else he'd just have to do it himself.

The aroma of fresh bread and seasoned soup stock clung to the air, stirring Elliot's senses. It reminded him that he was not only sleep deprived, but that he'd scarcely eaten since the night before. Hunger slammed him in the stomach.

"What are you making?" He shifted the leather briefcase in his hand.

"I was just going to bring the base to a simmer while we work."

"So you make clam chowder often?" He took a step forward, inspecting the crate of produce on the island. "But no tomatoes, I see."

Wren's head popped up so fast, a lock of her fiery hair curled down over her brow. She blew out her breath to push it off her eye but didn't move, appearing horrified at his suggested sin of marring a proper Boston clam chowder with vine-ripened tomatoes.

"It's seafood chowder. Even still . . . tomatoes?" The sudden reminder of the youth she'd spent in the UK heavily seasoned in her accent. "You are actually from Boston, yes? Or was that just a lie to wheedle your way into this kitchen?"

Elliot had to laugh at her sure-fired quip, though he kept it subtle. "You're from Boston, too, but not with that accent.

I'd wager it's difficult for people to guess you hold such strong convictions about chowder when you sound like you've escaped from an English moor somewhere."

She looked at home in the oversized space, with brick walls and high ceilings and white glass-front cabinets that showed off normal things like dishes and everyday serveware. The sight of her without stage lights, her golden eyes exposed and real, brought an unexpected ease he couldn't help but welcome. Perhaps it would stay for the remainder of the time they had to work together. If she was no longer on edge in his presence, it could speak well of his chances to glean the information he needed to break Stapleton's case.

"I'm surprised to see you chopping, with the arm and all."

"My arm is fine," she said, showing no evidence of pain. She simply kept her eyes fixed on the task in front of her. "It's already much better."

"Liar." Elliot shook his head. "If you're in pain, you could just ask for help. It wouldn't be admitting weakness if you did."

"Well, Agent Matthews, now that you've seen the worst of me, brandishing a blade and up to my elbows in celery and root vegetables, I assume we are in each other's confidence and can expect to work well together."

"It's Elliot, remember? And I'll have to taste the chowder first before making my final decision."

"Fine then." She gave a single nod to the open door leading out to the hall. "You can go through if you'd like. I thought we'd work in the downstairs library. I'll just finish up here and join you in a few moments."

Elliot nodded, taking his hat and briefcase with his notes on the case and walking toward the door.

"And in the unfortunate event that curiosity should entice

you to get lost, you'll find every doorknob is locked down the length of the hall," she called out behind him as he passed through the doorway.

The custom Wren Lockhart superiority was clearly back in her voice. Had he actually seen the real woman in her kitchen or only just imagined her?

CHAPTER 11

Elliot wasn't in the downstairs library.

By the time Wren had returned from seeing that all was in order upstairs, the embers in the fireplace crackled in an empty room. She marched out the door, fear sweeping through her insides.

What if Elliot had found his way through the hidden door in the library? Or worse yet, had gone upstairs? If he'd found out who Charlotte was . . . that she lived here at the estate and Wren had evaded answers about that part of her life . . .

She wasn't ready to open that door of her world to anyone.

The sound of curtain rings clinking halted Wren in her tracks. She poked her head out into the hall again, this time noticing a wide swath of sunlight that cut into the darkness at the far end. More clinking sounds echoed, followed by a sneeze.

It's where she found Elliot, standing smack-dab in the middle of her dining room with the French doors spread wide.

He'd removed his jacket and rolled the cuffs up on his forearms. Folders and stacks of paper had been arranged in neat piles across the length of her cherry dining table, and Elliot, unaware of her entrance, was sneezing under the onslaught of dust that clouded the air like the back room of a bakery.

"I said we'd work in the library. What in heaven's name are you doing in my dining room?"

"I'm about to get sick, that's what." Elliot bent over to brace hands on his knees through a cough, then stood and ran a hand through his hair. He moved on to the final pair of jacquard curtains and yanked them apart, allowing a crisp winter sunlight to flood in through the row of windows lining the back wall.

Wren stepped into the center of the forgotten room, all four slate-blue walls bathed in the late-afternoon sun. He stood with arms crossed over his chest, surveying the difference he'd made by allowing the sun to wash over an extended table and formal dining chairs for twenty and the large empty fireplace behind them.

Truth be told, he actually looked proud of himself for finding endless ways to nose into her private affairs.

The thought to blast him for never following instructions crossed her mind. She could have managed it, even though she'd essentially done the same thing by pushing the security detail off her estate. The words were about to part her lips, until she stopped cold.

Wren turned back to the French doors that had been spread wide, concern flashing back through her. "Just how did you get in here? The doors were all locked. I made certain of it."

He waved her off with a flip of his hand. "Oh, I used the key."

"You what?" she challenged, rendered nearly breathless.

"The one Irina messaged over. I figured these old stately houses use keys for more than one lock and it couldn't hurt to try. So I did, and it worked."

If Elliot could get into the dining hall, what stopped him from going in any other rooms he pleased?

"I'll take that back now." She held her hand out for the

key, then her attention duly shifted. "Wait—did you go anywhere else?"

"Of course not. I wasn't on a snooping mission. I was looking for a workspace and I found us one. I've been in here the whole time. Double doors." He pointed to the doorway. "Looked like it would be the biggest space. And please don't take offense, but I just can't work in that phony library of yours."

"Phony library! I'll have you know the artifacts on the walls have been collected from around the world. It contains herbs and plants from the Orient and the South Pacific and art of a quality so fine that it could be hanging in a European museum."

"Then maybe you should have left it there. Honestly, they're stage props at best. I don't know what you've got in those jars, but if I'd had any lunch, the smell would have made me lose it. And that big cat on the wall? I couldn't hope to focus with those glass eyes staring at us."

"That still does not give you the right to go prying in places you have no business to."

He moved to the table and slid out a chair opposite his. "You're right here." He patted the chair back.

Wren kept her feet planted, crossing her good arm over her injured one, enough that she hoped to show her displeasure. Honestly, for how pensive he'd always seemed in her presence, he'd turned the corner to more free-thinking ways in the ten minutes he'd invaded her home.

"I know you don't want to be coaxed into anything, Wren, so I'll just get to work and let you come sit when you're ready. In the meantime, I've got a lot to do."

He settled into his seat, took a pair of reading glasses from the tabletop, and slipped them on his nose, ignoring her after that. He set about scanning the contents of a file before him.

She waited. Tapped her foot through the silence. "Elliot, do you honestly propose to fight me at every turn? In my own home?"

"Good. You called me Elliot. That's progress." He turned a page. "And need I remind you what happened the last time you demanded to do something on your own? We ended up with a bumper full of bullet holes and you passed out from blood loss."

"I hardly think last night is relevant at the moment. And despite what you may have planned, I don't intend for my home to become operation central for the FBI's attempt to ferret out Horace Stapleton's crimes. I'll help you look for the truth, but only on my terms. And my terms are that you refrain from pushing in where you're not invited."

He looked up from a stack of papers, eyes over the rim of his glasses. "Very well, Wren. I can do that."

Finally. He'll see it my way.

"But I think you might want to reconsider that whole no-staff thing you're employing around this mausoleum. Seriously—it's a tomb."

"If it's a tomb, I like it that way. This room has been shut up for a reason. No one's been in here for years."

Elliot dropped the stack of papers on the tabletop, took off his glasses, and set them on top. "And why is that exactly?"

Wren stiffened her spine.

"You're not going to tell me. Classic." He sighed, then motioned her over. "Well, at least come in. Sit down, and rest your arm. Maybe consider listening to what we've managed to scrape together thus far. Because I'm about to be buried under it—no pun intended, of course. But if we're going to collaborate on who it is that wants one or both of us dead, we might want to take this seriously and stop talking about the drapes."

Elliot seemed to take her boldness in stride, until he leaned back in his chair. Glasses folded in his palms and waited, studying her.

She never favored close inspections.

Wren drew in a breath and, in the interest of ousting him from her home as soon as possible, gave in. She walked over to the table and slid into the chair opposite him.

If she expected cheek from him or a superior air that he'd managed to win the battle of wits, Wren received neither. Instead, Elliot smiled, welcoming her to their workstation without pretense.

"What do we know about Victor Peale?" she asked.

He slid a thick file folder across the table. Wren caught it under her fingertips, then opened the cover.

"You've got everything in that file. First things first—he didn't come back from the dead."

"It's humanly impossible," she mumbled to herself, thinking back on Harry's words from two years before.

"What was that?"

"Just something someone once told me—that it's not possible," she said, louder this time. "To come back from the dead, that is."

"Well, at least we agree on that much."

"You think there are two Victor Peales then—one in that grave whose life ended in 1903 and a different man who died in the cemetery on New Year's Eve?"

Elliot nodded. "Right. Stapleton wants us to believe they were one and the same, but it has to be two men going by the same name. It's the only possible explanation for a man to come back from the dead some twenty years after he was originally buried. And we're not diving into Stapleton's phony world of spiritualism. We've got to look at the hard facts and make this puzzle complete out of the pieces in front of us. Let's assume, for argument's sake, that there was only one man in history to have conquered death, and Victor Peale's not him."

"But many people ardently believe that's what Stapleton did, despite the way it worked out in the end."

Elliot sighed, frustration evident. "I'm aware of that. For whatever reason, the vast majority of the public trust him. It's blind trust, but he still has it—regardless of the fact that Houdini debunked him years ago and the fiasco at the cemetery was nothing more than an artful illusion gone wrong."

"Maybe Harry's memory is fading already . . ." It pained her to think of it, not for the showman, but more for her mentor and friend. "So, where do we start? What do we have that can make cracks in his story?"

"According to the marker at Mount Auburn Cemetery, the original Peale was born January 7, 1874, and died August 8, 1903. That man had no criminal background. No living relatives that we've been able to find. No acquaintances who can corroborate anything about him, except what it says on that gravestone."

"And what of the records from that section of the cemetery? What did they say?"

"Clever." Elliot grabbed a file near his left elbow. He turned it around so she could read the contents, pointing to the top of a letter from city government. "And yes. We checked on that. See? But records for that section of the cemetery were lost in a fire at the courthouse some six years ago now. They have nothing on it except that the entire section over the hill from Bigelow Chapel was full before the Spanish flu swept through in 1918."

"What about family plots? Aren't they customarily

purchased together? Surely there's another Peale nearby and we could cross-check their names against his."

"Sounds good in theory, but that lead dried up too." Elliot pulled out a four-square sheet of paper and unfolded it, spreading it wide over the top of their papers, revealing a topographic map of the landscape and cemetery plots.

"So, Stapleton was set up right here." He drew his index finger to outline a valley beneath the ridge and Bigelow's stone chapel fence. "And Victor Peale's grave was right in front of it. It's easy enough to go back and check the gravestones that are still there, which we did. There are no disturbed graves and no other Peales nearby. In fact, we couldn't find Victor Peale in any of the records for the city's history."

Wren let that sink in, her mind moving along with his. "Then we should ask—where's that first man's body now?"

He folded his hands together over the map. "Exactly. And we already questioned the doctor at the cemetery that day. The man said he'd be willing to stand up in court and stake his fifty-year medical practice on the fact that Peale was dead when he examined him."

"And you believe him?"

"I do. He seemed angry that it happened the way it did, with Stapleton making him appear foolhardy in front of every reporter in Boston. I don't think someone involved in a conspiracy to commit murder would be calling my office demanding to know when the trial will begin."

"At least we have one person on our side then," Wren said. "And what about Victor Peale, the latter? The one who reappeared and promptly died on New Year's Eve?"

"You mean, how did he die?" Elliot leaned back, raising his

hands behind his head. "That's the kicker. The medical examiner found nothing wrong with him after the fact. It's as if his heart just stopped. We had an initial toxicology report conducted to see what, if anything, was found in his system at the time of death. But the results showed nothing of substance. So we've sent it off to a lab in New York. We should know more when that comes back, but it's still a complicated bit of science and could be weeks before we have the answers we're looking for."

Wren moved the map out of the way, turning back to the file of documents in front of her. She scanned the sheets of paper—details of a medical examiner's report for the 1926 death and subsequent newspaper reports of the incident they both witnessed.

"It says here the man who died on New Year's Eve had no identification."

"None. All we found on his person was the book and note with your real name and that of Harry Houdini, a ticket stub to a baseball game at Philadelphia's National League Park, and his suit and shoes. That's it."

"What game?"

"A Boston Braves game, though the ticket's smudged and we can't read the date. Might seem insignificant, but the person who left it put it there for a reason. We're trying to uncover the connection. Even with that, the evidence we currently have only supports Stapleton's claims. Peale's suit was tailored from an exclusive North Yorkshire woolen mill that ceased operations by the early 1870s. There'd be no way to reproduce it, and we've had an expert tailor authenticate it. And his shoes were of the same era, traced to a manufacturer in Paris from 1868. If the aim was trickery, Stapleton's gone to quite an extent to cover all of his bases. It's as if he wanted us to check everything out, only to find the details are airtight."

Wren tapped her index finger against the table as she scanned the documents.

"And where does Amberley play into this? Have you found any connections between her or her late husband and Victor Peale?"

"We'd hoped to. Connor's been our gopher in the ground these last couple of weeks. He's got a nose for research, so I usually let him go and he brings back evidence every time."

"So what's he come up with? Anything we can go on?"

Elliot cocked an eyebrow in her direction. "Nothing yet. To be blunt, he's young and brash, and being swindled by a woman with excessive charms. I've had him tailing Amberley Dover for the last couple of weeks now, and I'm afraid he's going to fall into her gold-dipped clutches, if he hasn't already."

"Is that what he did last night then, trailed Amberley?"

"Yes," Elliot sighed. "Though I can't account for the in-between time."

"Agent Finnegan seems like a nice man. I do hope he knows what he's doing." Wren swept a lock of hair behind her ear and turned her attention back to the files in front of them.

"It makes you uncomfortable that Amberley's attractive, rich, and blinding the sense right out some poor man's head?"

"I wouldn't say it like that. No." She tiptoed around the truth. "What he chooses to do is his affair. I just think your partner should be . . . cautious in how he treads around Amberley, that's all."

Elliot paused and set his glasses on the tabletop. "Why? What do you know?"

Wren stopped herself. It was difficult to know what to say or how important any small piece of information might translate in Elliot's mind. He was always calculating things, smart, and thinking two steps ahead of nearly everyone. If she gave him one shred of unintended evidence, it might lock into place and make connections that would reveal far more than she'd ever intended.

"Wren?"

She snapped her head up, his voice drawing her out of her thoughts. "Yes?"

"Tell me."

Clearing her throat felt easier, so she did it and stalled a few seconds more. "Tell you what?"

"Whatever it is you're trying so hard to hide."

It's not that easy.

That's what kept careening through her mind. That it wasn't possible for her to simply let someone in and throw open every door to her past.

"They were just rumors," she clarified.

He furrowed his brow. "About Amberley? What rumors?"

Wren nodded, studying the face of the man across the table from her. "I thought you'd have heard about them already. Maybe come across them in one of your files down at the Bureau."

"Well, I haven't. We don't keep files on gossip, I'm sorry to say."

"It has to do with the day Harry took me to Margery Crandon's séance in 1924." She paused, choosing her words carefully. "It wasn't the first time I'd met Amberley."

"What are you talking about? It was the first time Houdini had brought you along in one of his fact-finding missions to defraud a spiritualist. You told me Amberley just happened to be there that day, as an acquaintance of the Crandons."

"That is true, but I'd also known her years before that, when I first came back to the States. And there were whispers floating around about her. She was Amberley Green though, a chorus girl on the circuit long before she met and married Stanley Dover."

Elliot nodded slowly, seeming to take her admission for what it was—a big step in her ability to trust anyone.

"Okay." He leaned back in his chair, the wood creaking in protest. "And what were the rumors?"

Wren swallowed hard, took a deep breath . . . and let go.

"They say she'd killed a man."

CHAPTER 12

With an accusation of cold-blooded murder tossed on the table, Elliot would need more to go on. A stack of rumors wouldn't amount to nearly enough of a case to bring before a judge.

"Murder?" He shook his head. "It's not possible, Wren."

"You think I'm lying?"

"Of course not. But rumors are rumors. You can't prove anything unless you have evidence." He opened a file, knowing fact would overshadow any rumors, and slid it across the table in front of her.

"We looked over everything we have concerning Amberley. See? Stanley Dover died in 1926, of a heart attack while he was miles away, on a train bound for Missouri. There were witnesses. And it was corroborated by a medical examiner after the fact. Case closed. There's no way Amberley could be implicated of any wrongdoing. A grieving widow who hosts a lavish birthday celebration just months after her husband's death may make her a poor wife, but not a murderess. You've got to give me more than that to go on."

Wren narrowed her eyes, staring him down from across the table.

She didn't appear angry that he'd taken up for the evidence in the case. Rather, he judged it as a personal challenge when Amberley had drawn a curtain of doubt between them. A challenge that Wren wouldn't consider backing down from now.

She looked as though evidence could be blown to bits for all she cared. "I never said she killed her *husband*."

"Okay . . . Then who did she kill?"

"There were rumors on the circuit. If you were in vaudeville during the war years, you heard of it. It wouldn't take much to have Connor dig it up if he were to ask Amberley himself."

"I'm sure not." He tapped his pencil against the table as he waited for her answer, his patience bleeding thin. "But I asked *you*, Wren."

"You said yourself that I don't have anything we can prove."

The last thing he'd expected was to have to dig for another name. To find another story to corroborate would only delay things. It dropped him right at the edge of total frustration. Time was precious, and they were losing it with every day. All the while Wren was sitting right in front of him, still clutching answers tight to her vest.

Elliot dropped the pencil and ran a hand over his face, lack of sleep taking its toll.

They were getting nowhere, and fast. All he could claim at the moment was frayed nerves, and that wasn't likely to help at all.

He clapped his hands together and stood. He could feel her watching as he flipped folders closed, piled stacks of papers back together, and shoved them in his leather satchel.

"Now what are you doing?"

"What does it look like?" Elliot refused to look up at her. "I think we're finished for today. You need your rest, and I'd like to claim more than an hour of sleep myself. We'll start again tomorrow. Maybe by then you'll have gained enough trust in the system to seek fact, instead of stirring an old rivalry."

She pushed back from her chair and swept around to his side of the table. "After that fiasco onstage last night, surely you know Amberley is the one keeping it going."

"But you're certainly not doing anything to stop it."

"So that's it? You're leaving when a potential murderer is out there, using high-society parties as a cover to kill? Someone sent a car filled with hired guns after us last night, Elliot. By some miracle, we survived. If she didn't do it—which is a long shot— then I guarantee she at least knows who did."

He slammed the folders down on the table and turned to face Wren, meeting her head-on. "I'd love nothing better than to find out who it was, but you keep dancing around the details with me, Wren. I'm weary of turning puzzle pieces in every conversation with you. Either lay it all out on the table or don't—but don't presume to play your stage games with me. I'm not some fool sitting in your audience. No more acts. No more show. I want truth from you, right now, or nothing at all."

"You say you want truth? I don't know a thing about you except that your aunt left you a rather beautiful seaside cottage that you never use. You claim no family. Want no entanglements save for your work, which you hold in a white-knuckled grip. Beyond that, you're a bigger mystery than I am. Yet you demand trust from me, just like that. Now who's playing games?"

"I'm trying to find a link between this case and why someone wanted to put a bullet in your head last night. It's not just about Stapleton any longer. You and I both know there's something bigger going on. Yet you refuse agents to watch your house. You won't hire any private security. So forgive me, but I think

Amberley is the least of your problems right now. We need to get past your defenses before we work on anyone else's."

Pounding a fist to the tabletop would have felt good in the moment, but it would do nothing by way of forcing Wren to spill her secrets. She'd be sure to bristle back.

Hard-pressed as he was to admit it, Wren was right. They were a little more alike than he'd initially bargained for, which made for a mixture of oil and water at the moment. Isolation had become both a habit and a comfort to him too. And there she was: a stranger who walked in similar shoes.

Wren was made-up before him, costumed and perfected in the swath of sunlight that beamed in from the windows. This picture was how the world perceived her. Yet it wasn't who she really was, and he could see that now.

Something new emerged from within her—the clear presence of indecision in her eyes.

It was the first time Elliot had seen her carefully controlled veneer crack at all. He cooled, not wishing to battle under the sudden glimmer of vulnerability.

"You're trying to sidestep me, Wren, when all I want to do is help. Why won't you let me do that?"

She opened her mouth to speak, then her chin trembled ever so slightly and she shut her mouth. After swallowing, she tried again. "Don't you understand? I'm trying to tell you that I *can't*."

"Can't what?"

She shook her head. Brought her good hand up to hastily wipe at the moisture gathering under her eyes, as if ashamed to show an inkling of real emotion to anyone.

He tried again, softer this time. "What are you afraid of?"

Wren didn't reply right away. Instead, she blinked back. Her countenance soft. Open, almost hopeful before him.

"Elliot . . ." Her golden eyes studied his face. She looked down for a breath, as if she'd come close to revealing something but thought better of it and retreated again. "Friend or foe—it's difficult to tell the difference sometimes. We don't always want to see what's right in front of us. That's what gives me pause about Connor associating with someone like Amberley Dover. He doesn't know it, but he's playing with fire when he skirts around her world."

"Is it the same feeling that gives you pause about me?"

She tried to turn away, diverting her attention to a folder on the table.

Elliot stopped her retreat by stepping in front of her. The illusion fell as he looked down at Wren, her golden eyes open and searching, allowing him to see past the mask to the depths of who she was beneath it.

What he saw was beautiful.

Breathtakingly beautiful. Real, but caged.

"I'll wait." He delivered his offer with the softest tone he had.

Surprised to find he'd said the words, even more that it wasn't all business in that moment, and he felt a whisper of breathlessness before her that he hadn't known for a long, long time.

It stirred something he thought had been lost, maybe scarred over forever.

"This is what we're here for. To get to the bottom of all this. And I hope, after last night, you know I'm on your side. Whatever you need to tell me, I'll wait until you feel safe enough to give it, and I'll protect it when you do."

She wavered, her eyes deftly breaking the connection with his.

"Did you hear me?" He coaxed her to look at him with the

softness of his words. "I said I'll protect you, if it's what you want. I'll be a friend to you."

A knock at the door cut through the growing threat of closeness between them.

"Ms. Lockhart?" Irina's voice carried in from the doorway, firm in breaking them apart. "You have another guest. I found him at the back door."

Wren moved away in a heartbeat, easing back by several steps, until she leaned in to the sideboard against the wall.

Connor stumbled past Irina, breaking into the dining room with quick-footed steps. "Sorry, Matthews. We've got a problem that can't wait."

Elliot wanted to wring his partner's neck for the intrusion. He'd come so close to making progress with Wren. But after the moment had shattered, a cold formality moved in to occupy the space between them. He wouldn't be able to draw her out again—at least not right away.

Wren kept her gaze from connecting with his, the only evidence of emotion in the tight grip she'd fused to the edge of the wooden buffet cabinet behind her.

"What is it, Connor?"

"Amberley. I've been tailing that dame all over Boston. To date, she's had the most boring social schedule a lug can imagine. I've been to dress shops, parlors, even something that looked like a big fashion fling. I thought it was all fluff." He tipped his hat back off his forehead. "Until this afternoon, that is, when she began checking over her shoulder everywhere she went."

"And this is something you couldn't telephone about?"

"No good," Wren interjected. "I had my phone disconnected. We've had too many calls from the press and I grew tired of hanging up the line."

"This all happened too fast to get to a telephone box anyways. I had to chase that dame down. She didn't know I was there, but she quickened those heel-wearing feet of hers and doubled back down a side street. And I caught up just as she slipped into a back room at the Union Oyster House." He raised his eyebrows, like that information just leveled the playing field. "You heard me right. Not exactly a five-star clambake, is it? They may boast of the best oysters on the East Coast, but that's still not enough to attract an upscale broad like her."

Wren kept her head turned away during their exchange, her focus lost in the landscape beyond the back windows. She flitted a glance over to Irina, then took a bold step forward, inserting herself into the center of the conversation again. "What was she doing there?"

"Meeting a trench coat in a back room." He glanced from Wren back to Elliot. "And before you ask, I didn't get a look at his face. All I could see from the shadows was a hat and dark hair. Could have been anybody. But he scared her well enough, that's certain. I've been watching that girl for weeks, and she's got a smile for every gent she passes on the street. Except this one. She wouldn't touch any food and didn't crack a smile once. And he disappeared out the back before I could get anything more from it all. But I'll tell you this—whoever that trench coat is lit a fire under her shoes."

Elliot exchanged glances with Wren, trying to read her thoughts.

They seemed to mirror his own: Maybe Amberley wasn't behind the hired car after all. What if she was just as entangled in the same web of something they all were? It looked as if a new thread of intrigue had just been added to the case, and he wasn't the least bit convinced Wren could stay out of the thick of it now.

She stood on silently, looking part incensed, part curious over the turn of events—a dangerous combination if he was going to get her to stay put in any safe spot for more than five minutes.

"Where is she now?" Elliot ran a hand through his hair.

"I caught her at her house. Trying to look discreet as she loaded a mass of pink hatboxes in the back of her car."

"She's skipping town." Elliot began gathering up their things. "We'll have to stop her."

He grabbed his jacket and hat from their perch on a dining chair nearby, intent on running out to catch up to Amberley before someone else did.

"Not anymore, boss." Connor shook his head. "I just arrested her."

"What?" Elliot shouted.

"Good," Wren chimed in at the same time.

Elliot sent her a look that questioned her assessment of the situation. Still, the timing couldn't have been worse.

"Honestly. Don't look at me like that. Innocent people don't run, Elliot. There has to be something you can hold her for, even if it's just questioning about what happened to us last night. This could be our chance to find out who she's running from and why. I'd say Agent Finnegan here did you a service by bringing her in."

"It's not that easy, Wren. If it was, I'd have done it already. But we're not ready to question her. We simply don't know enough to get her to talk."

"But if someone is watching her, then they'll know we've been tailing her too," Connor added. "And if they think she's likely to tell us anything, they'll go after her. Then we'll know for certain whether she's involved. And you forget—we do have something to hold her, at least for now."

"The punch . . ." Wren looked to Elliot, her eyes seeming to question whether she was right.

Connor nodded. "The spiked punch at her party."

"So now that we brought her in on some piddly charge—which we can't prove, by the way—you want to use her as bait? Do you have any idea the kind of lawyers this woman is likely to have on retainer?" Elliot slipped his hands in his pockets, sending Connor a look of displeasure.

Elliot was a stickler for traditional methods of criminal investigation. Dangling a socialite in front of an unknown threat wouldn't ensure they didn't end up with blood on their hands. He was certain Amberley Dover wouldn't like the emerging plan much either.

"Not bait exactly. But she's in a Bureau office. At the very least, we'll have her in a place where she doesn't feel as much of a big shot. She's likely to negotiate if she thinks she could save her own skin."

"Then it's simple. We've got to get to her first." Wren leaned forward to Victor Peale's folder on the table and flipped the cover open. "You have one death certificate already. We almost had another last night. And if we don't do this now, we could make it one more." She tilted her head ever so slightly.

"Fine. We'll hold her as long as we can, but she's not going to tell us anything." Elliot watched the shades of indecision cross Wren's features.

She stared off in the distance, her good hand braced at her chin, momentarily lost in thought. Suddenly, she looked up, triumph alive on her face. "Arrest me."

Elliot sighed. Ran a hand over his brow. "You're not helping."

"I'm serious." Wren crossed the room to his side and braced a hand at his elbow. "Arrest me. Take me in for questioning, then put me in a room where I can slip in and talk to her. Chances are she's scared enough now that she'll spill something useful, if she thinks it will save her neck. And then we'll come back here and figure this out together. I'm sure Agent Finnegan has somewhere he can keep Amberley safe after you let her go. Right?" She turned to Connor.

"I might know a guy who's got a place." He shrugged.

Elliot scoffed. "I'm sure you do have someplace in mind. I guarantee you it's all you've been thinking of."

"Well, what else could I do? It was either take her in or fit her for a pine box later. She's not Capone, you know. Regardless of lawyers on her payroll, she won't have much in the way of protection. I chose the handcuffs as a last resort. Anyway, it's done now. And seems like Ms. Lockhart here's got a plan that could actually work. If she can get the information we need, then I can keep Mrs. Moneybags safe so you two can work this mess out in the meantime."

"If it would get you to do a moment's worth of work, I'd consider it. But say I actually do agree to this half-baked plan— just what am I supposed to arrest you for, Wren? You said you wanted your kept name out of the papers. This isn't a good way to accomplish that, especially if you're innocent of any wrongdoing. I have to trust the men down at the Bureau, but who knows what Amberley will try to pull if she's backed in a corner? I can't guarantee your safety if you want to do this. If you ask me, sounds like you could get a repeat performance of last night, and I, for one, don't think it's worth it if you get yourself killed."

"What happened last night?" Connor ping-ponged his glance between them.

No doubt it would shock him to know the truth—Wren had

a fresh bullet wound in her arm and Elliot had driven her car through the winding streets of Boston, dodging gunfire until the back bumper looked like Swiss cheese.

A bright smile filled Wren's face as she whispered, "Wrong-doing . . ."

Connor gave Elliot a clueless look. Irina, too, was quiet, standing behind the group without a readable emotion on her face.

"Wren?" Elliot asked, though he wasn't sure he wanted the answer.

"I'm a bootlegger."

Connor's eyes widened, but he crossed his arms over his chest and lowered his chin, trying to hide a smile. Elliot, however, didn't find the admission as comical as he did. He eyed Wren, sure he couldn't have heard her correctly.

He remembered their first conversation in her library, when she'd mentioned how she abhorred drink. But now she wanted him to believe she was embroiled in the illegal manufacture and sale of alcohol?

It was another illusion, and a terribly concocted one at that.

"I'm sorry, but you're a what?"

"You heard me. A bootlegger." She looked a little too happy with herself. When he didn't make any move to accept her admission, she switched over to a fast frown. "It's true. I share ownership in a theater downtown. The Castleton. I take full responsibility for the hollowed-out legs of the chairs in the VIP rooms. If you send investigators down there, you'll find they're full of alcohol."

With ginger movements to accommodate her wounded shoulder, Wren held her wrists out before him. "So you see, gentlemen, I've been running an illegal speakeasy in the back halls of vaudeville. I'm guilty of a crime and I've confessed, so now you are obligated to take me in."

Her jaw tense, Irina stepped forward, her customary approach of melting into the background apparently too much to stand any longer. "No, Wren. Don't do this for Amberley. You don't have to do this."

Wren looked from Irina back to Elliot and Connor, determination stamped on her face. "Yes I do. And I'm not doing it for her. I'm doing this for us. For the case. Because the ways of frauds like Stapleton need to be exposed. And if we can prove he didn't bring Victor Peale back from the dead, even if we save him in the process, then we still win. The truth will be known and Stapleton's career will be over. He'll stop manipulating the public."

Irina sighed. "What do you need me to do?"

"Everything here at the estate has been taken care of, as of this morning. Just look after yourself. And if Agent Matthews sends a car of agents to watch over the house, you have my permission to allow them to stay."

Wren turned and locked gazes with Elliot, then slung a glance down to her wrists. Familiar gold charms winked out from the cuffs of her shirt-sleeves. She looked up again, revealing a twinkle in her eyes.

"Go ahead, Agent Matthews. Lock me up. And feel free to toss away the key."

CHAPTER 13

APRIL 2, 1916

36 BUGLE STREET

SOUTHAMPTON, ENGLAND

"I won't be made a fool!"

It was a riotous shout that garnered Wren's attention the instant she'd stepped through the front door of the Duke of Wellington public house. She peered through the small crowd gathered in a back corner of the establishment, trying to see the cause of the commotion past men in threadbare coats, uniformed soldiers, and sailors counting down the hours before they shipped out to the front.

Glasses thudded against the wood of the bar and spoons clinked porcelain bowls as men ate. Murmurs of conversation in French and Spanish—and bawdy pub talk in English—painted the background with the character Wren had expected of a refreshment room in Southampton's dock district. It was rampant with emigrants desperate for passage to a safe haven from the war, with walls that would shield the eyes for a time, sequestering thought on the scores of wounded who never seemed to stop arriving in the streets outside. The odor of fish hung on the air like a plague, working to turn even the hungriest stomachs sour.

Wren turned away from the activity in the back of the pub.

It wasn't the way she'd have chosen to spend her birthday. But with her uncle's death so recent and the war turning the world upside down around her, how could a birthday ever be the same again? She aimed to find a quiet corner somewhere, with a bowl of stew—even if it only had potatoes and thin broth—and a cider to toast her final birthday spent overseas. The plan was to eat quickly, stay out of notice on her way to her boardinghouse a street over, and find her passage on a merchant ship in the morning, leaving the world of war behind for a future back in America.

Another bellow and a fist jingling cutlery on a tabletop drew her attention back to the crowd.

"She's taken my ticket for passage—"

A young woman's voice cut in from the center of the small crowd. "You lost it without my help, *you mongrel!*"

"I've never murdered a woman in my life, but I'd make an exception for you, lass."

"Well, who's to stop you now? Don't let the package deter you," the voice fired back, sure and strong. "I don't care if you claim you're King George—your threats mean nothing. I can take care of myself!"

Wren edged around the small crowd until she could catch a glimpse of the activity at its center.

The voice had indeed belonged to a woman—one of slight build and exotic descent, who was flipping a deck of cards on a tabletop. More than seeing a female take charge of the rowdy and cidered-up travelers, it piqued Wren's notice that she thought she'd seen the young woman before. In London, perhaps? Or was it just that the streets of Southampton harbored any manner of foreigners escaping the war in France and one weary traveler looked like the next? Either way, she couldn't have been more than Wren's age—which was entirely too young to have been threatening a group of grown men in a public house.

If she had taken some man's travel money, as he'd argued, Wren feared how the young woman was going to talk herself out of such a mess.

Wren could follow the woman's impressive sleight of hand—one that was similar to her own *thimblerig*, only this girl used cards and clever distraction with her words instead of shifting a pea under shells.

It made sense that the gentlemen were red-faced with anger.

The young woman was good. Too good. She was swindling them full stop, and she had a pile of winnings mounded in front of her to prove it: two watches on gold chains and a few jewelry baubles glimmering in the firelight. Scraps of folded paper—steamship tickets?—and a smattering of coins, a utility knife, salted meats, and canned fish made up the lot. With a war on, the food was as valuable as a gentleman's finest timepiece, and she owned it all.

A gristly man leaned over the table, placing a tight fist on either side of the winnings, glaring down at the woman from behind a beastly beard. "I—want—my—ticket." Tiny flecks of spittle flew with each drawn-out syllable.

She eyed him, the challenge flashing with consideration in her light-green eyes. "Double or nothing." She tapped her index finger on the table with each word. "Choose a man here. Anyone. If he can best my magic, I'll give it all back. If not, you leave me be. And"—she narrowed her eyes—"you apologize for your rudeness."

Murmurs pulsed through the crowd. In truth, they pulsed through Wren, too, coursing with anger at the young woman's use of one word . . .

Magic.

"I'll do it."

Wren was shocked to find that she'd not just thought the words, but she'd actually spoken them aloud and stepped into the light, where every ale-addled brow turned in her direction. They looked at her, dressed in a man's tweed jacket and trousers, hair tucked up under a woolen hat, no doubt thinking she was nothing but a spry and gangly young man with a death wish.

"You?" the beastly man scoffed.

Surely he saw Wren the way the rest of them had. She swallowed hard but continued staring down the lot of them.

"That's right."

The young woman peered around the room, scanning face after face.

"Is there anyone to argue with my magic? Surely not this boy here. I extend an offer to stand up now, gentlemen. After all, it's your wares you stand to lose to a novice."

"I am no novice." Wren glared back. Confident as ever. "And I *never* lose. I'll get your winnings back, or I will personally pay each of you for the whole of your losses."

The challenge was accepted with no dissention—only a raised eyebrow or two. The men eased back, clearing the way for her to step up to the table. And she obliged. It was, after all, a grand test before she'd be faced with Harry Houdini once again. This should tell her one way or another whether she was ready. And though her uncle's inheritance left her far from being an heiress, it was still enough to cover the expense of a few stragglers' pocket change if need be.

"Very well. Challenge accepted."

A smooth smile creased the young woman's lips.

"The aim is simple. You choose a card. Show it to these men so they'll remember it. Then slip it back in the stack." She flipped the deck out in a series of shuffles, then smoothed it out in a half-mooned fan across the table. "You may shuffle. And cut the deck wherever you choose. But the card cannot hide from me. I can retrieve it from the deck every time on the first attempt—with *magic.*"

Wren almost laughed. "Magic?"

"That's right."

"No. It's not nearly magic." Wren walked up to the tabletop and gathered the cards in her hands, reshuffling. "It would be pointless, gentlemen, to check this woman's shirt-sleeves. Or to ask her to stand and inspect the underside of the table—which I'm sure men of your knowledge would have already thought of, no doubt. You'd have found your attempts wasted because that's not her game. She's not stashing away extra cards in the shadows somewhere."

"Exactly," the young woman echoed, her haughtiness firmly in place.

Wren shuffled the deck with expert hands. Flipping the cards in a row on the wooden table, long fingers moving with dexterity.

"Instead." She laid down a card—the ace of clubs. "She hides them in plain sight. But I shall enlighten you. She plays on your unschooled ignorance of illusions, gentlemen."

"I hardly think this is—"

Wren flipped another card, staring back, silencing the young woman by revealing the ace of hearts.

"And also on your greed . . ."

And another, the ace of spades.

"Even your hope that you can eventually best her . . ." And the final card, the ace of diamonds. Wren laid it out for all to see. It was timed with a muffled gasp from the men. "But you will never win. As you can see, that kind of luck is quite impossible."

If another could shuffle the deck with such precision and reveal an entire suit with ease, it cast palpable doubt that the young woman's magic was anything but artful trickery.

"How'd she do that?" a man cried.

And another, "She's got magic too!"

"Magic? No, sir." Wren drank in a deep breath, then flipped another card. "I'd never claim that."

Another ace of spades.

And then another ace of clubs. Then hearts. And finally, diamonds.

"But I will tell you that you've been tricked. Every single one of you. She's had extra cards all along. It's much easier to find the card she wants when they're already stacked against you."

Tempers flared at once as they realized the deck had been stacked with multiples of the same cards, and the men stepped forward—ale and anger emboldening them.

Wren stepped in front of the young woman, who actually stood up with her, realizing the men's threats had quickly turned murderous.

"Just a moment, gentlemen. You'll get everything that's owed to you." She glanced over her shoulder, connecting with the defiant green eyes of the woman standing behind her. "Yes?"

The young woman hesitated only seconds, then nodded. She watched, keenly and with a tense jaw, as the men swept up the bounty she'd collected. Some cheered, falling their way back to the bar for another pint. Others grumbled, stuffing their goods in their pockets. And the last one, a man with teeth still grinding behind his beard, glared daggers at the young woman as he swiped a folded paper from the tabletop and shuffled away.

The woman hurried to sweep up the few things she had with her: a leather satchel worn at the edges, a tatty wool cape, and a few coins that had been left on the table. She sifted through the handful to see what was there, then tossed a button out of the mix.

"Well, you got your way, whatever it was. So leave me be," she bit out in Wren's direction, attention fixed on her palm.

A small glass bottle, stoppered with a cork, dropped from her bag and rolled across the floor. Wren stooped to retrieve it.

"It's an odd thing to carry." She handed the bottle back, noticing when the young woman went to put it away, she had a trove of others tucked in her satchel.

"It's not odd. My mother was a healer. Herbs and plants." She shrugged, as if it were the most commonplace trait to find in a pub. "She taught me."

"A healer?" Wren tipped her head to the side, something striking a familiar chord about her. Her mind kept working to place her. "Where? In London, perhaps?"

"And other places. She was a singer with a traveling show."

"But you're not English."

The young woman looked up, fire in her eyes.

"My mother was from the islands, or can't you tell with those sharp eyes of yours? All I know is that haul could have fed me for a month. Now I'll have to start all over in a different pub— preferably one that's far away from you."

"I feel certain we've met somewhere before."

She shook her head. "I've never seen you before in my life,

London or any other place. Wish I hadn't seen you now. I'd have remembered if I met another girl who was as good with cards as I am." She lowered her voice to a whisper. "Who do you think you're fooling with a getup like that? You're no young man. You'd have already been conscripted to some trench in France if you were. Or at the very least, signing your morals up for service in the Women's Auxiliary Army Corps."

Touché.

Wren allowed a slight smile without meaning to. "I suppose we're both found out then."

"Not with those fools at the bar. They're no real judge of ability. You saw how I was doing."

"But you claimed the use of magic and I'm sorry, but it just wasn't true. I had to say something."

"Who are you, the pope?" she demanded, lip curled. "The magic police? It's not a crime to survive, you know. With bombs blowing the world apart at our front and back, who knows when another supply ship will come in? I just lost the first meat I've seen in two months' time, thanks to you and your scruples. And I'm still without a way out of this blessed port, which means I have more work to do before I find a pillow to rest my head for another two days at least. Now, if you'll let me pass." She shoved by, heading for the door.

Wren had a sinking feeling in her gut because the young woman was right.

The streets of Piccadilly may have been a learning ground for her, but Wren always had a home to return to. The streets were cruel when they wanted to be; merely about survival for some. No matter if the young woman had used trickery or not, Wren's quest for truth had swiped provision from her, and she couldn't leave her with next to nothing now.

"Would you claim the use of magic if you didn't have to?"

The young woman turned. "What?"

"Do you claim magic because you want to or because you have to in order to survive?"

"There's a difference? I'll starve either way."

"Not if you don't want to." Wren pulled the piece of paper from the inside pocket of her coat. "Tomorrow morning. That's when another merchant ship is expected."

"And just how do you know that? Crystal ball?" the young woman snapped and her eyes drifted to the paper Wren held out.

"A business associate of my uncle's owns a shipping company, and he's bringing in supplies for the troops. This will secure you passage on his boat, leaving from the White Star Dock tomorrow morning. If you're set up with the proper paperwork to travel to America, then this is your ticket out of here."

She stared back at Wren. "Why would you help me?"

"Because I shouldn't have pushed in. Not in that way. It felt like the right thing to do at the time, but I see better of it now. I offer this as reparation for what you lost."

She took the paper from Wren's hand, examining it.

"Don't you need it?" She looked up. "How will you sail?"

Wren took another paper from her pocket. "That one was for my uncle. He's recently passed, so I'm bound for America on my own, and a job, eventually. It will just go to waste unless you take it." Wren pushed the ticket into the young woman's hand. "Please. With my apologies."

She folded the ticket, keeping a keen eye on Wren as she slipped it in an inner pocket of her mandarin-collar coat. "I go by Irina."

The measure of familiarity in the exchange of names took Wren by surprise. "Wren."

"Wren. A scavenger bird that takes flight with others' goods. That's rather Machiavellian, isn't it?"

She shrugged, the comment not even scratching the surface of her skin. It did tell her that despite appearances, the young con artist was smart and had absorbed cultured speech somewhere along the way. That combination was curious. "No more than your profession."

Irina looked to a back corner of the pub and nodded to an empty table by the fireplace. "Well, Wren. What do you say to a bowl of their watered-down stew and a cider before they run out? Perhaps you can tell me about this job. If it's anything like the skills you just showed off, I think I'd like to hear about it—whether magic is involved or not."

❄

"Remember what I said," Elliot whispered in Wren's ear as they exited the downtown Bureau's second-floor elevator. "I'm putting you in my office—the room next to Amberley's. It's got one window. There's a lever at the bottom and it's not locked, just in case."

"Just in case what? I need to shimmy down a drainpipe from the second floor?" She frowned. "Honestly. At least I know how to maneuver my way out of a proper fix. I've done it before. I suppose I can manage it again today."

"As much as I'd love to see the ever-composed Wren Lockhart make one of her quick escapes, I hope it doesn't come to that. I think your shoulder needs rest, and hanging from a second-story ledge isn't the best way to accomplish it. Nevertheless, the window's there. I always like to plan two steps ahead."

"I understand." She nodded as he walked her through the office.

Usually she could feel the eyes of every passerby burning through her. She wasn't inconspicuous by any means. But the office was so busy, it seemed the one time Wren could waltz through a crowd and not have whispers follow her the entire way. Elliot escorted her past smoky offices and rows of occupied desks, ringing telephones and the punching of typewriter keys generating a steady *click-clack* hum in the background.

"Just try to ignore them," he added, reading her thoughts. "It is a weekend, but they're still too busy to notice us anyway."

"It's been quite a long time since I've cared whether I receive stares or not. That worry died a long time ago." She willed defiance to triumph with each step she took through the precinct.

"And I can guess what you're thinking," he said, a laugh just hidden in his voice. "That you'd like to wring Amberley Dover's pretty little neck for ensnaring you in the middle of all of this. But we need her alive. And our conversation from earlier, about the fact that she's rumored to be a murderess? We'll continue that later. Just please don't make me sorry for going along with this."

"You won't be. I've known Amberley for a long time, and there've been sparks of friction between us from the start. But I know what we need, and no matter what, I'll work to get it."

He opened the door to his office and flipped the light switch on the wall. She stepped in front of him, looking around.

"Do me one favor, Wren?"

She turned, finding him hovering in the doorway. The intensity in Elliot's eyes softened, and he lowered his voice to a whisper. "Don't open this door unless you're absolutely sure it's me on the other side, okay?"

"I won't."

He gave her a quick nod to show his confidence, then clicked the door closed behind him. Wren heard the key turn and click in the lock, and all at once, she was alone.

A quick look around told her what she already knew: Elliot was meticulous, detailed, and heavily invested in his work. There was nothing personal about. No family photographs. Not even a coffee mug or potted plant on the windowsill. Just a small desk lamp with a frosted glass teardrop shade, a jar of sharpened pencils and a Remington typewriter tucked away in a back corner, and endless stacks of papers, files, and books that created a sense of neat and proper organization around the small room.

More stacks of papers seemed to occupy every inch of the desktop.

Volumes of law books lined the bookshelves in neat rows. On a wall opposite the desk, case photographs and hand-written notes were pinned about like a haberdashery paper mosaic. A glance told Wren it wasn't the Stapleton case, however. She suspected that was because, for his own reasons, Elliot wanted to keep it private. The files they'd looked over in her dining room must have stayed in the leather briefcase he kept with him.

Wren shook out of her momentary distraction and went to work, remembering what she had to do. She unhooked the cuff link from her left wrist and pulled the metal pick from its hiding place in her sleeve.

With a bum shoulder and her senses on high alert, it took her a bit longer to unlock the handcuffs, even though Elliot had thankfully left them a bit loose at the wrists. But she was soon free, rubbing at the skin where the memory of cold metal lingered.

Wren moved to the inner door, pausing to hold her ear against the panel of wood separating the two rooms.

Nothing.

If Amberley was in there, she was alone. Alone and quiet.

It took Wren only a few seconds to pick the lock—what a relief to find it was old and gave quite easily. She slipped into the adjoining room, then eased the door closed behind her. Amberley's gaze darted to the door the second Wren had stepped through, a look of instant irritation flaming through her rouged cheeks.

For all of Amberley's airs about dressing for every occasion, Wren had to do a double take when she saw the society queen positioned at the table in the center of the room.

Her hair was mussed out of her usually sculpted waves, several strands having fallen down to graze the fox-trimmed coat of orange paisley draped across her shoulders. It had been pulled over a deep purple-and-black beaded dress in a clash of luxurious fabrics, giving her the appearance of a confused socialite who'd dressed for two different parties. A rolled paper cigarette hardened the look, a trail of smoke spiraling up as she exhaled, then fanned away the smoke with her manicured fingertips.

"I should have known," Amberley scoffed, her lips pressed in a haughty smile.

Wren stepped forward, undeterred.

"When that ferret of an agent—*Shenanigans* or something— showed up at my door and went on about taking me downtown for spiked punch at my party, I should have known it would be for something like this."

"I'm surprised I'm standing here too," Wren whispered, crossing the room to slip into the chair across from her. "The least you could do is keep your voice down. You're supposed to be in here alone."

She scanned the layout of the room.

It was a noticeably larger space than the one in which Wren

had been put, and their voices would carry if too loud. A light fixture hung overhead, but it let off so little light that it made the room feel cold and the figure of Amberley Dover lonely in it.

Wren glanced over her shoulder to the door leading to the hall, the movement of shadows through the pebbled glass passing in waves every few seconds. The inability to see through it made her uneasy.

"Expecting the boogeyman to join us?"

"I wouldn't be so lukewarm about this if I were in your shoes."

"We'll see how lukewarm I am when I have those agents hauled into court. My lawyers will have a free-for-all with this. I'll sue the federal government for every cent. And then some. I had an afternoon tea scheduled with the mayor's wife—one I couldn't get out of. You know that little twerp dared to put cuffs on me, with her sitting right in my parlor? I'll start with him and then move on up every ladder from there."

"The agent you're referring to won't let anyone come in. The way I heard it, hauling you downtown was a courtesy Agent Finnegan offered for your own protection. And the fact Agent Matthews let me find my way into this very room should tell you they're on your side. You might think of holding your tongue from now on and show some gratitude that they're willing to protect you."

Amberley set her jaw, staring across the table as if she could look straight through Wren to the wall behind. She scoffed. "Protect me from what?"

Wren leaned in, looking Amberley dead in the eyes. "From bullets whizzing by your head. At least, that's what I had to dodge on the way home from your party last night."

An unmistakable ripple of surprise swept over Amberley's face, lightening the hardened edges that had been there.

"You mean to tell me that wasn't you who arranged it?"

"I don't like you, Wren. That's no secret. But there's something I don't like even more, and that's getting my hands dirty. Murder is most decidedly dirty business."

"There's been more than one rumor about your experience with it before."

Amberley straightened her shoulders. "And just like their opinion of you, the public will believe whatever they want to believe, won't they? Regardless of whether it's true. I could tell you that I had nothing to do with Al's death, but what good would it do? You've obviously made up your mind. You made up your mind about me from the moment you waltzed into *my* auditorium. And you've been an iron thorn in my side since. Someone else's too, I'd say, if they tried to shoot you down."

Instinct told Wren that Amberley wasn't the one pulling a hit man's strings. In truth, she looked a bit wild in the eyes. Wild, caged, and scared in the interrogation room.

That kind of honest she couldn't hope to hide.

"I hope I'm not sorry for it later, but I actually believe you about last night. And so do the agents who brought me here."

"And about Al?"

Wren shook her head. "They don't know about him or your past relationship—at least not the details. That's your story to tell. But the agents want to see if you're ready to talk about Stapleton, though heaven knows why I'm sticking my neck out this far to even ask you."

"Is that why they hauled me in here? To turn me into an FBI snitch? I'm smarter than that." She flicked her gaze down, tapping cigarette ash into a glass ashtray on the table. She met

Wren's eyes again, though she looked wary, as if her ability to hold an air of superiority in place was crumbling.

Wren leveled her glare at Amberley.

"These FBI agents know you're smart—or at least, you were, before you thought it a wise idea to pack your car and run. By my estimation, you're pretty sure to have half of Boston's underworld chasing you before the night's over."

Amberley shrugged with a delicate tip of the shoulders, then fluffed the fox-trim of her coat against her collarbone.

"Well. Everyone knows a lady never goes anywhere without her best hat."

Wren leaned in, elbows to the table.

"This isn't the time for games, Amberley. If you know something about Victor Peale's death, you need to spill it right now, and then maybe you'll actually live to spend all of your late husband's money."

"Are you in league with the badges now? Can't blame you, though. They're a couple of lookers, aren't they?" She blew out a puff of smoke and examined the room, as if there were eyes watching them through the walls. "What a historic turn of events. Wren Lockhart actually has a heart beating underneath that bow tie of hers. It's starting to pitter-patter for the first time, eh?" Amberley shook her head, a lurid tone punctuating her words.

She used her nails to pick a piece of tobacco that had gone astray from her cigarette and stuck to her tongue.

Wren knew her words were meant to sting, but something still managed to prick at her, that perhaps she was more transparent than she wished to be.

"If you think you'll get a better offer from the man you met at the Union Oyster House today, then by all means, do feel free to go ask him instead."

Amberley's eyes narrowed. "How did you know that?"

"Agent Finnegan has been tailing you. And he's seen enough to know you're in some serious trouble. I'm about the last person you wanted to see. Believe me, I don't want to be here either. But you may want to listen to what I have to say because shocked as I am to admit it, we might be the only allies you have right now." Wren waited for the pointed admission to crack Amberley's defenses. "So tell me. Why did you help Horace Stapleton at his show in the cemetery? What does he have on you?"

"Nothing." Her eyes drowned with indecision. She dropped her voice low. "It's other complications that have become problematic for me."

She looked as though she was ready to spill something further, until her eyes focused on the door behind Wren's back. A small bit of card stock slid under the door, sailing to a stop in the middle of the linoleum floor.

Wren jumped up and crossed over to pluck it up. It bore a single word scratched in ink.

Run.

CHAPTER 14

A shadow darkened the pebbled glass of the door leading to the hall.

"One of your guys?" Amberley whispered.

Wren shook her head. "I would have guessed one of yours."

"But I don't have guys!" Amberley's whisper shot out in a fever pitch. "I'm a widow. I'm on my own, Wren."

If you're on your own, then that's finally something we have in common . . .

Wren shifted her glance back to the door. The figure was more than a head taller than Elliot and much stockier than Connor. The only thought that moved through her mind was that Elliot told her not to open the door unless she was certain he was on the other side. And now with a warning in hand, their precious little time could be slipping away.

The doorknob jiggled and she locked eyes with Amberley, seeing that instant fear flashed in them.

Wren jumped to her feet and hauled the shaken socialite up at the elbow. The cigarette fell from her fingertips, the last bit of flame in the end scattering ashes and sizzling out as it dropped onto the tabletop.

"Come on," she whispered, tugging Amberley through the inner door to Elliot's office.

There was no time. Wren closed and locked it behind them, then scanned the room, her mind firing quickly at her options. There were no other means of escape, and the thought of trekking blindly through the unknown halls of the Bureau seemed riskier than hiding out in a locked office. The best they could do was try to push the corner of the desk closer to the door. It wouldn't stop bullets from flying, but it could help slow up someone if he tried to come through.

"Help me." Wren elbowed Amberley, then tipped her head to the desk in the center of the room. "This may give us a head start if someone tries to push in."

Amberley didn't question, just nodded and put her back into moving the desk's edge to block the door. Her strength was deceptive. And though Wren's shoulder protested, she grimaced rather than crying out as the pain intensified, and the desk finally gave in to their joint effort.

"What is the matter with you?" Amberley paused, brow furrowed.

"I'm fine. It was just a little present from some of the guns that chased us down last night."

"What? You mean you weren't just posturing? You were actually shot?" Amberley's hand flew to cover her mouth, her whisper urgent. "Then the people who came after you last night . . . Is that who's in the room next door this very minute?"

"Let's hope we don't have to find out. But if we don't want a repeat performance for both of us this time, we need to get out of here. Now."

She crossed to the window and tugged at the Venetian blinds until they cinched up out of the way. The shelf between them and a path to the window was stacked high with papers, files, and books.

"Sorry, Elliot." Wren used her good arm and swept the painstakingly organized stacks of case files to the ground. Paper rained down like a ticker-tape parade, covering the floor in a sea of white.

The lever clicked when Wren pushed the window wide, allowing a cold blast of air to invade the room. She poked her head outside and looked left to right, her heart sinking.

You were right, Elliot. She couldn't believe his quip about the unlocked window actually came true. Classic. Now it was their only way out. There were no drainpipes, but there was a wide ledge and a low rooftop in the building next to them. They'd have to climb down, then cross over to a grove of trees down to the street.

If that was the only escape route available, they'd have to take it.

"You don't mean we're actually climbing out on that ledge, do you?"

"You bet we are." Wren hauled Amberley up to her side. She pushed her in the small of her back until the tips of her shoes kissed the wall. "And you're going out first."

Amberley drank in a deep breath. Despite looking as though she might swoon clean off the ledge, she climbed up, balancing the heels of her gold-tipped oxfords along the windowsill. Wind brushed the coat about her legs and played with the wavy brown locks of hair in a frenzy against her neck.

A flood of relief washed over Wren when she saw a familiar car appear through the trees. It came to a stop in the shadowed grove beneath them with the outline of a familiar face through the window.

She watched as Elliot angled the car so he could see them through the maze of tree branches above. He edged forward until he was in a good position and idled the car. She presumed he was waiting to intercept them the moment their shoes touched the ground.

"I'll tell you this," Amberley said, her breath fogging in the frigid night air. She shivered at Wren's side, easing her heels in careful steps along the ledge. "If we manage to live through this night, I just may reconsider my stance on murder. Right now, Horace Stapleton is number one on my list."

"While I don't advocate that, you just might get your chance to claim justice against him." Wren tightened her grip on the brick exterior as she slid out on the ledge behind her.

"I know how he brought Victor Peale back. Or how he tried to make it look like he did. I assume bringing you in was his attempt at revenge for attempting to ruin him. Except he waited until Harry was gone to resurrect his own name. But if your agent friends want a statement from me, I need a guarantee of full immunity first. If I see one night in jail, I swear I'll put everything in a vault and they'll never hear a peep out of me."

"Well, standing on a ledge isn't the place to tell it. But you'll have to come clean as soon as we're on firm ground. You know it was bound to come to this." Wren nodded to the shadow of the car through the trees as they moved. "Head for the car. That'll be our ride out of here."

"Right. But I . . ." Amberley nodded, edging over to the roof they'd have to traverse from the ledge. She hesitated. "I hated you, you know."

It was the least surprised Wren had found herself since New Year's Eve. "I know."

"I'm not the only one."

"I know that too." Her words were flat. Said on a sigh. "But envy is a poor substitute for doing the right thing."

"I'm not in the mood for a lecture. You became Harry's little protégé, and so many others faded away behind the stage curtain. I ended up kicking up my heels for dime shows at the Castleton just to stay off the streets."

"I thought I heard that somewhere."

"Well, thank Providence I met Stanley Dover and got out of there, even when so many others didn't. Yet all the while, you seemed content to languish in the darkest parts of the show-man's world. Dressing how you wished. Living in your big house on the hill. Uncaring what anyone thought, when I wanted you to fade as badly as the rest. I tried to humiliate you last night, in front of everyone in Boston society, because of it. And still you bested me. But you should know now that I could have darkened you, and I didn't."

"I have no interest in competing with you, Amberley, let alone to best you in anything. I'm content to live my life without drama."

"And yet you know I've become privy to your family's secrets. I have only to whisper the blackness of the Charles name to bring down a scandal upon Wren Lockhart if I choose. The public may not know who you are, but I do. Remember? I heard Houdini say your real name that first day you showed up to join his show. I never forgot what I heard, or what I learned it meant."

Wren refused to show that any mention of her past affected her. "Scandal or not, I've never cared much what society thought of me."

"Secrets will keep until someone is ready to use them. They always do. Whether Horace Stapleton is behind the car chasing you, I don't know. But I had nothing to do with it. I'd still see you hang in the court of public opinion, of course, but I won't tie a real noose."

Amberley had the power to destroy the fragile cage Wren had built to protect herself, and she knew it too. In the smallest instant, the walls could be torn down. Her whole life's illusion, shattered. Only, the truth didn't sting as much as Wren always thought it would.

Maybe she was stronger somehow.

Maybe the sins of Horace Stapleton could be unfurled, and Amberley's willingness to help them could prove the key. Harry Houdini had always been interested in the most profound levels of truth, scientific or otherwise. And the deeper they trekked into the dark world surrounding Victor Peale's death, the more Wren realized people were not the real enemy. It was her choice how she lived, whether she'd carry the burden of bitterness against Amberley or allow truth to soothe the gaping wounds between them.

"Step there." Wren pointed Amberley to a level surface leading down to the flat roof. "This doesn't make up for past wrongs. Nothing can change that now. But I won't live under the shadow that you propose. If you choose to ruin me, so be it."

Amberley paused, turning to look Wren square in the eyes. The breeze carried stray locks of hair off her brow, sweeping it back in winding tendrils off her face. "Then why? Why are you helping me?"

"Because it's the right thing to do," Wren said. "And it's what Harry would have wanted."

Amberley's nod and the feel of the cold night air flowing around them reminded her that time wasn't on their side.

"Let's go. That desk won't hold them off forever." She gripped an arm around a sturdy limb of a nearby tree. "You'll just have to restrain your hatred of me—at least until we're out of our current fix. After that, all bets are off."

"I think I can handle that, if you can."

Wren extended her hand out to Amberley. It should have been against her better judgment, but she held fast. "I can't believe I'm actually saying this, but welcome aboard."

※

"I want to talk to him," Amberley demanded, tipping her chin toward Elliot. "Alone."

The socialite narrowed her eyes, daring Connor or Wren to challenge her the moment they stepped inside the back door of the seaside cottage.

Elliot watched for shades of objection to darken Wren's face. He saw none. Tall and sanguine, she stood in the doorway with her injured arm cradled in her good one, remaining silent. He considered it a marked response that she didn't challenge Amberley's behavior and decided to follow suit.

"Very well, Mrs. Dover. Just this way." Elliot motioned her to the parlor.

"And I'll just go in to make sure everything's . . . ," Connor piped up, following them into the room.

Wren stepped up, easing her good arm to hook under his elbow. "You've been here before, Agent Finnegan?"

"Uh . . . no. But I'm sure Elliot will give you a tour later if you want." He tried to wiggle his way out of her grasp to see into the parlor in which Amberley had just disappeared.

"Actually, I'd love one now. And I assume we'll just have to find the kitchen together. Yes? I could certainly use a cup of tea."

"Good idea." Elliot pointed down the hall past the stairs.

"Kitchen's in the back. Connor, you keep Ms. Lockhart here safe while she makes us some tea." When Connor looked like he wanted to argue another solution that included staying at Amberley's side, Elliot added, "And don't bother having the grounds keeper or his wife do it. Wren likes to live on the wild side—without anyone doing anything for her. She won't take to disturbing service staff when the two of you can manage it together."

He knew what Wren was up to.

She smiled, a honeyed version Elliot knew was much too submissive to have been anything close to real.

"Rightly so." She tugged Connor down the hall with her.

Best to separate the would-be lovers, even if the potential sparks were one-sided. Connor wasn't thinking clearly, and the last thing Elliot needed was a love-sick agent clouding judgment during an interrogation. If Amberley was ready to talk, he couldn't allow obstructions to what she had to say.

Wren slipped Elliot a slight nod to tell him he'd have as much time as he needed in order to get something out of their cagey socialite. He nodded back, trying not to notice how easily they could play off each other's thoughts without missing a beat.

They turned the corner. Did Wren know he watched her all the way?

Lovesick agent . . .

Before, he might've judged that as only Connor's fate. Heaven help Elliot if the growing familiarity he had with Wren made him begin to doubt what they were there to do.

Elliot brushed it off and trailed into the parlor.

Amberley had settled in a wingback chair by the fireplace, smoking a cigarette in the dark. After shrugging out of his coat, he tossed it on a bench by the stairs and undid the cuffs of his

shirt. It was cold, so he knelt and twisted old newspapers as
kindling.

"Well, you got what you wanted." Elliot layered logs and
paper in the hearth. "I'm here. I assume you'll tell me why."

"I will. Don't you worry about that."

Amberley's words weren't the problem. It was her tone—
secure and unafraid—that made him doubt their conversation
would go the direction he wanted it to.

"What's this about, Amberley? What kind of game are you
playing?" He scratched a match against the stone hearth and
lit the edges of the newspapers. A flame caught, and an orange
glow began to fill the room.

"Who says I'm playing games?"

"Aren't you? In the interest of saving everyone a lot of time,
why don't you just tell me what you want."

Amberley tipped her head to the side, as if indecision held
her prisoner from answering. "Oh, this is about what *you* want,
Agent Matthews. I'll give you something for free. Just *one* something. The rest is going to cost you—full immunity—if I give
a signed statement as to what I know about Horace Stapleton.
That's my offer. Take it or leave it."

He brushed his hands together and moved to the chair across
from her, then sat with elbows braced at his knees. "And what do
we get for free, since you're being so magnanimous?"

"You choose," she said, her singsong voice punctuated with a
smile. She flitted her glance toward the end of the hall and to the
corner around which Wren had just disappeared.

"If I could choose, I'd have you hauled before a judge who
would force it out of you. But I consider myself magnanimous,
too, for giving you the opportunity to come clean while you
still can—at least before the trench coat from the Union Oyster

House finds you. He's still out there, you know. We could put you out on the street right now and just wait for something to happen. I promise you that you're not likely to get a better offer from the people who have you running scared."

"Oh, believe me, my position has had me up nights. But I do so love to be helpful, Agent Matthews. So I'll let you choose the topic of our conversation: Horace Stapleton or—" She leaned back in the chair, satisfied, it seemed, with the cards she was playing. Smoke curled around her. "I'll tell you the dirty family details of our caged little Wren back there, better known as one Jennifer Charles."

CHAPTER 15

APRIL 21, 1916

KEITH'S THEATRE

WASHINGTON, DC

"You say you're here to work with Harry Houdini?"

The guard at Keith's Washington, DC, theater looked like he might believe them. Wren had only to offer the man a confident smile and a worn business card with the entertainer's name for she and Irina to be allowed access to the auditorium.

"That's correct, sir. We both are—my business manager and I." She watched intently as he flipped the card back and forth in his fingertips.

"Business manager?" He eyed Irina, looking her up and down as though she were a creature from a far-off jungle.

Irina crossed her arms over her chest, green eyes staring him through.

"Does this one talk?"

"If there's anyone worth talking to," Irina grumbled, prompting Wren to lightly stomp the side of her foot.

"Of course she does, sir. What a silly question." Wren laughed it off, doing her best to make light of the situation.

If only the man had known the truth of the matter, that Irina could talk herself out of nearly any situation, he'd have let them pass without a second thought.

"Come a long way, have you, with that accent?"

"I have," she stated, then added a mock sigh of nervousness to flavor the story. "We have, actually. But if we're asked to wait much longer, I'm afraid we'll be tardy on our first day."

"I thought all of the stage crew had arrived days ago."

"That's my understanding, too, but we've just arrived from Boston. It wasn't possible to catch a train until today."

"And why is that?"

Wren raised her chin. "My guardian's funeral. We came to the capital as soon as we were able."

She'd been honest about why she was only making it to Houdini's stage now. As for stretching the rest of the truth—that the entertainer had no idea they were there . . . Wren would keep that choice tidbit to herself.

The guard's hard edges softened, and he handed the card back to her, the speculative air gone from the creases around his eyes and mouth. "I've never seen a young woman in pants before, walking around plain as day. You aren't one of those free-thinking Lucy Burns suffragists, are you?"

"I'd have thought it rather commonplace for a variance in dress in the entertainment world. And I'm not a part of the stage crew. I'm an illusionist." She offered him a sweetened smile. "And I don't know about Lucy Burns, but I'd say the sooner women can start to wear what best suits them, the better off we'll all be."

Wren picked up the leather suitcase she'd set at her feet.

She clutched the case that held her very dear belongings packed inside, as if she was ready to be on her way.

"If Mr. Houdini's here, you'll find him back in the auditorium. Doors at the back. You can go on in."

"Thank you. And I'll be sure to relay how helpful you were."

"Helpful he was not," Irina echoed under her breath, the moment they'd walked through the red carpeted lobby to the auditorium doors. "Did we come all this way to be treated like this?"

"Forget him. No more card tricks at a Southampton boardinghouse for you and no more Piccadilly street corners for me. We're up for better things—starting now."

"I almost believed that once."

Wren tipped her head to the side, bestowing the best authoritative glare she owned. "Well, believe it again. Deep breath." She pushed the doors open. "Shall we?"

Irina shook her head. "Not this time. You go." She nudged. "He gave you his card, and it's you he'll want to see. I'll wait here. Managers stay in the shadows of their stars."

Beyond the double doors, a world was bustling.

Vaudeville was alive with all manner of costumed showmen and dancers and stage crews hammering, painting, and unpacking who knew what. Men tinkered around with lights and rope, organizing mechanical things along the back of the stage. Above them, voices carried from a catwalk over a grand balcony to workers managing the lighting. Others were moving about, carrying crates and such, some inspecting and cleaning seats in the audience, others gathered around a crate table, sharing a quick cup of coffee and a few cantankerous laughs.

Police presence was everywhere, with uniformed men inspecting rows of auditorium seating in front of them. Irina slipped into a seat in the back row, waving her on. "Go, Wren. Dream chase down that aisle."

Wren nodded and strode down the aisle, trying to look as though she belonged right where she was. She kept her head held high, though, in truth, her insides were closer to mush.

What if Houdini wasn't here? Worse yet—what if he didn't remember her?

Wren had been dressed as a shoe-shine boy at the time. In the years since, she'd grown into a young woman. A tall and lanky, trouser-wearing entertainer, but still a young woman. Chances were the famous illusionist had seen so many faces in the crowd in his lifetime, and possibly handed his business card to numerous other fans, that he mightn't remember a young red-headed scamp from the streets of Piccadilly.

She drew in a steadying breath and advanced to the edge of the stage.

A young woman of about Wren's age, wrapped in a flowy gauze dress and sporting a Gibson Girl bouffant, practiced a pirouette on the front corner of the stage. She continued her twirling, balancing a hand on the back of a wooden chair, unaware that Wren stood just beneath her.

Wren waited, seeing the beautiful costume and the young dancer's porcelain skin and dark hair. Her beauty was breathtaking—quite opposite from what Wren's was with gangly limbs, a splash of freckles, and flaming hair. She owned no flowing gauze dresses. Hers was a suitcase full of gentlemen's trousers and shirts—the costume she'd donned in secret for years. And now, despite disapproving looks and proper women who gasped everywhere she went, Wren had fused the getup to her offstage persona by wearing it every day.

In contrast, this dancer looked as though she'd been born to decorate a stage. She was lovely and practiced, graceful in each controlled movement she made.

"Excuse me?" Wren asked.

The young woman halted in her steps, looking down with winded breaths. "Yes?"

"I'm here to see Mr. Houdini."

Concentration broken, she reached for a towel from the nearby chair and dabbed it to her neck. "He's not taking visitors just now. If you have a delivery, you should leave it at the front desk. This area's for crew only."

"I do have a delivery, but this one needs to go into Mr. Houdini's hand."

The young woman stood over her with attitude in a cocked hip, her glare boring into Wren's figure from above.

"You'd jolly-well listen then, because we don't take deliveries back here. And if that suitcase means you've got aspirations that you'll be staying on, you best turn right around and scoot back out those doors. We don't take drifter types around here either. We're serious performers."

Wren slammed her suitcase to the floor at her feet, the loud echo drawing attention from several workers nearby. They paused, curious, but went back to work. She stood tall under the onslaught of the dancer's glare, but refusing to be intimidated, Wren straightened her spine and narrowed her own eyes in response.

"Good. Because that's what I am." She folded her arms across her chest. "And I'm not leaving until I speak with Mr. Houdini."

"Sure about that?" Something flashed in her eyes. Anger? Respect even? Whatever it was, it stayed on as she used her pinky fingers to make a shrill whistle, drawing the attention of a couple of men on the stage crew. She tipped her head in Wren's direction.

"What is it, Amberley?"

"Al? We've got a straggler here with pants and a sour disposition. Seems unable to find the door on her own."

"What's this?"

Wren looked up, her attention drawn stageside.

And there he was, Harry Houdini himself.

He'd simply walked onstage, as unassuming as a man could be in a white shirt and work trousers, clipboard in hand. He connected eyes with the dancer first, asked the question, then turned to Wren for an answer.

The man named Al started trotting over, but Mr. Houdini raised a hand to halt him.

Wren actually stopped breathing for a moment. Then the cadence of the inhale-exhale hitched in her chest. Would they send her packing straightaway?

"This girl says she has a delivery for you, sir." The dancer eyed Wren, a knowing superiority in her tone. "Al here was just about to show her to the stage door. But she claims she's not leaving. One of those stubborn Brits we've heard so much about."

He glanced down at the suitcase on the floor by her feet. "Thank you, Miss Green. You may leave this one to me. I'll help this young lady find where she's supposed to be. You and Al see what mischief needs cleaning up with the backstage props."

The dancer nodded to him and, without another word, padded off in her stockings to the hidden places somewhere behind the stage curtain.

"How may I help you, miss?"

Wren stood tall, stretching out to hand the business card to him. "I brought this."

Seconds ticked by, Wren's arm feeling horribly weighted against the time for him to make a decision to take the card or not. Finally, he stepped over to the wooden chair the young woman had been using for balance and set his clipboard on the seat. He then stooped, taking the card from her hand.

His eyes lightened when he read the name printed on its center. He turned the worn edges over in his fingertips. "This is one of my cards from years ago." He looked down at her. "Wherever did you get it?"

"You gave it to me, sir. In Piccadilly. Six years ago."

His eyebrows ticked up with what she hoped was recollection.

"Six years ago, you say? And you kept it all this time?"

In the years she'd traveled with her uncle, from Paris to sites across England and finally back to Boston, the card always stayed with her. It represented more than a job or a future. To Wren, it was evidence that she hadn't dreamt it all up. That she'd actually crossed paths with the world's most famous illusionist one sunny afternoon in Piccadilly. And if she wanted that dream badly enough, she had an open invitation to claim it now.

"Yes, sir. You told me to find you when I turned sixteen, that you'd have a job waiting for me. My birthday was a couple of weeks back, but nevertheless, here I am."

"You're after a job?"

"I am, sir. On the stage. I won't accept anything less." She looked him dead in the eyes, projecting every ounce of confidence she possessed.

He stood still for a moment, considering. "And your skills?"

"I'm an illusionist and escapologist. I can free myself from handcuffs. A locked door. Even a jail cell, though I've only tried it once. I'm a crack hand at cards and a *thimblerig*, but I'd like to learn and be more. I haven't a vanishing act just yet, but I'm still working it out."

"You're young. You have no family?" He looked at the

auditorium seating behind her. "Shouldn't you have someone here with you?"

"Begging your pardon, sir. I was alone on the streets of London at ten years old. I hardly think I should have a guardian tagging along after me at sixteen." She half turned, gesturing over her shoulder. "I've come as a professional. My manager is in the back, and she's ready to discuss my terms for a contract."

He smiled outright. "Alright. So you have a manager. That means something, I suppose. But how do I know I can trust you? Plenty of reporters would love to get backstage at a Harry Houdini show and reveal all the secrets of our illusions to the world. Why should we suppose you are who you say you are?"

She took a step toward the stage. "I want an honest wage for honest work. I know you to be a performer of integrity, and I won't work for anyone who's less than. No tricks or cons. And no magic—only top-notch entertainment. And as a matter of advice, Mr. Houdini, I'd put someone with more competence at the auditorium door out there. The gentleman who questioned me didn't dig very deep into my story. He believed whatever I told him, and I walked straight back here as a result."

His eyes twinkled, amusement she hoped signaled that he remembered a long ago meeting in Piccadilly.

"Well, miss. I never forget an introduction. If I truly gave you this card, then I'll remember your name."

Wren thought it over, recalling the details of their first meeting so many years ago. He'd asked for her name then, too, which she'd given. But he'd cautioned her that vaudeville was about more than a stage story—a showman's world was wrapped up living the illusion at all times. And it was he who'd said to come back with a name all her own.

A new name for a new life.

She drew from her gumption, stating with a clear voice, "My name is Wren Lockhart, and I'm an illusionist—" She stopped. "Apprentice with the Harry Houdini traveling show."

His face registered nothing right away. Not hesitation or, worse, distrust. But he didn't show signs of recollection either.

Everything she'd hoped and wished for over the past six years was wrapped up in this one moment. And the one man who could change the course of her life wasn't giving any sign as to whether he'd turn her away or welcome her into the world she was determined to make her home.

"Jennifer Charles," he said at last, a smile spreading wide across his face. "It's nice to see you again."

Harry handed the card back, then left his hand extended, offering a handshake.

She stretched out to accept it, though she was screaming inside. He might have picked up on her excitement with the slight tremble of her hand in his, but he said nothing of it. Just stood again, picked up his clipboard, and addressed her the final time for that day.

"It's nice to be seen, sir. And the other name—" She lowered her voice to a whisper. "I'd just assume we keep that quiet, if you don't mind. I'm Wren Lockhart now, no one else."

"Very well, Ms. Lockhart. We can accommodate you. Amberley Green, the dancer you just met, is a stage assistant and performer. She'll be backstage with one of our crewmen, Al. They will show you the ropes. The crew meets for a dress rehearsal at five o'clock sharp. If you found us by reading the papers, then you know we're performing for President Wilson and the First Lady tomorrow, and we'd best be on our toes. With that in mind, I see I must remind our security staff about the importance of screening guests in a stricter fashion."

"Good." She smiled back. "Because I have a mind to talk to the president about women's rights. Maybe seeing a progressive Brit in trousers will inspire support for the Yankee girls' right to the vote."

The myth of a man turned, ready to get back to work. "Welcome aboard, Wren Lockhart. And to your manager as well," he called over his shoulder before disappearing behind his stage curtain once again. "Come on back."

Wren turned, beaming.

Irina swept up the aisle and met her, nodding approval. "And you thought I was a cool talker. Wren, that was marvelous."

She whisked up Wren's suitcase for her, then they climbed the stairs together and swept behind the curtain after the stage legend.

Wren's world of secrets gained another player, and another door.

Wren felt oddly at home, lingering in the shadows. Silently absorbing the tail end of Amberley's interrogation with the FBI. From the moment Connor had slipped out of the kitchen and returned to the parlor, their socialite's irritation had grown and now had evolved into a one-sided shouting match.

Wren could have told them it would end up that way.

It had been little more than twenty-four hours after the party at the Statler Hotel, yet it felt like years had passed since then. And here she was, haunting the doorway of the seaside cottage, watching the stern flex of Elliot's profile outlined by the same firelight from the night before. He drummed a pencil on the armrest of his chair while he waited for Amberley to answer their questions.

Connor stood back. Watching and waiting. Honestly, Wren couldn't have guessed what he was thinking at the moment.

"You have my answer, gentlemen." Amberley jumped to her feet. "Now, if you intend to keep me here under house arrest, I would like to go to my own room." She eyed Connor. "Preferably with a door that locks from the inside." She stormed from the room, her heels echoing down the hall.

Connor shoved his hands in his pockets, his frustration apparent. His early interest in the socialite had been obvious. But once she figured out their little trick at the Bureau office, she made it known she wanted nothing to do with him.

"Guess I'll be taking first watch," he mumbled to Elliot and turned to leave.

He noticed Wren then and tipped his head on his way out.

It wasn't a common gesture for her to smile, but Wren couldn't help it. Under the circumstances, she figured a genuine show of support might soften the blows Amberley had landed. Connor was a might outspoken and a little rough around the edges, but he was a complement to Elliot in that they both sought truth at their core. That made the emotions he did show in the moment quite believable.

The floorboards creaked as he ducked out and Elliot turned, the firelight casting a warm glow on the side of his face. He moved to stand at her entrance.

She stilled him with a lifted palm. "Don't get up." Wren crossed over to the settee opposite him, then eased onto the cushion, tucking her legs under her.

"One guess says Connor's idea of a first watch is to post

himself outside Amberley's door and wait until he catches her trying to escape."

"From what I heard I hate to ask, but did she say anything useful?"

"Some. Not enough to turn the case one direction or another. At least not yet," Elliot answered, though his eyes said he was holding something back. He didn't look right at her, instead seemed lost in the depths of the fire dance.

"But Amberley agreed to talk?"

He nodded. "She's proving a bit of a reluctant informant. But once I get the prosecutor to agree and a judge to guarantee her immunity, then yes. I think she'll talk. Until then, I'm not sure what we have. I'm betting on the fact it's enough to keep Stapleton behind bars and to find out who's responsible for that wounded shoulder of yours."

Wren braced a hand at her brow, frustrated with the jumble of puzzle pieces.

"Did she explain the rumors surrounding her when she worked on vaudeville?"

"She did, though she didn't much take to the fact you'd alluded to a former beau who left vaudeville and promptly died in a farm accident when she was a hundred miles away."

"I didn't say she did it—only that there were suspicions."

"Well, we're looking into it. The only man who fits that description is a former member of Houdini's stage crew—an Al Gruner. Do you remember him?"

"Vaguely."

"And that's about all we've unearthed so far. There are rumors that he died in an accident on his brother's farm, or that he met an untimely end at the hands of a socialite in a big city. Problem is, the trail stops there. It stops with Amberley, unfortunately."

Elliot raised his eyebrow. "Add questions of her character and a swift marriage to the very wealthy Stanley Dover, and you've got the makings of a good mystery novel."

Why they couldn't just demand Amberley comply with an official investigation still puzzled her. Between a dead man in Mount Auburn Cemetery and the car chase after the party, one would think Amberley would do anything possible to ensure her own safety. When people were dying, matters of reluctance should be the first to fly out the window.

Elliot turned to her, forcing a weary smile. "We may not have answers on everything, but until we know more, you did your part, Wren, and I'm grateful."

"The note was a nice touch. Amberley never questioned whether we were being tailed at the Bureau office. I almost bought it myself. You had me checking over my shoulder a couple of times, until I saw your car pull up and figured it out." She bit back a laugh.

"The note under the door was Connor's idea."

"And the man at the interrogation room door?"

"An oblivious agent who was slipped a few bucks to keep his eye on the door. She wouldn't have known, but something in Connor's face gave it away when Amberley insisted we call the mayor and tell him about corruption at the Bureau. She was mad as a hornet when she figured that part out—that once we had her in custody, it was a bit of an overacted plan to nudge her into talking."

"I can imagine. Oh, poor Connor." Wren laughed outright then, doing her best to hide a smile behind her hand.

"At least here we should be able to lie low for a few days, figure this out."

"Won't someone wonder where Amberley is? She was picked

up in dramatic fashion, in front of the mayor's wife and a parlor full of ladies. She's not likely to forgive that anytime soon. And her social circles will no doubt be speculating as to her location."

"We had her telephone her house to tell her staff she'd skipped out on holiday. Though I'm not sure this is the kind of getaway she's used to. She'll have to be holed up here until we secure a signed statement from her. That could take days. Or weeks, if she gets wise and tries to string it out."

It was the first time Wren allowed herself to relax after hours of running.

Amberley might have been too incensed to be charmed by the cottage, but the sound of the ocean waving past the windows soothed Wren's sensibilities, and the scent of salty air drifted in to remind her that she was safe, for the moment, in the quiet seaside hideaway.

Suddenly, her body awoke.

Every bump and bruise seemed to cry out, the soreness in her shoulder taking center stage, as if she'd climbed down a hundred trees instead of just one. Her stomach rumbled with the reminder that she hadn't eaten in hours. And a wave of exhaustion tempted her to lean back farther and allow her lids to drift closed.

"While I don't relish the idea of having to hide away here, I understand why we have to for right now. And actually"—she glanced around—"it's nice. Smaller than the grand house of oddities I live in."

"I shouldn't have said that." He leaned back in his chair, joining her to scan the wall of built-in bookcases and the windows overlooking the water. "Any place can be home if you see it that way. This old place is full of memories. I spent summers here when I was a boy. It still feels like home somehow."

Wren imagined the woman's gentle touch that had chosen

the drapes to clothe the windows or the flowered wallpaper that wrapped the room in an endless spring. Even the settee that warmed her by the fire was welcoming, soft, and unassuming. It was a rare glimpse into Elliot's personal life to imagine him tearing through the parlor and halls as a boy or dashing into the waves under the summer sun.

"What was her name?"

He tipped his head to the side. "Whose?"

"Your aunt."

"Agatha." He looked around as the firelight created shadows across the room. "It's odd to think of this place as mine now. I seldom come back. And I certainly never bring anyone here."

"And now you have a house full, with two strong-minded women who loathe each other and a rookie agent with lovesickness to contend with. We're quite a party of first-time guests."

Elliot laughed, baring a smile she hadn't expected. It barred her from finding offense in the fact that he welcomed her wit.

"And I assume that laughter means you'll be glad to know Amberley and I came to an agreement of sorts when we were locked in that Bureau office together."

"Which is?"

"We agree to disagree on just about everything. That goes without saying. But we also agree not to strangle one another before breakfast. I have no plans to murder your star witness over a plate of bacon and eggs, in case you were worried."

"And if she has plans to murder you?"

"Then she'll be quite sorry."

He whistled low. "I won't tell you how much of a unicorn that statement is for Amberley Dover to be sorry for something."

"Indeed. Sorry or not, I just wish she'd give us something we could use."

"She will." He gazed back at her, his brow furrowed slightly, as if something kept him questioning their exchange.

"Are you . . . are you sure she didn't say anything?"

"Nothing of importance, Wren. At least nothing that changes this case in my eyes. And what you said the night we spoke backstage at the Bijou is true: secrets always come up for air. And I have a feeling the full weight of Horace Stapleton's are about to make an appearance, and they'll tip the scales one way or another."

CHAPTER 16

"Jenny?" Olivia Charles whispered over her shoulder, drawing her daughter's attention from *The Welsh Fairy Book* she'd received from her uncle. It had already become a treasure, gently cradled in her lap.

Her little flame-haired Jenny with bouncing waves and a freckled-over smile set her book aside and slid off the four-poster bed, then padded over to the open French doors. She lingered in the drifting edge of the curtains.

"Come here, Jenny," Olivia whispered, scared to speak any louder, for the magic of the moment would be broken if she did. She gazed out over the second-story stone balcony to their backyard garden below.

Spring had just breezed in on the calendar, though the sun had no inclination to burn off the morning mist just yet. It was steadfast, a painted backdrop around the garden grounds every morning. The fog surrounded the trunks of aged trees in a haze of white, limbs climbing up out of the ghostly vapor. The tree's arms stretched and yawned toward the sky, spring buds dotting all the way up to the tips of the branches.

It was there, what Olivia wanted to show her daughter—a sprightly little wren, nestled just out of reach along the end of a branch. She held her hand open and still before the little bird, a crumbled butter cookie offering she'd tucked inside her palm.

"Do come see, Jenny," she whispered again. And when she heard her daughter's buckle shoes finally clip against the balcony floor, she hushed her with an outstretched hand. "Quiet as you can now. We don't want to frighten her."

"What is it, Momma?"

"Look." Olivia nodded toward the little bird hopping and bobbing on the limb. "There she is. See? That's our little wren."

Jenny tilted her head, confused. "But she's a wild bird, isn't she?"

"Of course she is, but that's just what she has to show the rest of the birds. That she is wild like them. But underneath? She is smart—she will not give away her secrets easily. And I think she really longs to be someone's pet. She has a soft heart beating beneath her breast. I can see it. She's come back to visit every day this week. Only kindness will do that."

"Why does she return?"

Olivia leaned back, shocked by the notion of such a question. "Isn't it obvious? She likes us, of course. Because she hasn't even tasted the tea cookie yet, or she'd come back without hesitation. I always leave one for her. Just there—on the stone ledge." Olivia smiled at seeing the delight on her daughter's face. "And do you know what she does?"

Jenny was breathless with wonder; Olivia could tell.

"What does she do?" she breathed out.

"She never touches it," Olivia said. But sensing her daughter's disappointment, she added, "I think she looks exceptionally hungry today, though. I believe that she's ready to trust us enough that she'll eat from your hand."

"My hand?" Jenny shook her head. Perhaps she was fearful to take on the responsibility should the wren get skittish and fly off again.

It felt right, so Olivia reached out and cupped her daughter's hand to roll the cookie crumbs in it. "Now wait. Just lay your hand out, open to the sky. When she's ready, she'll come to you. But you have to let it be her choice as to whether she sees you as a friend or a foe. She'll open up to you when she's ready." Olivia leaned in closer from behind, cheek just grazing the softness of her daughter's. "Let us see what she chooses."

The wren danced from perch to perch, teetering on the edge of trust. She flitted down from the tree branch to the stone railing and, finally, took little hops toward them.

Jenny stood frozen, delight held just at bay as she waited for the bird to choose whether to eat from her hand.

"What shall we call our new friend? What about Jenny?" Olivia squeezed her arm around her daughter's shoulder.

"For me?" Jenny whispered, her voice caught in the magic of the moment.

"Of course. She could be our happy secret—our very own *Jenny Wren*." They watched the little wren, tiny feet dancing and head bobbing around the tips of Jenny's fingers. "She's got fire in her, see? I think she's got the same spirit as you. So the name fits."

Jenny turned to look back in the nursery and the bed that cradled her sleeping sister. "Won't Charlotte want a pet named after her too?"

Olivia thought about it, how at only six years old her

daughter had simply fallen into reading and scarcely a year later, delighted in every fairy-tale story she could get her young hands on. The stories were both lovely and frightening at the same time—tales of princesses and knights on white steeds. Of tiny birds and lonely tower balconies. And always off on the horizon lay the presence of darkness. A threat that was poised to roll into the story, making a hero or heroine arise.

Olivia hated that she could watch her daughter now, with such innocence that teetered on the verge of being shattered. But still, the hope of light kept her going. It reminded her that for any of the darkness in the world, there was always light to counter it.

Even in the darkness of their home and family, Olivia could look out over a second-story balcony and find light in a little wren, just as she could in the way the breeze caught the nursery curtains, dusting the edge of her youngest daughter's bed with a veil of gauzy yellow.

A mop of auburn hair lay still against the pillow.

Charlotte's breathing was even and still.

"Your sister will grow up one day, Jenny. When she does, she'll need us to help her believe in fairy tales too. She'll need to know that there is light in the world. And we should be the ones to show her. We'll train some beautiful winged creature to be her pet. A butterfly, perhaps? One that floats on golden wings? She'd like that."

"I wish I could float away sometimes. Like the sprites in our fairy stories. Or our winged friends . . . ," Jenny whispered, stone-still as their wren tiptoed around its butter cookie prize.

Me too, little bird.

The morning was wearing thin. Olivia could feel it. The sun was rising, cutting higher through the trees now—almost time for their sunrise spell to be broken.

A door slammed inside the house, echoing down the hall. The cadence of heavy footfalls on the stairs shattered the beauty of their stolen moment, replacing it with the errant echoes of yelling just past the nursery door.

There was another grand slam and the birds took flight, scattering to perches well above the balcony. Olivia watched them, tears gathering in her eyes as they fled, wishing she and her sweet daughters could sail away with them.

"Momma." Jenny pointed up to the empty branches, the cookie crumbs falling from her palm to scatter about the ledge. Wind toyed with them like forgotten dust. "Our birds!"

"Don't worry." She tugged her at the arm, ushering her back inside. "They will come back tomorrow. You'll see. We are friends now. Our Jenny Wren will not want to miss out on another visit. Perhaps Charlotte will be awake then and she can meet her too."

A crash reverberated down the hall.

Olivia's heart sank. It sounded as if her new pitcher and basin had met their demise against her bedroom floor.

"Does that mean Father's home?" Jenny asked, her voice sounding too grown up, her eyes keenly watching the closed door.

"Yes," Olivia mumbled, her whisper painful even for her own ears to hear. "It sounds like your father is home." She eased them into the nursery, closed the double doors, and locked the outdoor balcony world tight behind them.

It wasn't safe to bring the girls around Josiah when he was like this.

A full night of revelry at his theater ensured he'd be home late—not until morning. It also ensured his temper would flare, and his weakness for strong drink would make him the thing they most feared in Jenny's beloved fairy tales: the monster that swept in with each sunrise.

"Stay here, Jenny." She brushed her fingertips under Jenny's chin, raising her eyes to look at her. "No matter what you hear, stay here with Charlotte. If she wakes, you read her one of your fairy-tale stories. Maybe even tell her about our secret wren if she cries."

"Of course, Momma."

"And you remember what I've said? You always look out for one another. It's what wrens do, isn't it? They share the darkness if they have to, just as they share the moments of light. Share light with her, okay?"

Pounding reverberated against the nursery door.

Olivia's breathing quickened.

She ran a palm over the apple of Jenny's cheek, loving the way freckles danced across the bridge of her nose. Why couldn't the moment be drawn out? Why did she have to turn away from those freckles, the innocence they held?

No matter what her heart longed for, the moment refused to linger. If she wanted to keep Josiah out of the nursery, she'd have to go. Every time her husband came home in such a state, their fairy-tale world fractured a little more. And with each new break, Olivia wondered if she'd walk out the nursery door for the last time.

When would it all end . . . ?

"Remember—stay here, little Wren. No matter what you hear, don't step through this door. Promise me?"

Jenny nodded, her little eyes glazing with tears.

Olivia took a deep breath as the pounding continued.

She notched her chin, ready to fight the dragon again. Wondering if she'd walk away wounded, or whether it would be the final time her heart was slain.

FEBRUARY 12, 1927

BIJOU THEATRE

WASHINGTON STREET

BOSTON, MASS.

Elliot stepped into Wren's heavily veiled backstage world for the second time.

On this turn, she wasn't sparring with federal agents or sifting through mountains of paperwork at her dining room table. Instead, she sat upon the spindle chair, squeezed between the oversized stage wardrobe and oblong table spread with the wares for her stage show.

She was silent, her gaze fixed in the kaleidoscope of fractured light cast by the crystal vase from the nearby tabletop. Her crimson costume was crisp and clean. Boots shining. Lips painted. To anyone, Wren appeared ready for spotlights to rain down. But Elliot knew better; this was the look of a performer who was miles away, lost in her own world. The only movement her gentle brushing of gloved fingertips over the pages of a book in her hands.

"Wren?"

She jumped at his voice, snapping the volume shut. "Yes?"

"I didn't mean to startle you. It's . . ." He hesitated, arcing a thumb toward the stage. "Almost showtime."

"I know." She popped up to slip the book in a hidden drawer in the oblong table. Wren ran a gloved hand over her cheek and cleared her throat. "I could hear the crowd. But thank you."

"Did I disturb you?"

Wren finally turned, the display of confidence back in her straightened spine. She gave a light tug to each cuff, further perfecting her composure.

"No." She attempted to laugh it off with nonchalance. "But I am glad you're here. I've been thinking."

"You're reconsidering your performance tonight? Good. Because—"

"Not particularly. I still plan to perform. But I was actually remembering something Harry said to me once. That to come back from the dead is humanly impossible. He told Bess that if he passed, he'd try to connect back with her in spirit if he could."

"You don't say. Do you think he has, come back to visit his wife?"

Wren sent him a look that said such a question was ill appreciated. But she answered anyway. "Not to my knowledge. I was never very close with Bess, so I wouldn't push in to ask her. But to come back as Victor Peale did?" She shook her head. "It's impossible, Elliot. No matter what Stapleton claims or what information Amberley will share. If the greatest illusionist in the world believed it to be impossible, how can I entertain ideas that are anything less?"

"I agree with you. That's why I brought this." He stepped closer to her and held out the newspaper clipping from August 8, 1903.

She scanned the headline: "Black Saturday Disaster," and the lines below it, reading aloud: ". . . 12 dead and 232 injured when a balcony support gave way during a doubleheader baseball game between the Boston Braves and Philadelphia Phillies at Philadelphia's National League Park . . ." Wren looked up. "Yes, I recall hearing something about it. I was quite young when it happened, but it's still talked about to this day, even after the war. It's terrible, but I don't understand what it has to do with us."

"The baseball game. Remember? The ticket stub in Peale's book?"

"That's connected to this? It couldn't be."

"Someone wants us to believe it is. Here. Have a look." He pulled another news clipping from his pocket, knowing this was the one that would get the reaction. "The date was smudged on the ticket. Even so, Connor's been digging into the newspaper archives, looking for newsworthy events between the two teams and then cross-checking that for any mention of Peale. And we got a hit on it just this afternoon. I knew you'd want to know, so I came right over."

When her eyes widened, he knew she'd found it: one of the twelve killed when the balcony collapsed was a man named Victor A. Peale, and his photograph was a dead ringer for the man they'd both watched die at the cemetery on New Year's Eve of 1926.

"Why . . . it's him, isn't it?" She shook her head. "But how is it possible? This was more than twenty-three years ago. How in the world could a man look exactly the same after that much time?"

"So goes Stapleton's argument. He'll think it's another notch in his win column, no doubt."

Wren slapped the newspaper clippings down on the table, then shot to her feet. "I don't know how it's possible. But surely you see someone planted this. They wanted you to find it. And with every piece of evidence stacked up in favor of Stapleton, I'm more compelled than ever to go out on that stage. I have to declare truth through my actions—that these are illusions, and that's all they are. No magic. No spiritual trickery or deals with the afterlife. Just a show to entertain. I've never lied about what I do out there. And I'd never seek to deceive a crowd in the way he is so capable of doing. Just like you said, there's but one man who could claim power over the grave. And I assure you—*Horace Stapleton isn't him.*"

"You're angry."

"You bet I'm angry," she shot back, arms tense at her sides.

"I was going to say, you're angry . . . and yet you still won't consider canceling, will you? Even when the evidence in favor of Stapleton's claims keeps building and whoever's out there could try to silence your voice against him?"

"Seems to me if someone was going to try to get rid of an illusionist, they'd simply find a way to slip in when no one was around and make her disappear. They'd certainly not bother while she's onstage in front of a packed auditorium with hundreds of witnesses and the press with flashbulbs at the ready. Seems like I'd be safer out there than just about anywhere."

It wasn't wise for Wren to perform tonight.

They both knew it.

She hadn't been allowed a full week to heal from a bullet wound, and yet it was already proving an uphill battle to convince her out of her rather stubborn willfulness regarding the car chase. Elliot couldn't leave her unprotected now, for too many reasons, despite the pigheadedness that seemed to be slowly growing on him. Maybe she'd at least hear him out this time before she declined an offer of protection.

"While I admire your tenacity, Wren, that's the very reason I'm going to stay right here until the curtain closes."

Tell her why.

Elliot sighed, warring with himself.

"But you know no one can touch me out there. The stage is the safest place to be right now."

Tell her why . . . Tell her what you know about Jennifer Charles.

Still Elliot battled with his thoughts. The closer he tried to get, the more Wren was inclined to bolt in the other direction.

"I'm not convinced hired guns are all that clever to begin with. I think they'd try anything, witnesses or not. That's why I'm not leaving. You need someone on your side."

Wren tensed her jaw and turned away. She reached for the crystal vase, then moved in front of the spindle chair, blocking his view. Crystal meeting wood gave off the lightest sound. She left the vase there, breaking up what light there was in a thousand brilliant sparkles.

"And who will ensure you keep your nose out of my props? I know it must be eating at you from the inside, but you'll just have to stay content with being the only person who knows about the cuff links."

He tipped his head to the door leading to the back of the stage, the one that Irina swept in and out of while attending to her duties. "You mean . . . ?"

"No one knows. Not even Irina," she said, but before he could read anything into it, her face brightened with a smile. "And if I hadn't been knocked out at the time, you wouldn't know about them either. Since I can't change that now, I'll just have to trust you will hold it in the strictest confidence and not let your curiosity stray any further."

"I won't get involved unless I absolutely have to. You said yourself it's safe out on that stage. Well, here's your chance to prove your theory."

Shades of willfulness fell across her face, almost making

him laugh. He backed off, hands in the air. "I'm here strictly as a member of law enforcement tonight. You and Amberley are paramount to our case against Stapleton, and that means we're not leaving either of you alone for one second. So you can go ahead to your stage if you have to, but I'll always be here waiting when you're through."

In a blink, it became all too apparent what he'd said.

Always.

The audience murmured and the band began to cue up past the curtain, punctuating the sudden grip of silence that had fallen between them.

Whether Elliot had meant the admission as more than just a job didn't matter. For reasons even he couldn't explain, there was the smallest measure of truth in the one word. That thinking about Wren's bandaged shoulder felt like a punch to the gut every time. That the sight of her bloodied tuxedo jacket was something he wished he could expunge from his memory. That he couldn't forget the way her hair had fallen across her brow when she'd passed out in his arms. That she bore a will stronger than anyone he'd ever known, with talent and determination that cast her ownership over every stage, but she also possessed the unexpected presence of a softer side.

The side so few were privileged to see.

The side he longed to see more of.

Wren stood before him, her eyes shining under the dimmed light from the sides of the stage. And it hit him as he looked at her—they were alike. Both self-professed loners and workaholics who finally had something that stirred a bit of life in them again.

Wren Lockhart, and not the whole of Stapleton's case, was the real reason for the shift in his thinking. Unbelievable.

"What did you just say?" she asked, breathless.

"I said I'll be right here." A pause. The summoning of bravery, and then, "If you want me to be."

"Please don't . . ."

"Why?" He searched her face for an answer. "Why can't I say it if it's true?"

"Because we're working together for a very short time. Because I don't *want* anyone else. I have to rely on myself."

"Yet you speak to me of faith? Isn't that relying on more than just yourself?" He shook his head. Felt a pull drawing him a measured step forward. "You can't walk on both sides of the street, Wren. I'm not asking you to change anything. Not who you are or what you do. I know I can't prevent you from stepping onto that stage tonight. I'll try to sway you every time if it's in your best interest, but I won't bully you out of your will. All I'm saying is that as long as you want me to, I'll be right here waiting when you're through."

She crossed her arms over her chest, as if bravado would continue protecting her. Even tried to look away, scanning the backstage area as if she needed one last check of the stage props, though her meticulous nature would have ensured she'd already done so before that very moment.

Elliot saw it, plain as day.

The ever-composed Wren Lockhart he'd come to know was crumbling before his eyes. It wasn't like her to shed vulnerability, yet she did. Earnestly. And that spoke volumes.

Finally, she exhaled. "When I was young, I moved to England to live with my uncle. It was not long after my mother died and everything about my world had changed."

"I'm so sorry, Wren," he whispered, empathy carving a slow trail through his chest like a surgical knife.

"Thank you. It was a long time ago. I've taught myself not to think on it much. But then the case—these past weeks . . ." She ran a gloved fingertip over the back of the spindle chair, lost in thought. "Memories have come to life and it seems I have nowhere left to run from them. They haunt me."

Elliot studied her, ignoring the fact that she'd avoided his confession entirely and instead had chosen that moment to revive a childhood memory. But whatever must have been going through her mind, he didn't stop her.

He stood still.

Drawn to silence in the shades of light falling from the backstage rafters. Telling his feet to hold fast when all they wanted to do was charge forward. He had to wait for Wren to come to the door of her past and invite him to step through of her own volition.

There was no pushing his way in this time.

"I remember my uncle had many business associates in France and traveled often before the war. It was very much a golden time, the calm before the world's storm of the Great War. And my uncle knew I loved stories of kings and castles, that sort of thing. He took me to see the palace of Versailles once. Have you heard of it?"

"I've heard of it. Yes," he said, his voice strong but making sure it was void of coaxing. She wasn't likely to take to that.

"I'd never seen anything like it. It was so different from my view of the world—of Boston at night and the back halls of vaudeville theaters. My view was always darkness. But this world seemed gilded with daylight. Marble and manicured gardens and surfaces dripping with gold . . . It was like something I'd read in a fairy tale. But it's odd that when in comparison to all that splendor, the memory that holds me fast is of something you only find when you look past the gold leaf. It was a painting, an arch positioned above the door to a salon at each end of a lavish hall."

"The Hall of Mirrors?"

"Yes. You've heard of it too." A faint smile eased over her lips with the remembrance.

He nodded. "I do read a fair bit."

"It's said that when any visiting dignitary came to Louis VIX's palace, they were invited into one of the two grand salons flanking the hall. Above one door is a painting celebrating the king's gift of peace bestowed upon Europe from France, portrayed in a regal, very heroic pose. Over the other is the depiction of the king atop a magnificent steed, fierce and charging ahead in battle, trampling over his adversaries along the way."

"So based upon the invitation into either salon, that country would know exactly where they stood with France."

Wren nodded softly. "Yes. One room for peace, the other for war. They'd immediately know whether they were considered a friend or foe, and they could expect their audience with the king to go accordingly. There was no guesswork after that because the paintings spoke without the necessity of words."

"And that's why—?" Elliot stopped short when something more open registered in her eyes. He glanced around the large space before he brought his gaze back to rest on her. "It's why you bring everyone into your library first. That's your war room, isn't it?"

She didn't deny it. Illusions were one thing, but dealing with real emotion was something else entirely. And she didn't look able to master this.

"I don't have friends, Elliot. Everyone is a foe in the beginning, you understand. It's not personal. It's just meant to help me survive another day. If I make sure I don't rely on anyone other than myself, I'm assured I'll never be let down."

"And yet I'm still allowed in your backstage at the moment. You didn't invite me in, but you haven't exactly asked me to leave either."

"Then why are you here?"

He took a step closer, until the hairline part in the curtains cast of swath of light that no longer cut across the floor between them but split up the side of his shirt-sleeve. Elliot looked down at it, then back to her, as if it were an invisible line he'd intentionally crossed.

"I told you," he whispered. "Security."

"Mine or yours?"

Elliot held up his index finger for a brief second, then brushed back a lock of hair that had fallen over her cheek.

"Do you want me to leave? Just tell me to go back to the library and I will."

Wren blinked back, saying nothing, giving him no indication what she might be thinking. She turned back to the table and pulled out the drawer. Her gentle fingertips grasped the worn edges of the book she'd put there.

She stopped before him, offering it.

"*The Welsh Fairy Book*." He read the title, raising his brow slightly. "What's this?"

"It's a favorite of mine. And it's very dear to me. So I wonder if I could trust you to hold on to this until after the show. Keep it safe."

"Why do you want me to take it?"

Head shaking ever so slightly, she whispered, "It's what I can give right now."

Those words wrecked him.

Without thinking better of it, Elliot gave in. He moved forward, his shoes brushing the tips of hers, and leaned in. Dangerously close. So she had to lean back a breath with him, clutching the tabletop at the small of her back.

He allowed his lips to graze hers as he eased his fingertips over the spine of the book at the same time, taking it in hand. "Then I'll take that as an invitation to stay," he whispered a breath away from her lips, just as the familiar music began to play out against the ceiling vaults in the auditorium. "I believe that's your cue, Ms. Lockhart. Please try not to break a leg. The federal government would like you to remain in one piece."

He melted back into the shadows just as quickly, leaving Wren frozen in her spot behind the center part of the curtain. He watched her visibly shift tracks to the task at hand, dipping her head and closing her eyes, waiting in her signature pose as the curtain drifted apart.

Though she was a consummate professional, the tiniest shred of hopefulness cut into his chest when he took his place at the stage wing, with enough of a vantage point to see her place under the spotlight.

She'd smiled—a whisper-soft display of contentment that he hoped was in the lingering memory of the moment that passed between them. She inhaled, music swelling, even as her teeth just caught the edge of her bottom lip.

It was no use to deny that the woman in red was more than a means to an end for the case. Even with her eccentric ways and masked persona, Wren Lockhart had begun to mean more to Elliot than he dared say.

He gripped the book in his hand, the blue cover and thick spine worn, printed with the name William Jenkyn Thomas and the ethereal title in block gold letters: *The Welsh Fairy Book*.

Fairy tales were stories where anything was possible, even the fanciful dreams of childhood. But how could Elliot tell her that he wasn't just there as a precaution? That he had a terrible instinct growing in his core: more threats were looming. Bringing them to a war room whether Wren wanted it or not. And if she longed for a fairy-tale hero, he wasn't it.

Not by a long shot.

Stay with me, Wren. A battle was raging, bringing a fight she didn't know was already on its way.

Elliot swallowed hard as he saw a little girl skipping down the center aisle with a basket of mingled peonies and roses hooked under her elbow, drawing the crowd into the opening act with Wren eloquently weaving her story from the stage.

"Stay with me . . . ," he whispered, holding tight to the book from her past.

Even when I have to tell you that I already know what Jennifer Charles is hiding.

CHAPTER 17

Wren's shoulder protested, slamming her with pain even while wrapped in the soft cradle of water.

She'd been chained to the bottom of the glass water chamber, both ankles and wrists bound in thick coils of metal, and covered in water that had been pumped in until it was full and rippled just over the top of her head.

The audience became a jumble of figures—watercolor shapes bleeding into one another from her submerged view. With the errant hammering of her heart and the muffled gasps from the audience piercing through the water, it proved a losing battle to keep her hands calm.

Instead of the lock clicking open as it always did, Wren felt it tighten and fight back. Terror slammed through her mind.

This isn't my lock . . .

A new lock, untested and firm, became a different kind of enemy—one that rendered her injured arm near useless. Her shoulder refused to help, every motion she'd practiced time and time again turned into a fresh battle against dexterity now.

The pick caught in the lock, jarring slightly, and to her horror—slipped from its secure perch between her forefinger and thumb. And it was gone, disappearing into the depths of the water tank, leaving her hand painfully empty.

With the minimal stage lighting, Wren knew it was impossible for the crowd to see the tiny glint of metal as it cut down through the water. She'd planned it that way. It had always been her fail-safe. If the first pick was dropped or caught on the tape in her glove, there was no need to panic. She always had a spare in the other hand. Candlelight onstage would become her ally, too, providing a backdrop just dim enough to conceal the falter and save the illusion.

But this time panic gained its first true foothold on her stage.

She had a second pick to turn to, but she couldn't move her left arm enough to reach it from under the tape in her other palm. Her first tiny savior had already sunk to the bottom of the chamber and without it, she'd have little chance to free herself with the second one.

Wren turned her head to both sides, pleading with the water-color splotches for help. Surely Elliot was there. He'd be standing off in the wings somewhere, waiting with everyone else, expecting her to emerge triumphant to the adulation of the crowd. If only she could see him through the wash of color splotches . . . Cry out for help . . .

His voice was in her head. *I'll always be waiting. If you want me to.*

Wren pulled her wrists in a violent battle against the hand-cuffs. Her legs, too, warred with the restraints. But fighting wasn't enough.

Not this time.

If her body had craved oxygen after the one-minute mark, now ticking nearer to two minutes, her lungs were screaming now.

There were no illusions in that instant.

It was the first time Wren could feel the shock of death creeping in, both terrifying and real.

Wren's mouth sought air, and almost without her control, she gasped, finding a punishing intake of water to burn her insides. Though chained, she kicked her legs furiously and her arms seemed to twitch on their own. And as the watercolor world of the audience melted into a subdued blackness that enveloped like a curtain, Wren's eyelids fluttered, then finally closed.

She barely heard the deep crack of an ax shattering glass . . .

※

FEBRUARY 12, 1927

CHERRY HILL

CANTON, MASS.

The near miss onstage had shaken Wren's nerves to the point she could no longer stay away from the oversized brick building in Cherry Hill, and the one person she'd hidden away within its walls.

Not when she'd come so close to disaster.

One second Wren had been fighting a watery grave, and in the next, she'd been pulled from the tank with a rush of spilling water, coughing and sputtering, with the feel of the hardwood stage to catch her tumble. She learned later that Elliot had been there, standing watch in the wings of the stage. And in the instant she'd given up hope, he tore onto the scene and ripped the ax from the stage handler's grip, then swung it down to slice into the glass.

It was impossible to think of anything else—how a hand

had patted her cheek, and when her eyelids fluttered open, she'd found Elliot's look of intense concern fade to relief. The fear she'd seen staring back at her couldn't have been masked. Not when he was there, bracing a hand at the small of her back while she doubled over in a fit of coughing as the curtain came together in front of them. Not as he helped her stand but held back from sweeping her up, somehow knowing she'd need to walk off the stage on her own two feet.

That kind of momentary security shouldn't have found its way behind her carefully drawn defenses. But it had scared her enough that she needed an escape. A trip fifteen miles south of the city on a dusky evening could almost guarantee her anonymity—especially when she'd opted to leave any costume of Wren Lockhart's at home.

That night she could only be Jenny.

The wind kicked up as she hurried down the sidewalk.

A swift gust fled through the grove of trees, rustling their bare limbs, carrying with it the scent of rain. The light rumble of thunder filled the night behind her as whisper-soft pricks of raindrops dusted her cheek.

It was lucky she'd just missed the rain.

Wren eased her fingertips around the iron scrollwork to push the gate wide and step through.

No more water. Not tonight.

"Wren—wait."

At the whisper of her name she spun. "I knew someone was following me."

"I know you did." Elliot shook his head. "You kept doubling back and I had some time keeping up."

Wren ran her hands down to smooth her coat, needing a few long seconds to ease her nerves. Relief washed over her that it was a friend instead of an enemy who'd trailed behind, especially since she'd just been through a car chase and a jail break, and now a near miss with drowning in her own stage show. Thank goodness she still had enough wits about her to recognize a shadow when she had one.

"What on earth are you doing here, Elliot? And why do you keep sneaking up on me?" She breathed out, then frowned once her faculties of clear thought returned.

"You got out of a car two blocks back when you know you shouldn't be out alone—" Elliot stopped midsentence and stared, suddenly incredulous.

Wren saw the fast work of understanding descend over his face as she straightened her hat. Finally, he'd noticed what was different—that *she* was quite different close up, and it blasted her with vulnerability she hadn't prepared for.

Gone was the heavy stage makeup.

She had no dark lines to rim the corners of her eyes. No enhanced lashes, perfectly painted lips, or circles of rouge dotting her cheeks. She didn't wear the tailored gentleman's attire everyone had come to expect from her. Instead, she wore a ladies' day coat and frock that bathed her legs in shades of nude gauze and blush-pink silk. A beige cloche hid the pin-tucked curls she'd swept back at her nape. Only gentle wisps had freed themselves in the wind and stirred at the base of her neck.

Elliot was mere inches away this time, looking down at her the way she'd not allowed anyone to see. Without her mask. Without a single guard or defense in place. He'd stopped, taking in what she'd always fought to keep hidden, and that terrified her.

"Wren? You're—" He wrinkled his brow. Even took a step back. "Is that you?"

She cleared her throat and lifted her chin a touch higher. "What are you doing here? We're miles away from the city."

"I know we are." He shook his head and held out her book, safe in his outstretched hand. "I promised to give you this after the show. I had to drop it for a moment when . . . Well, the point is, I have it now. And I'm returning it to you, as promised."

She took it in hand and wrapped the book under her arm in a protective manner. "How did you know where to find me?"

He looked down on her as the rain-laden wind caught up his hair and tossed it upon his brow. "After what happened, I only wanted to check on things to make sure you were safe. I hadn't thought to come so far as to catch up to you unless I had to."

"And when you did catch me? What then?"

Elliot seemed to be weighing if words would help his cause in explanation, or push her away again.

"I hadn't thought that far ahead."

She shook her head, turning away.

Elliot reached out, his hand connecting with hers. But this was a graze, the softness of his fingers entreating her to turn back to him as his grip slid down to cover her gloved hand. His thumb brushed against her palm in a gentle tug, turning her around to face him.

The streetlamp illuminated his face. His was a look that said the hand still grasping hers was intentional.

Unable to think, she slipped her hand from his. "Elliot, you . . . kissed me tonight."

"I did, didn't I? That changes things, for me anyway. Especially when you could have died out there on that stage. Is it always so dangerous, this vaudeville life of yours?"

She shrugged. "Only since I teamed up with you, it seems. But it was nothing. A lock got switched somehow. It shouldn't happen, but my shoulder kept me from being able to open a new one I hadn't planned for. I could have done it, if I wasn't still healing."

"Do you plan everything?"

"I try to. When I can."

"Forgive me for saying it flat out, but you seem bent on finding new ways of killing yourself since I've known you. And believe me, if that were to happen, I'd be very upset. Please try to plan a quiet evening at home for a change."

"But you see, tonight reminded me that I don't need anyone to save me. Or protect me. That will never change in my eyes. If you hadn't broken that glass, it would have only taken me seconds more to be free. I could have done it on my own. And I still walked off that stage under my own volition."

"Only because I knew that's what you'd want, so I let you do it."

"And if you only wanted to check on the state of affairs at my home, you're quite far away from the city at the moment."

He shook his head. "Please don't be angry with me for caring, Wren. I wanted to check on the state of affairs with you," he whispered, a smile tempering the corners of his mouth. "Can't have my partner drop out now. You're too important to this investigation."

Elliot tilted his head to the engraved wood sign beyond the gate. *Rock Creek Manor. Est. 1862.* "Not a new lead in the case, is it?"

Wren shook her head. "I wish it was."

"Then what are you doing here? If it's not too much to ask. You left your car a few blocks back and you're not dressed for—" He faltered, shifting tracks in his words. "I assume this isn't a performance for Wren Lockhart since you're trying to sneak about unnoticed. Which isn't smart, I might add, given the state of things."

Wren gazed up at the elaborate brick manor, with long window-lined wings branching out on both sides, the soft glow of electric lights from the arched windows cutting through the quick fall of darkness.

The sky echoed with thunder, mingling with the growing scatter of breezes.

The promise of rain had her cinch the collar of the day coat up higher round the neck.

"Please. Elliot, this can't end up in the papers. Wren Lockhart may be owned by the public, but what's inside those walls isn't for sale to anyone." She glanced from the threatening sky to the haven of the manor, then back to connect with his eyes.

"When are you going to get it through your thick head that I'm not your enemy, Wren? I'm trying to help."

What are you going to do, Wren?

She tapped the toe of her shoe against the brick walkway, darting her glance from Elliot's face back to the glow of lamplight coming from the Rock Creek Manor windows.

Wren exhaled, trying not to think about the enormous risk she was undertaking.

"Well, if that's true, then you'd better come inside."

CHAPTER 18

A wail reverberated from somewhere down the hall. It jarred the air, the greeting ghostly and uninviting.

Evening was not the usual time for visitors, Elliot guessed, as the waiting area was empty. Perhaps the manor had a different feel as night drew closer. Or were there odd sounds all the time? He walked through the set of double doors behind Wren, curious to see if he was right about why she'd come. She stepped up to the desk and spoke to a nurse and he hung back, hands in his pockets, scanning the room.

It was easy to see that Rock Creek Manor wasn't a sanitarium of the type Elliot had visited in his aunt's final days. An asylum, no matter how clean and respectable, had a very different air about it.

A sanitarium was to make the sick well again; this place reminded visitors that patients rarely left the walls around them, if ever.

Wren walked back toward Elliot, drawing his attention.

"We can go back now." She held a paper visitor's pass out to him. "But we can only stay for a bit. Visiting hours are officially over, but they've made an exception tonight."

"Lead the way." He nodded and took the pass.

Wren turned, walked forward, and took the large door's knob in hand at the same time Elliot had reached out to open it for her. His hand rested over hers for a long second. She looked up at him, her golden eyes piercing back, vulnerability evident. She'd removed her gloves. In the instant that Elliot could almost feel the skin of his palm burning against hers, realization washed over him.

This was the first time Wren had brought anyone here. Not to the actual building—but to this point in her private, offstage life.

Elliot had an idea of who they were here to see, but it had never crossed his mind that this could be the first time Wren trusted anyone enough to sweep back the curtain and reveal the depths of this part of her world. It was as if the whole of her heart was attached to that doorknob, and not just her hand. "There's a first time for everything."

She nodded, her pretty face and dotting of freckles still peeking out from under the brim of her cloche. He held the side of the door, allowing her to precede him.

The hall was distant, met by a breezeway with windows lining the right side and beyond, doors—some open, others closed—lining the left. It, too, was stark—clean, but lacking warmth. Drizzle cried down the outside of the glass, the ink-black night serving as the backdrop beyond the windows.

"Are we going to someone's room?"

"Yes. We are. And if that's too much for you, it's okay. I won't think ill of you if you turn around now. But I have to keep going." Wren kept walking at his side, the book he'd given her cradled in her left arm.

She kept her view focused on the elevator doors at the far end of the hall. And somehow, in the grand mess of the case and as they took steps together into Wren's compartmentalized world, it felt simple and right to reach out and take her hand.

So he laced his fingers with hers. Would she pull away or allow him the simple gift of walking alongside her?

"I'm not going anywhere," he said again.

Wren accepted his hand without look or spoken words.

They walked in step as if they'd done it hundreds of times before, to the elevator and the second-floor hall, without breaking stride.

Wren slowed and slipped her hand from his when they came to a door at the end of the hall. It had been cracked open, and she tapped her fingers against it, then pushed it wide.

The room was larger than he expected. Still small as a bedroom, but made welcoming by a wall of windows in an angled semicircle, with cushioned benches along all sides. A grid of bars hung inside the glass, but the windows weren't shuttered against the rain. A web of tissue paper streamers of white stars, pink flowers, and blue-and-yellow nautical flags were strewn across the ceiling on strings of twine. Soft lamplight glowed from a light fixture high overhead. Stacks of picture books were piled on a small desk. And dolls, meticulously arranged, stood guard from the bureau, adding unexpected enchantment to the space.

A young woman with auburn hair sat upon a cushioned window seat with a folded paper hat over her long waves, her nose buried in a storybook.

Wren whispered, "Hello, my darling."

The young woman looked up, blank-faced for a moment, then warmed with a bright smile when she saw them. "Jenny!" She dropped her book, which slapped the linoleum floor, and then covered a reactionary giggle with her fists over her mouth.

Wren slipped out of her coat and hat, then laid them over

the foot of the bed along with *The Welsh Fairy Book*, then moved in and swept the young woman in an embrace.

"Jenny, I've been reading about Peter Pan. And Wendy. And the boys who wear hats and crow at the moon! I was going to crow tonight too." She glanced toward the windows, sorrow lining her features. "But the moon hides behind the storm clouds."

Elliot stood back from what felt like a private moment, watching Wren brush a lock of hair off the young woman's brow. Listening as she talked of a marauder by the name of Captain Hook and a beautiful fairy called Tinker Bell, in a manner that was animated and childlike. Genuine tenderness filled Wren's eyes, such that he'd guessed at but had never before witnessed from her.

Wren smiled and eased the young woman around to face the spot where he stood in the doorway. "I would like for you to meet someone." Wren presented her with an arm wrapped around the waist of her soft ivory dress. "This is my friend, Elliot. He's come to visit."

The young woman's glance darted about, apprehensive because of the stranger in their midst.

"He won't hurt you." Wren nodded when the girl turned toward her, unease making her draw in ever so slightly. "He's our friend. Okay? You can trust him."

Wren took a deep breath. And Elliot guessed why, because he already knew what she was about to say.

"Elliot, this is Charlotte." She looked up, chin lifted, adding a brave: "My sister."

He took a slow step forward and nodded in greeting. "It's very nice to meet you, Charlotte."

Elliot had always heard of asylums. They were rumored to be horrible places, where those afflicted with lunacy lived out their days wandering halls and bellowing out from attic windows. But the room in which he stood now wasn't horrible. It was hushed and kept, like a child's Neverland nursery that time couldn't touch.

Wren stood in the center of it, her arm around someone she loved, and looked back at him with questions in her eyes.

Frightened as a bird, Charlotte stood still, hat in place, book on the floor in front of her. It brushed against the tip of her stocking feet.

"My name is Elliot. May I come in and hear about your stories? Jenny just showed me her *Welsh Fairy Book* tonight." He set his hat on the bed and picked up Wren's book. "Would you like to read it?"

Charlotte nodded, her face brightening with something akin to recollection.

Her eyes twinkled, dancing with delight.

She reached out with a tentative hand, cautious until she held the book, then hopped over and curled up in her window seat and began poring over the pages.

"It's the pictures she adores," Wren whispered. "William Pogany's illustrations are her favorite."

Wren slid down to the foot of the bed and absently wrapped her hand around one of the metal spindles at the footboard, watching her sister. Elliot sat in a rocker near the bureau. He braced his elbows on his knees, leaning in toward Wren, drawing into conversation with her through the space that separated them.

"You must think me terrible, to hide her away like this."

"I'd never question a decision you make, Wren. I'm sure it was for good reason that she's here."

"She's always been with me. I promised myself I'd never send her away. But I had no choice, not after what happened the night of Amberley's party. If she loses me, who will look after her? I moved her here from my home in Beacon Hill that morning. No one knows she's Wren Lockhart's sister. Here, she's unknown. She's safe. Whoever came after me will not find her. And the newspapers could let us alone, too, at least until this is all over. I've managed to keep her hidden from them for this long. What's a few more months?"

She brushed her hand against the side of Charlotte's face, then wound a lock of deep-auburn hair behind her ear.

"I knew you had a sister once. Charlotte was listed as Jennifer Charles's next of kin in the old newspaper articles we found about your family. I assumed she'd just grown up. Maybe married and moved away, and that you preferred not to speak of her. So I never asked."

"That's our protection, to be forgotten. It's why no one asks."

"Forgotten?" He shook his head at the thought. How could anyone—especially Wren—possibly be forgotten?

"I made a promise to our mother that I'd always look after Charlotte. She's always traveled with me, regardless of where the shows are. I stay in Boston as often as I can, but I must work. If I don't have this career, then it's not just me who loses. She loses too. That's why I have no staff. No extraordinary expenses except what would keep up the ruse of wealth among society. I make enough to live on and we have my uncle's inheritance, but even that won't last forever. I don't mind to be thought an eccentric, as long as it means Charlotte is hidden from the spotlight and is taken care of in the best manner possible. Being forgotten is the only way to do that."

"That's why you keep your house shuttered? Your dining room never in use?"

Wren smiled like she expected him to say that. "Most of the rooms are empty. You just haven't seen them all. If I shut up my home, no one asks questions about our past and that's where it stays. Locked tight where the prying pens of the newspapers can't find us."

"We all have pasts, Wren." The weight of her sadness gripped him from across the room. "I never thought of you as a person who'd run from anything."

"You don't see it. No one does, really. I've become quite good at hiding who I am, and for most of my life, I've walked—or run away from things—with my head down." A soft shrug tipped those delicate shoulders she owned. "But that's not living, is it? I could have died on that stage tonight, and I kept thinking about her. Who'd take care of Charlotte if I were gone? No one even knows I've moved her here, except you. She doesn't even know who Wren Lockhart is, poor thing."

"I heard it said once that some people die at twenty-five but aren't buried until seventy-five. Is it something like that?"

A soft laugh escaped her lips. Weighted and humorless. "In a way, I think part of me died at six years old." She gazed at Charlotte's serenity in turning page after page of the fairy book. "But then I look at her—so beautiful. Young in mind. Untouched by grief because she can't understand it. I lost my innocence long ago, and yet she'll never lose hers. She's locked away in the past, and all I've done is try to run from it. We are opposites in a way, but we're the same too."

Was it the right time to return her candid admissions with honesty of his own?

"Would you look at me?" Elliot drew her gaze from Charlotte to lock with his. "Can you tell me what happened to her? Your mother."

Wren swallowed hard. "She died protecting us."

It was a far cry from a full explanation of her mother's death, but it was enough. Even though he knew far more than she thought he did, it still explained her pain, the look of sorrow that had soaked in the depths of her eyes, and the reasons why Charlotte was so infinitely dear.

"I said I was sorry before, and I meant it. Because I understand some of that pain. I lost my parents as well."

She tilted her head, taken aback. "You?"

"I was still in France in the fall of 1918. I went to war as an officer, and I felt the responsibility to stay with my men, to see it through all the way. So I wasn't there when it happened. My father and mother were traveling home after a party one night. Their auto was run off the road and rolled down an embankment. They were both killed."

"I'm so sorry. But . . . what do you mean 'run off the road'? Was it an accident because of the weather?"

"No, Wren. There were witnesses, but none who were willing to come forward. My father supported the Wartime Prohibition Act that was headed for a congressional vote that November. Many stood to lose everything if it went through and became law. So he was eliminated before the vote. It still passed, though, so what was it for really?"

Say it out loud . . . But the words refused to come.

He couldn't—didn't dare say what guilt still plagued him.

"They were *murdered*."

Elliot didn't say that word, as a rule.

Never talked about himself. Not even to Connor, though many in the Bureau whispered that he was the agent whose parents had been killed for a vote to Prohibition.

"Elliot . . ."

The bed creaked as she moved. He felt her closeness, the touch of air that breezed by as she settled down to the floor at his feet. Even the warmth of her eyes, watching him so closely.

Elliot reached in his pocket. He retrieved the ivory-faced lighter that had belonged to his father, turning it over to catch the light so she could see it glint. "By the time I returned home from war, the funeral was long over and everything about life had changed. I'd always planned to go into politics like my father. But nothing made a difference for my parents. I wasn't there to protect them, and now they're gone."

Elliot allowed a light laugh to escape his lips, his former naivety difficult to remember.

"How wide-eyed I was back then. Like Connor is now. I wanted to change the world, or some such nonsense. So I joined up at the fledgling Bureau and never looked back. I threw myself into work and that became my king. Problem was, I wasn't ready. I thought I was, but I froze up during one of my first calls—a rookie called to a hostage situation between a man and his wife. I hesitated, he fired, and she died. In a blink. It was that fast . . . You don't make a decision—or you do—and the consequences are lifelong. I suppose I've been working myself raw in the years since, to try and make up for it in some way—guilt-work for the innocence lost."

"Guilt? I understand something of that."

"And all the while, I still carry this light with me. Just a small flame now. A flicker of who I once was. My father always used to say that we had a duty to our fellow man, to carry light every-where we go. He took it literally. And now I do, too, hoping it will help me remember." He dropped the lighter back in his pocket.

Wren returned his gaze and, heaven help him, he loved see-ing her without.

Without pretense or makeup. Without any mask.

"It's not nearly nonsense to want to do some good in the world, Elliot." She paused and he let the balm of those words sink in. "We just can't save everyone. No matter how we might want to."

"Yes, but I spend my days chasing rumrunners and interrogating vaudeville performers. It's not exactly what I expected, this protecting the people thing. But you've done well in it, Wren. Your mother would be proud to see what you've become and how much you obviously care for your sister."

Wren wrinkled her brow, as if his words struck a hidden place that she hadn't expected. She stared down at her hands clasped in her lap. She ran her fingertips over her palm, as if assuaging the memory of his touch with her own.

"Our mother used to say that a hero doesn't always have to slay a dragon to save the day." She swept a lock of hair behind her ear in an honest gesture, then pursed her lips and looked back at him, her gaze endearing. "Sometimes he just walks through the fire alongside you, and that's enough."

Time seemed to slow to a standstill between them.

Elliot had always thought that touch was the most intimate way a man and a woman could connect. A kiss. A hand across the base of the neck or a brush of fingertips against the small of the back. But if his thundering heart gave any indication, the moment of honesty Wren had shared in that single look made the air crackle with tension, of the kind he'd never known before.

Soft thunder rumbled against the windows, shattering the silence.

Charlotte clapped her hands together. "Did you hear that? More rain." Charlotte closed the book and held it out, her teeth just biting her bottom lip in excitement. "Jenny. Tell me a story.

The one about how the hero slays the dragon and wins the princess's heart! It's my favorite."

Wren took the book and thumbed through pages to the middle, then began telling the story of a red dragon and a fierce hero with a sword, as if from memory. It was a beautiful thing to witness, how Wren became Jenny Charles for a time, how she could fall into storytelling and forget anyone else was there watching.

It made him smile when she produced a paper bird for Charlotte, seemingly out of an empty hand. She flipped her wrist over and a small folded creation appeared in her fingertips—snowy white and perfect, with little wings and a perky notch to its head.

Her sister clapped in awe, then held it out to show off to him. "My sister makes things out of nothing. See? This is our own little bird. A wren. We used to have one outside our window. With a great tree and a balcony off our tower room. But we don't hit, do we, Jenny? We never hit or push."

"That's right, Charlotte. A hero never causes hurt; she only lessens it."

"And if I promise never to push again, can we go home? I don't like it here as much as my room at our house. They won't let me eat raspberry tea biscuits in between meals like you do."

Wren smiled—a maternal glow taking over her face. "Yes, darling. We'll go home soon. Together."

As rain pattered the asylum windows and Charlotte delighted over the story of heroes and dragons, Elliot realized that Wren may be skilled as an illusionist, but she still created her own magic. And this kind wasn't on a stage in front of hundreds of admirers. It was soft and quiet, in hushed moments talking of fairies and wrens and all manner of whimsical things.

She could make beauty grow out of nothing.

Flowers out of crystal vases and tiny paper birds out of ash in the palm of her hand. And even in him. Elliot hadn't realized until that moment how deeply his affection had grown for her. How it had awakened from a scarred nothing. And no matter what was poised to happen with Horace Stapleton's case, everything had changed.

No way could he walk away from her now.

CHAPTER 19

MARCH 5, 1927

BEACON HILL

BOSTON, MASS.

Rain dotted and dripped down walls of leaded glass.

The indoor conservatory greeted Elliot with cathedral vaults of brick and stone, and a glass roof that echoed the sounds of an almost-spring storm. The space was hushed but alive with new growth, with Wren's hallmark roses and peonies filling every corner with color and the high ceilings with fragrance. Tiny birds flitted about the rafters, chirping as they mingled with little leaves and the gangly limbs of small potted trees.

Irina had shown Elliot to the downstairs library as usual, but the shut-up door in the library's corner had been left ajar, almost as if he'd been expected. Even welcomed to step inside. He'd turned the corner, taken aback by the enchantment of the glass house first, then by the true understanding of where he stood. And all of a sudden the news he'd brought of the case meant very little in comparison.

And his breath was stolen away.

Wren knelt on the ground, digging in the soil of one of the beds.

Not knowing he was there, she hummed something—a soft, slow song in harmony with the birds, beautiful and perfect in the charmed garden hideaway. Her flaming hair was loose to her shoulders, in soft waves that moved when she did, framing the delicate lines of her face.

He stood still. Thoughts tangled. Words hopelessly escaped him. Coat dripped from the rain in a miserable puddle at his feet.

For a reason Elliot couldn't know, she looked up. With her gloved hands still buried in earth to the wrist, she turned golden eyes and freckles and her unmasked face toward him. As if she'd felt his eyes had settled upon her.

"I didn't mean to disturb you . . . But I had to share something that couldn't wait. And the door was open."

Wren rocked back on her heels, sitting up.

"I know it was." She pursed her lips. "I asked Irina to leave it that way from now on. Just in case. So you could walk through the library the next time, and if you want, every time after that."

"How could I have missed something like this?" He shook his head. "I didn't know it was here. The brick wall and the trees outside cover it completely."

"You're not supposed to know. No one is. It's one of the reasons I chose this estate house—because it could give me solace in a place no one would even know existed. Here, we're safe."

"But it's connected to the library. You keep your treasure that close to where every guest is put when they come into this house?"

"Few people come to this house, Elliot." She nodded, a smile easing over her lips. "But it's an old trick of the trade: secrets are best hidden in plain sight. Every illusionist worth their salt knows that."

The rain continued its dance, dotting the walls with the longing of a spring song around them. She glanced at the teary glass. "You got caught in some rain, I see."

He cleared his throat. "Yes. It's raining just as much as it has all week. Who knows when it will stop."

It seemed appropriate to remove his hat so he did, then turned it in his hands. He hadn't the slightest clue what to say. How to act. Even how to approach her.

Wren removed her gloves and brushed any bits of soil from her palms to the apron that covered her blouse and trousers. She paused, as if wavering over some thought, then inhaled and left the gloves on a glass tabletop nearby. Then, with marked intention, she stopped in the center of the room.

They were untangling a web of deception and death in Stapleton's case. Now wasn't the time to form an attachment. But all was forgotten, somehow pushed out in the rush of just seeing her again.

It had been too many long days since he'd brought her home from the visit with Charlotte. They'd barely spoken on the drive back to Beacon Hill. And he'd fallen into work for days thereafter, trying to avoid thoughts of her since. Trying to reconcile that their worlds were too different. His was based on justice. And hers, no matter how willing to change, was still too dark to ever welcome him fully.

If Stapleton went to trial, she'd be called as a potential witness. And if he was convicted, Wren's connection to the world of magic would no doubt ensure a black mark was placed upon her. If that happened, he knew what came next: she'd run.

She'd turn back, drawing within, locking all the doors in her life. Pulling away from the world.

Pulling away from *him*.

Was he really poised to fall for someone who was a breath away from running at all times?

Wren brushed a lock of hair back from her brow, eyes searching his face. "Well, what did you think?" Vulnerable and sweet, she added, "That the door would remain closed forever?"

He shook his head. "I didn't know it opened to anything like this."

"Yes, well." She looked off into the distance. "The Castleton closed this week. Did I tell you that?"

"No. You didn't."

"It was our family's old theater. I know it's right—the building should have been condemned ages ago. But I suppose I just wasn't ready to say good-bye . . ." She traced her finger along the edge of the tabletop. "I am now. And I think it's because of you. I couldn't shut you out any longer. Not after you met Charlotte. She's all of me, you see: a mixture of the old Jenny and the new Wren. I want to tell you the truth of who I am. If you're here to listen."

To get further involved was irresponsible, wasn't it?

Standing so close to her—even from across the glass room—he wasn't sure anymore.

"Wren, I . . ."

Elliot saw how futile it was then, and his mind lost out.

If she was going to run, so be it. But it was going to be straight into his arms.

He dropped his hat and allowed the leather briefcase strap to slip from his shoulder and slam against the brick floor beneath them.

Any hesitation faded and he charged forward. Giving in.

Arms enfolding. Heart slamming and will crumbling, and kissed her. With every single breath he could possibly lay claim to.

Wren melted in his arms, without breathing, it seemed. She threaded her fingers through the hair at his nape and held on like the world was about to collapse around them, fragile as the glass walls standing up against a storm.

After so many days without her smile, to see it again had him forget anything but her. The fragrance of flowers clinging to her hair . . . the sweet taste of her lips . . . the hint of tomorrow all around them. And while it nearly killed him, he finally broke away for air, staring back, forehead grazing hers. Searching the freckled and lovely face that looked on him.

She was Wren Lockhart—the woman ardently against any form of entanglement. But wasn't she also Jenny, the woman whose entire world was entangled with his at the moment? The one who read fairy stories to her sister, treating her with gentle hands and honeyed words? The illusionist who talked of beauty and worth from a humble stage? The woman whose air was of mystery, unless she chose to open her world and heart to someone else—like she'd done with him?

It seemed a certainty that falling for her could end badly for both of them.

Elliot edged back, trying desperately to save himself.

It wasn't the Wren everyone knew that he was in danger of now. It was the woman behind the mask that held him captive, the one with the past and the unconventionality that softened, it seemed, only for him.

The one who had the power to destroy any fresh stirring of life in him now.

I'm sorry were the first unfortunate and half-witted words to come to mind. And he'd actually let them slip from his lips.

"Don't be sorry. I told you—I left the door open. I wanted you to walk through it." She leaned up on the tips of her toes again, her lips inches away, not fazed by his doltish reply in the least. Her fingertips slid down, winding under the lapels of his coat. Her eyes continued searching his face.

"I knew you had to work, but that you'd come back to me." She pressed her lips at the corner of his mouth.

"Wren, I see where I'm standing right now, and I don't take this lightly," he said, feeling too inept for words.

"I know. But it was time." She looked around, as if introducing him to the most secret part of her heart—the blooms and life growing strong and bold from every corner. "You've seen the war room out there. And I wanted you to see this instead. Here. It's my peace. And you know the real me behind it."

"You don't know everything, Wren. There's too much to say and I can't think . . ."

"The thinker is without thought? However did I manage to cause that?"

He hesitated, the reality of seeing Jenny Charles, and not Wren Lockhart, too much for his heart to handle. "I meant, we need to talk."

"Talk . . . Okay then." A few small words and she was wounded that quickly. "We can start with the case first—if that's easier for you."

Elliot stepped back to his bag, knelt, and opened it. The papers inside were mostly dry—only the edges had absorbed enough water to ripple the paper. He reached for the sheet on top, then stood and walked over to her.

"What's this?" She wrinkled her brow.

"Read it."

Wren grasped the paper in gentle fingertips, then flipped the sheet up in front of her eyes, scanning the words on the typed page as Elliot recited them in his mind. *". . . an effect on the peripheral nervous system consistent with toxicity—not of foxglove, but of the Batrachotoxin-R family, resulting in cardio toxic effects similar to digoxin toxicity and acute cardiac arrest."*

She looked up, her eyes wide. "What do these notes mean? That Victor Peale was poisoned?"

"It looks that way."

"You're sure it's this drug—Batrachotoxin-R?"

Elliot nodded. Just once. "The toxicology report was sent to Alexander Gettler, a renowned toxicologist in New York. And though the original report named the foxglove plant as the probable culprit, there were some inconsistencies. The effects on Peale's body were similar to the foxglove—arrhythmia, cardiac arrest—but we were at a loss because there wasn't a trace of it in his system. So Gettler's office researched the case, and after examining the evidence, he found it. A drug of that kind is rare and more than potent. There's no antidote, so once it's administered, that's it. Which means Victor Peale's death was no accident. And now we have conclusive proof."

He gazed down at her as a pained look washed clean over the lovely lines of her face. "I've shocked you."

"No . . . But I—"

She lost her breath. He knew why.

It was one thing to suspect foul play, but it was quite another to have proof of cold-blooded murder. Elliot hated that it could become commonplace in his line of work, but Wren wasn't used to such blunt matters of life and death. Whether Stapleton was the culprit or not, it could change things once the truth behind a case began to unravel. He'd seen it before, the lengths a man could go to dispose of another human life.

She didn't look to be dealing with it very well. Her skin had gone pale and her hand trembled slightly as she handed the paper back.

"But if this drug was in Victor Peale's system, as you say, and he was in fact dead when the doctor examined him, how was he able to stand and walk out on that stage? Did the examiner give his opinion on that?"

"A drug was administered, he believes, to slow Victor's heart. To give him the appearance of having been dead already. He's concluded it was a rush of adrenaline that awakened Peale in that coffin. It was enough to give him the ability to walk out on that stage, but not enough to overcome the effects of the first drug, which ultimately proved fatal."

"The doctor gave him a dose of adrenaline while he was in the coffin? Surely not."

He shook his head. There was only one person who'd been within close enough proximity to administer the drug on that stage. And she wasn't talking—yet.

"Not the doctor, Wren."

"Amberley." Wren drew in a deep breath. "You're sure."

"Yes. She had the opportunity. Now we just need to know the motive behind it."

"You said the drug is rare. If that's true, then you should be able to determine who would have access to it and find out who's responsible from there. If that's the case, Amberley would have left a trail leading right to her."

"That's what we're looking at now. But as I said, it's quite rare. Not seen much here in the States." He glanced through the open door. "Do you have any botany books in your library?"

She nodded, the magic of the moment that had passed

between them long shattered by the foreboding talk of death. "Yes. This way."

Wren led him to the library and flipped on the table lamp before she turned to the bookshelf. He watched her, wishing for the life of him that he could read her thoughts now.

She ran her index finger over the spines of several books. Scanning the shelves for the right title. He noted the way she flowed through the sections of shelved books.

"I thought the library was just for show."

She shrugged it off, still searching through her books. "It is. Except for these—the books. They've always been mine." Wren hooked a finger over the spine of a thick book and drew it down into her hand. "And it's not a plant-borne toxin. You'll find it comes from a bird. I believe this book will have what you need."

"*Islands of the South Pacific?*" Elliot read the title on the spine, then stared back at her. "How did you know?"

Wren turned away, running her fingers over another spine, one blue and worn, lovely and familiar. She pulled the book down from the shelf and lovingly ran her hand over the cover.

"Wren, how did you know where that toxin came from? I didn't tell you."

He asked a second time, but she didn't answer. Just hugged the book to her chest as she approached him. She slipped *The Welsh Fairy Book* on top of the botany volume in his hands, then eased up on the tip of her toes and pressed a soft kiss to his cheek.

Tears were building in her eyes as she said, "This is for you. In case you should need some reading later."

"But this is your book. Yours and Charlotte's. Why would you give it to me?"

Wren smiled, tears falling from her lashes. "I want you to

have it. And no matter what happens, I need to know that there's someone who will look after Charlotte. That someone will tell her stories, so she'll know there cannot be dark without the light that will overcome it. Whatever darkness there is, God's light shines brighter. It has to. He's the Hero in every story—especially this one. I'm . . ." Her voice hitched, emotion catching fire. "I'm entrusting her to you."

Elliot discarded the books on the desk, fear hitting him like a lightning strike. He'd never seen Wren cry.

Her reaction shattered him.

He cupped his hands under her elbows, drawing her close. And without care for pretenses or propriety, he stayed there. Close enough to feel the warmth of her breath against his neck. He ran a finger under her eye, catching a tear before it cut a path down her cheek.

"Wren . . . please. God help me, I need you to tell me why you're giving me this. What is it you're holding so close?"

A knock cut through the air between them.

Irina stood in the doorway to the glass house, a look of shock on her face. "Excuse me, Ms. Lockhart, but . . ." She looked at their stance, huddled in the center of the dim room and diverted her eyes. "A call just came in. It's urgent."

Wren was quiet for long seconds, then nodded. She stepped back, spine straight again, voice solid, and said, "Yes. I'll take it. Thank you."

"No. It was for Agent Matthews."

Elliot started, turning toward the doorway. "Me?"

Irina nodded uncomfortably, twisting her hands in front of her. "Yes, sir. It was from the Federal Bureau office. I'm sorry but . . . they say Agent Finnegan's been shot. They don't know if he's still alive."

"What?" He broke away from Wren. "What do you mean they don't know if he's still alive? What happened?"

"It's all they would tell me, sir. Except that you're needed at the Bureau office immediately and you'll be briefed once you get there."

God, please no . . .

Elliot's chest burned with anger.

Not Connor. Not the kid with barely a year at the Bureau and enough gusto for ten field agents. Not on his watch.

He slammed his fist against the desk.

Not again . . .

"Wren, I'm sorry, but I have to go."

"Of course you do. Go," she whispered, mumbling through shock.

"I have to make sure he's okay. I can't—"

"I can't be responsible for anyone else's death" was what he wanted to say but stopped short, clearing his throat of unfettered emotion.

"I'll see to Connor first. We'll have to make arrangements to move Amberley as soon as possible. The cottage isn't safe any longer." He started toward the door. "But please stay here. I can't take the chance that you'll be out on the streets alone, not after all this. I can't handle this if I'm worried about you."

"I promise. We'll stay here."

He nodded. Still blown apart inside but soothed enough to know she wouldn't be caught up in the turn of events. "I will come back, Wren. When I can. And we'll continue this conversation. I just have to—"

"Go. I understand. You're wasting precious time here when Connor needs you." Wren ushered him through to the glass house. She lifted his hat and leather briefcase from the latent trail of raindrops. "Go. Agent Finnegan will have my prayers. You both will."

"I'll get word to you, just as soon as Amberley is settled."

Irina cut in behind them. "It won't do any good, sir. They said Mrs. Dover's gone missing too."

❋

Wren leaned back against the library desk, moments after Elliot had gone.

He'd swept out into the rain, leaving in haste to get to Connor's side. His worry, the pained look upon his face . . . She couldn't possibly forget it. Guilt, it had a pain all its own. One she'd seen reflecting back at her in the mirror for too many years. The weight of it crushed her heart for him. If the worst happened to Connor, God forbid it, Elliot would never forgive himself.

The searing burn of guilt would finish him.

Staring through the doorway to the glass house, Wren watched the melody of the birds' flight.

Why hadn't they tried to escape?

They never did. Not even in her stage show. They flew over balconies. Under theater ceilings. Turning endless circles in cages of glass . . . But the birds never found freedom. They floated from branch to branch, content in their caged world, when if they'd been brave but once, they could have flown out the next time the door had been opened . . .

Why, when freedom was so close, did they cling to their chains?

Wren tore her gaze from the winged creatures, the fight to suppress emotion a losing battle. She let go for a rare moment, allowing herself to weep into her hands.

It had felt too right, the way Elliot had held her.

Kissed her.

How he'd accepted all parts of her without reproach. And now, knowing the part she'd played in one man's death, and if Connor, too, were to meet the same fate . . . It was all too terrible to endure.

Wren inhaled deeply, summoning the courage to cross the room to the apothecary table on the far wall.

The jars' labels were clearly marked. She ran her finger over the glass rim of each one, looking for a specific bottle . . . *pitohui*. Her instincts must have been wrong. There simply had to be an explanation. She'd find the bottle, full and stoppered as it always had been. The apothecary table was a prop, after all. It didn't contain any real substances. She'd find it and by the time Elliot returned, she'd have come to a different conclusion.

Except, the spot lay defiant before her eyes; a clear glass bottle had been slipped in to take the place of the old one.

And her heart sank.

The other bottle and its contents were a mere prop no longer.

They were gone, likely used on Victor Peale weeks before. And the toxicology report Elliot had just shown her proved the truth. That only one other person in the world knew a toxin like that was part of the ruse in Wren's library. Only, it wasn't an illusion this time. The toxin was real—terribly real and potent enough to bring death without turning back.

A split second of horror gripped her, and Wren shuddered.

She turned, thinking to dash back into the glass house for her walking stick before she confronted Irina, but a hard blow struck her in the side of the head, halting her steps.

Wren tumbled down hard, until she was crawling on all fours.

A wave of nausea threatened to make her wretch as her vision blurred, swirling the colors of the rug into shapeless forms. As she collapsed there, the last thing she expected to see was the face of her friend, her green eyes intense and unapologetic, holding the bloodied hilt of a sword she'd stripped down from the library wall.

Wren reached out toward Irina, her arm lifeless and heavy as it fell back down in a *thud* against the floor. A warm trail dripped down the side of her face, running over the bridge of her nose. She wiped at it, blood mixed with tears, darkening her palm.

And a black sleep became her friend.

CHAPTER 20

MARCH 6, 1927

BOSTON CITY HOSPITAL

745 MASSACHUSETTS AVENUE

BOSTON, MASS.

Elliot hadn't been to a hospital for what felt like ages, though his aunt had only passed the year before. But he walked through sterile halls, dodging uniformed nurses and patrons in the halls for the second time in twenty-four hours. It was supposed to be a place that made the sick well again. Yet he found his stomach twisting in knots over the hope that Connor had turned a corner and was finally awake.

Elliot nodded to the officer on duty outside the hospital room door and slipped in. Connor's eyelids fluttered at the sound of the creaking door, and he opened them. His face faded into a sleepy smile.

"You look tired." It was no surprise Connor's voice sounded like raked-over gravel. He winced, pain hitching him when he tried to talk.

Elliot hadn't even known he'd held his breath until that moment. He exhaled, relief washing over him at the sight of his partner, not in a morgue, but alive and talking, even if he was broken and bruised in a hospital bed.

"Under the circumstances, I think that's what I'm supposed to say to you."

"And I'm supposed to reply that I feel like death and probably look close to it."

Connor must have felt well enough if he could toss out quips at the drop of a hat. That at least was something to be grateful for. He readjusted against the pillows at his back and patted a heavily bandaged thigh. "Guess I won't be chasing any rumrunners down for a while—leastwise, not on foot. Maybe the Bureau has an equine unit I can look into."

"I think we'll get you a nice, quiet desk job after all this."

"You can leave right now if you start talking rubbish like that. A man can only take so much."

"Well, no one's going to ask you to run anywhere right now." Elliot slid a chair up beside the bed. "How are you feeling?"

"Like a good hangover times ten." Connor tried to shake his head and grimaced against the bandages compressed to the side of his collarbone. "But don't go all partner on me. It's just a scratch. I'll be out of here tomorrow and back on the job by the end of the week. And we'll finish this case like men."

"It didn't look like a scratch when I first saw you last night. And the doctors seemed to think it was serious enough that they transferred you to a larger hospital in the city."

"So it's a scratch in two places," he grumbled. "Forget it. I don't want to talk about me right now. Tell me you've got good news or get out of here until you do."

Elliot hesitated.

Of course Connor wanted to appear strong as an ox, though he was likely as worried as Elliot was. Those involved in the case seemed to be dropping like flies. It was the unspoken concern permeating the room, for sure—Amberley was still out there somewhere. Trouble was, Wren was too, and Elliot still didn't know what to make of it all.

"I was going to wait to tell you, but since you're awake . . ."

Despite his wounds, Connor sat up a little straighter. "Amberley?"

Elliot shook his head. "She's missing. We've got agents out looking, but I'm sorry. There's nothing so far. I'd be lying if I said I wasn't on edge for a new reason now too." His heart felt a stab just to say it out loud. "Wren's unaccounted for."

"Unaccounted for? Is that a nice way of saying she's been pinched too?"

"I stopped by the estate house this morning, and it was locked up tight. No sign of her. Her car wasn't in the carriage house. It's set me to worry, though. I went to the Bijou, thinking she may have been preparing for a show. But no one's heard anything. I was in the theater district so I stopped over at the Castleton, out of distraction more than anything. But it's closed, just as she said. Boarded up from the outside. I don't know what to make of it. It's as if she just faded into the night."

Connor tore his gaze away to stare at a blank spot somewhere out the window on the far wall. "It doesn't mean anything concrete. Wren knows her own mind. Who's to say she didn't step out for something? A new lead, perhaps? Or maybe it's as common as posting letters or going for a dress fitting."

"Wren doesn't wear dresses," Elliot shot back, frustration growing.

"You know what I meant."

"She wouldn't have gone out, Connor. Not for errands and certainly not for something as unnecessary as building her wardrobe. I asked her to stay put. She promised me she would."

"But did you see anything out of the ordinary? Broken glass? Door ajar? Anything like that?"

"I looked, but no."

"If nothing's amiss, she's fine—which is a darn sight better than Amberley's situation at present. If something had happened to Wren, there'd have been evidence. Like at the cottage. Was there . . . ?" Connor coughed for a moment, then cleared his throat. "Was there blood in Amberley's room?"

"No. Just in the hall where you were shot. But since she's the only one we know for sure is missing, could you tell me what happened?" Elliot leaned forward and dropped his voice, more out of habit than fear that they'd be overheard. "Anything would help. It may lead us to them."

They sat in quiet for several seconds, the ringing of a telephone and muffled voices coloring activity out in the hall.

"That's how it started at the cottage—the sound of glass breaking." Connor cut into the silence with his usually gruff fashion. "We doused the light and I made Amberley hide while I checked it out. I heard footsteps coming up the stairs, gunshots fired, and the lights went out after that—only they were mine this time. That's how fast it happened. If anything happened to Wren, I guarantee you there'd be no time for tidying up a library or a carriage house."

"I have no proof she's been taken, other than the fact that my gut keeps nagging me. We need to know more, so I'm headed to the Bureau now. I've had Josiah Charles brought in for questioning."

Connor gave a gentle nod. "Bold move. If she is missing, you think her father's involved?"

"He's rumored to be a despicable character, and believe me—if what I've read in the old file is true, I'd like to gift him with a fist to the jaw for what he did to his family. I still might at some point. But we have no other option. If I'm to make any connection out of all this, I have to learn everything I can about the hidden parts of Wren's past."

Connor sat back. He nodded again, his face looking too weary for the bit of youth that still clung to him. Half-moons shadowed the undersides of his eyes in purple as he stared across the room. "Then what you're saying is, we're in some serious trouble if we're counting on that man to save our case."

"It's not off base to say so, no." Elliot braced his elbows on the knees, finding clarity in staring at the floor, of all things.

Connor sighed, which was never a good sign. "Prettier than Clara Bow and gutsier than Lon Chaney . . . I think I should have asked that girl to marry me." He turned back, locking gazes with Elliot.

Elliot knew he was serious. Serious and stupid, over a woman who was sure to break his heart.

"What, Amberley? Connor . . . They must have you on a slew of drugs to come up with a statement like that." Elliot chalked it up to temporary insanity. He couldn't think about Connor's lovelorn sighs, not when he had to get back to the jail and question Wren's father as quickly as possible.

"I know what you think, but I'm not beating my gums here for nothing. I know I'm not a big shot like that Dover gent was. I've got nothing to offer her. But you didn't see her when we were in that hallway at the cottage. She wanted to stand up to those lugs. A princess from a parlor wanted to take on a couple of hired guns with her bare hands. I finally got her to stay in that room. I stood on the other side of the door to block anybody coming in. That's the first time I've ever met a dame with that kind of fire. You mean to tell me I should let those heels walk right out the door without even giving it a fair shot?" He shook his head. "I'm not that strong."

"Connor, you're tired. And you've just been through a trauma. You'll be thinking more clearly in a few days. We'll make sure there's a man posted outside the door. In the meantime, you just get some sleep, hmm? I'll send word as soon as we hear anything." Elliot patted Connor's arm and stood to go.

"Sleep isn't going to fix this. Look, if anyone's to blame, you are, for making me chase Amberley all over the city. Now I've got it for her. She's clipped my heart like no other dame has, for better or worse. Although I think right now I'm feeling the worse," he said with the hope of a smile, but it faded almost as quickly. "Wish I could go with you. I hate the thought of missing a potential shootout."

"I know you do. But we've got a bigger problem. You can't race in for a rescue if you don't know where the starting line is."

"Just think like they would. You're smart, Elliot. Put it together and you'll make the right connection. Remember what you told me at the cemetery when all this started? Our job is to notice what other people don't. You do that and you'll find Amberley for me." Connor's eyebrows tipped up, like he could read Elliot's thoughts even while muddleheaded, and knew where they'd lead. "And find Wren for you, I think. But I'd never embarrass you by saying that last part out loud."

Connor's affection for Amberley seemed impulsive, but there was a measure of authenticity rooted in what he'd said.

Elliot's own affections had turned toward Wren in a way he'd never bargained for, which made the stakes that much higher.

Time was short. "I ought to go."

"Just promise me I won't see you back here, unless of course it's to drive me home. We can't have our entire team out for the count." Connor could be serious when he wanted, even if he added a slight half grin on to the end.

"I promise" was all Elliot could manage to say before he left Connor's room. It was one vow he hoped he could keep, for all their sakes.

He wished he could promise that Wren and Amberley would be fine. That he wasn't shaken by their absence. That this was far more to him than closing a case file. There were pasts. And pain. And if Elliot was honest with himself, the hope of a different kind of future than one he'd ever planned.

If he was ever going to get around to telling Wren what any of that meant, he'd have to find her first. Only problem was, he had no idea where to start looking.

CHAPTER 21

APRIL 3, 1907

256 W. NEWTON STREET

BOSTON, MASS.

Olivia woke from pain when she tried to move.

Her cheek was on fire and her eye swollen so she could barely see, though the hardwood floor cooled the side of her face. She slid over to the wall, trying to push herself up to a sitting position, until a sharp pain cut through her chest. It stole her breath and she cried out before she could help it.

She looked down the stairs. *Please don't let Josiah hear me.*

Olivia waited in the hall. Not a sound greeted her—no breath of wind to kiss the windows. No birds chirping outside on the balcony. Not even the creaking and settling of an old house. Just silence. Odd, uninviting silence.

She looked up to the open window at the end of the hall.

Dusk had fallen.

The sky was gray and soon to welcome the night.

Could it have been that long? She'd passed out or been knocked out. And had she lain here all day?

Olivia's thoughts turned to the girls. They'd have been locked in the nursery since morning. With no food. And no indication that she was ever coming back for them. Jenny was responsible—her trusted girl even at six years old. But Charlotte was a young three years old. So innocent. They must have been terrified. It would do no good to frighten them. She'd best clean up quickly, then slip into the nursery with a dinner tray.

She fought to get up, clawing at the flowers on the wallpaper to help her climb. A shriek reverberated down the hall.

"Momma?"

Olivia turned her face toward the cry, tears immediately glazing over her eyes. Her little cherub, Charlotte, at the end of the hall with her auburn hair and tiny shoulders outlined by the dim glow of fading daylight cast behind her. Her bottom lip trembled, and she clung to her doll like a lifeline.

"No, baby. Don't look at me," Olivia cried out, hiding her face.

She didn't know if she was covered in blood or her skin swollen beyond recognition. Either way, Charlotte wouldn't understand. She'd be terrified to see that her mother had turned into a monster.

"Momma!" Charlotte dropped her doll, the china head shattering on the hardwood floor. She padded down the hall in her stockings, reaching for Olivia.

"No! Go back to Jenny. Stay with her where you're safe." She pleaded with her sweet little girl.

Olivia stared up at the ceiling, wishing the wooden vaults would open up, revealing the heavens above. *God, protect my daughters. Shield their precious eyes so they don't know. Don't see . . . Help them not know who their father really is.*

Charlotte swept up to her, tiny fingers and thumbs shaking as they reached out for her face. "Momma," she cried, tears falling unrestrained. She brushed her fingertips over the swollen part of Olivia's eye, then pulled them back, her palms covered in red. "Hurt, Momma."

There was no choice now. Olivia called out, "Jenny? Jenny, come here."

Whether Josiah woke or not, she couldn't stand for her younger daughter's fragile view of the world to be broken. Jenny's had been shattered years before, but at the very least, Olivia had hoped she'd have a new story.

Maybe the book of fairy tales Franklin had given her could be their new start. They were supposed to read it together, to think on gentler things. Good, strong things. Of heroes who rode in on white steeds and slayed dragons. And together, they'd ensure Charlotte never had to know the truth.

But now, all of that looked to have been broken too.

Charlotte wiped her hands on her dress, smearing crimson palm prints on her smocked yellow. She held her trembling hands out, palms to the ceiling, unsure what to make of the mess on her hands.

"Jenny?" she called again, trying to stand. Olivia wrapped an arm around her middle, stuffing down the pain in her ribs when she hoisted Charlotte up on her hip and began to shuffle her back down the hall. She braced a hand against the carved newel post to catch her breath.

"Where do you think you're going?"

Josiah appeared, slinking around the corner with fists braced at his sides. He stood in a swath of light at the bottom of the stairs, leering up at her.

He was dressed in the best trousers he owned, shirt starched and tie perfectly straight. He'd cleaned up well. Maybe sobered up too. Though he'd smoothed himself out to see to the evening performances at the Castleton, Olivia saw nothing suave or gentile about him. Not when she remembered the way his fist had swung down on her, leaving her in ruins on the floor of the hall.

Olivia straightened her stance as much as she could, though the pain tried to convince her she'd not be able to stand for long.

"The girls are hungry, Josiah. I assume they've not had anything to eat."

"I'll see to that. Go to bed. You look unwell."

Instincts kicked in, and Olivia released the newel post to grip Charlotte with both arms, cupping a palm at the back of her nape in a protective manner. "No."

"I don't have time for this, Olivia." He checked his pocket watch. "I won't be late for the next show. Now do as I've said."

If she was ever going to stand firm, it had to be then. Her daughters deserved a better life. And if she had to stand up to the dragon to win it for them, so be it.

Olivia took a careful step backward, ardently shaking her head.

Something flashed in his eyes, though it wasn't the same anger she saw in one of his alcohol-induced rages. No, this spoke of contempt—derision that could bite with a single glance. "Put her down." Josiah took a marked step onto the bottom stair, as if to chase her defiance with merely the suggestion of brutality.

Olivia wrapped her arms tighter around Charlotte's little body. Her little heart was beating like a bird fluttering against her chest. Charlotte looped her arms around Olivia's neck, lacing her fingers in the hair at her nape, and buried her head in the crook of her neck.

"Go, Josiah. Go to your theater." She tried to keep the pleading from her tone. She was shaky but needed to appear calm. Calm and strong enough to stand up to him.

"But it's not my theater, is it? Your family left it to you. And your broken heart left with my brother, didn't it? When he sailed for London, there was nothing left for me."

"We won't stop you. Please, just go."

Josiah slinked up two steps, straightening his waistcoat as if the effort to come after her was making him untidy. "I will not tell you again." His steps surer, every measure of the climb made him more agitated.

"Please." She took a step back. "Just let her go. I'll put Charlotte down if you promise to let her go."

He flitted his gaze to the cracked nursery door at the end of the hall, then returned it to her. "Where is Jenny?"

Olivia didn't know, but she could guess. "She's asleep. She was tired today."

Another step. Another flash of anger at the climb.

Charlotte began to cry, hiccupping quietly against Olivia's ear. It broke Olivia's heart, what was left unshattered up to that moment. She swept her fingertips over her shoulder, bracing Charlotte in a protective hold.

"Hush, now," she whispered, staring at Josiah as she pressed a kiss to her temple.

"This is your last chance, Olivia."

He took another few steps.

Faster.

His footfalls pounded, his temper too far gone to back down.

Emotion threatened to close off her throat. She couldn't speak. Could barely see out of her swollen eye. And all she could feel were the cries of her daughter, racking her little chest.

Olivia's body refused to feel pain at the moment. Her entire body, from fingertips to feet, tremored as he walked closer. She backed up another step. And another. Until the wall was at her back. There was nowhere left to run.

His strength was too much—it always had been. And there was no more time for words.

Josiah reached out with rough hands, gripping Charlotte by the arm and ankle on one side, aimed at ripping her free.

Her little hands tangled in Olivia's hair, grasping as she cried out.

"No!" Olivia screamed, tightening her arms around Charlotte's middle, holding on as if they were about to tumble over the edge of a cliff.

Dragons are all show... She battled with Josiah for Charlotte's weightless little body. *They posture and breathe bloody fire, but they can never stand up to a true hero.*

Olivia had given up her future to marry a man she might have loved but ultimately couldn't, because he stamped out any spark of it before it caught aflame. She pledged to fight for her daughters, stepping in front of the dragon each time he roared, acting as a shield between them. But now, the moment had arrived. And her girls would hide away no more. Either she was going to stand up to Josiah or she never would.

She swung her arm back and connected her bloodied fist with the underside of his chin with a primal cry, *"No!"*

His head snapped back, the clip having hit its mark.

Whether it hurt, she couldn't guess. Her puny punches were nothing compared to his. But it was enough to make him stumble back a few steps, shock branding his face. And then, as if a storm cloud had swept over them, the hall darkened and rage like she'd never seen consumed him.

The Josiah she'd known for the past six years was gone. In his place, the shell of a man with vengeance seething from his heart. His hands, rough and calloused, wrapped around Charlotte's body and yanked.

"Charlotte!" Olivia reared back, Charlotte falling from her grasp with such force that she reeled to the top of the stairway. And with one slip, Olivia's foot catapulted her from the top step.

Suddenly Jenny was there. Sleepy and rubbing her palms to her eyes. She screamed out for her momma as Olivia flew down the mountain of stairs without wings.

Falling had never been the fear.

Not even death.

Olivia welcomed it then, the peace that came from closing her eyes and knowing in an instant she'd be gone. The fairy-tale world she'd tried to create for her daughters would be broken.

The dragon had won—the heroine was finally felled.

�֎

Wren awoke to the odor of musty carpet pressed against the side of her face.

Cool water dripped and ran down the bridge of her nose, stirring her. She licked her lips, dried blood cracking at the corners of her mouth.

"Oh, thank the Almighty," came a breathless voice hovering over her. "You're alive."

Wren cracked her eyelids, silently praying that they wouldn't show her what she feared. Amberley looked down on her with worried eyes, her stringy hair hanging lifeless about her shoulders. She held out a cloth that had been soaked in water.

Wren tried to take it, but her wrists were bound behind her back, with rope so tight it burned into her skin.

"I was trying to wipe some of that off for you." Amberley reached out to bathe the side of Wren's head. "They didn't use handcuffs, I'm afraid. They thought you'd know how to get out of them. And there was no use in me trying to free you. The ropes are too tight."

Wren closed her eyes against the pounding in her head. "I cannot possibly look worse than I feel right now."

"When you didn't wake, I started to worry. Thank God you're alive."

She was right; they were alive. But this time it was a darn sight worse that sitting in a Bureau interrogation room battling with each other's wits. Their present circumstances could prove far more deadly.

Amberley looked terrified, but at least she was holding herself together. Her gaze kept flitting across the room to a closed wooden door, as if she were waiting for something evil to walk through it.

Wren eased to a kneeling position and took in their surroundings. Tiny beams of sunlight cut through cracks in the plank ceiling overhead, indicating it was daytime somewhere beyond their room. But there were no windows, and a single door was tucked back in the shadows.

Worn clapboard walls and threadbare carpet of red paisley surrounded them on all sides. Painted letters cried out from the wall above their heads, but the once-red paint faded to a shadow of broken words. A haphazard mound of dusty old chairs heaped high behind them, marking the only furnishings. Dirt, rodent excrement, and rolls of water-damaged paper were piled in the far corners of the room.

"I have no idea where we are," Amberley said as if trying to sound brave, though her voice nearly cracked. "They kept me blindfolded. It was night anyway, so I couldn't have seen much had I wanted to. I tried to listen, though, to see if something sounded familiar when they brought me in."

Given what Elliot had surmised about the possibility Amberley was involved in Victor Peale's death, Wren wasn't ready to trust her entirely. But she wouldn't need to in this case. Wren could have walked the walls blindfolded, for all around her were the worn and wooden bones of her memories. And in seeing this particular room again, her heart began to bleed from the inside out.

"We're at the Castleton."

"What? No." Amberley shook her head. "I used to work at that run-down vaudeville hamlet. I'd know if there was a room like this one backstage. I've never seen this place before."

Wren sighed. The carpet. The rolls of show posters discarded in the corner. Even the chairs—once gold but now dingy and forgotten . . . They all cried out from her memory, of the early days when her uncle had told her about the hidden door under the stage. She'd gone exploring in the back halls, discovering the shrouded corners of her family's old entertainment world.

"You were a dancer. That's why you wouldn't know this room. Only illusionists ever used this space. Illusionists, their stage assistants, or the owners."

"But . . ."

"We're under the stage, Amberley. Any illusionist with a disappearing act would have known of it. There's a square cutout in the planks above our heads. It's hidden, so they could drop down from the stage. The door at the back leads to a hallway behind the VIP rooms. There's another hidden door behind the stage curtain. After I came home and worked with Houdini's show, my father refused to hire another illusionist. So this just became a lost storage area. Shut up and forgotten." Wren tilted her head toward the lettering on the back wall. "See that? Old banners for the shows. They were used long before a marquee was outside. That one was for my uncle's act."

"Your uncle's?" Amberley squinted, trying to read what was left of it.

"It doesn't matter now. We have to find a way out of here. If I can get out of these ropes, then I can come up with a plan. No one knows the Castleton like I do—even in the dark. Maybe we could stack the chairs . . . climb up through the trapdoor to the stage . . . That is, if it's not bolted from the outside, but it might be too high. We may have to pick the lock on the door."

Working it out aloud triggered a reminder.

Wren lifted her wrists until the rope connected to her ankles went taut. "Amberley, can you see gold cuff links? There, on my shirt?"

Please, God . . . Let Irina have overlooked them.

Amberley ran her hand over Wren's wrist. Wren twisted her upper body to lock gazes with her. "Well?"

Amberley's face broke into a smile of pure disbelief. "So that's how you did it." She shook her head. "You scheming little minx. I knew there had to be something you had onstage at my party. I just couldn't work it out. Imagine that—these cuff links were all it took to humiliate me."

"What does it matter now? We need to work together to get out of here." She leaned her back closer to Amberley so she could unfasten the cuff link from her sleeve. "Just get them off, please. The left one has a metal file affixed to the end. See it? We can saw through the ropes. I have a pick we could try to use in the lock on the door."

"That would do no good." Amberley tugged at her wrists. "I heard someone moving around out there."

Wren grimaced through the shot of pain when the action tugged at her shoulder, though only because she thought Amberley wouldn't see it.

"I'm sorry. I forgot," Amberley whispered.

Wren exhaled through the dull reminder of pain. "It's alright. But, Amberley, I must ask you something—" She froze, cutting her words off because of the sound of something—footsteps?— moving across the floorboards above their heads.

Dust rained down like flour on air. They just sat together, neither able to breathe, Amberley's hands sweaty and gripping Wren's, waiting to learn if their captors meant to break in on their fledgling escape plan.

The footsteps died away seconds later, and the hold of Amberley's nails to Wren's palm eased. She worked at the ropes silently after that, the two of them hoping to make a getaway before anyone knew Wren was awake.

"Did you hear about Connor?" Amberley whispered, so softly while she worked.

Wren nodded. Just once, and clamped her eyes shut.

She couldn't think about Connor right then, shot and possibly bleeding out somewhere. The image was too terrible to entertain. Heaven help her if the same guns came after Elliot too. He didn't know she'd been plucked up either, and if he came looking, he might not come to the conclusion that Irina was involved. That put him at as much risk as the rest of them.

"Is he . . . alive?"

"I don't know. I heard about it and then all of this happened."

"Connor stood outside in the hall, blocking my door. Men broke into the cottage and he refused to let them pass. He . . ."

Wren could hear sobs backing up in Amberley's throat, her hands trembling with them. "I heard footsteps and gunfire . . . and then I heard something slump against the door and everything went quiet.

"I tried the window, but the sill had been painted shut. And I'd have broken the glass, but it would have been too high to jump without killing myself. So I broke the porcelain wash basin on the side of the bureau and backed into the wardrobe with the shards in my hand."

The pain in Amberley's voice was too raw to ignore.

"I don't believe it's your fault, what happened. Connor was doing his job. Blame the people who did this to him."

"But I should have fought harder. I was no match for them. I'm not strong like you. I fell apart and they just dragged me out. They dragged me over him, Wren. Just lying there in his own blood. And I tried to grab hold . . . to take him with us . . . I scratched one of them with everything I had in me, and I screamed for Connor all the way down the stairs. And we just left him there." Amberley stopped filing and wept quietly, the action tugging at Wren's heart.

Perhaps there was more to Amberley's misguided attachment to Connor after all. It could have been fear talking. Or shock. But Amberley seemed genuinely crushed by Connor having been hurt solely to protect her.

"Amberley, I have to believe we'll see him again," she whispered. "Look at me."

Amberley opened her eyes, blinking through the dim light.

"If there was no darkness, there would be no opportunity for light to overcome it. This is the time for heroes to rise, okay? And Connor was your hero last night. So if you promise me you'll calm down, we can do what we need to in order to get out of here, and I'll take you to him first thing. If there's anything you need to tell him, you can do it yourself. But you have to work with me, okay? Just keep cutting the ropes."

Once she felt the pressure of sawing at her wrists, she continued. "Now, what about the grounds keeper and his wife at the cottage? Are they okay? Surely they heard what happened if you were screaming."

"Connor had sent them away, for their own safety."

"Then at the very least they won't have been harmed. But what else? Were any other agents at the house?"

She shook her head. "Connor didn't think it was safe to let anyone know where we were—even fellow agents. After what happened to you and Elliot after my party that night, he seemed to suspect everyone."

"How many gunmen were there?"

"Two that I know of. But I've never seen either before."

"Okay. So we have at least two hired men, maybe more. What else?" Wren strained to listen to any sound that might drift down through the wood panels.

"I've seen Irina, but only when they brought you in. I don't know who else is out there, but I did hear her talking."

"With whom?"

Amberley shifted her kneeling position, like her legs were falling asleep. She moved over Wren's right shoulder and went to work sawing at the ropes again. "I heard her and another man. They were speaking French."

Wren did a double take. "French?"

Amberley scoffed behind her, keeping her voice to a rough whisper. "I'm sure they thought some former chorus girl turned wealthy widow couldn't have any education. Well, being married to Stanley Dover was no cakewalk, you know. He was always traveling for business. And I got bored, so I hired tutors to help me acclimate into society. That included art instruction, music, and the ever-dreaded French lessons."

"So you know what they said?"

She hesitated, then eked out, "Yes."

"Well?"

"*Si elle ne parle pas, alors nous la tuer.* It means—"

"I know what it means." Wren exhaled low.

If she doesn't talk, we'll kill her . . .

The ropes gave then and Wren let out a sigh of relief, reveling in the feel of freedom at the wrists. She gingerly pulled her left arm forward, the wound on her shoulder more tender after being so tightly restrained. She turned her wrists in circles, feeling the burn of raw skin that seared from where the ropes had been.

Never mind that. She could think about pain tomorrow.

Wren held out her hand. "The file?"

Amberley handed it over and Wren went to work, starting on the mass of ropes binding her ankles.

"What are we going to do, Wren? If they want me to spill about Stapleton, I won't have anything new to give them. They already know everything I do."

Wren paused, looking up to confront Amberley. "And that's what I was going to ask you. What you know. Because it must be something, or else they wouldn't have gone to the trouble to abduct you and bring you here. The only way I can get us out of here is if you tell me right now what you're holding back— immunity or not."

Was it guilt or just plain surrender that caused Amberley to shake her head? "It was the adrenaline. You know, the second shot Victor Peale was given? Elliot must have figured it out by now. He'd have told you that's what happened."

Wren was angry with herself for trusting Amberley Dover any measure at all.

She continued filing the ropes. "I knew it."

"But I didn't do anything!" Amberley gripped Wren's wrist. "I'll swear to it in court if have to. Stapleton was trying to blackmail me because of my late-husband's debts. He paid me to administer the shot. But I swear I didn't touch Victor Peale. You know that because you had to have seen me. When it came down to it on that stage, I couldn't believe it was all actually happening and I stepped back. One of the gravediggers must have done it or Stapleton himself, because it sure wasn't me."

Wren eyed her, the force of her frustration at the boiling point.

"I know you're angry. I am, too, for what happened to Connor. All I can say is that I was scared. I admit it. And very much alone. I couldn't tell the FBI what I knew and risk being pulled into Stapleton's case. And I couldn't tell anyone that someone was threatening me, because I was scared of whoever killed Victor Peale. But this?" Her shoulders slumped. "I don't know what I could've possibly told Irina that would have her say something like that, in French or in English."

"They weren't talking about you, Amberley. They were talking about me."

"You? Why?" Incredulous, Amberley stared back.

"I already know what they want."

"Which is . . . ?" Amberley began, her voice tight. "Look, you said we're in this together. If that's true and if Connor—" Her words hitched for a split second. "If he took a bullet for me, then at the very least, I deserve to know what it was for."

"You're in no position to make any demands when you've been holding out on us until you get your signed immunity deal."

Amberley shook her head in a glimmer of shame. "I don't know anything, Wren. I was just playing a hand."

If they weren't facing possible death at the hands of unknown captors, Wren might have strangled her. "Playing a hand?" She stopped filing the rope and gripped Amberley's wrist. "You are playing with people's lives, Amberley! This isn't some petty game. Don't you understand that?"

"Of course I do—now. But I'm in trouble too. Stanley had amassed gambling debts all over the city. Several to some underworld characters who want it all back—with exorbitant interest. It will take nearly every penny I have just to pay them off. It was only for the money that I agreed to anything. I knew that wheedly little Stapleton from ages ago just like you, when we were all on the vaudeville circuit. He telephoned with the idea and I figured it couldn't hurt, as he was more than willing to reimburse me for the use of my name and association in the papers. I had no idea when I went up on that stage that he'd set his sights on murder, the miserable little troll." She kicked at a stray bit of rope near her shoe. "I hope he's rotting in that jail cell."

"Then it really wasn't you who gave Victor Peale the toxin before the show or the shot of adrenaline in the coffin?"

The shock that washed over Amberley's face was so authentic, Wren was sure she couldn't have made it up. "You mean you didn't know about the toxin?"

"I swear it." She shook her head, locks of hair dancing over her shoulder.

"Alright. Enough about Stapleton for right now. But you mean to tell me that's what your meeting was about at the Union Oyster House? Your husband's debts?"

"Well, now they're mine, but yes. They want to collect."

It all made sense. Amberley hadn't been running from

Stapleton. She'd been running from people for the oldest reason in the book—money. And thinking it was the only card she had left to play, she feigned possession of more information than she had in order to protect herself.

Wren sighed. Typical Amberley.

"What were you going to do when Elliot got a judge to agree to give you immunity? He'd have figured out pretty quickly that you were a lying snake."

"I'll ignore that last comment, but yes—my lawyers have been delaying the process. They said they could bury it in the courts another few months at least. And the last thing I would do was let someone pin something on me, so I wanted protection from the beginning."

"And in the meantime, you left Elliot holding the bag."

"Look. I dislike this horrible mess as much as you do, but whatever I might have said to Agent Matthews doesn't matter now. You said they came after you. But I don't know why I'm here. That's the honest truth. The fact that anyone other than a loan shark would come after me is more than a surprise." She shrugged. "Everyone likes me."

"I'll try not to give us away by outright laughing at that." Wren rolled her eyes. "But it's me they want. Or rather, what I know about Harry. I'm sure of it."

"Harry Houdini?" Amberley rocked back on her heels. "Then it's true? You know how he managed his illusions?"

Wren kept filing away at the ropes, the final strand becoming more threadbare as the seconds ticked by.

"Well, I'll take that as a yes since you're not going to answer. But what could they possibly want with some old magic tricks— especially since he's gone?"

"They think they can reveal them to the world, to discredit

his name. Or manufacture their own illusions with his methods. I don't know. Maybe become greater than Houdini was? I can't claim to understand why it would be that important to take a man's life over. If you ask me, I think Horace Stapleton is the fall guy for someone else entirely. And we know now that Irina is involved, we just don't know with whom. The timing, though, so soon after Harry's death, tells me they were interested in resurrecting Horace Stapleton's career when the great Houdini was no longer around to discredit him a second time."

The ropes gave and Wren unfurled them from around her ankles, savoring the ability to stretch her legs in front of her. She slipped the cuff links back on her wrists. It was the safest place to keep them, should she need them later on.

"You trusted her. Irina. She betrayed that trust, and . . . Well, there's nothing else to be said, is there? When trust is shattered . . . it changes you. I suppose you'll finally understand the kind of bitterness I've felt these past years. I should have let go of it. I see that now."

Wren had trusted Irina, yes. As much as anyone, really. But she couldn't think about that betrayal now, nor the years they'd forged a friendship in the back halls of vaudeville. Pain would make her weak, and Wren needed every ounce of strength she had, both in her body and in the confines of her heart.

"Yes, well. Bitterness isn't going to help us out of this mess, so I'd just assume talk about Irina's motivations later." Though a bit shaky, Wren bent her legs under her and wobbled to stand, testing out her weary limbs.

Amberley followed suit, looking around the musty room with her. "So now what?" she whispered.

"We find a way out of here."

CHAPTER 22

Something was wrong.

Elliot's gut kept nagging him, replaying every possible scenario concerning Wren as he hurried through the halls of the Boston Bureau office. Thoughts of her whereabouts inflicted punishing fears as he swept past a sea of people: witnesses, agents on telephones, and secretaries pecking typewriter keys.

She wouldn't just leave . . . not after last night.

Over and over, Elliot told himself there was a logical explanation for her absence, and he vowed to find it. He'd find *her*.

The one man they'd finally picked up and brought into the downtown office that morning ignited a flicker of hope within him. Elliot stilled the rabid beating of his heart as he came to an interrogation room door, opened it on a determined intake of air, and stepped inside.

"Who are you?"

Terse words greeted Elliot, along with pinched features, a tense jaw, and soul-tired eyes of a man who needed no introduction.

Josiah Charles sat, arms crossed over a wretched dirty shirt and suspenders, eager to dislike anyone who'd walked through the door. He could boast some of his daughter's coloring, though what looked to have once been flaming hair had dulled to tufts of ruddy gray over the ears and a beard that was overgrown with salt and pepper. He was missing any spark of kindness that could light his daughters' features.

"I'm Agent Elliot Matthews, with the Federal Bureau of Investigation. And I'd like to thank you for coming in today, Mr. Charles."

He scoffed. "As if I had any choice in the matter."

"I'm sorry about the inconvenience." Elliot clicked the door closed behind him and just stood there, hands buried in his pockets.

Wren was all that mattered, not the posturing of two men on opposite sides of the law.

"What does the federal government want with me?"

"To be blunt, sir, your daughter's whereabouts are presently unknown."

A cough rumbled low in Josiah's throat, as if it had been building up for days. Or years. "Unknown, eh?" he asked, his voice gravelly. "I knew she was working with you badges. I told her to steer clear, to keep to her own affairs and stay out of it, but that girl always has been too headstrong for her own good. Never once listened to a thing I said. How do you boys know she hasn't just skipped town? Wren's done it before."

"Because she left Charlotte behind, sir."

"What does that matter? Wren spent much of her young years in London, away from her sister. So don't pretend she's got a heart all of a sudden."

Elliot shoved the slight away. Wren had a heart. But this man didn't believe it. Certainly couldn't see it. Elliot would have to try another tactic.

"Wren's been working with us for the last several weeks on

a case that involves some persons close to her on the vaudeville circuit. Last night my partner was shot trying to protect one of our witnesses for a case involving a showman by the name of Horace Stapleton. That witness also happens to be one of your former employees—a Mrs. Amberley Dover née Green. She's recently gone missing and we believe, because Wren is also unaccounted for this morning, that their disappearances are linked. It's very unlikely Wren has left town. Or if she has, I'd say she didn't do so willingly."

Josiah eyed him, a half-sober paternal glare easing down his face. As if he knew anything about who his daughter really was and had chosen that moment to be a knowing parent. "What you don't realize is, a day absent in Wren's life doesn't mean anything. She does what she wants. Goes where she wants. And she'll turn up eventually—if she wants to be found. She always does."

"Not this time." Elliot pulled out a wooden chair opposite Josiah and sat, then opened his briefcase. "Her house is shut up. I looked in on the estate house this morning and she's gone, when I specifically asked her to stay put."

"Like I said, don't mean nothing. Not with that girl."

"But you see, it does." Elliot took Wren's book from inside and set it on the desk in front of Josiah. "Because she gave me this right before I left. I didn't know why at the time, but I do now."

As expected, Josiah reacted. Just a slight pinch to the jaw and leaning back in his chair, as if hovering close to the book brought physical discomfort to him. "What's that?"

"I think you know it's Wren's. And I think you know why it's so important to her."

Josiah frowned, a twisted, curvy line of his lips that showed his contempt.

Elliot flipped halfway through the volume. Finding the page

he was looking for, he stopped, then turned the book around so it was right side up to Josiah. "This is Wren's handwriting." He pointed to the words penciled in at the top of the page. "Yes?"

Josiah squinted at the words, weary eyes attempting to focus.

"Her account starts here." Elliot indicated the elegant handwriting covering nearly all the margin space, flipped several pages, and stopped again. "And goes through to the conclusion of that story. Ending right here."

"An account of what?"

"Of the last day of her mother's life, Mr. Charles. A day in which she watched her mother die."

Josiah froze, then slammed the book closed. He pushed it back across the desktop. "I want this on the level. No funny police work or tricky angles." He leveled a firm, though oddly glassy-eyed glare at Elliot. "Do you intend to prosecute me for my wife's death?"

"Should we?"

Josiah leaned in, incensed. "You don't know what you're talking about—"

"No. I don't." He tapped his index finger atop the book. "But *she* does. Wren's words are an indelible eyewitness account of your wife's death."

"From the storied eyes of a child."

Anger flashed in Elliot's mind. He suppressed it, gritting his teeth. "From the guilt of a woman who's blamed herself for two decades. She's recorded it all here. How she watched her sister push her mother down the stairs, and because Wren had fallen asleep that day, she was too late to stop it. I've read the newspaper archives, Mr. Charles. And the old police file. It makes sense now, why you and Wren have worked together all these years. She was protecting Charlotte from possible prosecution because she misinterpreted what she saw. You are correct. This account is from the storied eyes of a child. But you—*you*—let her believe in a lie her entire life!"

The truth of what Wren had been through stung. Her pain was held so close, chaining her to a wound that would never heal. And this man was directly responsible.

It made Elliot sick to look at him.

"Now, Mr. Charles, I have a few questions for you."

Josiah leaned back in his chair, scratching at the scruff on his chin while he calculated in the muddled confines of his drink-soaked mind. "You said I'm not here for prosecution. So what do you want with me?"

"I need to know everything you can tell me about Amberley Dover and Wren's stage manager, Irina. Knowing their association to Harry Houdini and yours to vaudeville, you were the one person I thought could make some useful connection for us."

"I don't know that I can tell you much of anything." He glanced up at the corner of the ceiling, as if his memories had drifted there. "Amberley came to work for me in 1920, after she'd been let go from the Houdini show. By then she'd lost any star power she might have had."

"But you hired her anyway."

"Yes. She was a terrible flirt from the stage, but that drew in the gents enough to fill some seats for a time."

"What did she do?"

Josiah snickered low, as if the answer were obvious. "What do you think? She swished her skirts, of course. What other talent could that cat have except to shimmy around on a stage?"

Elliot's hand drifted to Wren's book before he could stop it, his palm resting on the cover. It felt like a part of her was here somehow, still beside him. The pain raw and her past so near, he wanted to hold it close. To protect it in some way.

"And what about Irina? We can't find anything definitive on her—not even a last name. But I didn't question her at the start because Wren had explicit trust in her. She put me off of it."

"That woman showed up with Wren when she came back to Boston, during the war. All I ever heard was that Wren met her somewhere overseas. Beyond that I didn't care enough to find out." He exhaled on a deep sigh. "That Amberley is a piece of work, though. She didn't take to Wren coming back here at all, especially since she'd made a name for herself, even without Houdini's help. I assume Amberley hated her for being pushed out. But she still doesn't know that Wren came here and demanded I give that rotten little socialite a job."

Elliot did a double take. "What did you just say?"

"You didn't know?" Josiah took a tin from his shirt pocket and opened it. He rolled tobacco in paper as he talked. "The Castleton was going under years ago, long before we closed down. Wren swooped in. Saved it with the money she'd inherited from my dear, departed brother. I hated to do it, but the theater needed the funds. I swore I'd never take a cent from her again and I haven't. She owns the ramshackle building now, she and my Charlotte, though the girl is addle-brained and can't make any decisions for it. It's why I always ran the books.

"Wren said she wouldn't get in the way, except for two things: that Amberley would have a job there for as long as she wanted and that she'd never know the reason why. So my daughters inherited a small fortune from my brother's estate and I inherited a prima-donna dancer with superior airs. Figures. Thankfully, that rich Dover fella came in for a show and liked what he saw—enough that they were married a month later and I was finally free of her."

Elliot leaned forward, resting his elbows at the knees as he sorted through his thoughts.

What was he missing?

Amberley didn't seem the type to have orchestrated Stapleton's show. She wouldn't have had the know-how or, frankly, cared enough to get involved. She was tactical but not trained, unable to give a man a lethal dose of anything. And while she harbored obvious resentment against Wren, she didn't seem the type to do much but attempt public humiliation. At that she'd failed miserably.

His thoughts bounced around, mentally taking him over the last moments he'd shared with Wren in the library. Of her tears and the insistence that he take the book with him . . . Of the time they'd spent backstage at the Bijou and in the sitting room of the seaside cottage. Everything they'd talked about came down to one thing: Wren didn't trust anyone easily, but she'd trusted *him*. She'd given him the book for a reason, and it wasn't until that moment that Elliot finally understood why . . .

"She didn't trust Irina."

"What kind of thing is that to say? Of course she trusted Irina. Worked with her for more than ten years, letting her in the backstage area of every show. You'd have to trust a person to make her your manager—especially as an illusionist."

Wren had said it backstage at the Bijou—even Irina didn't know everything. She didn't know about the cuff links and she certainly didn't know about the book, because no suspicions were raised when Wren handed it off to him right in front of Irina.

"She knew . . ."

"Who knew what?"

"Wren. She had to have known Irina was involved when she gave me the book. She wasn't asking me to look after Charlotte because of a would-be threat. There was one right in the room."

Josiah exhaled, as if the exchange was draining his patience. "Involved in what?"

"She was trying to get me out of the house before she confronted Irina. She was trying to keep me safe, too, at the expense of herself."

When Irina had burst in the library with the news about Connor's shooting and Amberley's disappearance, she couldn't have taken a telephone call. Wren told him herself she'd disconnected the phone weeks prior, because they'd tired of the press calls.

Elliot ran a hand through his hair, regret boiling over. "She was saying good-bye."

Wren had done it for him.

The endearment of it made him want to shake some sense into her for putting herself at risk but still kiss the life out of her at the same time. She'd given him the book and let him walk right out the back door, leaving her alone in the grasp of a monster.

"The toxin used in Victor Peale's death comes from a bird found on the Fiji islands. That's why Wren gave me the book on the South Pacific, because it was familiar to her once I'd given the description. She was trying to tell me that Irina was involved."

"I don't know what that all means, but could it be you're finished with me? I have things to do."

A resurgence of energy claimed Elliot. Irina had to be involved in Peale's death, and she couldn't let Wren walk away from the estate house with that kind of information. She'd keep

Wren close. And she'd have had to make a decision quickly, meaning that she had help. Help that would have taken Wren from the estate house.

Help that had to be right here in Boston.

"... *hidden, in plain sight.*"

Elliot jumped to his feet. "Mr. Charles, where did Wren get this book? Was it a gift from someone—your wife, perhaps? I need to understand why she chose this one. I don't know why, but I think it could lead us to her somehow."

Josiah licked the paper on his cigarette, taking his time about answering. For once, it didn't seem an act of defiance, but he did show evidence that the mention of the book had affected him. Elliot could see long-protected bitterness clawing to the surface.

"Franklin," he grumbled, opening his desk drawer to root around for something. He scattered things in the drawer with his fingertips, creating a minor racket. "My brother. He brought it for her."

"Wren's uncle . . ." Surprise tinged his thoughts. "How old was Wren when she received it?"

"How should I know?" Josiah barked out. "And what does that matter now?"

Elliot reached in his pocket and retrieved his lighter, then flipped the flame to burn before his face. Josiah stopped, leaned into the flame, singeing the end of his cigarette until it caught fire. He took a long draw.

"The thing is, Mr. Agent, my brother always loved those girls. *My* girls. And *my* wife. All because he'd missed his chance. When he finally realized it, he came back from his fancy life across the sea and thought he could swindle them away from me." He pounded his fist on the table. "But I'm a man who keeps what's mine."

"What do you mean, your brother missed his chance? His chance for what?"

"To have a family." Josiah leveled a direct glare at Elliot, his eyes piercing through the curls of smoke rising around the desk.

"But he could have had a family. Why would any of that stop him?"

"Because Wren is his daughter."

CHAPTER 23

It shouldn't have been a great surprise, though hearing the truth confirmed was something altogether different from Elliot relying on instinct. Suddenly dominoes began to fall into place, laying questions flat along with them.

"Does Wren know this?"

"Of course not. I'd never give either of them the satisfaction of telling her the truth about where she's come from."

"But surely Wren deserves—"

"Deserves what? To know that my wife always pined for another man? She tried to hide it but I knew. We were a comedy act together, Franklin and me. In the early days, pratfalls and gags, that sort of nonsense. But some producer of a London show took a liking to Franklin's smile and offered him a contract with a performance company in England. So he broke up the act and away he went to strike his fortune, leaving Olivia behind. By the time he came back, she was already married to me and carrying her first child—by the name of Jenny."

Elliot listened with a guarded ear.

He'd read the newspapers.

He knew of the rumored physical abuse Olivia Charles

suffered, that she'd taken a fall down a flight of stairs and broken her neck one night, but that the fall itself likely wasn't the cause of a swollen eye and bruised ribs already pronounced on her body. No matter what Josiah said, his words couldn't explain that away in Elliot's mind.

He balled a fist under the edge of the desk where Josiah couldn't see. Much more of this and he'd be thrown in jail for letting his own punches fly on an aging drunkard.

Elliot refocused his thoughts, turning back to the front cover so he could open the first page to Josiah. Block letters spelled out WREN LOCKHART.

"Then where did she come up with this? Why would she choose that name in particular?"

"How should I know? The girls had a whole line of trees that grew up from the garden to their second-story bedroom window. Maybe they liked those stupid birds that always flew around, building nests in the eaves that I had to climb up and rip out. Why else would she choose such a silly name?"

Elliot's heart stopped.

The trees . . .

They'd covered every angle of the case, from Victor Peale's book and the scrap of paper with the names, to the pinpoint-precision of the man's wardrobe and the doctor's testimony that Peale was dead before he'd been brought back. Even the ticket stub found on the body had been authenticated and the photo in the paper a perfect likeness for Peale. Every base had been covered—but one.

And now Elliot had a feeling he knew exactly what it was.

He gathered up the book and turned toward the door, rushing through his excuses for leaving in such a whirlwind.

"Wait just a minute." Josiah stood with such force it toppled the aged chair behind him. "I want to know one thing before I let you leave," he demanded, his voice rough. "Why are you really going after Wren?"

"Because she has information that is paramount to this investigation, Mr. Charles. She's also an innocent citizen, and I believe her disappearance is the result of foul play. It would be an injustice if we didn't find her as soon as possible, especially when she could be in grave danger. So the reason I'm going after her is because it's my job to keep her alive."

"No. I'm not asking why you Federal Bureau folk are looking for her. I asked why *you* are. Seems to me there'd be better things for the federal government to do." Josiah took a last draw before extinguishing the end of his cigarette in the overflowing ashtray on the table. "It's more than that, isn't it? You care for my daughter?"

Even if someone had stolen his tongue, Elliot couldn't have said less in that moment.

The last thing he expected was to have a heart-to-heart with a man the likes of Josiah Charles. He stood taller somehow, even for his medium stature, and waited with some pitiful attempt at paternal authority in place. "Well?"

"You've made it quite clear that she's not your daughter, so I'll ignore the audacity of your question. Wren is a grown woman, and I believe the time for parenting is long past." He offered his sincerest words. "I will say that if I love Franklin's daughter, she's going to hear it from me first. And I promise you one thing—I'll make sure no harm comes to her. Wherever she is, I'll find her. So I thank you for your time. You're free to go."

Elliot gave a slight nod for propriety's sake, then stepped through the door and started down the hall.

"She won't marry you! Even if you ask," Josiah tossed out

behind him. "Vaudes are all the same. They never trust any-one enough to love. I'm proof of that. And so was her mother. That girl will end up in an early grave because of it, just like that Houdini fella did. Wren Lockhart is damaged goods."

Elliot froze. Then turned. Slowly.

Fury was quick to rise from his gut, for the little girl who'd watched hatred and abuse perpetrated on someone she loved, right before her eyes. For the innocence Wren had spoken of when they'd visited Charlotte that was stolen by this man right here, dirty and stinking of drink and only half sober as he tossed out righteous indignation.

It took everything in Elliot to keep his fists cemented at his side. But his feet? They moved. They carried him with steps so sure that Josiah Charles actually took a lopsided leap backward, toppling the chair back with a crooked shove with the thought a fist could fly in his direction.

Elliot stopped mere inches away from the man's face, incensed for what he'd put his girls through. Elliot's breath tore in and out of his lungs, teetering on the cliff of letting his anger fly. But all he could think of in that moment was Wren, how beautiful and untainted she'd been when she'd welcomed him in the peace of her glass house.

The vision of her was more powerful than revenge, and he knew she wouldn't want him to do it.

"With all due respect, Mr. Charles, you might be the last per-son on this planet who can speak to me about love. Wren isn't like anyone else. If she trusts enough to love, she'll do it with the whole of her heart—even though you've nearly damaged it beyond repair. So you'll have to excuse me, because I believe I know where she is. Wren needs a hero for once in her life, and I'll do whatever it takes to ensure she finally gets one."

CHAPTER 24

The abandoned halls of the Castleton were black as night.

That Wren remembered from the last time she'd visited. But traversing the halls now, stage-side right without a pinprick of light and only their hands to follow along the walls—it made even the hair on the back of her neck stand to attention. Every sense remained on high alert, as they would be for one walking blind. Listening for every sound. Thinking they could hear footsteps every other breath. Pausing. Not breathing. Praying, and then breathing again. Hearing the possibility of danger in the creaking of the old walls as it fought with a spring breeze outside.

"Are you sure you know where you're going?" Amberley's voice was squeaky, drawn down to the softest whisper she could manage and still be heard.

"Shhh! Of course I do," she answered in a rough whisper of her own.

Wren kept edging her hands along the wall, feeling aged planks that had slight warps to the sides, worn and water-damaged velvet of curtains draped at certain intervals, and open spaces that led to stage-prop areas and doorways to halls greeting more blackness.

Amberley trekked close behind, so close that she plodded a heel to Wren's ankle every few steps. Wren ignored it, biting her lip as she kept moving.

It has to be here somewhere . . .

"Where's that blasted door?" Wren's hand eased over the tell-tale cold grasp of a metal knob and she exhaled. Finally, relief. The door to the VIP-room hall. It was there, hidden in the shadows right where she'd remembered it, as if it had been waiting for her after all those years.

She turned the knob, jiggling lightly. It turned but refused to give. The door was bolted from the inside, as usual. But no matter. It just took a bit of know-how to open without a key. Wren felt for the crack of the door, found it, and slipped her file all the way to the top until it clinked against metal. She applied light pressure, an old hinge squeaking as it lifted the metal bar on the inside.

And there they were, door open, with freedom but a few darted steps away.

There was but one window at the end of the hall, a tall, arched portal of stained glass that was once beautiful and inviting as it looked out over the bustle of Scollay Square. But the glass, too, had been hidden, existing now behind wooden boards nailed up on the outside. There was just enough light to illuminate a door outlined at the far end of the hall, cast in shadows of red and gold, yellow and blue from the stained glass.

Beyond . . . the alley. And freedom.

"Good." The satisfaction was sweet. Wren's skills were useful, if one was locked in an old theater. "Amberley? Come on. We can make a run for it before they even know we're gone."

The blackness seemed even deeper with Amberley's silence.

"Amberley? I said let's go," she whispered, slight and low, desperate to reach out for her in the dark.

"I'm here," she whispered, though her voice sounded too far behind.

Wren turned, darting through the door to the hall. Heart in her throat, she plowed into the wall of a man's chest.

Any gasp she might have let out died in her throat. Instead, the man who'd managed to sneak up on them, and done God knew what to silence Amberley, was about to get the fight of his life.

She reared back, breath nearly lost as she balled her fist and let her knuckles fly. They connected with flesh and bone, blasting her good arm with fiery pain, the bones in her hand jarring. It shot pain down her arm and a dull *thud* against what she hoped was a tender spot on an unsuspecting someone's jaw.

"Wren! What's the matter with you! It's me."

"Elliot?" Her breathing finally rocked her. Taking over. Reminding her that she, too, was flesh and bone and that her will was so much stronger when he was by her side. "What are you doing here?"

A thimble full of dim light flooded in from cracks in the boarded window at the end of the hall, illuminating his features. He had a hand on his jaw, eyes clamped shut, a pinched expression on his face. "The least you could have done was warn me."

"Warn you?" She threw her arms around his neck. "I could kiss you right now!"

He shook his head, cheek brushing against the side of her face. "No. Not when I've just had my bell rung like a telephone box." He still rubbed his jaw. "Where'd you learn to punch like that?"

Senses came back to remind Wren where they were and that time was not on their side. "It's a great story and I'll tell you later. But right now—where's Amberley?"

"I'm here." Her voice drifted from behind Elliot's back.

"Good. Then let's go. There's the door—" She pointed out in the dim light cast from the stained glass. "It leads to the alley. I can take us the rest of the way, behind the buildings until we're a safe distance away."

"I know. I came from the alley. No one's there." He exhaled.

Was he as relieved to see her in one piece as she was to see him?

"Then let's just get out of here. You tell me the rest after we've gotten Amberley to safety."

They'd have to run for the door. Wren would have flown down the hall, leaving the dark, back-halls world of the Castleton behind, if the door hadn't opened on its own, flooding the hall with golden daylight.

Wren felt Elliot's hand ease around her wrist from behind. Softly. With just enough of a touch to let her know he was still there, no matter what came.

Sunlight illuminated the open doorway to the alley—and the forms of Irina, the glint of metal from a cocked pistol, and a young woman with a pink dress and auburn hair.

No . . .

Wren bit her bottom lip or else she'd cry out. Elliot moved his hand down to her palm, lacing fingers with hers, and squeezed.

"Charlotte," she breathed out, her bottom lip trembling.

"Good. You're awake." Irina's voice was calm and hand unwavering as it held the gun on Wren's sister. "And now I have your attention."

She stepped through the door with Charlotte in tow, then slammed the door on their flight to freedom.

CHAPTER 25

To a six-year-old, the sight of her mother falling down a flight of stairs was otherworldly.

But it had happened. In a flash. Before anyone could stop it. And the aftermath was both immediate and bone chilling in its finality. It was as if they all hung on time for a moment as imaginary dust settled, and the cloud of doubt lifted enough that even Jenny could discern what just occurred.

Her mother lay lifeless, a beautifully scarred heroine, her body quiet and still on the hardwood in the entryway. Charlotte had fallen, too, but only a step or two. She clung to the wooden spindles outlining the staircase and cried out in the silence, a single, heartbreaking sob: "Momma?"

Jenny couldn't breathe. Couldn't even think.

She watched as her father ran down the stairs, taking the

steps two at a time. The old wood groaned out in protest as he tore over it, falling to his knees on the ground floor. He shook their mother. First lightly, his hands cautious as he ran them over her forehead and cheeks. Though her weighted feet moved in slow-motion, Jenny slipped her book under one arm and walked to the stairs. She stepped down, one . . . two . . . three steps. And when she was at Charlotte's side, she held out her hand.

Charlotte's hands were fused to the spindles—white-knuckled, as if she were grasping for her own life.

"Come, Charlotte," she said, feeling strength well up inside her. From where? She didn't even know. It just seemed sensible to take her sister away.

As their father pounded fists to the floorboards, crying out with pain, Jenny slipped her hand in her sister's tiny cherub palm and squeezed.

"Come with me," she whispered.

Charlotte trusted her. She nodded, tear tracks still wet upon her face. And together they walked the longest path Jenny could have imagined, from the top of the stairs all the way to the nursery door at the end of the hall.

Jenny closed it, drowning out the pitiful noise of their father's shouts. There was no key to turn in the lock, so she looked to their desk and pushed the yellow-painted chair up under the old brass knob. And as if the night beckoned her, she crossed the room to the double doors and swung them open.

The coolness of evening flooded in, catching up the gauze curtains on a breeze.

The sun had gone to sleep.

Trees were talking with the wind and tiny singsong spurts of birdsong mingled through the waving leaves. It was as if their garden sang through the night, even as pounding continued on the door downstairs and the entry suddenly filled with the sound of footsteps and adult voices.

Somehow, in the midst of death's grip, the call of something beautiful and untainted swept into the nursery room.

Jenny stood on the balcony and listened, hearing their father's wailing from somewhere below, fighting with the soft call of birds in the trees. And she watched, tears peppering her eyes, as a tiny wren dropped out of the treed sky and landed on the stone rail before her.

"Come here, Charlotte," Jenny whispered, for fear the tiny bird was still too wild to trust and a loud voice could cause alarm. It hopped about, bobbing its head. "I want to introduce you to a friend. This is our little wren."

Charlotte wiped her eyes with her rolled fists. "We have a bird?"

Jenny nodded, the flood of emotion finally gripping her heart. "Yes. Come see. We'll talk of lovely things," she whispered, pained. Because of what she saw. Because Charlotte had been at the top of the stairs and their mother was at the bottom. And there was no other explanation than the horrific thought that Charlotte was to blame.

Though she couldn't have known what she'd done, Wren's little sister had shattered both their worlds.

"I'll tell you a fairy story from our book. It's about a princess and a dragon. And a hero who comes to save the day. But you cannot speak of this day again. Understand? Not ever."

"Never?"

Jenny shook her head. "No. All we will say is that we will never push someone again. Do you understand?"

Charlotte nodded. As though she understood at a level

deeper than her mind would allow. This her sister had felt with her heart, for her eyes teared. Her hands trembled, still covered in smeared crimson. "We never push . . ."

"Come." Wren held her hands, ushering her to the wash-basin. "I'll wash them. And we'll talk of lovely things from now on."

The promise of simple things, of fairy-tale worlds and sweet dancing birds beckoned Charlotte from her tears. She came to the window and stepped out on the balcony. "I do like your stories," Charlotte said. And then, with a far softer tone, asked, "Is Momma asleep?"

Jenny leaned down, slipping her arm around her sister's tiny shoulders. "I would like for you to meet our wren. She will always watch over us," she whispered. "Her name is Olivia."

"Agent Matthews, I'll ask you to remove your weapon—slowly, because we don't want our dear Charlotte to be frightened—and slide it over to me."

Without a word, Elliot followed the order, immediately taking the gun from his shoulder holster. He knelt, sliding the gun out on the hardwood floor. It sailed forward, then fell dead with a *thud* against the wall.

Irina stooped to retrieve it, the flash of metal dulled by the dim light of the Castleton's back hall, the sunlight shut out by the closed door behind her. "You can come out now," Irina called, her voice oddly shrill and calm at the same time. "I've stopped them."

Wren stood frozen, watching her entire world crumble. The door closest to Irina opened, and three men stepped into the hall. Two she recognized from a snowy New Year's Eve in Mount Auburn Cemetery—just as she'd suspected, the gravediggers had been hired for the job.

The other, a man who'd hung back behind Irina, finally stepped into the light.

Always one to act without restraint, Amberley let out a shriek. "Al . . . But you're supposed to be dead."

He was thinner now and far more composed than Wren remembered. So unlike the hired hand they'd known in Harry Houdini's show. Gone were the scuffed boots and work shirts with suspenders. They'd been replaced by a genteel air, even if it did seem manufactured. He wore a crisp tailored suit and a top hat, twirled a walking stick in his fingertips, and walked forward to Irina's side in shoes that had been polished to a right shine.

"Al Gruner?" He chuckled. "I haven't heard that name in some time—not since word got out in the papers that I'd died in a farming accident some years back. Right about the time our Amberley here had discarded me as an old stagehand in favor of a neat and tidy life with a railroad tycoon."

Anger swept over Amberley's face and she stepped out, as if to swing a fist at the man. Elliot moved in, holding her back at the elbow. She turned an ankle on the heel of her shoe, blasting out, "You mean to tell me that I've been forced to endure rumors—the blackening of my character—for years, while you were building a vaudeville empire? You have some nerve to come back here now . . ."

Gruner chuckled, ignoring her.

Wren exchanged glances with Elliot. Wishing she could read his mind. Wondering how to think like an agent so they could see a way out of the proper fix they were in.

"I'm glad to see you haven't lost your fire, Amberley. But I've changed a bit since the old days. And you forget—crew members are never photographed and hardly seen even when backstage. Who would remember my face but you? So it's Mr. Albert Moriarty now, of A. M. Theatre Productions. You may know one of our top talents, Mr. Horace Stapleton. Well, that is, he was one of our top talents before our Wren here decided to team up with the late Mr. Houdini and sully our showman's name. I will forgive the slipup since you may not have known of my one-time success as a private investor in certain vaudeville shows across the country. But you decided to ruin that, didn't you, Jenny? It wasn't until Irina came to me with an idea to save my venture that I thought it was time to come back to life—so to speak."

"But Victor Peale—"

"Him? A nobody. Some nameless scamp off the streets. But in searching through photographs of those buried in Mount Auburn Cemetery and with a stroke of luck, we found that he bore a striking resemblance to the real Victor Peale, dead some twenty years." Al scoffed. Had the nerve to laugh over a dead man. "If you promise a starving man the world, you'll find he'll agree to just about anything."

Enough of this. I need to get Charlotte out . . .

She won't understand.

"Whatever it is you want from me, you can have it. Just let them go. This is between us, isn't it, Irina? This is our ten-year courtship with the truth finally come to light."

"And what truth is that?"

"Magic," Wren breathed out. "Do you remember? I asked you once if you would claim the use of magic if you didn't have to."

"And now you know the answer. I believe in magic, but only because I believe in myself more. If the fools in a crowd will toss their coins in my direction because they believe in an illusion, I'll use that and more to convince them of truth."

Charlotte whimpered. "I don't like it here, Jenny," she cried out. "I want to go home, with you."

"It's okay, Charlotte. I'm here." Tears tumbled down Wren's face, unencumbered now, not seen since a day in April more than twenty years before.

Wren stepped forward, drawn from the solidarity of Elliot's strong form by the soft cries of her sister. "It's going to be alright. Just think of Olivia, okay? Think about our winged friend. The memory of our wren will give you strength."

She eased her hands up, taking slow, measured steps, until she was away from both Elliot and Amberley.

"And yet with each step, things become less and less okay." Irina lavished a smile on Charlotte as she pressed the gun's barrel closer to her auburn waves, halting Wren's advance.

"Please. Let them go. It's me you want, isn't it? Well, I'm right here."

"That's where you're wrong. We can't possibly let any of you go. Not Charlotte, because she's our honored guest at the Castleton today. And not Mrs. Dover, because however much she dislikes you, she's guaranteed to dislike us more. We can't have an extra witness around telling tales to juries." Irina lifted her gaze past Wren. "And we certainly can't let you go, can we, Agent Mathews? Because you've already worked all of this out, haven't you?"

Wren could hear her own breathing. It escaped her lungs with force, years of pain and fear billowing up from her insides, forcing strength from her. She looked to Elliot, wishing she knew what he was thinking. Praying through the moment for some glimmer of his direction to reach her.

But there was none.

Elliot stood still, his body blocking Amberley's. His jaw just the slightest bit flexed. And then he nodded, once, and said, "You tunneled underground."

A wide smile spread the width of Irina's face. "Yes, we did. Al here was our lead on that, given that he's worked as a crewman for many a stage. But do you mind telling me how you knew?"

"The tree, in the cemetery. You tunneled from the vaults under Bigelow Chapel, right into the tree line. That one in particular got in the way, so either it had to go or was an accident. But the ground was frozen; it couldn't be replaced until spring. A glance at the list of former employees on the grounds crew at Mount Auburn Cemetery showed a familiar name, one we hadn't thought to make a connection to until now, especially since he'd worked there years back."

"Jack Adler, our gardener at Wren's Beacon Hill estate." Irina smiled. "Well done, Agent Matthews. I knew from the work you shared with our Wren that you'd checked with the mayor's office and Mount Auburn Cemetery right away. It didn't take much money to seal his lips. And paying off a few hungry men assured that the grounds hadn't been disturbed before New Year's Eve because that's what the press was told to believe. And it was confirmed by the mayor's office, of course, thanks to some behind-the-scenes socializing on Mrs. Dover's part. She was very helpful to gain the support of the mayor's wife, though the poor woman was quite oblivious except to believe whatever a well-placed socialite would tell her. All we had to do was press on the thumb of Stanley Dover's debts a bit to gain Mrs. Dover's participation."

"I didn't know it was her, Wren. I swear it." Amberley's cries came out with unrestrained urgency. "The man at the Oyster House—"

Elliot held his hand out for Amberley to stop. She obeyed, retreating back into silence.

A *pop*, then the sound of broken glass in one of the rooms cut into the silence.

Irina shifted her glare from Wren to Al and the men they'd brought, the gravediggers who still hovered in the shadows behind. Something or someone was in one of the VIP rooms, it seemed, because she looked the tiniest bit derailed.

"Go. Now. See who that is." Irina gave the order, nudging Elliot's gun with the side of her foot. "And take this."

The men obeyed, one stooping for the weapon while the other walked back toward the door.

Wren's focus was solely on Charlotte, and the hand that still held a gun to her sister's temple. She was but feet away. A few more steps and Wren might've been able to think of some way to free her little bird. Maybe jump in, try to take the brunt of a bullet for Charlotte. To be brave like their mother had been.

Every thought of the past and the present mingled together in her mind. Her thoughts were jarred when Elliot's arm wrapped around her waist from behind, quickly pulling her back with him.

"Get down," was all he managed to say against her ear before one of the men turned his hand around the knob and opened the door.

And the Castleton's once-lovely VIP hall became the next casualty of Irina's war, exploding into flames.

CHAPTER 26

Shards of stained glass shattered, raining over them like bits of colored ash.

"Charlotte!"

Elliot heard Wren's guttural screaming at once. He'd covered her beneath the force of the blast, but now she was clawing at the hardwood like a caged animal, trying to crawl forward into the path of the flames, desperate to reach her sister.

Smoke tainted the air, singeing his lungs with each coughing breath.

The explosion had blanketed the far end of the hall in flames, just as Elliot had planned. It created the diversion they'd needed. A slow burn of the fire he'd set in the VIP room exploded once it hit the accelerant of corn whiskey in the hollowed-out chair legs.

Al Gruner and the men had disappeared behind the flames and smoke. Whether they'd managed to crawl to the door in the alley, he couldn't tell. Not through the intensity of flames and thick black smoke that billowed up, along with the force of the fire clawing up the sides of the wall.

Never mind them.

If they were still alive, the horde of federal agents waiting on the street would make quick work out of finding them a pair of handcuffs. What he needed to worry about was happening there in front of him: Wren's desperate cries as Irina dragged Charlotte away, down the depths of a smoke-filled hall.

For all of the adrenaline that must have carried through her veins, Wren was fighting him like a lion. She pulled away, crying her sister's name over and over.

"Wren, stop! Please, stop."

Grasping for her ankle was futile. She tore out of his grasp, pulling herself up to run in pursuit. She disappeared down the depths of an adjoining hall, her boot falls fading against the loud popping of the growing fire.

Instinct told him to help Amberley out first. No matter what came, he couldn't be responsible for another's life. If it was Wren's choice to go after Irina empty-handed, then God help him, he couldn't stop her now.

He said a silent prayer because it was all he could do—leaving his love in God's care—and slipped his arms under Amberley's legs to scoop her from the ground. She fell into a riot of coughs against his chest. "Hold on. You're going to be okay."

Amberley twisted her arms around his neck, and he ran to the only outlet they had.

A mosaic of glass pieces covered the ground under the remnants of the window. He kicked at the last shards of glass on the sill, sending colors flying. He took to the boards next, pounding them with a barrage of kicks, even as their world tumbled down into flames at his back.

He coughed, lungs screaming, Amberley a deadweight in his arms. Thinking of fresh air. Only clean, breathable air.

Kick. Kick, Elliot.

Shades of memories passed over his thoughts: His parents. An innocent who'd once died because of his inexperience . . . his inability to protect another. His fear at being able to protect Wren now.

No one else dies because of me.

The boards finally gave way against one final slam of his foot and fell in a clatter on the sidewalk.

The fire sizzled and danced as he carried Amberley out, a red dragon eating up the Castleton's bones behind them. It wouldn't be long before the entire building was consumed by the darkness of smoke and ash.

But just as Wren had written in the margins of her fairy-tale book, darkness could never win. He had faith in that now. For if there was darkness, that could only mean the presence of light was near enough to overcome it.

Wren would rise from the ashes of her past. And just as he'd told her before, Elliot would always be waiting in the wings when she was through with her flight.

He deposited Amberley a safe distance from the building, then turned back to the heart of the flames. The dragon roared as he leapt back through the window: a hero charging into battle.

CHAPTER 27

The fire created an eerie backdrop of evil hisses and an orange glow down the hall.

Wren kept running through the darkness. Ducking in dressing rooms. Throwing open doors along the hallway and bumping into walls. She tried to listen past the sound of flames hungrily consuming the back of the Castleton.

"Charlotte?" she cried out, but heard no answer.

She tore a strip of linen from her shirttail, then covered her mouth against the growing threat of smoke that was singeing her insides.

A loud *pop* froze Wren in her tracks.

Her breathing shallowed, the linen strip falling from her fingertips to drift to the floor.

The stage . . .

The sound had echoed; only an expansive space could do that. Irina must have been close to the auditorium. On that stage. Or in the balcony, perhaps.

God, please don't let that have been a gunshot.

She tore through the darkness, heading for the stage door. A voice echoed, a man crying out, "You'll not hurt her!"

Two more *pops* echoed in succession, ripping the breath from Wren's lungs.

The stage finally opened up before her, the grand auditorium hazy with smoke. Irina stood in its center, Charlotte sitting at her feet, cradling something in her lap.

Wren took slow steps and peered around the curtain.

Her breath stalled in her lungs when the scene came into view, for it wasn't a something Charlotte held but a someone. A man's legs lay sprawled out, his boots still and lifeless against the stage. Crimson marred his torso. And her sister sat, so still, so quiet, running her fingertips over a man's brow.

"Elliot?"

She started to move faster, her heart screaming, but was halted by Irina's order to stop. "That's far enough, or I'll give you what he got." She trained the gun on Wren without batting an eyelash.

Wren couldn't think. Why hadn't she looked to see what Elliot was wearing? It had been too dark. Too much had happened, and she hadn't even really looked at him . . . She didn't tell him how she felt . . . and now, would she ever?

Sirens wailed in the background, a mournful cry that called through the walls: firemen had been called. No doubt as black smoke curled up into the sky.

"Please, let me call for help. You can still stop this, Irina. You don't have to do this. There's still redemption—even for this. Just let me save him."

"Redemption? Don't talk to me about redemption. It's not real, unless you grasp it for yourself. Anything I could have become was wiped away the day Olivia Charles died."

The sirens, the smoke, and the crackling of timber became a

storm around them. But even with it, Wren's heart stopped when she heard the words.

"Please . . . I don't understand. Just let me help him . . ."

"He got what he deserved. And Jenny Charles? She is just as guilty. She moved to London and the man who had loved *my* mother, who had promised us the world—he walked away. Decided that he didn't need an opera singer and her daughter. Raising his niece was all the family he wanted. So we were cast off, and you were moved into his grand estate. My mother died— used, broken, and penniless—in a workhouse not two years later. When we should have had everything, I was left on the streets. To survive alone. And all the truth I needed to know was in finding my own redemption.

"I followed you to Southampton. And you were so smug with your morality and your plans to work with the great Houdini, not knowing that all the time, my grand illusion had just begun. Wasn't mine greater that his? I fooled even the great Wren Lockhart."

Irina turned, pointing at the boots on the stage. "I was patient. For ten years. But eventually, I knew I'd come back to redeem two lives—mine and my mother's. And you, Jenny Charles, were the root of my misery. Just like he was."

Wren swallowed hard, and a sinking feeling washed over her.

The man held in Charlotte's embrace wore boots. Old, scarred, over-the-knee riding boots. Showman's boots. The kind of costumed wares found on a vaudeville stage—or in a theater manager's office. But these boots were tired and worn.

God, no . . .

Though it took every ounce of courage she possessed, Wren refused to slink away. And she refused to stop. She took one step forward. And another. Until the daylight cast down through a hole in the roof shone enough for her to see her father's lifeless body.

And for the second time in her life, sweet Charlotte had blood covering her hands. She stood and raised them, showing the darkness of crimson that had covered her palms.

"Charlotte . . . please. Back away, dear."

"No, she may not." Irina's hands trembled, ever so slightly, as she turned the barrel on Charlotte.

Tears came then. Emotion tearing from her heart up to cloud her eyes, choke her voice, and rip apart anything she might have had left.

"But why? Why did you wait until Harry was gone? You could have been done with me in England. Away from Charlotte. She's an innocent! Can't you see? She couldn't hurt anyone. I was wrong . . . so wrong. And it should have been me alone that you pursued. So why come here, work with me, befriend me for years . . . Was any of it real?"

"Real? Yes. It was all real for me. Because I lived the illusion. I fooled this girl here. Why, even you were fooled. And all because the world would never believe in magic as long as Harry Houdini was alive. And his secrets died with him, just as they must now with you."

"*No—Wren!*" Elliot appeared, her love, a ghostly shadow tearing up from the back of the auditorium, a gun in his hand—though useless that far away.

But it wasn't a bullet that Wren needed most. His call distracted Irina enough that she looked away for the rarest of seconds, opening a split-second window for Wren to take a single step forward.

One step was all she needed.

Wren slammed her boot to the stage, pressing on the trigger for the illusionist's secret door. And as if on cue, without a word spoken, Charlotte pushed Irina with all her might.

The furious sound of Irina's scream echoed as the trapdoor opened and she fell into the depths of the stage below.

And the Castleton's auditorium was quiet once again. With ash and flames threatening closer. Sirens beat against the walls and sunlight was choked out by the growing haze of smoke in the air.

"I'm sorry, Wren," Charlotte whimpered. "We never push. We never push . . ."

"It's alright." Wren's voice splintered on a sob and she ran forward, then pulled Olivia's little bird into her arms. "You did good, my dear. Very, very good. Remember? A hero never causes hurt; she lessens it. That's what you did."

Elliot tore down the aisle and leaped onto the stage.

He stopped first to look through the secret door. Whatever he'd seen must have satisfied him that Irina was no longer a threat because he ran to Josiah's side. He eased her father down from Charlotte's lap, looking for signs of life.

But she didn't need confirmation. Wren had seen death before. She'd watched it play out. Tasted every horrifying moment as their mother fell. Remembered the look of a pair of eyes that no longer owned a soul.

"Come, Charlotte," Wren beckoned, tugging her back. "Come with me now. You're safe."

Wren couldn't remember much of what happened next.

It was a blur, the moments of Elliot helping them outside. Passing by firemen and water hoses as they moved in, attempting to save the buildings of Scollay Square. Amberley was safe, if not terribly shaken up. And both federal agents and police pushed back the press. They'd arrived to a frenzy, much like Stapleton's show on New Year's Eve.

Shackled men were led away as their flashbulbs danced.

The newsmakers watched as Elliot returned to their side and slipped a coat over Charlotte's shoulders. And then he stood in front of Wren, soot-covered and eyes searching every inch of her face. Taking his thumb to wipe at the dried blood and layers of black dust marring her brow. With empathy for her loss so real, and so deeply felt, Wren could never forget the look upon his face.

"But how did he know?" Wren's will was broken. Fear, pain, memories . . . They'd come back to life the instant her father had stepped in front of Charlotte, shielding her from Irina's gun. "Please, how did he know where to find us?"

"Because when I was walking out the door to come after you, I told him that I loved you. And if you were going to hear from anyone, you'd hear it from me first. And he stopped me. He told me the truth, that he knew the moment he saw your writing in that book. You're not to blame, Wren."

He cupped her cheeks with his palms, truth and anguish connecting his eyes to hers. "Do you hear me? It was his choices. His rage. His sin that killed Olivia Charles. Not yours. And he came here to tell you that. To absolve you of this guilt you've held on to all these years."

She wept, tears rolling down, mingling with the soot and skin of his palms holding her face.

"So can you, Wren? Can you let it go?" Elliot's eyes searched her face, pleading for an answer. "You can be free if you want to. But it's your choice. I'll never ask you to be less than who you are. And if you need to step out on a stage, I'll always be waiting when you come back. If you want me to."

Elliot opened his arms wide. Waiting. As the smoke and sirens and flashbulbs mingled with the sounds of chaos. And without a word or a second thought, Wren slipped into the safe haven his arms provided and closed her eyes as her past burned to the ground.

CHAPTER 28

April 20, 1927

Suffolk County Jail

Boston, Mass.

It was jarring, the finality in the sound of an iron door being closed and locked behind her.

Wren and Elliot followed the uniformed officer down a hall-way to a wooden door with clear glass—a private visitor's room. Elliot opened it, holding it wide as the officer nodded her inside.

"You're sure you want to do this? You don't have to, you know."

She loved the way he could say so much with so few words. His brow was wrinkled, showing concern, but not enough to say he didn't have full confidence that she could handle what they'd come here to do. His eyes were never judging—just open enough that Wren knew he only wanted what was best for her and would always try to support it.

"I know I don't have to. But it is why I got all dressed up

today, isn't it?" She'd dressed in Wren Lockhart's hallmark gentleman's clothes and stage-ready cherry smile, stepping out in public for one of the first times since the news story broke outlining the deception of one Irina Blackwood, a former vaudeville manager, and Albert Gruner, the proprietor of A. M. Moriarty's Theater Productions. Both Gruner and Irina had been charged alongside Stapleton, all facing their own trials for kidnapping and conspiracy to commit murder, with evidence that continued mounting against the lot of them.

Wren was prepared to testify in court, though she bore scars that needed healing. A cut from the hilt of a sword had permanently marked her brow and tiny scratches were still evident on one cheek, but her makeup had covered them well. Only eyes that looked on her as closely as Elliot's could see them now.

"Do you want me to stay?" He looked over at the striped denim-clad prisoner sitting at a table in the center of the room.

Wren squeezed Elliot's hand, drawing his attention back to her face. "I love that you asked, but no. This is something I need to do on my own."

He nodded. And just like always, he understood, saying nothing more about it. "I'll be just outside if you need me."

Wren waited until the door clicked closed behind her, then walked across the space to the empty chair at the table. She looked down at the woman, her usually sun-kissed skin pale from months behind bars.

"May I sit down?" She gripped the chair back.

"It is why you've come, isn't it?"

Wren slid onto the chair opposite Irina.

For the first time in years, her friend appeared dead in the depths of her striking green eyes. Wren couldn't help but wonder if the next time they'd connect like that would be from across a courtroom, with her in a witness stand and Irina fighting to avoid a death sentence.

"Thank you for agreeing to see me," Wren began. "I . . ."

There was much to say—a history between them that went back years, long before Harry Houdini, before home became a stage. But now that the opportunity had come to say what she knew she must, the words were lost on her tongue.

Start again. Pray for the words, and start again.

"Elliot told me the truth. That on the day of his death, Josiah Charles told him who my real father was. But I think you already suspected that, didn't you?"

"Why have you come? To brag? To hold it over me that I'm in here and you're out there?"

"Not to brag. And not even to seek resolution with you. I believe the courts will seek justice for what you've done, and they'll judge you accordingly. I'm here on another matter."

Irina narrowed her eyes, doubt covering her features. "If you're not here about the case, then . . ."

"I am here because of the years following my mother's death. I don't blame you for my father's sins. He owned them alone, and the result was that our family was torn apart. But I needed to ask you a question—one that no one else can answer rightly."

Irina crossed her arms over her chest.

"The man you named Victor Peale died on Horace Stapleton's stage. That is a fact. And it's for the courts to decide who administered the drug that killed him and to unravel the events of what happened in the weeks after. A jury will unfurl the story of why you had hired guns chase us down on the streets and why you attempted to have me die onstage by slipping in a new lock when no one was looking. But an illusionist's secrets can always be explained. You know this. From the piping system that gave Victor Peale the ability to breathe in that coffin, to the gravedigger who administered the shot of adrenaline on the stage that day . . . It would have had to be someone with medical training, a healer, perhaps. Someone standing in line with the rest of the gravediggers in the shadows behind Amberley Dover. Someone who opened that coffin yet remained unnoticed because she hid in plain sight."

Irina remained silent.

"I assume the book had significance. To give Victor Peale a book penned by Arthur Conan Doyle was a none-too-subtle message about a friendship that had fallen out. It was directed at me, wasn't it? It was to be a message about us. We'd fallen out long ago, only I didn't know it."

"That would have been a clever possibility."

"You don't have to confirm what I already know. But I must ask, what was he going to say? Victor Peale. If his heart hadn't stopped when it did, what was he going to say about the afterlife? Or, should I ask, what did you tell him to say about it?"

"I can't answer that, of course, as this case is ongoing. But I would have said there is no power over the grave that we can't harness for ourselves."

"And you truly believe that?"

"It sounds as though you have your theories all worked out. Is that why you came, just to accuse me one last time before we meet in a courtroom?"

Wren shook her head. "No. I came to absolve you."

Irina laughed, a curious chortle void of humor. It was a touch arrogant, given the state of her, stripped of her former affluence and now, known only as the number on a striped shirt. "Absolve me?"

Wren nodded. "Yes."

"And why would I care what you think? You're an illusionist. You take money for the same reasons as the rest, yet you call it entertainment. But we're all magicians weaving spells and crafting lies, making people believe in something that's a vapor. You should know that people will only believe in what they can see with their eyes. I know there's a stage waiting for you out there and there's plenty of money yet to be made. They won't hang a woman, so you'll be making it long after I'm finished rotting behind these bars."

"But I never claimed a connection with the afterlife, Irina, except to have received the gift that is available to every soul who walks the earth—including you. So I'll say what I've come to say, and then I suppose we'll meet again in court."

"Then say it and get out."

Wren looked at her friend, seeing the years that had passed between them now hollow in the depths of her eyes. "I forgive you."

"What?" Her eyes flashed with the first bit of emotion Wren had seen.

"I said that I forgive you. For all of it. I won't live with bitterness for a single day."

"You think I need your forgiveness?" She slammed her fist to the table. "Guard? We're done here!"

The door swung open, and Wren turned to see Elliot sweep into the room. He stood by, his glare serious.

Wren shook her head softly, letting him know she was still okay. That some things she still had to do on her own, and this was one of them. If she truly wished for restoration and a life that wasn't an illusion, Wren could be the only one to let her past go.

She stood, feeling weightless, as if bitterness had withered like flowers in a crystal vase and fallen, cast off like a pile of ash on the floor. "I'm sorry, Irina. You may not have needed grace today, but I did—if I'm ever going to be free."

CHAPTER 29

OCTOBER 6, 1927

PALACE OF VERSAILLES

VERSAILLES, FRANCE

The grand salon doors were open at either end of the *Galerie des Glaces*—the Hall of Mirrors—in Versailles' grand palace.

The last searching rays of evening sunlight streamed in through the span of arcaded windows. With the wall of mirrors at Wren's back, light fractured against pillars of gold and low-hanging crystal chandeliers, enhancing the timeless luxury that still clung to the golden hall of Louis XIV's seventeenth-century world.

Wren looked from the central windows to the lush landscape beyond the back façade, dusk hiding what remained of the gardens' summer secrets. Hers would be a stage set under the vault of a starry sky, where she'd perform her illusions for a crowd of illustrious guests: high-society Parisians, government officials, and dignitaries who'd arrived to see the famed American illusionist's show. It was the final show in her late-summer tour—the pinnacle of the career she'd built over the last many years.

Whether gilded at the moment or not, the name of Wren Lockhart had become synonymous with a dying art. She knew that soon vaudeville would be no more. What Horace Stapleton and so many others had fought to keep tight in their grasp was slowly fading away. Radio and cinemas with talking pictures were poised to steal the entertainment limelight. It had already begun in cities like Boston and New York, London and even Paris, where patrons flocked not to a live vaudeville stage but to entertainment that thrilled in modern ways. Traveling trick shows weren't likely to find bookings at such honored former palaces for much longer, if ever again.

The winds had begun to shift, enough that Wren wondered what would be left when it was all over. It weighed on her thoughts as she waited for showtime now, taking slow steps the length of the hall, her boot falls echoing off the ceiling.

This moment was the one she'd longed for once. It was her dream, to see the hall again. To stand in its center, then walk its length and decide which salon to enter at the end. Each entryway possessed its own painting—one for pretending and one for truth. One for war, the other for peace. And like the Sun King in his mirrored world, Wren could choose which one to enter.

Wren could step into a future showered with peace, like the last rays of sunlight that bathed the hall around her. Her mother's death did not have to be in vain. Nor Victor Peale's, or even Josiah Charles's. And she knew Franklin was her father in name now, though he'd always been in her heart. It changed everything to know who she really was. Wren wanted to use the events of the last months as a reminder for what truly mattered. That what Elliot had whispered once was true—the girl behind the mask had worth far greater than what the world said on a stage.

Her freedom was, as Socrates had said, in the beauty of a life lived without pretending.

Wren looked from left to right as the sun sank deeper, the swift fall of darkness outside emphasizing the glow of the crystal and gold-tipped chandeliers down the length of the hall.

"Jenny."

She spun on her heel, staring toward the salon at the end of the hall. Elliot was there, spinning a bright-pink flower in his fingertips. He emerged into the glowing light reflected by the mirrors. "I don't know what it is, but it looked like a peony."

"You picked it from the gardens . . ." He didn't deny it. That made her smile. "You'll be thrown in a French prison for defacing a national landmark."

Elliot shrugged, as if the threat were paltry. "You're worth it."

He came toward her, his stride sure, eyes focused on her. Wren nodded, fiery waves grazing wetness that had found its way to her cheeks.

"They sent me to fetch you. You ready? It's about that time."

"I know. I was just . . . thinking."

"I wasn't sure where you were. Looks like I guessed correctly when I found the backstage area empty." He came still closer. He held up a slip of paper in his hand, stopping in front of her. "As your temporary manager, I am bound to tell you that we shouldn't be late. But I did want to share this before you went on."

"Business?"

His shook his head. "An urgent telegram. Apparently we're being summoned back to Boston." Elliot cleared his throat, trying his best not to smile. "It reads, and I quote: 'I should have listened to you. Stop. You'd better be home by Christmas. Stop.

I'll never make it through this wedding without you two. Stop.'
Signed Connor Finnegan."

Elliot folded the telegram and slipped it into his tuxedo pants
pocket. "I told him Amberley would have him walking down the
aisle in the grandest society wedding Boston has ever seen to
date. He said now that he wishes he'd gone to the courthouse like
we did, and maybe he, too, could be spending his honeymoon on
a European tour."

Wren laughed, unable to suppress the image of Connor
Finnegan saying "I do" in front of five hundred of Amberley's
closest friends. "I am sorry for him, of course." She smiled. "But
I have to say that since Mrs. Amberley Finnegan will be our business partner, I might have to hold my tongue a little better in the
future. I think maybe I'll start right now."

"You're sure you want to go into business with Amberley,
especially when you know what you'll be in for?"

"I do. I think it's right. We know now that Stanley Dover's
debts were not quite as life-altering as she'd been threatened into
believing. Still, she's trying to make amends. Allowing her to
fund our rebuilding of the theater as the Castleton Gardens is a
small price to keep the peace. And I'm freeing up my husband to
get back to the job he loves. Everyone wins."

"Then you're not sorry?" He held a hand out to her.

Wren looked down at it, his palm open to the golden ceiling.
It felt more right than ever to lace her fingers with his, now that
she could do it anytime she pleased. "No. I'm not. How could I
be when this reminds me that we walked hand-in-hand down
a hallway once? A hallway that was much grander than this
because I was staring down my past, and you wouldn't let me do
it alone."

"I remember."

"I wasn't sorry then and I'm not now. I'm Wren Lockhart to everyone out there." She tilted her head toward her stage set up in the gardens. "For better or for worse, I'm a vaude. I can't turn back time and change who I've become. So I'm going out on that terrace to give a show. It's who I am."

He edged a step closer, the tips of his shoes grazing hers with soft intention. "And that woman onstage who enchants every crowd is exactly who I love. So just go out there. Be Wren Lockhart as long as it brings you joy. And I'll be waiting in the wings of every stage when you do. But please—don't think you can't be Jenny with me too. Someday you might be ready to leave Wren behind, but I won't ever push you to change. Loving someone is accepting all of who she is, not just the best or the easiest parts. Do you hear me? I love you, my Jenny Wren, and that's loving your pain too. All of it. Just as you accept me with mine."

Elliot slipped his arm around the small of her back, leading her down the hall. "I can't forget that first night I stepped up onto your stage."

Laughter came easy and sounded so right as it bounced off the high ceiling. "You pushed your way in as a counterfeit volunteer."

"You said your heart was already spoken for, that first time I stepped on your stage and offered you a flower. Do you remember?"

She nodded. "Yes. I do."

"I know you were playing to the crowd, but there was some truth behind what you said, wasn't there? Please don't tell me I busted up a secret courtship of some sort."

"It was like the tales in *The Welsh Fairy Book*: there was the *promise* of a hero one day. Someone who would walk down a hall with me. Who'd take my trembling hand in his. Maybe listen while I talk of fairy stories with my little sister. And he'd tell me to sell my home if it made me happy. To bring Charlotte to live with us in a little cottage by the sea, because he understands me so completely that he didn't even have to ask to know it would be exactly what I'd want." Wren met his smile with one of her own.

One of their stagehands came into view of the doorway at the end of the hall. It was time.

"I have to go." She leaned in, pressing the whisper of a kiss against his mouth with a butterfly's touch. "Will you be here when I'm through?" She leaned back, savoring the openness of his eyes looking only at hers.

Elliot tugged at the tip of a fiery wave that had settled on her cheek and brushed it back with a finger against her brow. "Yes, Wren. I'll always be right here, waiting when the curtain goes down. And we'll walk through whatever door we choose from this moment on—together."

Wren stepped onstage with music playing and a crystal vase of flowers ready to grow. Elliot was there. Watching and waiting but allowing her to be all of who she was. Feeling at peace as a little girl danced down the aisle. As flowers grew and matured. As false lives withered and died away.

And in the next breath, ashes flew.

She tossed it up, letting go, the crowd riotous in awe.

A wren rose from the ashes, fluttering and soaring over the applause, its wings beating in time with the music . . . daring to go as high as freedom would allow. And she watched, heart full, as moonlight cast the shadowed outline of tiny wings on the manicured gardens below.

The Wren was finally whole.

AUTHOR'S NOTE

One of my favorite stories about Harry Houdini wasn't in one of his most infamous escapes or lockdown jailbreaks. It's actually a story from his youth, of a young boy who, much like our own sons, had quite a taste for the interesting and adventurous.

At barely seven years old, Ehrich Weisz (later to become the world-famous Harry Houdini) was a known daredevil and lock-breaking kid who one night, "unlocked all the doors to the shops" along College Avenue in the town of Appleton, Wisconsin. Upon seeing a street circus pass through town, he decided then and there that a life of adventure was for him. And on October 28, 1883, Houdini made his show-business debut with the Jack Hoeffler 5-Cent Circus, taking home a purse of thirty-five cents.

Said to have been athletic and nimble from birth, he was fascinated by the tightrope walker who defied death in that street circus, stringing up a wire between buildings and walking across, seemingly without worry for the outcome of certain death should he fall. The prospect fascinated and exhilarated Harry so that he went home, promptly strung a rope from two trees, and climbed up to traverse the distance in the same way a tightrope walker would.

343

Harry fell. Hard. The ground broke his fall but not his spirit. He got up, dusted himself off, and vowed to try again. In fact, he was soon dangling from a rope in his mouth, not knowing the showman in the street circus had used an iron-jaw mouthpiece to perform his tricks. It's said that Houdini lost his front teeth as a result of that death-defying feat. (Fortunately they were not permanent teeth and new ones soon grew back to complete his smile.)

What I love about these insights into a person's past is that the talents and passions we're born with are often harnessed at a very tender age. We have a great amount of documentation about Harry Houdini's life story, and we have the luxury to go back and see the telltale signs in youth of the fantastic entertainer he would later become. But our story begins in this book—not in the early days of a showman's buildup to fame, but in the winter of his life, when deep questions of spiritualism and faith dominated much of his time and attention.

The Illusionist's Apprentice held an exciting new challenge for me as an author. It allowed me to stretch and try a new flavor of mystery writing, much like stringing a rope between two trees in Houdini's backyard. And the development of Wren's fictional story gave me the opportunity to do what I love best—to research and incorporate historical fact into a story—but also to paint a visual world that evokes the magic of another time, another place . . . The Jazz Age (and Boston in particular) is one such place I've dreamed of painting with words for quite some time.

Wren Lockhart is fiercely independent and bold—in many ways, like Mr. Houdini himself—but she also has a softness to her I very much wanted to uncover throughout the story. It intrigues me that a character could live a public life as someone completely different from who they were behind closed doors, but that their talent could manage to effectively bridge both of those worlds.

While Jenny "Wren" Lockhart is a purely fictional character, there are two aspects to her character that are rooted in historical fact. In this book, Wren's professional relationship with Harry Houdini was inspired by real-life entertainer Dorothy Young, who at seventeen years old was hired as a stage assistant to the famous illusionist and toured with him for years. Houdini's quote that to come back from the dead was "humanly impossible" were words actually spoken to Dorothy. Many of the acts in Wren's stage show are a culmination of illusions from the stage, in books, and even from modern-day movies in tricks that derived from Houdini's initial popularization.

Second, with history that is personal to our family, the story behind Jenny's nickname is also true. In this book, Olivia Charles gave her daughter the nickname Jenny Wren. I learned after I began writing the story that Jenny Wren is the name of a beloved character from Charles Dickens's *Our Mutual Friend* (1865), and interestingly enough, the character also suffered abuse from a father who battled alcoholism. The same name was passed down from my great-grandfather, James "Shorty" Thompson, a coal miner from Newcastle, England, who tamed a wild wren into a pet, teaching her to sit on his shoulder and eat from his hand. He named her Jenny Wren—which became my own sister's childhood nickname. The thought that a young girl could be both caged and still wild at heart gave me the idea for a character whose life mimicked this idea in fantastic ways.

Giving her this name fit on so many levels.

Readers will also recognize several character references in this novel that are true to history, first and foremost Harry Houdini himself. In this book, we imagine what an encounter might have been like with the world-famous talent had it occurred offstage, on a sunny London street in Piccadilly. As such legend surrounds the showman side of his persona, it was incredible to imagine what Houdini's wit and personality might have been like in real life.

Other historical names have been wrapped into the story, including Bess Houdini (Harry's beloved wife); Boston's forty-fourth mayor, Malcolm E. Nichols (1926–1930), and his second wife, Carrie Williams Nichols; known spiritualists George Valentine, Ann O'Delia Diss Debar, Joaquín Argamasilla, and Mina "Margery" Crandon (also known as "The Witch of Lime Street"), the latter whom Harry Houdini most famously debunked in 1924. (Horace Stapleton, too, is a fictional character, though his public-debunking experience would have been similar.) Also alluded to in this story is famed writer Sir Arthur Conan Doyle, Houdini's longtime friend who had a falling out with the entertainer over their differing views of spiritualism in the late 1920s. Harry Houdini died on October 31, 1926, the two men never to reconcile. (Readers with an interest in Doyle's writing may also recognize several antagonists' names in this novel as those of Sherlock Holmes's adversaries from several of his books.)

As a wise editor once told me, historical fiction has to know when to bend the line between fact and storytelling. We've pulled in a real book to fit the timeline of this story: *The Welsh Fairy Book* by W. Jenkyn Thomas, originally published in 1907. It was illustrated by William "Willy" Pogany, a celebrated Hungarian illustrator readers may also recognize as a character from one of my previous novels, *The Ringmaster's Wife*. While we've woven historical fact to flavor a 1920s vaudeville world, we've also gone down a fictional road to tell Wren and Elliot's story, and I love that we've had the opportunity to cross into both worlds in this book.

Thank you, dear readers, for walking this story road with us.

❧——ACKNOWLEDGMENTS——☙

The heartbeat of this story began in the midst of a summer brainstorming retreat with—surprise, surprise—a few suspense writers.

Imagine two historical authors (Sarah E. Ladd and myself) finding ourselves immersed in the world of suspense with talented authors: Colleen Coble (a Houdini-like mentor in this author's life), Ronie Kendig, Lynette Eason, Michelle Lim, Robin Carroll, and Carrie Stuart Parks (who also reached out to her crime lab network to find answers to my 1920s toxicology questions), all gathered in a living room to brainstorm books, with coffee and chocolate in steady supply. As it was my first official foray into mystery writing, this gathering of authors ushered me into their world in the first five minutes by adding a cemetery, a corpse, and at least one death within the very first chapter of the book.

I laugh at the memory of how wide-eyed Sarah and I must have looked, two historical authors in the midst of such suspense awesomeness. Not only did the plot for *The Illusionist's Apprentice* come alive in that living room, but the rest of Wren's character began to take form before my eyes. Thank you, suspense ladies.

The experience turned me into a firm believer in two things: brainstorming sessions and fellowship with friends.

Every book has a layer of story itself in how it came to be. This book was developed with my wonderful publishing team at HarperCollins Christian Publishing: Daisy Hutton, Becky Monds, Jodi Hughes, Amanda Bostic, Paul Fisher, Stephen Tindal, and our vintage-loving Kristen "Goldie" Golden. You are absolutely the best work family a writerly gal could ask for. I love every day that has you in it. To dear editors (and beloved friends) Becky Monds, Julee Schwarzburg, and Jodi Hughes: I'm so blessed to have been able to take another book journey with you. From "Once upon a time" to those magical words "The End," you keep me sane, help me learn, and make the story-building process a greater joy than I could have ever imagined. Thank you! (And to Julee, I send a hug for your patience and kind teacher's heart. You've made me a believer in the power of good editing!) To Rachelle Gardner, my wildly supportive agent: I owe you much for those dig-deep phone conversations to encourage me along this road. You go above and beyond the call of duty, and I couldn't be more blessed than to get to call you a friend.

To Katie Ganshert, Cara Putman, Beth K. Vogt, Sarah E. Ladd, Melissa Tagg, Courtney Walsh, Katherine Reay, Casey Herringshaw, and Jeane Wynn: The last year has been a blessing because of your fellowship. Thank you for the prayers, for the calls, for sharing the love when life gets "real." The time spent researching and writing this book helped me learn the meaning of true sisters-in-Jesus love.

A very special thanks must go to my friends Gary and Lanette Almon, owners of Kölkin Coffee Shop. The Almon family welcomed me in, sharing smiles and support, and worked very hard to keep me alive with coffee during the thick of the manuscript-writing process—even giving me my own preferred table right beneath the kayaks on the wall. As far as hidden coffee-shop corners go, this find is a piece of heaven. Thanks for everything, guys! And also to Livie, the superstar barista who readers will recognize as a familiar name (Olivia) in this book. Buying this writer a coffee on a certain Thursday meant more than you could ever know. Thanks for becoming a part of our story by naming this character!

To my support system of mentors and friends: Maggie Walker, Sharon Tavera, Colleen Coble, Allen Arnold, Mary Weber, Kerry Newland, Kelli Deary, and the students and staff at Christian Academy of Louisville's Rock Creek campus. You have all become part of this story, and I thank you for your fellowship along the way.

To my family: You put up with my quirky writer ways, overlook the messy house when Mom's up against a project deadline, and love me no matter what. I'm blessed by my four amazing guys: Brady, Carson Dallas, Colt, and best friend, Jeremy. I also send my most sincere gratitude to my mom, Lindy, for showing me how to be brave during valley-walking. Thanks for being my first reader and best friend. I am so proud of you. And to my sis, Jenny: The magic of memory-making that only sisters could share is at the absolute heart of this book. We love you, Jenny Wren!

And were he here, I'd want to thank Harry Houdini for providing the backbone to this story. He left such a legacy behind—of mystery and grand illusions and of excellence in creative craft—that made him the greatest in his field. I enjoyed reading his writings, diving in to biographies about his life, and especially researching the deep spiritual questions he asked about life and the conquering of death that permeated popular culture in the

1920s. I'll always be grateful to Harry and to our fictional Wren Lockhart for showing me it's okay to ask questions and to dream along the way.

There's only One who claims victory over the grave—and lucky us that Horace Stapleton wasn't him!

With joy,

Kristy

FURTHER READING

Houdini, Harry. *A Magician Among the Spirits*, Fredonia Books (NL), 2002.

Houdini, Harry. *The Right Way to Do Wrong: A Unique Selection of Writings by History's Greatest Escape Artist (Neversink)*, Melville House, 2012.

Jaher, David. *The Witch of Lime Street: Séance, Seduction, and Houdini in the Spirit World*, Crown, 2015.

Kalush, William, and Sloman, Larry. *The Secret Life of Houdini: The Making of America's First Superhero*, Atria, 2006.

DISCUSSION QUESTIONS

1. Though she lives in a world of mystery and illusion, Wren's faith continues to push her story forward, even when confronted by the seemingly ironclad facts of Horace Stapleton's case. It isn't until she crosses paths with Elliot and his fact-based logic that she realizes how deeply held her convictions are. How would Wren's story have ended differently if she'd only relied on what she could see—and prove—with her eyes? Was her faith a major factor in her pursuit of the truth behind Stapleton's illusions?

2. Though the world sees Wren Lockhart as an illusionist on a stage, Jenny Charles is the real woman who lives behind the scenes. How are the personas of these two women different, and how does Elliot manage to see the authenticity behind both? In what ways do Wren and Elliot finally unmask who they truly are?

3. Harry Houdini lived a life of adventure from the stage. In this story, however, we imagine him as a wise mentor offstage, helping to shape Wren into the skilled entertainer she would one day become. As Houdini began to ask deeper questions about faith and spirituality in his final years, how did the debunking

of false mediums affect Wren's view of their shared vaudeville world? Though the story opens months after Houdini's death, how was he ever-present in Wren's journey?

4. The atmosphere of Boston in the late 1920s was flavored by the sights, sounds, and settings of vaudeville, from the experiences of many secondary characters: Connor, Amberley, Irina, Josiah, Al, Olivia, and Franklin. Which characters were living a life of illusion themselves, and why?

5. Wren and Charlotte experienced tragedy in their young lives at the hands of their father. Though she was able to overcome the pain of her past, how did Wren eventually learn to trust again? Did Olivia's sacrifice for her daughters impact Wren's ability to reopen her heart to others?

6. In the years following World War I and the aftermath of the Spanish flu outbreak, many families were left grieving from unfathomable loss. A running theme in the story is the hinging of faith in the One who did conquer the grave. How does Wren's deeply rooted faith affect her ability to see past the claims of false spiritualists in order to help Harry Houdini debunk them? Does her faith impact Elliot's ability to heal from loss in his own life?

Also Available from Kristy Cambron, the

Hidden Masterpiece Novels!

A mysterious painting breathes hope and beauty into the darkest corners of Auschwitz—and the loneliest hearts of Manhattan.

Bound together across time, two women will discover a powerful connection through one survivor's story of hope in the darkest days of a war-torn world.

ABOUT THE AUTHOR

Photo by Whitney Neal Photography

Kristy Cambron fancies life as a vintage-inspired storyteller. Her novels have been named to *Library Journal* Reviews' list of Best Books of 2014 and 2015 and have received nominations for RT Reviewers' Choice Awards Best Inspirational Book of 2014 and 2015. She holds a degree in Art History from Indiana University and has fifteen years of training and communications experience for a Fortune 100 corporation. She lives in Indiana with her husband and three football-loving sons.

Visit her website: www.kristycambron.com
Twitter: @KCambronAuthor
Facebook: Kristy-Cambron